Count Lev Nikolayevich Tolstoy (9 September [O.S. 28 August] 1828 – 20 November [O.S. 7 November] 1910), usually referred to in English as Leo Tolstoy, was a Russian writer who is regarded as one of the greatest authors of all time. He received multiple nominations for Nobel Prize in Literature every year from 1902 to 1906, and nominations for Nobel Peace Prize in 1901, 1902 and 1910, and his miss of the prize is a major Nobel prize controversy. Born to an aristocratic Russian family in 1828, he is best known for the novels War and Peace (1869) and Anna Karenina (1877), often cited as pinnacles of realist fiction. He first achieved literary acclaim in his twenties with his semi-autobiographical trilogy, Childhood, Boyhood, and Youth (1852–1856), and Sevastopol Sketches (1855), based upon his experiences in the Crimean War. Tolstoy's fiction includes dozens of short stories and several novellas such as The Death of Ivan Ilyich (1886), Family Happiness (1859), and Hadji Murad (1912). He also wrote plays and numerous philosophical essays. (Source: Wikipedia)

Literary works:
The Autobiographical Trilogy
Childhood (1852)
Boyhood (1854)
Youth (1856)
War and Peace (1869)
Anna Karenina (1877)
Resurrection (1899)
Family Happiness (1859)
The Cossacks (1863)
The Death of Ivan Ilyich (1886)
The Kreutzer Sonata (1889)
The Devil (1911)
The Forged Coupon (1911)
Hadji Murat (1917)

A RUSSIAN PROPRIETOR
AND OTHER STORIES
LEO TOLSTOY

PRINCE CLASSICS

PRINCE CLASSICS

First Printing: 2019

ISBN 978-93-89370-05-8 (paperback)

ISBN 978-93-89370-06-5 (Hardcover)

ISBN 978-93-89370-07-2 (eBook)

Published by Prince Classics

www.princeclassics.com

Contents

A Russian Proprietor
And Other Stories

PREFACE.

The following tales are, with one exception, taken from the second volume of Count L. N. Tolstoï's collected works, and are representative of his literary activity between 1852 and 1859.

The first story, though only a fragment of a projected novel to be called "A Russian Proprietor," is perfect and complete in itself. One cannot help feeling that it is autobiographical; Count Tolstoï himself, it will be remembered, having suddenly quitted the University of Kazan, in spite of the entreaties of his friends, and retired to his paternal estate of Yasnaya Polyana, near Tula. The aunt whose letter is quoted in the first chapter must have been Count Tolstoï's aunt, mentioned in the second chapter of "My Confession."

The "Recollections of a Scorer" and "Two Hussars" are both evidently reminiscent of Count Tolstoï's gambling-days. Both must have been suggested by some such terrible experience as that told of the count's gambling-debt in the Caucasus.

"Lucerne" and "Albert" are likewise evidently transcripts from the author's own experience. The strange benefactor in each, and the shadowy Prince Nekhliudof, are all Count Tolstoï in phases quite distinct from what he is at present.

"The Three Deaths," written in 1859, has little of the sombre power of "Iván Ilyitch." The scalpel which was so remorselessly applied to the soul in the latter is wholly hidden. It is realism pure and simple; and the contrast between the death of the peasant and of the lady is left to inference, made all the stronger by the unexpected and grandiose finale in the death of the tree.

In interesting contrast to these characteristic stories is the little gem entitled "A Prisoner in the Caucasus," which is found in Vol. IV. of the Count's works under the heading "Tales for Children." The style is perfectly simple and lucid; the pictures of life in the Tatar village among the mountains are intensely vivid, painted with strong and masterly touches; and the reader will not soon forget the little laughing maiden Dina, with the rubles jingling in her braided hair. She stands forth as one of the most fascinating of the author's creations.

NATHAN HASKELL DOLE.

Boston, Dec. 5, 1887.

A RUSSIAN PROPRIETOR.

I.

Prince Nekhliudof was nineteen years of age when, at the end of his third term at the university, he came to spend his summer vacation on his estate. He was alone there all the summer.

In the autumn he wrote in his unformed, boyish hand, a letter to his aunt, the Countess Biéloretskaïa, who, according to his notion, was his best friend, and the most genial woman in the world. The letter was in French, and was to the following effect:—

"Dear Auntie,—I have adopted a resolution upon which must depend the fate of my whole existence. I have left the university in order to devote myself to a country life, because I feel that I was born for it. For God's sake, dear auntie, don't make sport of me. You say that I am young. Perhaps I am still almost a child; but this does not prevent me from feeling sure of my vocation, from wishing to accomplish it successfully, and from loving it.

"As I have already written you, I found our affairs in indescribable confusion. Wishing to bring order out of chaos, I made an investigation, and discovered that the principal trouble was due to the most wretched miserable condition of the peasants, and that this trouble could be remedied only by work and patience.

"If you could only see two of my peasants, David and Iván, and the way that they and their families live, I am convinced that one glance at these two unfortunates would do more to persuade you than all that I can tell you in justification of my resolve. Is not my obligation sacred and clear, to labor for the welfare of these seven hundred human beings for whom I must be responsible to God? Would it not be a sin to leave them to the mercy of harsh elders and overseers, so as to carry out plans of enjoyment or ambition? And why should I seek in any other sphere the opportunity of being useful, and doing good, when such a noble, brilliant, and paramount duty lies right at hand?

"I feel that I am capable of being a good farmer;[1] and in order to make myself such an one as I understand the word to mean, I do not need my diploma as B.A., nor the rank which you so expect of me. Dear auntie, do not make ambitious plans for me: accustom yourself to the thought that I am going on an absolutely peculiar path, but one that is good, and, I think, will bring me to happiness. I have thought and thought about my future duties, have written out some rules of conduct, and, if God only gives me health and strength, I shall succeed in my undertaking.

"Do not show this letter to my brother Vásya: I am afraid of his ridicule. He generally dictates to me, and I am accustomed to give way to him. Whilst Vanya may not approve of my resolve, at least he will understand it."

The countess replied to her nephew in the following letter, also written in French:—

"Your letter, dear Dmitri, showed nothing else to me than that you have a warm heart; and I have never had reason to doubt that. But, my dear, our good tendencies do us more harm in life than our bad ones. I will not tell you that you are committing a folly, that your behavior annoys me; but I will do my best to make one argument have an effect upon you. Let us reason together, my dear.

"You say you feel that your vocation is for a country life; that you wish to make your serfs happy, and that you hope to be a good farmer.

"In the first place, I must tell you that we feel sure of our vocation only when we have once made a mistake in one; secondly, that it is easier to win happiness for ourselves than for others; and thirdly, that, in order to be a good master, it is necessary to be a cold and austere man, which you will never in this world succeed in being, even though you strive to make believe that you are.

"You consider your arguments irresistible, and go so far as to adopt them as rules for the conduct of life; but at my age, my dear, people don't care for arguments and rules, but only for experience. Now, experience tells me that your plans are childish.

"I am now in my fiftieth year, and I have known many fine men; but I have never heard of a young man of good family and ability burying himself in the country under the pretext of doing good.

"You have always wished to appear original, but your originality is nothing else than morbidly developed egotism. And, my dear, choose some better-trodden path. It will lead you to success; and success, if it is not necessary for you as success, is at least indispensable in giving you the possibility of doing good which you desire. The poverty of a few serfs is an unavoidable evil, or, rather, an evil which cannot be remedied by forgetting all your obligations to society, to your relatives, and to yourself.

"With your intellect, with your kind heart, and your love for virtue, no career would fail to bring you success; but at all events choose one which would be worth your while, and bring you honor.

"I believe that you are sincere, when you say that you are free from ambition; but you are deceiving yourself. Ambition is a virtue at your age, and with your means it becomes a fault and an absurdity when a man is no longer in the condition to satisfy this passion.

"And you will experience this if you do not change your intention. Good-by, dear Mitya. It seems to me that I have all the more love for you on account of your foolish but still noble and magnanimous plan. Do as you please, but I forewarn you that I shall not be able to sympathize with you."

The young man read this letter, considered it long and seriously, and finally, having decided that his genial aunt might be mistaken, sent in his petition for dismissal from the university, and took up his residence at his estate.

II.

The young proprietor had, as he wrote his aunt, devised a plan of action in the management of his estate; and his whole life and activity were measured by hours, days, and months.

Sunday was reserved for the reception of petitioners, domestic servants, and peasants, for the visitation of the poor serfs belonging to the estate, and the distribution of assistance with the approval of the Commune, which met every Sunday evening, and was obliged to decide who should have help, and what amount should be given.

In such employments passed more than a year, and the young man was now no longer a novice either in the practical or theoretical knowledge of estate management.

It was a clear July Sunday when Nekhliudof, having finished his coffee and run through a chapter of "Maison Rustique," put his note-book and a packet of bank-notes into the pocket of his light overcoat, and started out of doors. It was a great country-house with colonnades and terraces where he lived, but he occupied only one small room on the ground floor. He made his way over the neglected, weed-grown paths of the old English garden, toward the village, which was distributed along both sides of the highway.

Nekhliudof was a tall, slender young man, with long, thick, wavy auburn hair, with a bright gleam in his dark eyes, a clear complexion, and rosy lips where the first down of young manhood was now beginning to appear.

In all his motions and gait, could be seen strength, energy, and the good-natured self-satisfaction of youth.

The serfs, in variegated groups, were returning from church: old men, maidens, children, mothers with babies in their arms, dressed in their Sunday best, were scattering to their homes; and as they met the bárin they bowed low and made room for him to pass.

After Nekhliudof had walked some distance along the street, he stopped, and drew from his pocket his note-book, on the last page of which, inscribed in his own boyish hand, were a number of names of his serfs with memoranda. He read, "Iván Churis asks for aid;" and then, proceeding still farther along the street, entered the gate of the second hut[2] on the right.

Churis's domicile consisted of a half-decayed structure, with musty corners; the sides were rickety. It was so buried in the ground, that the

14

banking, made of earth and dung, almost hid the two windows. The one on the front had a broken sash, and the shutters were half torn away; the other was small and low, and was stuffed with flax. A boarded entry with rotting sills and low door, another small building still older and still lower-studded than the entry, a gate, and a barn were clustered about the principal hut.

All this had once been covered by one irregular roof; but now only over the eaves hung the thick straw, black and decaying. Above, in places, could be seen the frame-work and rafters.

In front of the yard were a well with rotten curb, the remains of a post, and the wheel, and a mud-puddle stirred up by the cattle where some ducks were splashing.

Near the well stood two old willows, split and broken, with their whitish-green foliage. They were witnesses to the fact that some one, some time, had taken interest in beautifying this place. Under one of them sat a fair-haired girl of seven summers, watching another little girl of two, who was creeping at her feet. The watch-dog gambolling about them, as soon as he saw the bárin, flew headlong under the gate, and there set up a quavering yelp expressive of panic.

"Iván at home?" asked Nekhliudof.

The little girl seemed stupefied at this question, and kept opening her eyes wider and wider, but made no reply. The baby opened her mouth, and set up a yell.

A little old woman, in a torn checkered skirt, belted low with an old red girdle, peered out of the door, and also said nothing. Nekhliudof approached the entry, and repeated his inquiry.

"Yes, he's at home," replied the little old woman in a quavering voice, bowing low, and evincing timidity and agitation.

After Nekhliudof had asked after her health, and passed through the entry into the little yard, the old woman, resting her chin in her hand, went to the door, and, without taking her eyes off the bárin, began gently to shake her head.

The yard was in a wretched condition, with heaps of old blackened manure that had not been carried away: on the manure were thrown in confusion a rotting block, pitchforks, and two harrows.

There were pent-houses around the yard, under one side of which stood a wooden plough, a cart without a wheel, and a pile of empty good-for-nothing bee-hives thrown one upon another. The roof was in disrepair; and one side had fallen in so that the covering in front rested, not on the supports, but on the manure.

Churis, with the edge and head of an axe, was breaking off the wattles that strengthened the roof. Iván was a peasant, fifty years of age. In stature, he was short. The features of his tanned oval face, framed in a dark auburn beard and hair where a trace of gray was beginning to appear, were handsome and expressive. His dark blue eyes gleamed with intelligence and lazy good-nature, from under half-shut lids. His small, regular mouth, sharply defined under his sandy thin mustache when he smiled, betrayed a calm self-confidence, and a certain bantering indifference toward all around him.

By the roughness of his skin, by his deep wrinkles, by the veins that stood out prominently on his neck, face, and hands, by his unnatural stoop and the crooked position of his legs, it was evident that all his life had been spent in hard work, far beyond his strength.

His garb consisted of white hempen drawers, with blue patches on the knees, and a dirty shirt of the same material, which kept hitching up his back and arms. The shirt was belted low in the waist by a girdle, from which hung a brass key.

"Good-day," said the bárin, as he stepped into the yard. Churis glanced around, and kept on with his work; making energetic motions, he finished clearing away the wattles from under the shed, and then only, having struck the axe into the block, he came out into the middle of the yard.

"A pleasant holiday, your excellency!" said he, bowing low and smoothing his hair.

16

"Thanks, my friend. I came to see how your affairs[3] were progressing," said Nekhliudof with boyish friendliness and timidity, glancing at the peasant's garb. "Just show me what you need in the way of supports that you asked me about at the last meeting."

"Supports, of course, sir, your excellency, sir.[4] I should like it fixed a little here, sir, if you will have the goodness to cast your eye on it: here this corner has given way, sir, and only by the mercy of God the cattle didn't happen to be there. It barely hangs at all," said Churis, gazing with an expressive look at his broken-down, ramshackly, and ruined sheds. "Now the girders and the supports and the rafters are nothing but rot; you won't see a sound timber. But where can we get lumber nowadays, I should like to know?"

"Well, what do you want with the five supports when the one shed has fallen in? the others will be soon falling in too, won't they? You need to have every thing made new,—rafters and girders and posts; but you don't want supports," said the bárin, evidently priding himself on his comprehension of the case.

Churis made no reply.

"Of course you need lumber, but not supports. You ought to have told me so."

"Surely I do, but there's nowhere to get it. Not all of us can come to the manor-house. If we all should get into the habit of coming to the manor-house and asking your excellency for every thing we wanted, what kind of serfs should we be? But if your kindness went so far as to let me have some of the oak saplings that are lying idle over by the threshing-floor," said the peasant, making a low bow and scraping with his foot, "then, maybe, I might exchange some, and piece out others, so that the old would last some time longer."

"What is the good of the old? Why, you just told me that it was all old and rotten. This part has fallen in to-day; to-morrow, that one will; the day after, a third. So, if any thing is to be done, it must be all made new, so that the work may not be wasted. Now tell me what you think about it. Can your

17

premises[5] last out this winter, or not?"

"Who can tell?"

"No, but what do you think? Will they fall in, or not?"

Churis meditated for a moment. "Can't help falling in," said he suddenly.

"Well, now you see you had better have said that at the meeting, that you needed to rebuild your whole place,[5] instead of a few props. You see, I should be glad to help you."

"Many thanks for your kindness," replied Churis, in an incredulous tone and not looking at the bárin. "If you would give me four joists and some props, then, perhaps, I might fix things up myself; but if any one is hunting after good-for-nothing timbers, then he'd find them in the joists of the hut."

"Why, is your hut so wretched as all that?"

"My old woman and I are expecting it to fall in on us any day," replied Churis indifferently. "A day or two ago, a girder fell from the ceiling, and struck my old woman."

"What! struck her?"

"Yes, struck her, your excellency: whacked her on the back, so that she lay half dead all night."

"Well, did she get over it?"

"Pretty much, but she's been ailing ever since; but then she's always ailing."

"What, are you sick?" asked Nekhliudof of the old woman, who had been standing all the time at the door, and had begun to groan as soon as her husband mentioned her.

"It bothers me here more and more, especially on Sundays," she replied, pointing to her dirty lean bosom.

"Again?" asked the young master in a tone of vexation, shrugging his shoulders. "Why, if you are so sick, don't you come and get advice at the dispensary? That is what the dispensary was built for. Haven't you been told about it?"

"Certainly we have, but I have not had any time to spare; have had to work in the field, and at home, and look after the children, and no one to help me; if I weren't all alone"....

III.

Nekhliudof went into the hut. The uneven smoke-begrimed walls of the dwelling were hung with various rags and clothes; and, in the living-room, were literally covered with reddish cockroaches clustering around the holy images and benches.

In the middle of this dark, fetid apartment, not fourteen feet square, was a huge crack in the ceiling; and in spite of the fact that it was braced up in two places, the ceiling hung down so that it threatened to fall from moment to moment.

"Yes, the hut is very miserable," said the bárin, looking into the face of Churis, who, it seems, had not cared to speak first about this state of things.

"It will crush us to death; it will crush the children," said the woman in a tearful voice, attending to the stove which stood under the loft.

"Hold your tongue," cried Churis sternly; and with a slight smile playing under his mustaches, he turned to the master. "And I haven't the wit to know what's to be done with it, your excellency,—with this hut and props and planks. There's nothing to be done with them."

"How can we live through the winter here? Okh, okh! Oh, oh!" groaned the old woman.

"There's one thing—if we put in some more props and laid a new floor," said the husband, interrupting her with a calm, practical expression, "and threw over one set of rafters, then perhaps we might manage to get through the winter. It is possible to live; but you'd have to put some props all over the hut, like that: but if it gets shaken, then there won't be any thing left of it. As long as it stands, it holds together," he concluded, evidently perfectly contented that he appreciated this contingency.

Nekhliudof was both vexed and grieved that Churis had got himself into such a condition, without having come to him long before; since he had more than once, during his sojourn on the estate, told the peasants, and insisted upon it, that they should all apply directly to him for whatever they needed.

He now felt some indignation against the peasant; he angrily shrugged his shoulders, and frowned. But the sight of the poverty in the midst of which he found himself, and Churis's calm and self-satisfied appearance in contrast with this poverty, changed his vexation into a sort of feeling of melancholy and hopelessness.

"Well, Iván, why on earth didn't you tell me about this before?" he asked in a tone of reproach, as he took a seat on the filthy, unsteady bench.

"I didn't dare to, your excellency," replied Churis with the same scarcely perceptible smile, shuffling with his black, bare feet over the uneven surface of the mud floor; but this he said so fearlessly and with such composure, that it was hard to believe that he had any timidity about going to his master.

"We are mere peasants; how could we be so presuming?" began the old woman, sobbing.

"Hush up," said Churis, again addressing her.

"It is impossible for you to live in this hut: it's all rotten," cried Nekhliudof after a brief silence. "Now, this is how we shall manage it, my friend"[6]....

"I am listening."

"Have you seen the improved stone cottages that I have been building at the new farm,—the one with the undressed walls?"

"Indeed I have seen them," replied Churis, with a smile that showed his white teeth still unimpaired. "Everybody's agog at the way they're built. Fine cottages! The boys were laughing and wondering if they wouldn't be turned into granaries; they would be so secure against rats. Fine cottages," he said in conclusion, with an expression of absurd perplexity, shaking his head, "just like a jail!"

"Yes, they're splendid cottages, dry and warm, and no danger of fire," replied the bárin, a frown crossing his youthful face as he perceived the peasant's involuntary sarcasm.

"Without question, your excellency, fine cottages."

"Well, then, one of these cottages is just finished. It is twenty-four feet square, with an entry, and a barn, and it's entirely ready. I will let you have it on credit if you say so, at cost price; you can pay for it at your own convenience," said the bárin with a self-satisfied smile, which he could not control, at the thought of his benevolence. "You can pull down this old one," he went on to say; "it will make you a granary. We will also move the pens. The water there is splendid. I will give you enough land for a vegetable-garden, and I'll let you have a strip of land on all three sides. You can live there in a decent way. Now, does not that please you?" asked Nekhliudof, perceiving that as soon as he spoke of moving, Churis became perfectly motionless, and looked at the ground without even a shadow of a smile.

"It's as your excellency wills," he replied, not raising his eyes.

The old woman came forward as though something had stung her to the quick, and began to speak; but her husband anticipated her.

"It's as your excellency wills," he repeated resolutely, and at the same time humbly glancing at his master, and tossing back his hair. "But it would never do for us to live on a new farm."

"Why not?"

"Nay, your excellency, not if you move us over there: here we are wretched enough, but over there we could never in the world get along. What kind of peasants should we be there? Nay, nay, it is impossible for us to live there."

"But why not, pray?"

"We should be totally ruined, your excellency."

"But why can't you live there?"

"What kind of a life would it be? Just think! it has never been lived in; we don't know any thing about the water, no pasture anywhere. Here we have had hemp-fields ever since we can remember, all manured; but what is there there? Yes, what is there there? A wilderness! No hedges, no corn-kilns, no sheds, no nothing at all! Oh, yes, your excellency; we should be ruined if you took us there; we should be perfectly ruined. A new place, all unknown to us," he repeated, shaking his head thoughtfully but resolutely.

Nekhliudof tried to point out to the peasant that the change, on the contrary, would be very advantageous for him; that they would plant hedges, and build sheds; that the water there was excellent, and so on: but Churis's obstinate silence exasperated him, and he accordingly felt that he was speaking to no purpose.

Churis made no objection to what he said; but when the master finished speaking, he remarked with a crafty smile, that it would be best of all to remove to that farm some of the old domestic servants, and Alyósha the fool, so that they might watch over the grain there.

"That would be worth while," he remarked, and smiled once more. "This is foolish business, your excellency."

"What makes you think the place is not inhabitable?" insisted Nekhliudof patiently. "This place here isn't inhabitable, and hasn't been, and yet you live here. But there, you will get settled there before you know it; you will certainly find it easy"....

"But, your excellency, kind sir,[7] how can it be compared?" replied Churis eagerly, as though he feared that the master would not accept a conclusive argument. "Here is our place in the world; we are happy in it; we are accustomed to it, and the road and the pond—where would the old woman do her washing? where would the cattle get watered? And all our peasant ways are here; here from time out of mind. And here's the threshing-floor, and the little garden, and the willows; and here my parents lived, and my grandfather; and my father gave his soul into God's keeping here, and I too would end my days here, your excellency. I ask nothing more than that. Be good, and let the hut be put in order; we shall be always grateful for your kindness: but no, not for any thing, would we spend our last days anywhere else. Let us stay here and say our prayers," he continued, bowing low; "do not take us from our nest, kind sir."[8]

All the time that Churis was speaking, there was heard in the place under the loft, where his wife was standing, sobs growing more and more violent; and when the husband said "kind sir," she suddenly darted forward, and with tears in her eyes threw herself at the bárin's feet.

"Don't destroy us, benefactor; you are our father, you are our mother! Where are you going to move us to? We are old folks; we have no one to help us. You are to us as God is," lamented the old woman.

Nekhliudof leaped up from the bench, and was going to lift the old woman; but she, with a sort of passionate despair, beat her forehead on the earth floor, and pushed aside the master's hand.

"What is the matter with you? Get up, I beg of you. If you don't wish to go, it is not necessary. I won't oblige you to," said he, waving his hand, and retreating to the door.

When Nekhliudof sat down on the bench again, and silence was restored in the room, interrupted only by the sobs of the old woman, who was once more busy under the loft, and was wiping away her tears with the sleeves of her shirt, the young proprietor began to comprehend what was meant for the peasant and his wife by the dilapidated little hut, the crumbling well with the filthy pool, the decaying stalls and sheds, and the broken willows which could be seen before the crooked window; and the feeling that arose in him was burdensome, melancholy, and touched with shame.

"Why didn't you tell the Commune last Sunday, Iván, that you needed a new hut? I don't know, now, how to help you. I told you all at the first meeting, that I had come to live in the country, and devote my life to you, that I was ready to deprive myself of every thing to make you happy and contented; and I vowed before God, now, that I would keep my word," said the young proprietor, not knowing that such a manner of opening the heart is incapable of arousing faith in any one, and especially in the Russian, who loves not words but deeds, and is reluctant to be stirred up by feelings, no matter how beautiful they may be.

But the simple-hearted young man was so pleased with this feeling that he experienced, that he could not help speaking.

Churis leaned his head to one side, and slowly blinking, listened with constrained attention to his master, as to a man to whom he must needs listen, even though he says things not entirely good, and absolutely foreign to his way of thinking.

"But you see I cannot do all that everybody asks of me. If I did not refuse some who ask me for wood, I myself should be left without any, and I could not give to those who really needed. When I made this rule, I did it for the regulation of the peasants' affairs; and I put it entirely in the hands of the Commune. This wood now is not mine, but yours, you peasants', and I cannot any longer dispose of it; but the Commune disposes of it, as you know. Come to the meeting to-night. I will tell the Commune about your request: if they are disposed to give you a new hut, well and good; but I haven't any more wood. I wish with all my soul to help you; but if you aren't willing to move, then it is no longer my affair, but the Commune's. Do you understand me?"

"Many thanks for your kindness," replied Churis in some agitation. "If you will give me some lumber, then we can make repairs. What is the Commune? It's a well-known fact that".…

"No, you come."

"I obey. I will come. Why shouldn't I come? Only this thing is sure: I won't ask the Commune."

IV.

The young proprietor evidently desired to ask some more questions of the peasants. He did not move from the bench; and he glanced irresolutely, now at Churis, now at the empty, unlighted stove.

"Well, have you had dinner yet?" he asked at last.

A mocking smile arose to Churis's lips, as though it were ridiculous to him for his master to ask such foolish questions; he made no reply.

"What do you mean,—dinner, benefactor?" said the old woman, sighing deeply. "We've eaten a little bread; that's our dinner. We couldn't get any vegetables to-day so as to boil some soup,[9] but we had a little kvas,— enough for the children."

"To-day was a fast-day for us, your excellency," remarked Churis sarcastically, taking up his wife's words. "Bread and onions; that's the way we peasants live. Howsomever, praise be to the Lord, I have a little grain yet, thanks to your kindness; it's lasted till now; but there's plenty of our peasants as ain't got any. Everywheres there's scarcity of onions. Only a day or two ago they sent to Mikháïl the gardener, to get a bunch for a farthing: couldn't get any anywheres. Haven't been to God's church scarcely since Easter. Haven't had nothing to buy a taper for Mikóla [St. Nicholas] with."

Nekhliudof, not by hearsay nor by trust in the words of others, but by the evidence of his own eyes, had long known the extreme depth of poverty into which his peasantry had sunken: but the entire reality was in such perfect contrast to his own bringing-up, the turn of his mind, and the course of his life, that in spite of himself he kept forgetting the truth of it; and every time when, as now, it was brought vividly, tangibly, before him, his heart was torn with painful, almost unendurable melancholy, as though some absolute and unavoidable punishment were torturing him.

"Why are you so poor?" he exclaimed, involuntarily expressing his thought.

"How could such as we help being poor, sir,[10] your excellency? Our land is so bad, you yourself may be pleased to know,—clay and sand-heaps; and surely we must have angered God, for this long time, ever since the cholera, the corn won't grow. Our meadows and every thing else have been growing worse and worse. And some of us have to work for the farm, and some detailed for the manor-lands. And here I am with no one to help me, and I'm getting old. I'd be glad enough to work, but I hain't no strength. And my old woman's ailing; and every year there's a new girl born, and I have to feed 'em all. I get tired out all alone, and here's seven dependent on me. I must be a sinner in the eyes of the Lord God, I often think to myself. And when God takes me off sudden-like, I feel it would be easier for me; just as it's better for them than to lead such a dog's life here"....

"Oh, okh!" groaned the old woman, as a sort of confirmation of her husband's words.

"And this is all the help I have," continued Churis, pointing to the white-headed, unkempt little boy of seven, with a huge belly, who at this moment, timidly and quietly pushing the door open, came into the hut, and, resting his eyes in wonder and solemnity on the master, clung hold of Churis's shirt-band with both hands.

"This is all the assistance I have here," continued Churis in a sonorous voice, laying his shaggy hand on the little lad's white hair. "When will he be good for any thing? But my work isn't much good. When I reach old age I shall be good for nothing; the rupture is getting the better of me. In wet weather it makes me fairly scream. I am getting to be an old man, and yet I have to take care of my land.[11] And here's Yermilof, Demkin, Zabref, all younger than I am, and they have been freed from their land long ago. Well, I haven't any one to help me with it; that's my misfortune. Have to feed so many; that's where my struggle lies, your excellency."

"I should be very glad to make it easier for you, truly. But how can I?" asked the young bárin in a tone of sympathy, looking at the serf.

"How make it easier? It's a well-known fact, if you have the land you must do enforced labor also;[12] that's the regulation. I expect something from this youngster. If only you'd be good enough to let him off from going to school. But just a day or two ago, the officer[13] came and said that your excellency wanted him to go to school. Do let him off; he has no capacity for learning, your excellency. He's too young yet; he won't understand any thing."

"No, brother, you're wrong there," said the bárin. "Your boy is old enough to understand; it's time for him to be learning. Just think of it! How he'll grow up, and learn about farming; yes, and he'll know his a-b-c's, and know how to read; and read in church. He'll be a great help to you if God lets him live," said Nekhliudof, trying to make himself as plain as possible, and at the same time blushing and stammering.

"Very true, your excellency. You don't want to do us an injury, but there's no one to take care of the house; for while I and the old woman are doing the enforced labor, the boy, though he's so young, is a great help, driving the cattle and watering the horses. Whatever he is, he's a true muzhík;" and Churis, with a smile, took the lad's nose between his fat fingers, and deftly removed the mucus.

"Nevertheless, you must send him to school, for now you are at home, and he has plenty of time,—do you hear? Don't you fail."

Churis sighed deeply, and made no reply.

V.

"There's one other thing I wished to speak to you about," said Nekhliudof. "Why don't you haul out your manure?"

"What manure, sir,[14] your excellency? There isn't any to haul out. What cattle have I got? One mare and colt; and last autumn I sold my heifer to the porter,—that's all the cattle I've got."

"I know you haven't much, but why did you sell your heifer?" asked the bárin in amazement.

"What have I got to feed her on?"

"Didn't you have some straw for feeding the cow? The others did."

"The others have their fields manured, but my land's all clay. I can't do any thing with it."

"Why don't you dress it, then, so it won't be clay? Then the land would give you grain, and you'd have something to feed to your stock."

"But I haven't any stock, so how am I going to get dressing?"

"That's an odd cercle vicieux," said Nekhliudof to himself; and he actually was at his wits' ends to find an answer for the peasant.

"And I tell you this, your excellency, it ain't the manure that makes the corn grow, but God," continued the peasant. "Now, one summer I had six sheaves on one little unmanured piece of land, and only a twelfth as much on that which was manured well. No one like God," he added with a sigh. "Yes, and my stock are always dying off. Five years past I haven't had any luck with 'em. Last summer one heifer died; had to sell another, hadn't any thing to feed her on; and last year my best cow perished. They were driving her home from pasture; nothing the matter, but suddenly she staggered and staggered. And so now it's all empty here. Just my bad luck!"

"Well, brother, since you say that you have no cattle to help you make fodder, and no fodder for your cattle, here's something towards a cow," said Nekhliudof, reddening, and fetching forth from his pocket a packet of crumpled bank-notes and untying it. "Buy you a cow at my expense, and get some fodder from the granary: I will give orders. See to it that you have a cow by next Sunday. I shall come to see."

Churis hesitated long; and when he did not offer to take the money, Nekhliudof laid it down on the end of the table, and a still deeper flush spread over his face.

"Many thanks for your kindness," said Churis, with his ordinary smile, which was somewhat sarcastic.

The old woman sighed heavily several times as she stood under the loft, and seemed to be repeating a prayer.

The situation was embarrassing for the young prince: he hastily got up from the bench, went out into the entry, and called to Churis to follow him. The sight of the man whom he had been befriending was so pleasant that he found it hard to tear himself away.

"I am glad to help you," said he, halting by the well. "It's in my power to help you, because I know that you are not lazy. You will work, and I will assist you; and, with God's aid, you will come out all right."

"There's no hope of coming out all right, your excellency," said Churis, suddenly assuming a serious and even stern expression of countenance, as though the young man's assurance that he would come out all right had awakened all his opposition. "In my father's time my brothers and I did not see any lack; but when he died, we broke all up. It kept going from bad to worse. Perfect wretchedness!"

"Why did you break up?"

"All on account of the women, your excellency. It was just after your grandfather died; when he was alive, we should not have ventured to do it: then the present order of things came in. He was just like you, he took an interest in every thing; and we should not have dared to separate. The late master did not like to look after the peasants; but after your grandfather's time, Andréï Ilyitch took charge. God forgive him! he was a drunken, careless man. We came to him once and again with complaints,—no living on account of the women,—begged him to let us separate. Well, he put it off, and put it off; but at last things came to such a pass, the women kept each to their own part; we began to live apart; and, of course, what could a single peasant do? Well, there wasn't no law or order. Andréï Ilyitch managed simply to suit himself. 'Take all you can get.' And whatever he could extort from a peasant, he took without asking. Then the poll-tax was raised, and they began to exact more provisions, and we had less and less land, and the grain stopped growing. Well, when the new allotment was made, then he took away from us our manured land, and added it to the master's, the villain, and ruined us entirely. He ought to have been hung. Your father[15]—the kingdom of heaven be his!—was a good bárin, but it was rarely enough that we ever had sight of him: he always lived in Moscow. Well, of course they used to drive the carts in pretty often. Sometimes it would be the season of bad roads,[16] and no fodder; but no matter! The bárin couldn't get along without it. We did not dare to complain at this, but there wasn't system. But now your grace lets any of us peasants see your face, and so a change has come over us; and the overseer is a different kind of man. Now we know for sure that we have a bárin. And it is impossible to say how grateful your peasants are for your kindness. But before you came, there wasn't any real bárin: every one was

29

bárin. Ilyitch was bárin, and his wife put on the airs of a lady,[17] and the scribe from the police-station was bárin. Too many of em! ukh! the peasants had to put up with many trials."

Again Nekhliudof experienced a feeling akin to shame or remorse. He put on his hat, and went on his way.

VI.

"Yukhvanka the clever[18] wants to sell a horse," was what Nekhliudof next read in his note-book; and he proceeded along the street to Yukhvanka's place.[19] Yukhvanka's hut was carefully thatched with straw from the threshing-floor of the estate; the frame-work was of new light-gray aspen-wood (also from stock belonging to the estate), had two handsome painted shutters for the window, and a porch with eaves and ingenious balustrades cut out of deal planks.

The narrow entry and the cold hut were also in perfect order; but the general impression of sufficiency and comfort given by this establishment was somewhat injured by a barn enclosed in the gates, which had a dilapidated hedge and a sagging pent roof, appearing from behind it.

Just as Nekhliudof approached the steps from one side, two peasant women came up on the other carrying a tub full of water. One was Yukhvanka's wife, the other his mother.

The first was a robust, healthy-looking woman, with an extraordinarily exuberant bosom, and wide fat cheeks. She wore a clean shirt embroidered on the sleeves and collar, an apron of the same material, a new linen skirt, peasant's shoes, a string of beads, and an elegant four-cornered head-dress of embroidered red paper and spangles.

The end of the water-yoke was not in the least unsteady, but was firmly settled on her wide and solid shoulder. Her easy forcefulness, manifested in her rosy face, in the curvature of her back, and the measured swing of her arms and legs, made it evident that she had splendid health and rugged strength.

Yukhvanka's mother, balancing the other end of the yoke, was, on the contrary, one of those elderly women who seem to have reached the final limit of old age and decrepitude. Her bony frame, clad in a black dilapidated shirt and a faded linen skirt, was bent so that the water-yoke rested rather on her back than on her shoulder. Her two hands, whose distorted fingers seemed to clutch the yoke, were of a strange dark chestnut color, and were convulsively cramped. Her drooping head, wrapped up in some sort of a clout, bore the most monstrous evidences of indigence and extreme old age.

From under her narrow brow, perfectly covered with deep wrinkles, two red eyes, unprotected by lashes, gazed with leaden expression to the ground. One yellow tooth protruded from her sunken upper lip, and, constantly moving, sometimes came in contact with her sharp chin. The wrinkles on the lower part of her face and neck hung down like little bags, quivering at every motion.

She breathed heavily and hoarsely; but her bare, distorted legs, though it seemed as if they would have barely strength to drag along over the ground, moved with measured steps.

VII.

Almost stumbling against the prince, the young wife precipitately set down the tub, showed a little embarrassment, dropped a courtesy, and then with shining eyes glanced up at him, and, endeavoring to hide a slight smile behind the sleeve of her embroidered shirt, ran up the steps, clattering in her wooden shoes.

"Mother,[20] you take the water-yoke to aunt Nastásia," said she, pausing at the door, and addressing the old woman.

The modest young proprietor looked sternly but scrutinizingly at the rosy woman, frowned, and turned to the old dame, who, seizing the yoke with her crooked fingers, submissively lifted it to her shoulder, and was about to direct her steps to the adjacent hut.

"Your son at home?" asked the prince.

The old woman, her bent form bent more than usual, made an obeisance, and tried to say something in reply, but, suddenly putting her hand to her mouth, was taken with such a fit of coughing, that Nekhliudof without waiting went into the hut.

Yukhvanka, who had been sitting on the bench in the "red corner," [21] when he saw the prince, threw himself upon the oven, as though he were anxious to hide from him, hastily thrust something away in the loft, and, with mouth and eyes twitching, squeezed himself close to the wall, as though to make way for the prince.

Yukhvanka was a light-complexioned fellow, thirty years of age, spare, with a young, pointed beard. He was well proportioned, and rather handsome, save for the unpleasant expression of his hazel eyes, under his knitted brow, and for the lack of two front teeth, which immediately attracted one's attention because his lips were short and constantly parted.

He wore a Sunday shirt with bright red gussets, striped print drawers, and heavy boots with wrinkled legs.

The interior of Vanka's hut was not as narrow and gloomy as that of Churis's, though it was fully as stifling, as redolent of smoke and sheep-skin, and showing as disorderly an array of peasant garments and utensils.

Two things here strangely attracted the attention,—a small damaged samovár standing on the shelf, and a black frame near the ikon, with the remains of a dirty mirror and the portrait of some general in a red uniform.

Nekhliudof looked with distaste on the samovár, the general's portrait, and the loft, where stuck out, from under some rags, the end of a copper-mounted pipe. Then he turned to the peasant.

"How do you do, Yepifán?" said he, looking into his eyes.

Yepifán bowed low, and mumbled, "Good-morning, 'slency," [22] with a peculiar abbreviation of the last word, while his eyes wandered restlessly from the prince to the ceiling, and from the ceiling to the floor, and not pausing on any thing. Then he hastily ran to the loft, dragged out a coat, and began to put it on.

"Why are you putting on your coat?" asked Nekhliudof, sitting down on the bench, and evidently endeavoring to look at Yepifán as sternly as possible.

"How can I appear before you without it, 'slency? You see we can understand"....

"I have come to ask you why you need to sell a horse? Have you many horses? What horse do you wish to sell?" said the prince without wasting words, but propounding questions that he had evidently pre-considered.

"We are greatly beholden to you, 'slency, that you do not think it beneath you to visit me, a mere peasant," replied Yukhvanka, casting hasty glances at the general's portrait, at the stove, at the prince's boots, and every thing else except Nekhliudof's face. "We always pray God for your 'slency."

"Why sell the horse?" repeated Nekhliudof, raising his voice, and coughing.

Yukhvanka sighed, tossed back his hair (again his glance roved about the hut), and noticing the cat that lay on the bench contentedly purring, he shouted out to her, "Scat, you rubbish!" and quickly addressed himself to the bárin. "A horse, 'slency, which ain't worth any thing. If the beast was good for any thing, I shouldn't think of selling him, 'slency."

"How many horses have you in all?"

"Three horses, 'slency."

"No colts?"

"Of course, 'slency. There is one colt."

VIII.

"Come, show me your horses. Are they in the yard?"[23]

"Indeed they are, 'slency. I have done as I was told, 'slency. Could we fail to heed you, 'slency? Yakof Ilyitch told me not to send the horses out to pasture. 'The prince,' says he, 'is coming to look at them,' and so we didn't send them. For, of course, we shouldn't dare to disobey you, 'slency."

While Nekhliudof was on his way to the door, Yukhvanka snatched down his pipe from the loft, and flung it into the stove. His lips were still drawn in with the same expression of constraint as when the prince was looking at him.

A wretched little gray mare, with thin tail, all stuck up with burrs, was sniffing at the filthy straw under the pent roof. A long-legged colt two months old, of some nondescript color, with bluish hoofs and nose, followed close behind her.

In the middle of the yard stood a pot-bellied brown gelding with closed eyes and thoughtfully pendent head. It was apparently an excellent little horse for a peasant.

"So these are all your horses?"

"No, indeed, 'slency. Here's still another mare, and here's the little colt," replied Yukhvanka, pointing to the horses, which the prince could not help seeing.

"I see. Which one do you propose to sell?"

"This here one, 'slency," he replied, waving his jacket in the direction of the somnolent gelding, and constantly winking and sucking in his lips.

The gelding opened his eyes, and lazily switched his tail.

"He does not seem to be old, and he's fairly plump," said Nekhliudof. "Bring him up, and show me his teeth. I can tell if he's old."

"You can't tell by one indication, 'slency. The beast isn't worth a farthing. He's peculiar. You have to judge both by tooth and limb, 'slency," replied Yukhvanka, smiling very gayly, and letting his eyes rove in all directions.

"What nonsense! Bring him here, I tell you."

Yukhvanka stood still smiling, and made a deprecatory gesture; and it was only when Nekhliudof cried angrily, "Well, what are you up to?" that he moved toward the shed, seized the halter, and began to pull at the horse, scaring him, and getting farther and farther away as the horse resisted.

The young prince was evidently vexed to see this, and perhaps, also, he wished to show his own shrewdness.

"Give me the halter," he cried.

"Excuse me. It's impossible for you, 'slency,—don't"....

But Nekhliudof went straight up to the horse's head, and, suddenly seizing him by the ears, threw him to the ground with such force, that the gelding, who, as it seems, was a very peaceful peasant steed, began to kick and strangle in his endeavors to get away.

When Nekhliudof perceived that it was perfectly useless to exert his strength so, and looked at Yukhvanka, who was still smiling, the thought most maddening at his time of life occurred to him,—that Yukhvanka was laughing at him, and regarding him as a mere child.

He reddened, let go of the horse's ears, and, without making use of the halter, opened the creature's mouth, and looked at his teeth: they were sound, the crowns full, so far as the young man had time to make his observations. No doubt the horse was in his prime.

Meantime Yukhvanka came to the shed, and, seeing that the harrow was lying out of its place, seized it, and stood it up against the wattled hedge.

"Come here," shouted the prince, with an expression of childish annoyance in his face, and almost with tears of vexation and wrath in his voice. "What! call this horse old?"

"Excuse me, 'slency, very old, twenty years old at least. A horse that"....

"Silence! You are a liar and a good-for-nothing. No decent peasant will lie, there's no need for him to," said Nekhliudof, choking with the angry tears that filled his throat.

He stopped speaking, lest he should be detected in weeping before the peasant. Yukhvanka also said nothing, and had the appearance of a man who was almost on the verge of tears, blew his nose, and slowly shook his head.

"Well, how are you going to plough when you have disposed of this horse?" continued Nekhliudof, calming himself with an effort, so as to speak in his ordinary voice. "You are sent out into the field on purpose to drive

35

the horses for ploughing, and you wish to dispose of your last horse? And I should like to know why you need to lie about it."

In proportion as the prince calmed down, Yukhvanka also calmed down. He straightened himself up, and, while he sucked in his lips constantly, he let his eyes rove about from one object to another.

"Lie to you, 'slency? We are no worse off than others in going to work."

"But what will you go on?"

"Don't worry. We will do your work, 'slency," he replied, starting up the gelding, and driving him away. "Even if we didn't need money, I should want to get rid of him."

"Why do you need money?"

"Haven't no grain, 'slency; and besides, we peasants have to pay our debts, 'slency."

"How is it you have no grain? Others who have families have corn enough; but you have no family, and you are in want. Where is it all gone?"

"Ate it up, 'slency, and now we haven't a bit. I will buy a horse in the autumn, 'slency."

"Don't for a moment think of selling your horse."

"But if we don't then what'll become of us, 'slency? No grain, and forbidden to sell any thing," he replied, turning his head to one side, sucking in his lips, and suddenly glancing boldly into the prince's face. "Of course we shall die of starvation."

"Look here, brother," cried Nekhliudof, paling, and experiencing a feeling of righteous indignation against the peasant. "I can't endure such peasants as you are. It will go hard with you."

"Just as you will, 'slency," he replied, shutting his eyes with an expression of feigned submission: "I should not think of disobeying you. But it comes not from any fault of mine. Of course, I may not please you, 'slency; at all

36

events, I can do as you wish; only I don't see why I deserve to be punished."

"This is why: because your yard is exposed, your manure is not ploughed in, your hedges are broken down, and yet you sit at home smoking your pipe, and don't work; because you don't give a crust of bread to your mother, who gave you your whole place,[24] and you let your wife beat her, and she has to come to me with her complaints."

"Excuse me, 'slency, I don't know what you mean by smoking your pipe," replied Yukhvanka in a constrained tone, showing beyond peradventure that the complaint about his smoking touched him to the quick. "It is possible to say any thing about a man."

"Now you're lying again! I myself saw"....

"How could I venture to lie to you, 'slency?"

Nekhliudof made no answer, but bit his lip, and began to walk back and forth in the yard. Yukhvanka, standing in one place, and not lifting his eyes, followed the prince's legs.

"See here, Yepifán," said Nekhliudof in a childishly gentle voice, coming to a pause before the peasant, and endeavoring to hide his vexation, "it is impossible to live so, and you are working your own destruction. Just think. If you want to be a good peasant, then turn over a new leaf, cease your evil courses, stop lying, don't get drunk any more, honor your mother. You see, I know all about you. Take hold of your work; don't steal from the crown woods, for the sake of going to the tavern. Think how well off you might be. If you really need any thing, then come to me; tell me honestly, what you need and why you need it; and don't tell lies, but tell the whole truth, and then I won't refuse you any thing that I can possibly grant."

"Excuse me, 'slency, I think I understand you, 'slency," replied Yukhvanka smiling as though he comprehended the entire significance of the prince's words.

That smile and answer completely disenchanted Nekhliudof so far as he had any hope of reforming the man and of turning him into the path of virtue by means of moral suasion. It seemed to him hard that it should be wasted energy when he had the power to warn the peasant, and that all that he had said was exactly what he should not have said.

He shook his head gravely, and went into the house. The old woman was sitting on the threshold and groaning heavily, as it seemed to the young proprietor as a sign of approbation of his words which she had overheard.

"Here's something for you to get bread with," said Nekhliudof in her ear, pressing a bank-note into her hand. "But keep it for yourself, and don't give it to Yepifán, else he'll drink it up."

The old woman with her distorted hand laid hold of the door-post, and tried to get up. She began to pour out her thanks to the prince; her head began to wag, but Nekhliudof was already on the other side of the street when she got to her feet.

IX.

"Davidka Byélui[25] asks for grain and posts," was what followed Yukhvanka's case in the note-book.

After passing by a number of places, Nekhliudof came to a turn in the lane, and there fell in with his overseer Yakof Alpátitch, who, while the prince was still at a distance, took off his oiled cap, and pulling out a crumpled bandanna handkerchief began to wipe his fat red face.

"Cover yourself, Yakof! Yakof, cover yourself, I tell you."

"Where do you wish to go, your excellency?" asked Yakof, using his cap to shield his eyes from the sun, but not putting it on.

"I have been at Yukhvanka's. Tell me, pray, why does he act so?" asked the prince as he walked along the street.

"Why indeed, your excellency!" echoed the overseer as he followed behind the prince in a respectful attitude. He put on his cap, and began to twist his mustache.

"What's to be done with him? He's thoroughly good for nothing, lazy, thievish, a liar; he persecutes his mother, and to all appearances he is such a confirmed good-for-nothing that there is no reforming him."

"I didn't know, your excellency, that he displeased you so."

"And his wife," continued the prince, interrupting the overseer, "seems like a bad woman. The old mother is dressed worse than a beggar, and has nothing to eat; but she wears all her best clothes, and so does he. I really don't know what is to be done with them."

Yakof knit his brows thoughtfully when Nekhliudof spoke of Yukhvanka's wife.

"Well, if he behaves so, your excellency," began the overseer, "then it will be necessary to find some way to correct things. He is in abject poverty like all the peasants who have no assistance, but he seems to manage his affairs quite differently from the others. He's a clever fellow, knows how to read, and he's far from being a dishonest peasant. At the collection of the poll-taxes he was always on hand. And for three years, while I was overseer he was bailiff, and no fault was found with him. In the third year the warden took it into his head to depose him, so he was obliged to take to farming. Perhaps when he lived in town at the station he got drunk sometimes, so we had to devise some means. They used to threaten him, in fun, and he came to his senses again. He was good-natured, and got along well with his family. But as it does not please you to use these means, I am sure I don't know what we are to do with him. He has really got very low. He can't be sent into the army, because, as you may be pleased to remember, two of his teeth are missing. Yes, and there are others besides him, I venture to remind you, who absolutely haven't any"....

"Enough of that, Yakof," interrupted Nekhliudof, smiling shrewdly. "You and I have discussed that again and again. You know what ideas I have on this subject; and whatever you may say to me, I still remain of the same opinion."

"Certainly, your excellency, you understand it all," said Yakof, shrugging his shoulders, and looking askance at the prince as though what he saw were worthy of no consideration. "But as far as the old woman is concerned, I beg you to see that you are disturbing yourself to no purpose," he continued. "Certainly it is true that she has brought up the orphans, she has fed Yukhvanka, and got him a wife, and so forth; but you know that is common enough among peasants. When the mother or father has transferred the property[26] to the son, then the new owners get control, and the old mother is obliged to work for her own living to the utmost of her strength. Of course they are lacking in delicate feelings, but this is common enough among the peasantry; and so I take the liberty of explaining to you that you are stirred up about the old woman all for nothing. She is a clever old woman, and a good housewife;[27] is there any reason for a gentleman to worry over her? Well, she has quarrelled with her daughter-in-law; maybe the young woman struck her: that's like a woman, and they would make up again while you torment yourself. You really take it all too much to heart," said the overseer looking with a certain expression of fondness mingled with condescension at the prince, who was walking silently with long strides before him up the street.

"Will you go home now?" he added.

"No, to Davidka Byélui's or Kazyól's—what is his name?"

"Well, he's a good-for-nothing, I assure you. All the race of the Kazyóls are of the same sort. I haven't had any success with him; he cares for nothing. Yesterday I rode past the peasant's field, and his buckwheat wasn't even sowed yet. What do you wish done with such people? The old man taught his son, but still he's a good-for-nothing just the same; whether for himself or for the estate, he makes a bungle of every thing. Neither the warden nor I have been able to do any thing with him: we've sent him to the station-house, and we've punished him at home, because you are pleased now to like"....

"Who? the old man?"

"Yes, the old man. The warden more than once has punished him before the whole assembly, and, would you believe it? he would shake himself, go home, and be as bad as ever. And Davidka, I assure your excellency, is a law-abiding peasant, and a quick-witted peasant; that is, he doesn't smoke and doesn't drink," explained Yakof; "and yet he's worse than the other who gets drunk. There's nothing else to do with him than to make a soldier of him or send him to Siberia. All the Kazyóls are the same; and Matriushka who lives in the village belongs to their family, and is the same sort of cursed good-for-nothing. Don't you care to have me here, your excellency?" inquired the overseer, perceiving that the prince did not heed what he was saying.

"No, go away," replied Nekhliudof absent-mindedly, and turned his steps toward Davidka Byélui's.

Davidka's hovel[28] stood askew and alone at the very edge of the village. It had neither yard, nor cornkiln, nor barn. Only some sort of dirty stalls for cattle were built against one side. On the other a heap of brush-wood and logs was piled up, in imitation of a yard.[29]

Tall green steppe-grass was growing in the place where the court-yard should have been.

There was no living creature to be seen near the hovel, except a sow lying in the mire at the threshold, and grunting.

Nekhliudof tapped at the broken window; but as no one made answer, he went into the entry and shouted, "Holloa there!"[30]

This also brought no response. He passed through the entry, peered into the empty stalls, and entered the open hut.

An old red cock and two hens with ruffs were scratching with their legs, and strutting about over the floor and benches. When they saw a man they spread their wings, and, cackling with terror, flew against the walls, and one took refuge on the oven.

The whole hut, which was not quite fourteen feet[31] square, was occupied by the oven with its broken pipe, a loom, which in spite of its being summer-time was not taken down, and a most filthy table made of a split and uneven plank.

Although it was a dry situation, there was a filthy puddle at the door, caused by the recent rain, which had leaked through roof and ceiling. Loft there was none. It was hard to realize that this was a human habitation, such decided evidence of neglect and disorder was impressed upon both the exterior and the interior of the hovel; nevertheless, in this hovel lived Davidka Byélui and all his family.

At the present moment, notwithstanding the heat of the June day, Davidka, with his head covered by his sheep-skin,[32] was fast asleep, curled up on one corner of the oven. The panic-stricken hen, skipping up on the oven, and growing more and more agitated, took up her position on Davidka's back, but did not awaken him.

Nekhliudof, seeing no one in the hovel, was about to go, when a prolonged humid sigh betrayed the sleeper.[33]

"Holloa! who's there?" cried the prince.

A second prolonged sigh was heard from the oven.

"Who's there? Come here!"

Still another sigh, a sort of a bellow, and a heavy yawn responded to the prince's call.

"Well, who are you?"

Something moved slightly on the oven. The skirt of a torn sheep-skin[34] was lifted; one huge leg in a dilapidated boot was put down, then another, and finally Davidka's entire figure emerged. He sat up on the oven, and rubbed his eyes drowsily and morosely with his fist.

Slowly shaking his head, and yawning, he looked down into the hut, and, seeing the prince, began to make greater haste than before; but still his motions were so slow, that Nekhliudof had time to walk back and forth three times from the puddle to the loom before Davidka got down from the oven.

Davidka Byélui or David White was white in reality: his hair, and his body, and his face all were perfectly white.

He was tall and very stout, but stout as peasants are wont to be, that is, not in the waist alone, but in the whole body. His stoutness, however, was of a peculiar flabby, unhealthy kind. His rather comely face, with pale-blue good-natured eyes, and a wide trimmed beard, bore the impress of ill health.

42

There was not the slightest trace of tan or blood: it was of a uniform yellowish ashen tint, with pale livid circles under the eyes, quite as though his face were stuffed with fat or bloated.

His hands were puffy and yellow, like the hands of men afflicted with dropsy, and they wore a growth of fine white hair. He was so drowsy that he could scarcely open his eyes or cease from staggering and yawning.

"Well, aren't you ashamed of yourself," began Nekhliudof, "sleeping in the very best part of the day,[35] when you ought to be attending to your work, when you haven't any corn?"

As Davidka little by little shook off his drowsiness, and began to realize that it was the prince who was standing before him, he folded his arms across his stomach, hung his head, inclining it a trifle to one side, and did not move a limb or say a word; but the expression of his face and the pose of his whole body seemed to say, "I know, I know; it is an old story with me. Well, strike me, if it must be: I will endure it."

He evidently was anxious for the prince to get through speaking and give him his thrashing as quickly as possible, even if he struck him severely on his swollen cheeks, and then leave him in peace.

Perceiving that Davidka did not understand him, Nekhliudof endeavored by various questions to rouse the peasant from his vexatiously obstinate silence.

"Why have you asked me for wood when you have enough to last you a whole month here, and you haven't had any thing to do? What?"

Davidka still remained silent, and did not move.

"Well, answer me."

Davidka muttered something, and blinked his white eyelashes.

"You must go to work, brother. What will become of you if you don't work? Now you have no grain, and what's the reason of it? Because your land is badly ploughed, and not harrowed, and no seed put in at the right time,—

all from laziness. You asked me for grain: well, let us suppose that I gave it to you, so as to keep you from starving to death, still it is not becoming to do so. Whose grain do I give you? whose do you think? Answer me,—whose grain do I give you?" demanded Nekhliudof obstinately.

"The Lord's," muttered Davidka, raising his eyes timidly and questioningly.

"But where did the Lord's grain come from? Think for yourself, who ploughed for it? who harrowed? who planted it? who harvested it? The peasants, hey? Just look here: if the Lord's grain is given to the peasants, then those peasants who work most will get most; but you work less than anybody. You are complained about on all sides. You work less than all the others, and yet you ask for more of the Lord's grain than all the rest. Why should it be given to you, and not to the others? Now, if all, like you, lay on their backs, it would not be long before everybody in the world died of starvation. Brother, you've got to labor. This is disgraceful. Do you hear, David?"

"I hear you," said the other slowly through his teeth.

X.

At this moment, the window was darkened by the head of a peasant woman who passed carrying some linen on a yoke, and presently Davidka's mother came into the hovel. She was a tall woman, fifty years old, very fresh and lively. Her ugly face was covered with pock-marks and wrinkles; but her straight, firm nose, her delicate, compressed lips, and her keen gray eyes gave witness to her mental strength and energy.

The angularity of her shoulders, the flatness of her chest, the thinness of her hands, and the solid muscles of her black bare legs, made it evident that she had long ago ceased to be a woman, and had become a mere drudge.

She came hurrying into the hovel, shut the door, set down her linen, and looked angrily at her son.

Nekhliudof was about to say something to her, but she turned her back on him, and began to cross herself before the black wooden ikon, that was visible behind the loom.

When she had thus done, she adjusted the dirty checkered handkerchief which was tied around her head, and made a low obeisance to the prince.

"A pleasant Lord's day to you, excellency," she said. "God spare you; you are our father."

When Davidka saw his mother he grew confused, bent his back a little, and hung his head still lower.

"Thanks, Arína," replied Nekhliudof. "I have just been talking with your son about your affairs."[36]

Arína or Aríshka Burlák,[37] as the peasants used to call her when she was a girl, rested her chin on the clinched fist of her right hand, which she supported with the palm of the left, and, without waiting for the prince to speak further, began to talk so sharply and loud that the whole hovel was filled with the sound of her voice; and from outside it might have been concluded that several women had suddenly fallen into a discussion.

"What, my father, what is then to be said to him? You can't talk to him as to a man. Here he stands, the lout," she continued contemptuously, wagging her head in the direction of Davidka's woe-begone, stolid form.

"How are my affairs, your excellency? We are poor. In your whole village there are none so bad off as we are, either for our own work or for yours. It's a shame! And it's all his fault. I bore him, fed him, gave him to drink. Didn't expect to have such a lubber. There is but one end to the story. Grain is all gone, and no more work to be got out of him than from that piece of rotten wood. All he knows is to lie on top of the oven, or else he stands here, and scratches his empty pate," she said, mimicking him.

"If you could only frighten him, father! I myself beseech you: punish him, for the Lord God's sake! send him off as a soldier,—it's all one. But he's no good to me,—that's the way it is."

"Now, aren't you ashamed, Davidka, to bring your mother to this?" said Nekhliudof reproachfully, addressing the peasant.

Davidka did not move.

"One might think that he was a sick peasant," continued Arína, with the same eagerness and the same gestures; "but only to look at him you can see he's fatter than the pig at the mill. It would seem as if he might have strength enough to work on something, the lubber! But no, not he! He prefers to curl himself up on top of the oven. And even when he undertakes to do any thing, it would make you sick even to look at him, the way he goes about the work! He wastes time when he gets up, when he moves, when he does any thing," said she, dwelling on the words, and awkwardly swaying from side to side with her angular shoulders.

"Now, here to-day my old man himself went to the forest after wood, and told him to dig a hole; but he did not even put his hand to the shovel."

She paused for a moment.

"He has killed me," she suddenly hissed, gesticulating with her arms, and advancing toward her son with threatening gesture. "Curse your smooth, bad face!"

She scornfully, and at the same time despairingly, turned from him, spat, and again addressed the prince with the same animation, still swinging her arms, but with tears in her eyes.

"I am the only one, benefactor. My old man is sick, old: yes, and I get no help out of him; and I am the only one at all. And this fellow hangs around my neck like a stone. If he would only die, then it would be easier; that would be the end of it. He lets me starve, the poltroon. You are our father. There's no help for me. My daughter-in-law died of work, and I shall too."

XI.

"How did she die?" inquired Nekhliudof, somewhat sceptically.

"She died of hard work, as God knows, benefactor. We brought her last year from Baburin," she continued, suddenly changing her wrathful expression to one of tearfulness and grief. "Well, the woman[38] was young, fresh, obliging, good stuff. As a girl, she lived at home with her father in clover, never knew want; and when she came to us, then she learned to do our work,—for the estate and at home and everywhere.... She and I—that

46

was all to do it. What was it to me? I was used to it. She was going to have a baby, good father; and she began to suffer pain; and all because she worked beyond her strength. Well, she did herself harm, the poor little sweetheart. Last summer, about the time of the feast of Peter and Paul, she had a poor little boy born. But there was no bread. We ate whatever we could get, my father. She went to work too soon: her milk all dried up. The baby was her first-born. There was no cow, and we were mere peasants. She had to feed him on rye. Well, of course, it was sheer folly. It kept pining away on this. And when the child died, she became so down-spirited,—she would sob and sob, and howl and howl; and then it was poverty and work, and all the time going from bad to worse. So she passed away in the summer, the sweetheart, at the time of the feast of St. Mary's Intercession. He brought her to it, the beast," she cried, turning to her son with wrathful despair. "I wanted to ask your excellency a favor," she continued after a short pause, lowering her voice, and making an obeisance.

"What?" asked Nekhliudof in some constraint.

"You see he's a young peasant still. He demands so much work of me. To-day I am alive, to-morrow I may die. How can he live without a wife? He won't be any good to you at all. Help us to find some one for him, good father."

"That is, you want to get a wife for him? What? What an idea!"

"God's will be done! You are in the place of parents to us."

And after making a sign to her son, she and the man threw themselves on the floor at the prince's feet.

"Why do you stoop to the ground?" asked Nekhliudof peevishly, taking her by the shoulder. "You know I don't like this sort of thing. Marry your son, of course, if you have a girl in view. I should be very glad if you had a daughter-in-law to help you."

The old woman got up, and began to rub her dry eyes with her sleeves. Davidka followed her example, and, rubbing his eyes with his weak fist, with the same patiently-submissive expression, continued to stand, and listen to what Arína said.

"Plenty of brides, certainly. Here's Vasiutka Mikheïkin's daughter, and a right good girl she is; but the girl would not come to us without your consent."

"Isn't she willing?"

"No, benefactor, she isn't."

"Well, what's to be done? I can't compel her. Select some one else. If you can't find one at home, go to another village. I will pay for her, only she must come of her own free will. It is impossible to marry her by force. There's no law allows that; that would be a great sin."

"E-e-kh! benefactor! Is it possible that any one would come to us of her own accord, seeing our way of life, our wretchedness? Not even the wife of a soldier would like to undergo such want. What peasant would let us have his daughter?[39] It is not to be expected. You see we're in the very depths of poverty. They will say, 'Since you starved one to death, it will be the same with my daughter.' Who is to give her?" she added, shaking her head dubiously. "Give us your advice, excellency."

"Well, what can I do?"

"Think of some one for us, kind sir," repeated Arína urgently. "What are we to do?"

"How can I think of any one? I can't do any thing at all for you as things are."

"Who will help us if you do not?" said Arína, drooping her head, and spreading her palms with an expression of melancholy discontent.

"Here you ask for grain, and so I will give orders for some to be delivered to you," said the prince after a short silence, during which Arína sighed, and Davidka imitated her. "But I cannot do any thing more."

Nekhliudof went into the entry. Mother and son with low bows followed the prince.

XII.

"O-okh! alas for my wretchedness!" exclaimed Arína, sighing deeply.

She paused, and looked angrily at her son. Davidka immediately turned around, and, clumsily lifting his stout leg incased in a huge dirty boot over the threshold, took refuge in the opposite door.

"What shall I do with him, father?" continued Arína, turning to the prince. "You yourself see what he is. He is not a bad man;[40] doesn't get drunk, and is peaceable; wouldn't hurt a little child. It's a sin to say hard things of him. There's nothing bad about him, and God knows what has taken place in him to make him so bad to himself. You see he himself does not like it. Would you believe it, father,[41] my heart bleeds when I look at him, and see what suffering he undergoes. You see, whatever he is, he is my son. I pity him. Oh, how I pity him!... You see, it isn't as though he had done any thing against me or his father or the authorities. But, no: he's a bashful man, almost like a child. How can he bear to be a widower? Help us out, benefactor," she said once more, evidently desirous of removing the unfavorable impression which her bitter words might have left upon the prince. "Father, your excellency, I"—She went on to say in a confidential whisper, "My wit does not go far enough to explain him. It seems as though bad men had spoiled him."

She paused for a moment.

"If we could find the men, we might cure him."

"What nonsense you talk, Arína! How can he be spoiled?"

"My father, they spoil him so that they make him a no-man forever! Many bad people in the world! Out of ill-will they take a handful of earth from out of one's path, or something of that sort; and one is made a no-man forever after. Isn't that a sin? I think to myself, Might I not go to the old man Danduk, who lives at Vorobyevka? He knows all sorts of words; and he knows herbs, and he can make charms; and he finds water with a cross. Wouldn't he help me?" said the woman. "Maybe he will cure him."

"What abjectness and superstition!" thought the young prince, shaking

49

his head gloomily, and walking back with long strides through the village.

"What's to be done with him? To leave him in this situation is impossible, both for myself and for the others and for him,—impossible," he said to himself, counting off on his fingers these reasons.

"I cannot bear to see him in this plight; but how extricate him? He renders nugatory all my best plans for the management of the estate. If such peasants are allowed, none of my dreams will ever be realized," he went on, experiencing a feeling of despite and anger against the peasant in consequence of the ruin of his plans. "To send him to Siberia, as Yakof suggests, against his will, would that be good for him? or to make him a soldier? That is best. At least I should be quit of him, and I could replace him by a decent peasant."

Such was his decision.

He thought about this with satisfaction; but at the same time something obscurely told him that he was thinking with only one side of his mind, and not wholly right.

He paused.

"I will think about it some more," he said to himself. "To send him off as a soldier—why? He is a good man, better than many; and I know.... Shall I free him?" he asked himself, putting the question from a different side of his mind. "It wouldn't be fair. Yes, it's impossible."

But suddenly a thought occurred to him that greatly pleased him. He smiled with the expression of a man who has decided a difficult question.

"I will take him to the house," he said to himself. "I will look after him myself; and by means of kindness and advice, and selecting his employment, I will teach him to work, and reform him."

XIII.

"That's the way I'll do," said Nekhliudof to himself with a pleasant self-consciousness; and then, recollecting that he had still to go to the rich peasant Dutlof, he directed his steps toward a lofty and ample establishment, with two chimneys, standing in the midst of the village.

As he passed a neighboring hut on his way thither, he stopped to speak with a tall, disorderly-looking peasant-woman of forty summers, who came to meet him.

"A pleasant holiday, father,"[42] she said, with some show of assurance, stopping at a little distance from him with a pleased smile and a low obeisance.

"Good-morning, my nurse. How are you? I was just going to see your neighbor."

"Pretty well, your excellency, my father. It's a good idea. But won't you come in? I beg you to. My old man would be very pleased."

"Well, I'll come; and we'll have a little talk with you, nurse. Is this your house?"

"It is, sir."[42]

And the nurse led the way into the hut. Nekhliudof followed her into the entry, and sat down on a tub, and began to smoke a cigarette.

"It's hot inside. It's better to sit down here, and have our talk," he said in reply to the woman's invitation to go into the hut.

The nurse was a well-preserved and handsome woman. In the features of her countenance, and especially in her big black eyes, there was a strong resemblance to the prince himself. She folded her hands under her apron, and looking fearlessly at him, and incessantly moving her head, began to talk with him.

"Why is it, father? why do you wish to visit Dutlof?"

"Oh, I am anxious for him to take thirty desiatins[43] of land of me, and enlarge his domain; and moreover I want him to buy some wood from me also. You see, he has money, so why should it be idle? What do you think about it, nurse?"

"Well, what can I say? The Dutlofs are strong people: he's the leading peasant in the whole estate," replied the nurse, shaking her head. "Last summer he built another building out of his own lumber. He did not call upon the estate at all. He has horses, and yearling colts besides, at least six troïkas, and cattle, cows, and sheep; so that it is a sight worth seeing when they are driven along the street from pasture, and the women of the house come out to get them into the yard. There is such a crush of animals at the gate that they can scarcely get through, so many of them there are. And two hundred bee-hives at the very least. He is a strong peasant, and must have money."

"But what do you think,—has he much money?" asked the prince.

"Men say, out of spite of course, that the old man has no little money. But he does not go round talking about it, and he does not tell even his sons, but he must have. Why shouldn't he take hold of the woodland? Perhaps he is afraid of getting the reputation for money. Five years ago he went into a small business with Shkalik the porter. They got some meadow-land; and this Shkalik, some way or other, cheated him, so that the old man was three hundred rubles out of pocket. And from that time he has sworn off. How can he help being forehanded, your excellency, father?" continued the nurse. "He has three farms, a big family, all workers; and besides, the old man—it is hard to say it—is a capital manager. He is lucky in every thing; it is surprising,—in his grain and in his horses and in his cattle and in his bees, and he's lucky in his children. Now he has got them all married off. He has found husbands for his daughters; and he has just married Ilyushka, and given him his freedom. He himself bought the letter of enfranchisement. And so a fine woman has come into his house."

"Well, do they live harmoniously?" asked the prince.

"As long as there's the right sort of a head to the house, they get along. Yet even the Dutlofs—but of course that's among the women. The daughters-in-law bark at each other a little behind the oven, but the old man generally holds them in hand; and the sons live harmoniously."

The nurse was silent for a little.

"Now, the old man, we hear, wants to leave his eldest son, Karp, as master of the house. 'I am getting old,' says he. 'It's my business to attend to the bees.' Well, Karp is a good peasant, a careful peasant; but he doesn't manage to please the old man in the least. There's no sense in it."

"Well, perhaps Karp wants to speculate in land and wood. What do you think about it?", pursued the prince, wishing to learn from the woman all that she knew about her neighbors.

"Scarcely, sir,"[44] continued the nurse. "The old man hasn't disclosed his money to his son. As long as he lives, of course, the money in the house will be under the old man's control; and it will increase all the time too."

"But isn't the old man willing?"

"He is afraid."

"What is he afraid of?"

"How is it possible, sir, for a seignorial peasant to make a noise about his money? And it's a hard question to decide what to do with money anyway. Here he went into business with the porter, and was cheated. Where was he to get redress? And so he lost his money. But with the proprietor he would have any loss made good immediately, of course."

"Yes, hence,".... said Nekhliudof, reddening. "But good-by, nurse."

"Good-by, sir, your excellency. Greatly obliged to you."

XIV.

"Hadn't I better go home?" mused Nekhliudof, as he strode along toward the Dutlof enclosure, and felt a boundless melancholy and moral weariness.

But at this moment the new deal gates were thrown open before him with a creaking sound; and a handsome, ruddy fellow of eighteen in wagoner's attire appeared, leading a troïka of powerful-limbed and still sweaty horses. He hastily brushed back his blonde hair, and bowed to the prince.

"Well, is your father at home, Ilya?" asked Nekhliudof.

"At the bee-house, back of the yard," replied the youth, driving the horses, one after the other, through the half-opened gates.

"I will not give it up. I will make the proposal. I will do the best I can," reflected Nekhliudof; and, after waiting till the horses had passed out, he entered Dutlof's spacious yard.

It was plain to see that the manure had only recently been carried away. The ground was still black and damp; and in places, particularly in the hollows, were left red fibrous clots.

In the yard and under the high sheds, many carts stood in orderly rows, together with ploughs, sledges, harrows, barrels, and all sorts of farming implements. Doves were flitting about, cooing in the shadows under the broad solid rafters. There was an odor of manure and tar.

In one corner Karp and Ignát were fitting a new cross-bar to a large iron-mounted, three-horse cart.

All three of Dutlof's sons bore a strong family resemblance. The youngest, Ilya, who had met Nekhliudof at the gate, was beardless, of smaller stature, ruddier complexion, and more neatly dressed, than the others. The second, Ignát, was rather taller and darker. He had a wedge-shaped beard; and though he wore boots, a driver's shirt, and a lamb's-skin cap, he had not such a festive, holiday appearance as his brother had.

The eldest, Karp, was still taller. He wore clogs, a gray kaftan, and a shirt without gussets. He had a reddish beard, trimmed; and his expression was serious, even to severity.

"Do you wish my father sent for, your excellency?" he asked, coming to meet the prince, and bowing slightly and awkwardly.

"No, I will go to him at the hives: I wish to see what he's building there. But I should like a talk with you," said Nekhliudof, drawing him to the other side of the yard, so that Ignát might not overhear what he was about to talk about with Karp.

The self-confidence and degree of pride noticeable in the deportment of the two peasants, and what the nurse had told the young prince, so troubled him, that it was difficult for him to make up his mind to speak with them about the matter proposed.

He had a sort of guilty feeling, and it seemed to him easier to speak with one brother out of the hearing of the other. Karp seemed surprised that the prince took him to one side, but he followed him.

"Well, now," began Nekhliudof awkwardly,—"I wished to inquire of you if you had many horses."

"We have about five troïkas, also some colts," replied Karp in a free-and-easy manner, scratching his back.

"Well, are your brothers going to take out relays of horses for the post?"

"We shall send out three troïkas to carry the mail. And there's Ilyushka, he has been off with his team; but he's just come back."

"Well, is that profitable for you? How much do you earn that way?"

"What do you mean by profit, your excellency? We at least get enough to live on and bait our horses, thank God for that!"

"Then, why don't you take hold of something else? You see, you might buy wood, or take more land."

"Of course, your excellency: we might rent some land if there were any convenient."

"I wish to make a proposition to you. Since you only make enough out of your teaming to live on, you had better take thirty desiatins of land from me. All that strip behind Sapof I will let you have, and you can carry on your farming better."

And Nekhliudof, carried away by his plan for a peasant farm, which more than once he had proposed to himself, and deliberated about, began fluently to explain to the peasant his proposition about it.

Karp listened attentively to the prince's words.

"We are very grateful for your kindness," said he, when Nekhliudof stopped, and looked at him in expectation of his answer. "Of course here there's nothing very bad. To occupy himself with farming is better for a peasant than to go off as a whip. He goes among strangers; he sees all sorts of men; he gets wild. It's the very best thing for a peasant, to occupy himself with land."

"You think so, do you?"

"As long as my father is alive, how can I think, your excellency? It's as he wills."

"Take me to the bee-hives. I will talk with him."

"Come with me this way," said Karp, slowly directing himself to the barn back of the house. He opened a low gate which led to the apiary, and after letting the prince pass through, he shut it, and returned to Ignát, and silently took up his interrupted labors.

XV.

Nekhliudof, stooping low, passed through the low gate, under the gloomy shed, to the apiary, which was situated behind the yard.

A small space, surrounded by straw and a wattled hedge, through the chinks of which the light streamed, was filled with bee-hives symmetrically arranged, and covered with shavings, while the golden bees were humming around them. Every thing was bathed in the warm and brilliant rays of the July sun.

From the gate a well-trodden footway led through the middle to a wooden side-building, with a tin-foil image on it gleaming brightly in the sun.

A few orderly young lindens lifting, above the thatched roof of the neighboring court-yard, their bushy tops, almost audibly rustled their dark-green, fresh foliage, in unison with the sound of the buzzing bees. All the shadows from the covered hedge, from the lindens, and from the hives, fell dark and short on the delicate curling grass springing up between the planks.

The bent, small figure of the old man, with his gray hair and bald spot shining in the sun, was visible near the door of a straw-thatched structure situated among the lindens. When he heard the creaking of the gate, the old man looked up, and wiping his heated, sweaty face with the flap of his shirt, and smiling with pleasure, came to meet the prince.

In the apiary it was so comfortable, so pleasant, so warm, so free! The figure of the gray-haired old man, with thick wrinkles radiating from his eyes, and wearing wide shoes on his bare feet, as he came waddling along, good-naturedly and contentedly smiling, to welcome the prince to his own private possessions, was so ingenuously soothing that Nekhliudof for a moment forgot the trying impressions of the morning, and his cherished dream came vividly up before him. He already saw all his peasants just as prosperous and contented as the old man Dutlof, and all smiling soothingly and pleasantly upon him, because to him alone they were indebted for their prosperity and happiness.

"Would you like a net, your excellency? The bees are angry now," said the old man, taking down from the fence a dirty gingham bag fragrant of honey, and handing it to the prince. "The bees know me, and don't sting," he added, with the pleasant smile that rarely left his handsome sunburned face.

"I don't need it either. Well, are they swarming yet?" asked Nekhliudof, also smiling, though without knowing why.

"Yes, they are swarming, father, Mitri Mikolayévitch,"[45] replied the old man, throwing an expression of peculiar endearment into this form of addressing his bárin by his name and patronymic. "They have only just begun to swarm; it has been a cold spring, you know."

"I have just been reading in a book," began Nekhliudof, defending himself from a bee which had got entangled in his hair, and was buzzing under his ear, "that if the wax stands straight on the bars, then the bees swarm earlier. Therefore such hives as are made of boards ... with cross-b—"

"You don't want to gesticulate; that makes it worse," said the little old man. "Now don't you think you had better put on the net?"

Nekhliudof felt a sharp pain, but by some sort of childish egotism he did not wish to give in to it; and so, once more refusing the bag, continued to talk with the old man about the construction of hives, about which he had read in

"Maison Rustique," and which, according to his idea, ought to be made twice as large. But another bee stung him in the neck, and he lost the thread of his discourse and stopped short in the midst of it.

"That's well enough, father, Mitri Mikolayévitch," said the old man, looking at the prince with paternal protection; "that's well enough in books, as you say. Yes; maybe the advice is given with some deceit, with some hidden meaning; but only just let him do as he advises, and we shall be the first to have a good laugh at his expense. And this happens! How are you going to teach the bees where to deposit their wax? They themselves put it on the cross-bar, sometimes straight and sometimes aslant. Just look here!" he continued, opening one of the nearest hives, and gazing at the entrance-hole blocked by a bee buzzing and crawling on the crooked comb. "Here's a young one. It sees; at its head sits the queen, but it lays the wax straight and sideways, both according to the position of the block," said the old man, evidently carried away by his interest in his occupation, and not heeding the prince's situation. "Now, to-day, it will fly with the pollen. To-day is warm; it's on the watch," he continued, again covering up the hive and pinning down with a cloth the crawling bee; and then brushing off into his rough palm a few of the insects from his wrinkled neck.

The bees did not sting him; but as for Nekhliudof, he could scarcely refrain from the desire to beat a retreat from the apiary. The bees had already stung him in three places, and were buzzing angrily on all sides around his head and neck.

"You have many hives?" he asked as he retreated toward the gate.

"What God has given," replied Dutlof sarcastically. "It is not necessary to count them, father; the bees don't like it. Now, your excellency, I wanted to ask a favor of you," he went on to say, pointing to the small posts standing by the fence. "It was about Osip, the nurse's husband. If you would only speak to him. In our village it's so hard to act in a neighborly way; it's not good."

"How so?... Ah, how they sting!" exclaimed the prince, already seizing the latch of the gate.

"Every year now, he lets his bees out among my young ones. We could stand it, but strange bees get away their comb and kill them," said the old man, not heeding the prince's grimaces.

"Very well, by and by; right away," said Nekhliudof. And having no longer strength of will to endure, he hastily beat a retreat through the gate, fighting his tormentors with both hands.

"Rub it with dirt. It's nothing," said the old man, coming to the door after the prince. The prince took some earth, and rubbed the spot where he had been stung, and reddened as he cast a quick glance at Karp and Ignát, who did not deign to look at him. Then he frowned angrily.

XVI.

"I wanted to ask you something about my sons, your excellency," said the old man, either pretending not to notice, or really not noticing, the prince's angry face.

"What?"

"Well, we are well provided with horses, praise the Lord! and that's our trade, and so we don't have to work on your land."

"What do you mean?"

"If you would only be kind enough to let my sons have leave of absence, then Ilyushka and Ignát would take three troïkas, and go out teaming for all summer. Maybe they'd earn something."

"Where would they go?"

"Just as it happened," replied Ilyushka, who at this moment, having put the horses under the shed, joined his father. "The Kadminski boys went with eight horses to Romen. Not only earned their own living, they say, but brought back a gain of more than three hundred per cent. Fodder, they say, is cheap at Odest."

"Well, that's the very thing I wanted to talk with you about," said the prince, addressing the old man, and anxious to draw him shrewdly into a talk about the farm. "Tell me, please, if it would be more profitable to go to teaming than farming at home?"

"Why not more profitable, your excellency?" said Ilyushka, again putting in his word, and at the same time quickly shaking back his hair. "There's no way of keeping horses at home."

"Well, how much do you earn in the summer?"

"Since spring, as feed was high, we went to Kief with merchandise, and to Kursk, and back again to Moscow with grits; and in that way we earned our living. And our horses had enough, and we brought back fifteen rubles in money."

"There's no harm in taking up with an honorable profession, whatever it is," said the prince, again addressing the old man. "But it seems to me that you might find another form of activity. And besides, this work is such that a young man goes everywhere. He sees all sorts of people,—may get wild," he added, quoting Karp's words.

"What can we peasants take up with, if not teaming?" objected the old man with his sweet smile. "If you are a good driver, you get enough to eat, and so do your horses; but, as regards mischief, they are just the same as at home, thank the Lord! It isn't the first time that they have been. I have been myself, and never saw any harm in it, nothing but good."

"How many other things you might find to do at home! with fields and meadows"—

"How is it possible?" interrupted Ilyushka with animation. "We were born for this. All the regulations are at our fingers' ends. We like the work. It's the most enjoyable we have, your excellency. How we like to go teaming!"

"Your excellency, will you not do us the honor of coming into the house? You have not yet seen our new domicile," said the old man, bowing low, and winking to his son.

Ilyushka hastened into the house, and Nekhliudof and the old man followed after him.

XVII.

As soon as he got into the house, the old man bowed once more; then using his coat-tail to dust the bench in the front of the room, he smiled, and said,—

"What do you want of us, your excellency?"

The hut was bright and roomy, with a chimney; and it had a loft and berths. The fresh aspen-wood beams, between which could be seen the moss, scarcely faded, were as yet not turned dark. The new benches and the loft were not polished smooth, and the floor was not worn. One young peasant woman, rather lean, with a serious oval face, was sitting on a berth, and using her foot to rock a hanging cradle that was suspended from the ceiling by a long hook. This was Ilya's wife.

In the cradle lay at full length a suckling child, scarcely breathing, and with closed eyes.

Another young woman, robust and rosy-cheeked, with her sleeves rolled up above her elbows, showing strong arms and hands red even higher than her wrists, was standing in front of the oven, and mincing onions in a wooden dish. This was Karp's wife.

A pock-marked woman, showing signs of pregnancy, which she tried to conceal, was standing near the oven. The room was hot, not only from the summer sun, but from the heat of the oven; and there was a strong smell of baking bread.

Two flaxen-headed little boys and a girl gazed down from the loft upon the prince, with faces full of curiosity. They had come in, expecting something to eat.

Nekhliudof was delighted to see this happy household; and at the same time he felt a sense of constraint in presence of these peasants, men and women, all looking at him. He flushed a little as he sat down on the bench.

"Give me a crust of hot bread: I am fond of it," said he, and the flush deepened.

Karp's wife cut off a huge slice of bread, and handed it on a plate to the prince. Nekhliudof said nothing, not knowing what to say. The women also were silent, the old man smiled benevolently.

"Well, now why am I so awkward? as though I were to blame for something," thought Nekhliudof. "Why shouldn't I make my proposition about the farm? What stupidity!" Still he remained silent.

"Well, father Mitri Mikolayévitch, what are you going to say about my boys' proposal?" asked the old man.

"I should advise you absolutely not to send them away, but to have them stay at home, and work," said Nekhliudof, suddenly collecting his wits. "You know what I have proposed to you. Go in with me, and buy some of the crown woods and some more land"—

"But how are we going to get money to buy it, your excellency?" he asked, interrupting the prince.

"Why, it isn't very much wood, only two hundred rubles' worth," replied Nekhliudof.

The old man gave an indignant laugh.

"Very good, if that's all. Why not buy it?" said he.

"Haven't you money enough?" asked the prince reproachfully.

"Okh! Sir, your excellency!" replied the old man, with grief expressed in his tone, looking apprehensively toward the door. "Only enough to feed my family, not enough to buy woodland."

"But you know you have money,—what do you do with it?" insisted Nekhliudof.

The old man suddenly fell into a terrible state of excitement: his eyes flashed, his shoulders began to twitch.

"Wicked men may say all sorts of things about me," he muttered in a trembling voice. "But, so may God be my witness!" he said, growing more and more animated, and turning his eyes toward the ikon, "may my eyes crack, may I perish with all my family, if I have any thing more than the fifteen silver rubles which Ilyushka brought home; and we have to pay the poll-tax, you yourself know that. And we built the hut"—

"Well, well, all right," said the prince, rising from the bench. "Good-by, friends."[46]

XVIII.

"My God! my God!" was Nekhliudof's mental exclamation, as with long strides he hastened home through the shady alleys of his weed-grown garden, and, absent-mindedly, snapped off the leaves and branches which fell in his way.

"Is it possible that my dreams about the ends and duties of my life are all idle nonsense? Why is it hard for me, and mournful, as though I were dissatisfied with myself because I imagined that having once begun this course I should constantly experience the fulness of the morally pleasant feeling which I had when, for the first time, these thoughts came to me?"

And with extraordinary vividness and distinctness he saw in his imagination that happy moment which he had experienced a year before.

He had arisen very early, before every one else in the house, and feeling painfully those secret, indescribable impulses of youth, he had gone aimlessly out into the garden, and from there into the woods; and, amid the energetic but tranquil nature pulsing with the new life of Maytime, he had wandered long alone, without thought, and suffering from the exuberance of some feeling, and not finding any expression for it.

Then, with all the allurement of what is unknown, his youthful imagination brought up before him the voluptuous form of a woman; and it seemed to him that was the object of his indescribable longing. But another, deeper sentiment said, Not that, and impelled him to search and be disturbed in mind.

Without thought or desire, as always happens after extra activity, he lay on his back under a tree, and looked at the diaphanous morning-clouds drifting over him across the deep, endless sky.

Suddenly, without any reason, the tears sprang to his eyes, and God knows in what way the thought came to him with perfect clearness, filling all his soul and giving him intense delight,—the thought that love and righteousness are the same as truth and enjoyment, and that there is only one truth, and only one possible happiness, in the world.

The deeper feeling this time did not say, Not that. He sat up, and began to verify this thought.

"That is it, that is it," said he to himself, in a sort of ecstasy, measuring all his former convictions, all the phenomena of his life, by the truth just discovered to him, and as it seemed to him absolutely new.

"What stupidity! All that I knew, all that I believed in, all that I loved," he had said to himself. "Love is self-denying; this is the only true happiness independent of chance," he had said over and over again, smiling and waving his hands.

Applying this thought on every side to life, and finding in it confirmation both of life and that inner voice which told him that this was it, he had experienced a new feeling of pleasant agitation and enthusiasm.

"And so I ought to do good if I would be happy," he thought; and all his future vividly came up before him, not as an abstraction, but in images in the form of the life of a proprietor.

He saw before him a huge field, conterminous with his whole life, which he was to consecrate to the good, and in which really he should find happiness. There was no need for him to search for a sphere of activity; it was all ready. He had one out-and-out obligation: he had his serfs....

And what comfortable and beneficent labor lay before him! "To work for this simple, impressionable, incorruptible class of people; to lift them from poverty; to give them pleasure; to give them education which, fortunately, I will turn to use in correcting their faults, which arise from ignorance and superstition; to develop their morals; to induce them to love the right....

What a brilliant, happy future! And besides all this, I, who am going to do this for my own happiness, shall take delight in their appreciation, shall see how every day I shall go farther and farther toward my predestined end. A wonderful future! Why could I not have seen this before?

"And besides," so he had thought at the same time, "who will hinder me from being happy in love for a woman, in enjoyment of family?"

And his youthful imagination portrayed before him a still more bewitching future.

"I and my wife, whom I shall love as no one ever loved a wife before in the world, we shall always live amid this restful, poetical, rural nature, with our children, maybe, and with my old aunt. We have our love for each other, our love for our children; and we shall both know that our aim is the right. We shall help each other in pressing on to this goal. I shall make general arrangements; I shall give general aid when it is right; I shall carry on the farm, the savings bank, the workshop. And she, with her dear little head, and dressed in a simple white dress, which she lifts above her dainty ankle as she steps through the mud, will go to the peasants' school, to the hospital, to some unfortunate peasant who in truth does not deserve help, and everywhere carry comfort and aid.... Children, old men, women, will wait for her, and look on her as on some angel, as on Providence. Then she will return, and hide from me the fact that she has been to see the unfortunate peasant, and given him money; but I shall know all, and give her a hearty hug, and rain kisses thick and fast on her lovely eyes, her modestly-blushing cheeks, and her smiling, rosy lips."

XIX.

"Where are those dreams?" the young man now asked himself as he walked home after his round of visits. "Here more than a year has passed since I have been seeking for happiness in this course, and what have I found? It is true, I sometimes feel that I can be contented with myself; but this is a dry, doubtful kind of content. Yet, no; I am simply dissatisfied! I am dissatisfied because I find no happiness here; and I desire, I passionately long for, happiness. I have not experienced delight, I have cut myself off from all that gives it. Wherefore? for what end? Does that make it easier for any one?

"My aunt was right when she wrote that it is easier to find happiness than to give it to others. Have my peasants become any richer? Have they learned any thing? or have they shown any moral improvement? Not the least. They are no better off, but it grows harder and harder every day for me. If I saw any success in my undertakings, if I saw any signs of gratitude, ... but, no! I see falsely directed routine, vice, untruthfulness, helplessness. I am wasting the best years of my life."

Thus he said to himself, and he recollected that his neighbors, as he heard from his nurse, called him "a mere boy;" that he had no money left in the counting-room; that his new threshing-machine, which he had invented, much to the amusement of the peasants, only made a noise, and did not thresh any thing when it had been set in motion for the first time in presence of numerous spectators, who had gathered at the threshing-floor; that from day to day he had to expect the coming of the district judge for the list of goods and chattels, which he had neglected to make out, having been engrossed in various new enterprises on his estate.

And suddenly there arose before him, just as vividly as, before, that walk through the forest and his ideal of rural life had arisen,—just as vividly there appeared his little university room at Moscow, where he used to sit half the night before a solitary candle, with his chum and his favorite boy friend.

They used to read for five hours on a stretch, and study such stupid lessons in civil law; and when they were done with them, they would send for supper, open a bottle of champagne, and talk about the future which awaited them.

How entirely different the young student had thought the future would be! Then the future was full of enjoyment, of varied occupation, brilliant with success, and beyond a peradventure sure to bring them both to what seemed to them the greatest blessing in the world,—to fame.

"He will go on, and go on rapidly, in that path," thought Nekhliudof of his friend; "but I"....

66

But by this time he was already mounting the steps to his house; and near it were standing a score of peasants and house-servants, waiting with various requests to the prince. And this brought him back from dreams to the reality.

Among the crowd was a ragged and blood-stained peasant-woman, who was lamenting and complaining of her father-in-law, who had been beating her. There were two brothers, who for two years past had been going on shares in their domestic arrangements, and now looked at each other with hatred and despair. There was also an unshaven, gray-haired domestic serf, with hands trembling from the effects of intoxication; and this man was brought to the prince by his son, a gardener, who complained of his disorderly conduct. There was a peasant, who had driven his wife out of the house because she had not worked any all the spring. There was also the wife, a sick woman, who sobbed, but said nothing, as she sat on the grass by the steps,—only showed her inflamed and swollen leg, carelessly wrapped up in a filthy rag.

Nekhliudof listened to all the petitions and complaints; and after he had given advice to one, blamed others, and replied to still others, he began to feel a sort of whimsical sensation of weariness, shame, weakness, and regret. And he went to his room.

XX.

In the small room occupied by Nekhliudof stood an old leather sofa decorated with copper nails, a few chairs of the same description, an old-fashioned inlaid extension-table with scallops and brass mountings, and strewn with papers, and an old-fashioned English grand with narrow keys, broken and twisted.

Between the windows hung a large mirror with an old carved frame gilded. On the floor, near the table, lay packages of papers, books, and accounts.

This room, on the whole, had a characterless and disorderly appearance; and this lively disorder presented a sharp contrast with the affectedly aristocratic arrangement of the other rooms of the great mansion.

When Nekhliudof reached his room, he flung his hat angrily on the table, and sat down in a chair which stood near the piano, crossed his legs, and shook his head.

"Will you have lunch, your excellency?" asked a tall, thin, wrinkled old woman, who entered just at this instant, dressed in a cap, a great kerchief, and a print dress.

Nekhliudof looked at her for a moment or two in silence, as though collecting his thoughts.

"No: I don't wish any thing, nurse," said he, and again fell into thought.

The nurse shook her head at him in some vexation, and sighed.

"Eh! Father, Dmitri Nikolayévitch, are you melancholy? Such tribulation comes, but it will pass away. God knows"....

"I am not melancholy. What have you brought, Malanya Finogenovna?" replied Nekhliudof, endeavoring to smile.

"Ain't melancholy! can't I see?" the old woman began to say with warmth. "The whole livelong day to be all sole alone! And you take every thing to heart so, and look out for every thing; and besides, you scarcely eat any thing. What's the reason of it? If you'd only go to the city, or visit your neighbors, as others do! You are young, and the idea of bothering over things so! Pardon me, little father, I will sit down," pursued the old nurse, taking a seat near the door. "You see, we have got into such a habit that we lose fear. Is that the way gentlemen do? There's no good in it. You are only ruining yourself, and the people are spoiled. That's just like our people: they don't understand it, that's a fact. You had better go to your auntie. What she wrote was good sense," said the old nurse, admonishing him.

Nekhliudof kept growing more and more dejected. His right hand, resting on his knee, lazily struck the piano, making a chord, a second, a third.

Nekhliudof moved nearer, drew his other hand from his pocket, and began to play. The chords which he made were sometimes not premeditated, were occasionally not even according to rule, often remarkable for absurdity, and showed that he was lacking in musical talent; but the exercise gave him a certain indefinable melancholy enjoyment.

At every modification in the harmony, he waited with muffled heartbeat for what would come out of it; and when any thing came, he, in a dark sort of way, completed with his imagination what was missing.

It seemed to him that he heard a hundred melodies, and a chorus, and an orchestra simultaneously joining in with his harmony. But his chief pleasure was in the powerful activity of his imagination; confused and broken, but bringing up with striking clearness before him the most varied, mixed, and absurd images and pictures from the past and the future.

Now it presents the puffy figure of Davidka Byélui, timidly blinking his white eyelashes at the sight of his mother's black fist with its net-work of veins; his bent back, and huge hands covered with white hairs, exhibiting a uniform patience and submission to fate, sufficient to overcome torture and deprivation.

Then he saw the brisk, presuming nurse, and, somehow, seemed to picture her going through the villages, and announcing to the peasants that they ought to hide their money from the proprietors; and he unconsciously said to himself, "Yes, it is necessary to hide money from the proprietors."

Then suddenly there came up before him the fair head of his future wife, for some reason weeping and leaning on his shoulder in deep grief.

Then he seemed to see Churis's kindly blue eyes looking affectionately at his pot-bellied little son. Yes, he saw in him a helper and savior, apart from his son. "That is love," he whispered.

Then he remembered Yukhvanka's mother, remembered the expression of patience and conciliation which, notwithstanding her prominent teeth and her irregular features, he recognized on her aged face.

"It must be that I have been the first during her seventy years of life, to recognize her good qualities," he said to himself, and whispered "Strange;" but he continued still to drum on the piano, and to listen to the sounds.

Then he vividly recalled his retreat from the bees, and the expressions on the faces of Karp and Ignát, who evidently wanted to laugh though they made believe not look at him. He reddened, and involuntarily glanced at the old nurse, who still remained sitting by the door, looking at him with silent attention, occasionally shaking her gray head.

Here, suddenly, he seemed to see a troïka of sleek horses, and Ilyushka's handsome, robust form, with bright curls, gayly shining, narrow blue eyes, fresh complexion, and delicate down just beginning to appear on lip and chin.

He remembered how Ilyushka was afraid that he would not be permitted to go teaming, and how eagerly he argued in favor of the work that he liked so well. And he saw the gray early morning, that began with mist, and the smooth paved road, and the long lines of three-horse wagons, heavily laden and protected by mats, and marked with big black letters. The stout, contented, well-fed horses, thundering along with their bells, arching their backs, and tugging on the traces, pulled in unison up the hill, forcefully straining on their long-nailed shoes over the smooth road.

As the train of wagons reached the foot of the hill, the postman had quickly dashed by with jingling bells, which were echoed far and wide by the great forest extending along on both sides of the road.

"A-a-aï!" in a loud, boyish voice, shouts the head driver, who has a badge on his lambskin cap, and swings his whip around his head.

Beside the front wheel of the front team, the redheaded, cross-looking Karp is walking heavily in huge boots. In the second team Ilyushka shows his handsome head, as he sits on the driver's seat playing the bugle. Three troïka-wagons loaded with boxes, with creaking wheels, with the sound of bells and shouts, file by. Ilyushka once more hides his handsome face under the matting, and falls off to sleep.

Now it is a fresh, clear evening. The deal gates open for the weary horses as they halt in front of the tavern yard; and one after the other, the high mat-covered teams roll in across the planks that lie at the gates, and come to rest under the wide sheds.

Ilyushka gayly exchanges greetings with the light-complexioned, wide-bosomed landlady, who asks, "Have you come far? and will there be many of you to supper?" and at the same time looks with pleasure on the handsome lad, with her bright, kindly eyes.

And now, having unharnessed the horses, he goes into the warm house[47] crowded with people, crosses himself, sits down at the generous wooden bowl, and enters into lively conversation with the landlady and his companions.

And then he goes to bed in the open air, under the stars which gleam down into the shed. His bed is fragrant hay, and he is near the horses, which, stamping and snorting, eat their fodder in the wooden cribs. He goes to the shed, turns toward the east, and after crossing himself thirty times in succession on his broad brawny chest, and throwing back his bright curls, he repeats "Our Father" and "Lord have mercy" a score of times, and wrapping himself, head and all, in his cloak, sleeps the healthy, dreamless sleep of strong, fresh manhood.

And here he sees in his vision the city of Kief, with its saints and throngs of priests; Romen, with its merchants and merchandise; he sees Odest, and the distant blue sea studded with white sails, and the city of Tsar-grad,[48] with its golden palaces, and the white-breasted, dark-browed Turkish maidens; and thither he flies, lifting himself on invisible wings.

He flies freely and easily, always farther and farther away, and sees below him golden cities bathed in clear effulgence, and the blue sky with bright stars, and a blue sea with white sails; and smoothly and pleasantly he flies, always farther and farther away....

"Splendid!" whispers Nekhliudof to himself; and the thought, "Why am I not Ilyushka?" comes to him.

FOOTNOTES:

[1] khozyáïn.

[2] izbá.

[3] khozyáïstvo.

[4] bátiushka.

[5] dvor.

[6] bratets, brother.

[7] bátiushka.

[8] bátiushka.

[9] shchets for shchi.

[10] bátiushka.

[11] The lands belonging to the Russian commune, or mir, were periodically distributed by allotment, each full-grown peasant receiving as his share a tiagló representing what the average man and his wife were capable of cultivating. When the period was long—ten years for instance—it sometimes happened that a serf, by reason of illness, laziness, or other misfortune, would find it hard to cultivate his share, pay the tax on it, and also do the work required of him on his bárin's land. Such was Churis's complaint.

[12] barshchina: work on the master's land.

[13] zemski.

[14] bátiushka.

[15] bátiushka.

[16] raspútitsa.

[17] báruinya.

[18] Yukhvánka-Mudr'yónui.

[19] dvor.

[20] mátushka.

[21] Where the holy images and the lighted taper are to be found.

[22] vaciaso for vashe siátelstvo (your excellency).

[23] dvor.

[24] khozyáïstvo.

[25] Little David White.

[26] khozyáïstvo.

[27] khozyáïka.

[28] izbá.

[29] dvor.

[30] khozyáeva; literally, "master and mistress."

[31] Six arshin.

[32] polushubok.

[33] khozyáïn.

[34] tulup.

[35] Literally, "middle of the white day."

[36] khozyáïstvo.

[37] clod-hopper.

[38] baba.

[39] dyevka, marriageable girl.

[40] muzhík.

[41] bátiushka.

[42] bátiushka.

[43] eighty-one acres.

[44] bátiushka.

[45] bátiushka; Mitri Mikolayévitch, rustic for Dmitri Nikolayévitch.

[46] Proshchaïte, khozyáeva.

[47] izbá.

[48] Constantinople.

LUCERNE.

FROM THE RECOLLECTIONS OF PRINCE NEKHLIUDOF.

July 20, 1857.

Yesterday evening I arrived at Lucerne, and put up at the best inn there, the Schweitzerhof.

"Lucerne, the chief city of the canton, situated on the shore of the Vierwaldstätter See," says Murray, "is one of the most romantic places of Switzerland: here cross three important highways, and it is only an hour's distance by steamboat to Mount Righi, from which is obtained one of the most magnificent views in the world."

Whether that be true or no, other Guides say the same thing, and consequently at Lucerne there are throngs of travellers of all nationalities, especially the English.

The magnificent five-storied building of the Hotel Schweitzerhof is situated on the quay, at the very edge of the lake, where in olden times there used to be the crooked covered wooden bridge[49] with chapels on the corners and pictures on the roof. Now, thanks to the tremendous inroad of Englishmen, with their necessities, their tastes, and their money, the old bridge has been torn down, and in its place has been erected a granite quay, straight as a stick. On the quay are built the long, quadrangular five-storied houses; in front of the houses two rows of lindens have been set out and provided with supports, and between the lindens are the usual supply of green benches.

This is the promenade; and here back and forth stroll the Englishwomen in their Swiss straw hats, and the Englishmen in simple and comfortable attire, and rejoice in that which they have caused to be created. Possibly these quays and houses and lindens and Englishmen would be excellent in their way anywhere else, but here they seem discordant amid this strangely grandiose and at the same time indescribably harmonious and smiling nature.

As soon as I went up to my room, and opened the window facing the lake, the beauty of the sheet of water, of these mountains, and of this sky, at the first moment literally dazzled and overwhelmed me. I experienced an inward unrest, and the necessity of expressing in some manner the feelings that suddenly filled my soul to overflowing. I felt a desire to embrace, powerfully to embrace, some one, to tickle him, or to pinch him; in short, to do to him and to myself something extraordinary.

It was seven o'clock in the evening. The rain had been falling all day, but now it had cleared off.

The lake, blue as heated sulphur, spread out before my windows smooth and motionless, like a concave mirror between the variegated green shores; its surface was dotted with boats, which left behind them vanishing trails. Farther away it was contracted between two monstrous headlands, and, darkling, set itself against and disappeared behind a confused pile of mountains, clouds, and glaciers. In the foreground stretched a panorama of moist, fresh green shores, with reeds, meadows, gardens, and villas. Farther away, the dark-green wooded heights, crowned with the ruins of feudal castles; in the background, the rolling, pale-lilac-colored vista of mountains, with fantastic peaks built up of crags and dead white mounds of snow. And every thing was bathed in a fresh, transparent atmosphere of azure blue, and kindled by the warm rays of the setting sun, bursting forth through the riven skies.

Not on the lake nor on the mountains nor in the skies was there a single completed line, a single unmixed color, a single moment of repose; everywhere motion, irregularity, fantasy, endless conglomeration and variety of shades and lines; and above all, a calm, a softness, a unity, and a striving for the beautiful.

And here amid this indefinable, confused, unfettered beauty, before my very window, stretched in stupid kaleidoscopic confusion the white line of the quay, the lindens with their supports, and the green seats,—miserable, tasteless creations of human ingenuity, not subordinated, like the distant villas and ruins, to the general harmony of the beautiful scene, but on the contrary brutally contradicting it.... Constantly, though against my will, my eyes were attracted to that horribly straight line of the quay; and mentally I should have liked to spurn it, to demolish it like a black spot disfiguring the nose beneath one's eye.

But the quay with the sauntering Englishmen remained where it was, and I involuntarily tried to find a point of view where it would be out of my sight. I succeeded in finding such a view; and till dinner was ready I took delight, alone by myself, in this incomplete and therefore the more enjoyable feeling of oppression that one experiences in the solitary contemplation of natural beauty.

About half-past seven I was called to dinner. Two long tables, accommodating at least a hundred persons, were spread in the great, magnificently decorated dining-room on the first floor.... The silent gathering of the guests lasted three minutes,—the frou-frou of women's dresses, the soft steps, the softly-spoken words addressed to the courtly and elegant waiters. And all the places were occupied by ladies and gentlemen dressed elegantly, even richly, and for the most part in perfect taste.

As is apt to be the case in Switzerland, the majority of the guests were English, and this gave the ruling characteristics of the common table: that is, a strict decorum regarded as an obligation, a reserve founded not in pride but in the absence of any necessity for social relationship, and finally a uniform sense of satisfaction felt by each in the comfortable and agreeable gratification of his wants.

On all sides gleamed the whitest laces, the whitest collars, the whitest teeth,—natural and artificial,—the whitest complexions and hands. But the faces, many of which were very handsome, bore the expression merely of individual prosperity, and absolute absence of interest in all that surrounded them unless it bore directly on their own individual selves; and the white hands glittering with rings, or protected by mitts, moved only for the purpose of straightening collars, cutting meat, or filling wine-glasses; no soul-felt emotion was betrayed in these actions.

Occasionally members of some one family would exchange remarks in subdued voices, about the excellence of such and such a dish or wine, or about the beauty of the view from Mount Righi.

Individual tourists, whether men or women, sat alongside of each other in silence, and did not even seem to see each other. If it happened occasionally, that, out of this five-score human beings, two spoke to each other, the topic of their conversation consisted uniformly in the weather, or the ascent of the Righi.

Knives and forks scarcely rattled on the plates, so perfect was the observance of propriety; and no one dared to convey pease and vegetables to the mouth otherwise than on the fork. The waiters, involuntarily subdued by the universal silence, asked in a whisper what wine you would be pleased to order.

Such dinners invariably depress me: I dislike them, and before they are over I become blue.... It always seems to me as if I were in some way to blame; just as when I was a boy I was set upon a chair in consequence of some naughtiness, and bidden ironically, "Now rest a little while, my dear young fellow." And all the time my young blood was pulsing through my veins, and in the other room I could hear the merry shouts of my brothers.

I used to try to rebel against this feeling of being choked down, which I experienced at such dinners, but in vain. All these dead-and-alive faces have an irresistible ascendency over me, and I myself become also as one dead. I have no desires, I have no thoughts: I do not even observe.

At first I attempted to enter into conversation with my neighbors; but I got no response beyond the phrases which had been repeated in that place a hundred times, a thousand times, with absolutely no variation of countenance.

And yet these people were by no means all stupid and feelingless; but evidently many of them, though they seemed so dead, had got into the habit of leading self-centred lives, which in reality were far more complicated and interesting than my own. Why, then, should they deprive themselves of one of the greatest enjoyments of life,—the enjoyment that comes from the intercourse of man with man?

78

How different it used to be in our pension at Paris, where twenty of us, belonging to as many different nationalities, professions, and individualities, met together at a common table, and, under the influence of the Gallic sociability, found the keenest zest!

There, from the very moment that we sat down, from one end of the table to the other, was general conversation, sandwiched with witticisms and puns, though often in a broken speech. There every one, without being solicitous for the proprieties, said whatever came into his head. There we had our own philosopher, our own disputant, our own bel esprit, our own butt,—all common property.

There, immediately after dinner, we would move the table to one side, and, without paying too much attention to rhythm, take to dancing the polka on the dusty carpet, and often keep it up till evening. There, though we were rather flirtatious, and not over-wise, but perfectly respectable, still we were human beings.

And the Spanish countess with romantic proclivities, and the Italian abbate who insisted on declaiming from the Divine Comedy after dinner, and the American doctor who had the entrée into the Tuileries, and the young dramatic author with long hair, and the pianist who, according to her own account, had composed the best polka in existence, and the unhappy widow who was a beauty, and wore three rings on every finger,—all of us enjoyed this society, which, though somewhat superficial, was human and pleasant. And we each carried away from it hearty recollections of each other, perhaps lighter in some cases, and more serious in others.

But at these English table-d'hôte dinners, as I look at all these laces, ribbons, jewels, pomaded locks, and silken dresses, I often think how many living women would be happy, and would make others happy, with these adornments.

Strange to think how many friends and lovers—most fortunate friends and lovers—are sitting here side by side, without, perhaps, knowing it! And God knows why they never come to this knowledge, and never give each other this happiness, which they might so easily give, and which they so long for.

I began to feel blue, as invariably happens after such a dinner; and, without waiting for dessert, I sallied out in the same frame of mind for a constitutional through the city. My melancholy frame of mind was not relieved, but rather confirmed by the narrow, muddy streets without lanterns, the shuttered shops, the encounters with drunken workmen, and with women hastening after water, or in bonnets, glancing around them as they turned the corners.

It was perfectly dark in the streets, when I returned to the hotel without casting a glance about me, or having an idea in my head. I hoped that sleep would put an end to my melancholy. I experienced that peculiar spiritual chill and loneliness and heaviness, which, without any reason, beset those who are just arrived in any new place.

Looking steadfastly down, I walked along the quay to the Schweitzerhof, when suddenly my ear was struck by the strains of a peculiar but thoroughly agreeable and sweet music.

These strains had an immediately enlivening effect upon me. It was as though a bright, cheerful light had poured into my soul. I felt contented, gay. My slumbering attention was awakened again to all surrounding objects; and the beauty of the night and the lake, to which till then I had been indifferent, suddenly came over me with quickening force like a novelty.

I involuntarily took in at a glance the dark sky with gray clouds flecking its deep blue, now lighted by the rising moon, the glassy dark-green lake with its surface reflecting the lighted windows, and far away the snowy mountains; and I heard the croaking of the frogs over on the Freshenburg shore, and the dewy fresh call of the quail.

Directly in front of me, in the spot whence the sounds of music had first come, and which still especially attracted my attention, I saw, amid the semi-darkness on the street, a throng of people standing in a semi-circle, and in front of the crowd, at a little distance, a small man in dark clothes.

Behind the throng and the man, there stood out harmoniously against

80

the dark, ragged sky, gray and blue, the black tops of a few Lombardy poplars in some garden, and, rising majestically on high, the two stern spires that stand on the towers of the ancient cathedral.

I drew nearer, and the strains became more distinct. At some distance I could clearly distinguish the full accords of a guitar, sweetly swelling in the evening air, and several voices, which, while taking turns with each other, did not sing any definite theme, but gave suggestions of one in places wherever the melody was most pronounced.

The theme was in somewhat the nature of a mazurka, sweet and graceful. The voices sounded now near at hand, now far distant; now a bass was heard, now a tenor, now a falsetto such as the Tyrolese warblers are wont to sing.

It was not a song, but the graceful masterly sketch of a song. I could not comprehend what it was, but it was beautiful.

Those voluptuous, soft chords of the guitar, that sweet, gentle melody, and that solitary figure of the man in black, amid the fantastic environment of the lake, the gleaming moon, and the twin spires of the cathedral rising in majestic silence, and the black tops of the poplars,—all was strange and perfectly beautiful, or at least seemed so to me.

All the confused, arbitrary impressions of life suddenly became full of meaning and beauty. It seemed to me as though a fresh fragrant flower had sprung up in my soul. In place of the weariness, dulness, and indifference toward every thing in the world, which I had been feeling the moment before, I experienced a necessity for love, a fulness of hope, and an unbounded enjoyment of life.

"What dost thou desire, what dost thou long for?" an inner voice seemed to say. "Here it is. Thou art surrounded on all sides by beauty and poetry. Breathe it in, in full, deep draughts, as long as thou hast strength. Enjoy it to the full extent of thy capacity. 'Tis all thine, all blessed!"

I drew nearer. The little man was, as it seemed, a travelling Tyrolese. He stood before the windows of the hotel, one leg a little advanced, his head thrown back; and, as he thrummed on the guitar, he sang his graceful song in all those different voices.

I immediately felt an affection for this man, and a gratefulness for the change which he had brought about in me.

The singer, so far as I was able to judge, was dressed in an old black coat. He had short black hair, and he wore a civilian's hat that was no longer new. There was nothing artistic in his attire, but his clever and youthfully gay motions and pose, together with his diminutive stature, formed a pleasing and at the same time pathetic spectacle.

On the steps, in the windows, and on the balconies of the brilliantly lighted hotel, stood ladies handsomely decorated and attired, gentlemen with polished collars, porters and lackeys in gold-embroidered liveries; in the street, in the semi-circle of the crowd, and farther along on the sidewalk, among the lindens, were gathered groups of well-dressed waiters, cooks in white caps and aprons, and young girls wandering about with arms about each other's waists.

All, it seemed, were under the influence of the same feeling that I myself experienced. All stood in silence around the singer, and listened attentively. Silence reigned, except in the pauses of the song, when there came from far away across the waters the regular click of a hammer, and from the Freshenburg shore rang in fascinating monotone the voices of the frogs, interrupted by the mellow, monotonous call of the quail.

The little man in the darkness, in the midst of the street, poured out his heart like a nightingale, in couplet after couplet, song after song. Though I had come close to him, his singing continued to give me greater and greater gratification.

His voice, which was not of great power, was extremely pleasant and tender; the taste and feeling for rhythm which he displayed in the control of it were extraordinary, and proved that he had great natural gifts.

After he sung each couplet, he invariably repeated the theme in variation, and it was evident that all his graceful variations came to him at the instant, spontaneously.

Among the crowd, and above on the Schweitzerhof, and near by on the boulevard, were heard frequent murmurs of approval, though generally the most respectful silence reigned.

The balconies and the windows kept filling more and more with handsomely dressed men and women leaning on their elbows, and picturesquely illuminated by the lights in the house.

Promenaders came to a halt, and in the darkness on the quay stood men and women in little groups. Near me, at some distance from the common crowd, stood an aristocratic cook and lackey, smoking their cigars. The cook was forcibly impressed by the music, and at every high falsetto note enthusiastically nodded his head to the lackey, and nudged him with his elbow with an expression of astonishment that seemed to say, "How he sings! hey?"

The lackey, whose careless smile betrayed the depth of feeling that he experienced, replied to the cook's nudges by shrugging his shoulders, as if to show that it was hard enough for him to be made enthusiastic, and that he had heard much better music.

In one of the pauses of his song, while the minstrel was clearing his throat, I asked the lackey who he was, and if he often came there.

"Twice this summer he has been here," replied the lackey. "He is from Aargau; he goes round begging."

"Well, do many like him come round here?" I asked.

"Oh, yes," replied the lackey, not comprehending the full force of what I asked; but, immediately after, recollecting himself, he added, "Oh, no. This one is the only one I ever heard here. No one else."

At this moment the little man had finished his first song, briskly twanged his guitar, and said something in his German patois, which I could not understand, but which brought forth a hearty round of laughter from the surrounding throng.

"What was that he said?" I asked.

"He says that his throat is dried up, he would like some wine," replied the lackey who was standing near me.

"What? is he rather fond of the glass?"

"Yes, all that sort of people are," replied the lackey, smiling and pointing at the minstrel.

The minstrel took off his cap, and swinging his guitar went toward the hotel. Raising his head, he addressed the ladies and gentlemen standing by the windows and on the balconies, saying in a half-Italian, half-German accent, and with the same intonation that jugglers use in speaking to their audiences,—

"Messieurs et mesdames, si vous croyez que je gagne quelque chose, vous vous trompez: je ne suis qu'un pauvre tiaple."

He stood in silence a moment, but as no one gave him any thing, he once more took up his guitar and said,—

"À présent, messieurs et mesdames, je vous chanterai l'air du Righi."

His hotel audience made no response, but stood in expectation of the coming song. Below on the street a laugh went round, probably in part because he had expressed himself so strangely, and in part because no one had given him any thing.

I gave him a few centimes, which he deftly changed from one hand to the other, and bestowed them in his vest-pocket; and then, replacing his cap, began once more to sing the graceful, sweet Tyrolese melody which he had called l'air du Righi.

This song, which formed the last on his programme, was even better than the preceding, and from all sides in the wondering throng were heard sounds of approbation.

He finished. Again he swung his guitar, took off his cap, held it out in front of him, went two or three steps nearer to the windows, and again repeated his stock phrase,—

"Messieurs et mesdames, si vous croyez que je gagne quelque chose," which

he evidently considered to be very shrewd and witty; but in his voice and motions I perceived a certain irresolution and childish timidity which were especially touching in a person of such diminutive stature.

The elegant public, still picturesquely grouped in the lighted windows and on the balconies, were shining in their rich attire; a few conversed in soberly discreet tones, apparently about their singer who was standing there below them with outstretched hand; others gazed down with attentive curiosity on the little black figure; on one balcony could be heard the merry, ringing laughter of some young girl.

In the surrounding crowd the talk and laughter grew constantly louder and louder.

The singer for the third time repeated his phrase, but in a still weaker voice, and did not even end the sentence; and again he stretched his hand with his cap, but instantly drew it back. Again not one of those brilliantly dressed scores of people standing to listen to him threw him a penny.

The crowd laughed heartlessly.

The little singer, so it seemed to me, shrunk more into himself, took his guitar into his other hand, lifted his cap, and said,—

"Messieurs et mesdames, je vous remercie, et je vous souhais une bonne nuit." Then he put on his hat.

The crowd cackled with laughter and satisfaction. The handsome ladies and gentlemen, calmly exchanging remarks, withdrew gradually from the balconies. On the boulevard the promenading began once more. The street, which had been still during the singing, assumed its wonted liveliness; a few men, however, stood at some distance, and, without approaching the singer, looked at him and laughed.

I heard the little man muttering something between his teeth as he turned away; and I saw him, apparently growing more and more diminutive, hurry toward the city with brisk steps. The promenaders who had been looking at him followed him at some distance, still making merry at his expense. My mind was in a whirl; I could not comprehend what it all meant; and still standing in the same place, I gazed abstractedly into the darkness after the little man, who was fast disappearing, as he went with ever-increasing swiftness with long strides into the city, followed by the merry-making promenaders.

I was overmastered by a feeling of pain, of bitterness, and above all, of shame for the little man, for the crowd, for myself, as though it were I who had asked for money and received none; as though it were I who had been turned to ridicule.

Without looking any longer, feeling my heart oppressed, I also hurried with long strides toward the entrance of the Schweitzerhof. I could not explain the feeling that overmastered me; only there was something like a stone, from which I could not free myself, weighing down my soul and oppressing me.

At the ample, well-lighted entrance, I met the porter, who politely made way for me. An English family was also at the door. A portly, handsome, and tall gentleman, with black side-whiskers, in a black hat, and with a plaid on one arm, while in his hand he carried a costly cane, came out slowly and full of importance. Leaning on his arm was a lady, who wore a raw silk dress and bonnet with bright ribbons and the most costly laces. Together with them was a pretty, fresh-looking young lady, in a graceful Swiss hat with a feather à la mousquetaire; from under it escaped long light-yellow curls softly encircling her fair face. In front of them skipped a buxom girl of ten, with round white knees which showed from under her thin embroideries. "Magnificent night!" the lady was saying in a sweet, happy voice, as I passed them.

"Oh, yes," growled the Englishman lazily; and it was evident that he found it so enjoyable to be alive in the world, that it was too much trouble even to speak.

And it seemed as though all of them alike found it so comfortable and easy, so light and free, to be alive in the world, their faces and motions expressed such perfect indifference to the lives of every one else, and such absolute confidence that it was to them that the porter made way and bowed so profoundly, and that when they returned they would find clean, comfortable beds and rooms, and that all this was bound to be, and was their indefeasible right, that I involuntarily contrasted them with the wandering minstrel who weary, perhaps hungry, full of shame, was retreating before the laughing crowd. And then suddenly I comprehended what it was that oppressed my heart with such a load of heaviness, and I felt an indescribable anger against these people.

Twice I walked up and down past the Englishman, and each time, without turning out for him, my elbow punched him, which gave me a feeling of indescribable satisfaction; and then, darting down the steps, I hastened through the darkness in the direction toward the city taken by the little man.

Overtaking the three men who had been walking together, I asked them where the singer was; they laughed, and pointed straight ahead. There he was, walking alone with brisk steps; no one was with him; all the time, as it seemed to me, he was indulging in bitter monologue.

I caught up with him, and proposed to him to go somewhere with me and drink a bottle of wine. He kept on with his rapid walk, and scarcely deigned to look at me; but when he perceived what I was saying, he halted.

"Well, I would not refuse, if you would be so kind," said he; "here is a little café, we can go in there. It's not fashionable," he added, pointing to a drinking-saloon that was still open.

His expression "not fashionable" involuntarily suggested the idea of not going to an unfashionable café, but to go to the Schweitzerhof, where those who had been listening to him were. Notwithstanding the fact that several times he showed a sort of timid disquietude at the idea of going to the Schweitzerhof, declaring that it was too fine for him there, still I insisted in carrying out my purpose; and he, putting the best face on the matter, gayly swinging his guitar, went back with me across the quay.

A few loiterers who had happened along as I was talking with the minstrel, and had stopped to hear what I had to say, now, after arguing among themselves, followed us to the very entrance of the hotel, evidently expecting from the Tyrolese some further demonstration.

I ordered a bottle of wine of a waiter whom I met in the hall. The waiter smiled and looked at us, and went by without answering. The head waiter, to whom I addressed myself with the same order, listened to me solemnly, and, measuring the minstrel's modest little figure from head to foot, sternly ordered the waiter to take us to the room at the left.

The room at the left was a bar-room for simple people. In the corner of this room a hunch-backed maid was washing dishes. The whole furniture consisted of bare wooden tables and benches.

The waiter who came to serve us looked at us with a supercilious smile, thrust his hands in his pockets, and exchanged some remarks with the humpbacked dish-washer. He evidently tried to give us to understand that he felt himself immeasurably higher than the minstrel, both in dignity and social position, so that he considered it not only an indignity, but even an actual joke, that he was called upon to serve us.

"Do you wish vin ordinaire?" he asked with a knowing look, winking toward my companion, and switching his napkin from one hand to the other.

"Champagne, and your very best," said I, endeavoring to assume my haughtiest and most imposing appearance.

But neither my champagne, nor my endeavor to look haughty and imposing, had the least effect on the servant: he smiled incredulously, loitered a moment or two gazing at us, took time enough to glance at his gold watch, and with leisurely steps, as though going out for a walk, left the room.

Soon he returned with the wine, bringing two other waiters with him. These two sat down near the dish-washer, and gazed at us with amused attention and a bland smile, just as parents gaze at their children when they are gently playing. Only the dish-washer, it seemed to me, did not look at us scornfully but sympathetically.

Though it was trying and awkward to lunch with the minstrel, and to play the entertainer, under the fire of all these waiters' eyes, I tried to do my duty with as little constraint as possible. In the lighted room I could see him better. He was a small but symmetrically built and muscular man, though almost a dwarf in stature; he had bristly black hair, teary big black eyes, bushy eyebrows, and a thoroughly pleasant, attractively shaped mouth. He had little side-whiskers, his hair was short, his attire was very simple and mean. He was not over-clean, was ragged and sunburnt, and in general had the look of a laboring-man. He was far more like a poor tradesman than an artist.

Only in his ever humid and brilliant eyes, and in his firm mouth, was there any sign of originality or genius. By his face it might be conjectured that his age was between twenty-five and forty; in reality, he was thirty-seven.

Here is what he related to me, with good-natured readiness and evident sincerity, of his life. He was a native of Aargau. In early childhood he had lost father and mother; other relatives he had none. He had never owned any property. He had been apprenticed to a carpenter; but twenty-two years previously one of his hands had been attacked by caries, which had prevented him from ever working again.

From childhood he had been fond of singing, and he began to be a singer. Occasionally strangers had given him money. With this he had learned his profession, bought his guitar, and now for eighteen years he had been wandering about through Switzerland and Italy, singing before hotels. His whole luggage consisted of his guitar, and a little purse in which, at the present time, there was only half a franc. That would have to suffice for supper and lodgings this night.

Every year now for eighteen years he had made the round of the best and most popular resorts of Switzerland,—Zurich, Lucerne, Interlaken, Chamounix, etc.; by the way of the St. Bernard he would go down into Italy, and return over the St. Gothard, or through Savoy. Just at present it was rather hard for him to walk, as he had caught a cold, causing him to suffer from some trouble in his legs,—he called it rheumatism,—which grew more severe from year to year; and, moreover, his voice and eyes had grown weaker. Nevertheless, he was on his way to Interlaken, Aix-les-Bains, and thence over the Little St. Bernard to Italy, which he was very fond of. It was evident that on the whole he was well content with his life.

When I asked him why he returned home, if he had any relatives there, or a house and land, his mouth parted in a gay smile, and he replied, "Oui,

89

le sucre est bon, il est doux pour les enfants!" and he winked at the servants.

I did not catch his meaning, but the group of servants burst out laughing.

"No, I have nothing of the sort, but still I should always want to go back," he explained to me. "I go home because there is always a something that draws one to one's native place." And once more he repeated with a shrewd, self-satisfied smile, his phrase, "Oui, le sucre est bon," and then laughed good-naturedly.

The servants were very much amused, and laughed heartily; only the hunch-backed dish-washer looked earnestly from her big kindly eyes at the little man, and picked up his cap for him, when, as we talked, he once knocked it off the bench. I have noticed that wandering minstrels, acrobats, even jugglers, delight in calling themselves artists, and several times I hinted to my comrade that he was an artist; but he did not at all accept this designation, but with perfect simplicity looked upon his work as a means of existence.

When I asked him if he had not himself written the songs which he sang, he showed great surprise at such a strange question, and replied that the words of whatever he sang were all of old Tyrolese origin.

"But how about that song of the Righi? I think that cannot be very ancient," I suggested.

"Oh, that was composed about fifteen years ago. There was a German in Basel; he was a clever man; it was he who composed it. A splendid song. You see he composed it especially for travellers." And he began to repeat the words of the Righi song, which he liked so well, translating them into French as he went along.

"If you wish to go to Righi,

You will not need shoes to Wegis,

(For you go that far by steamboat),

But from Wegis take a stout staff,

Also take upon your arm a maiden;

90

Drink a glass of wine on starting,

Only do not drink too freely,

For if you desire to drink here,

You must earn the right to, first."

"Oh! a splendid song!" he exclaimed, as he finished.

The servants, evidently, also found the song much to their mind, because they came up closer to us.

"Yes, but who was it composed the music?" I asked.

"Oh, no one at all; you know you must have something new when you are going to sing for strangers."

When the ice was brought, and I had given my comrade a glass of champagne, he seemed somewhat ill at ease, and, glancing at the servants, he turned and twisted on the bench.

We touched our glasses to the health of all artists; he drank half a glass, then he seemed to be collecting his ideas, and knit his brows in deep thought.

"It is long since I have tasted such wine, je ne vous dis que ça. In Italy the vino d'Asti is excellent, but this is still better. Ah! Italy; it is splendid to be there!" he added.

"Yes, there they know how to appreciate music and artists," said I, trying to bring him round to the evening's mischance before the Schweitzerhof.

"No," he replied. "There, as far as music is concerned, I cannot give anybody satisfaction. The Italians are themselves musicians,—none like them in the world; but I know only Tyrolese songs. They are something of a novelty to them, though."

"Well, you find rather more generous gentlemen there, don't you?" I went on to say, anxious to make him share in my resentment against the guests of the Schweitzerhof. "There it would not be possible to find a big hotel frequented by rich people, where, out of a hundred listening to an artist's singing, not one would give him any thing."

My question utterly failed of the effect that I expected. It did not enter his head to be indignant with them: on the contrary, he saw in my remark an implied slur upon his talent which had failed of its reward, and he hastened to set himself right before me. "It is not every time that you get any thing," he remarked; "sometimes one isn't in good voice, or you are tired; now to-day I have been walking ten hours, and singing almost all the time. That is hard. And these important aristocrats do not always care to listen to Tyrolese songs."

"But still, how can they help giving?" I insisted.

He did not comprehend my remark.

"That's nothing," he said; "but here the principal thing is, on est tres serré pour la police, that's what's the trouble. Here, according to these republican laws, you are not allowed to sing; but in Italy you can go wherever you please, no one says a word. Here, if they want to let you, they let you; but if they don't want to, then they can throw you into jail."

"What? That's incredible!"

"Yes, it is true. If you have been warned once, and are found singing again, they may put you in jail. I was kept there three months once," he said, smiling as though that were one of his pleasantest recollections.

"Oh! that is terrible!" I exclaimed. "What was the reason?"

"That was in consequence of one of the new republican laws," he went on to explain, growing animated. "They cannot comprehend here that a poor fellow must earn his living somehow. If I were not a cripple, I would work. But what harm do I do to any one in the world by my singing? What does it mean? The rich can live as they wish, un pauvre tiaple like myself can't live at all. What kind of laws are these republican ones? If that is the way they run, then we don't want a republic: isn't that so, my dear sir? We don't want a republic, but we want—we simply want—we want"—he hesitated a little,—"we want natural laws."

I filled up his glass. "You are not drinking," I said.

He took the glass in his hand, and bowed to me.

"I know what you wish," he said, blinking his eyes at me, and threatening me with his finger. "You wish to make me drunk, so as to see what you can get out of me; but no, you sha'n't have that gratification."

"Why should I make you drunk?" I inquired. "All I wished was to give you a pleasure."

He seemed really sorry that he had offended me by interpreting my insistence so harshly. He grew confused, stood up, and touched my elbow.

"No, no," said he, looking at me with a beseeching expression in his moist eyes. "I was only joking."

And immediately after he made use of some horribly uncultivated slang expression, intended to signify that I was, nevertheless, a fine young man. "Je ne vous dis que ça," he said in conclusion. In this fashion the minstrel and I continued to drink and converse; and the waiters continued unceremoniously to stare at us, and, as it seemed, to make ridicule of us.

In spite of the interest which our conversation aroused in me, I could not avoid taking notice of their behavior; and I confess I began to grow more and more angry.

One of the waiters arose, came up to the little man, and, regarding the top of his head, began to smile. I was already full of wrath against the inmates of the hotel, and had not yet had a chance to pour it out on any one; and now I confess I was in the highest degree irritated by this audience of waiters.

The porter, not removing his hat, came into the room, and sat down near me, leaning his elbows on the table. This last circumstance, which was so insulting to my dignity or my vainglory, completely enraged me, and gave an outlet for all the wrath which all the evening long had been boiling within me. I asked myself why he had so humbly bowed when he had met me before, and now, because I was sitting with the travelling minstrel, he came and took his place near me so rudely? I was entirely overmastered by that boiling, angry indignation which I enjoy in myself, which I sometimes endeavor to stimulate when it comes over me, because it has an exhilarating effect upon me, and gives me, if only for a short time, a certain extraordinary flexibility, energy, and strength in all my physical and moral faculties.

I leaped to my feet.

"Whom are you laughing at?" I screamed at the waiter; and I felt my face turn pale, and my lips involuntarily set together.

"I am not laughing," replied the waiter, moving away from me.

"Yes, you are: you are laughing at this gentleman. And what right have you to come, and to take a seat here, when there are guests? Don't you dare to sit down!"

The porter, muttering something, got up, and turned to the door.

"What right have you to make sport of this gentleman, and to sit down by him, when he is a guest, and you are a waiter? Why didn't you laugh at me this evening at dinner, and come and sit down beside me? Because he is meanly dressed, and sings in the streets? Is that the reason? and because I have better clothes? He is poor, but he is a thousand times better than you are; that I am sure of, because he has never insulted any one, but you have insulted him."

"I didn't mean any thing," replied my enemy the waiter. "Perhaps I disturbed him by sitting down."

The waiter did not understand me, and my German was wasted on him. The rude porter was about to take the waiter's part; but I fell upon him so impetuously that the porter pretended not to understand me, and waved his hand.

The hunch-backed dish-washer, either because she perceived my wrathful state, and feared a scandal, or possibly because she shared my views, took my part, and, trying to force her way between me and the porter, told him to hold his tongue, saying that I was right, but at the same time urging me to calm myself.

94

"Der Herr hat Recht; Sie haben Recht," she said over and over again. The minstrel's face presented a most pitiable, terrified expression; and evidently he did not understand why I was angry, and what I wanted: and he urged me to let him go away as soon as possible.

But the eloquence of wrath burned within me more and more. I understood it all,—the throng that had made merry at his expense, and his auditors who had not given him any thing; and not for all the world would I have held my peace.

I believe, that, if the waiters and the porter had not been so submissive, I should have taken delight in having a brush with them, or striking the defenceless English lady on the head with a stick. If at that moment I had been at Sevastópol, I should have taken delight in devoting myself to slaughtering and killing in the English trench.

"And why did you take this gentleman and me into this room, and not into the other? What?" I thundered at the porter, seizing him by the arm so that he could not escape from me. "What right had you to judge by his appearance that this gentleman must be served in this room, and not in that? Have not all guests who pay, equal rights in hotels? Not only in a republic, but in all the world! Your scurvy republic!... Equality, indeed! You would not dare to take an Englishman into this room, not even those Englishmen who have heard this gentleman free of cost; that is, who have stolen from him, each one of them, the few centimes which ought to have been given to him. How did you dare to take us to this room?"

"That room is closed," said the porter.

"No," I cried, "that isn't true; it isn't closed."

"Then you know best."

"I know,—I know that you are lying."

The porter turned his back on me.

"Eh! What is to be said?" he muttered.

"What is to be said?" I cried. "You conduct us instanter into that room!"

95

In spite of the dish-washer's warning, and the entreaties of the minstrel, who would have preferred to go home, I insisted on seeing the head waiter, and went with my guest into the big dining-room. The head waiter, hearing my angry voice, and seeing my menacing face, avoided a quarrel, and, with contemptuous servility, said that I might go wherever I pleased. I could not prove to the porter that he had lied, because he had hastened out of sight before I went into the hall.

The dining-room was, in fact, open and lighted; and at one of the tables sat an Englishman and a lady, eating their supper. Although we were shown to a special table, I took the dirty minstrel to the very one where the Englishman was, and bade the waiter bring to us there the unfinished bottle.

The two guests at first looked with surprised, then with angry, eyes at the little man, who, more dead than alive, was sitting near me. They talked together in a low tone; then the lady pushed back her plate, her silk dress rustled, and both of them left the room. Through the glass doors I saw the Englishman saying something in an angry voice to the waiter, and pointing with his hand in our direction. The waiter put his head through the door, and looked at us. I waited with pleasurable anticipation for some one to come and order us out, for then I could have found a full outlet for all my indignation. But fortunately, though at the time I felt injured, we were left in peace. The minstrel, who before had fought shy of the wine, now eagerly drank all that was left in the bottle, so that he might make his escape as quickly as possible.

He, however, expressed his gratitude with deep feeling, as it seemed to me, for his entertainment. His teary eyes grew still more humid and brilliant, and he made use of a most strange and complicated phrase of gratitude. But still very pleasant to me was the sentence in which he said that if everybody treated artists as I had been doing, it would be very good, and ended by wishing me all manner of happiness. We went out into the hall together. There stood the servants, and my enemy the porter apparently airing his grievances against me before them. All of them, I thought, looked at me as though I were a man who had lost his wits. I treated the little man exactly like an equal, before all that audience of servants; and then, with all the respect that I was able to express in my behavior, I took off my hat, and pressed his hand with its dry and hardened fingers.

The servants made believe not pay the slightest attention to me. One of them only indulged in a sarcastic laugh.

As soon as the minstrel had bowed himself out, and disappeared in the darkness, I went up-stairs to my room, intending to sleep off all these impressions and the foolish childish anger which had come upon me so unexpectedly. But finding that I was too much excited to sleep, I once more went down into the street with the intention of walking until I should have recovered my equanimity, and, I must confess, with the secret hope that I might accidentally come across the porter or the waiter or the Englishman, and show them all their rudeness, and, most of all, their unfairness. But beyond the porter, who when he saw me turned his back, I met no one; and I began to promenade in absolute solitude along the quay.

"This is an example of the strange fate of poetry," said I to myself, having grown a little calmer. "All love it, all are in search of it; it is the only thing in life that men love and seek, and yet no one recognizes its power, no one prizes this best treasure of the world, and those who give it to men are not rewarded. Ask any one you please, ask all these guests of the Schweitzerhof, what is the most precious treasure in the world, and all, or ninety-nine out of a hundred, putting on a sardonic expression, will say that the best thing in the world is money.

"'Maybe, though, this does not please you, or coincide with your elevated ideas,' it will be urged, 'but what is to be done if human life is so constituted that money alone is capable of giving a man happiness? I cannot force my mind not to see the world as it is,' it will be added, 'that is, to see the truth.'

"Pitiable is your intellect, pitiable the happiness which you desire! And you yourselves, unhappy creatures, not knowing what you desire, ... why have you all left your fatherland, your relatives, your money-making trades and occupations, and come to this little Swiss city of Lucerne? Why did you all this evening gather on the balconies, and in respectful silence listen to the little beggar's song? And if he had been willing to sing longer, you would have been silent and listened longer. What! could money, even millions of it, have driven you all from your country, and brought you all together in this little nook of Lucerne? Could money have gathered you all on the balconies to stand for half an hour silent and motionless? No! One thing compels you to do it, and will forever have a stronger influence than all the other impulses of life: the longing for poetry which you know, which you do not realize, but feel, always will feel so long as you have any human sensibilities. The word 'poetry' is a mockery to you; you make use of it as a sort of ridiculous reproach; you regard the love for poetry as something meet for children and silly girls, and you make sport of them for it. For yourselves you must have something more definite.

"But children look upon life in a healthy way: they recognize and love what man ought to love, and what gives happiness. But life has so deceived and perverted you, that you ridicule the only thing that you really love, and you seek for what you hate and for what gives you unhappiness.

"You are so perverted that you did not perceive what obligations you were under to the poor Tyrolese who rendered you a pure delight; but at the same time you feel yourselves needlessly obliged to bow before some lord, which gives you neither pleasure nor profit, but rather causes you to sacrifice your comfort and convenience. What absurdity! what incomprehensible lack of reason!

"But it was not this that made the most powerful impression upon me this evening. This blindness to all that gives happiness, this unconsciousness of poetic enjoyment, I can almost comprehend, or at least I have become wonted to it, since I have almost everywhere met with it in the course of my life; the harsh, unconscious churlishness of the crowd was no novelty to me: whatever those who argue in favor of popular sentiment may say, the throng is a conglomeration of very possibly good people, but of people who touch each other only on their coarse animal sides, and express only the weakness and harshness of human nature. But how was it that you, children of a humane people, you Christians, you simple people, repaid with coldness and ridicule the poor beggar who gave you a pure enjoyment? But no, in your country there are asylums for beggars. There are no beggars, there can be none; and there can be no feelings of sympathy, since that would be a confession that beggary existed.

"But he labored, he gave you enjoyment, he besought you to give him something of your superfluity in payment for his labor of which you took advantage. But you looked upon him with a cool smile as upon one of the curiosities in your lofty brilliant palaces; and though there were a hundred of you, favored with happiness and wealth, not one man or one woman among you gave him a sou. Abashed he went away from you, and the thoughtless throng, laughing, followed and ridiculed not you, but him, because you were cold, harsh, and dishonorable; because you robbed him in receiving the entertainment which he gave you: for this they jeered him.

"*On the 19th of July, 1857, before the Schweitzerhof Hotel, in which were lodging very opulent people, a wandering beggar minstrel sang for half an hour his songs, and played his guitar. About a hundred people listened to him. The minstrel thrice asked you all to give him something. No one person gave him a thing, and many made sport of him.*'

"This is not an invention, but an actual fact, as those who desire can find out for themselves by consulting the papers for the list of those who were at the Schweitzerhof on the 19th of July.

"This is an event which the historians of our time ought to describe in letters of inextinguishable flame. This event is more significant and more serious, and fraught with far deeper meaning, than the facts that are printed in newspapers and histories. That the English have killed several thousand Chinese because the Chinese would not sell them any thing for money while their land is overflowing with ringing coins; that the French have killed several thousand Kabyles because the wheat grows well in Africa, and because constant war is essential for the drill of an army; that the Turkish ambassador in Naples must not be a Jew; and that the Emperor Napoleon walks about in Plombières, and gives his people the express assurance that he rules only in direct accordance with the will of the people,—all these are words which darken or reveal something long known. But the episode that took place in Lucerne on the 19th of July seems to me something entirely novel and strange, and it is connected not with the everlastingly ugly side of human nature, but with a well-known epoch in the development of society. This fact is not for the history of human activities, but for the history of progress and civilization.

"Why is it that this inhuman fact, impossible in any country,—Germany, France, or Italy,—is quite possible here where civilization, freedom, and equality are carried to the highest degree of development, where there are gathered together the most civilized travellers from the most civilized nations? Why is it that these cultivated human beings, generally capable of every honorable human action, had no hearty, human feeling for one good deed? Why is it that these people who in their palaces, their meetings, and their societies, labor warmly for the condition of the celibate Chinese in India, about the spread of Christianity and culture in Africa, about the formation of societies for attaining all perfection,—why is it that they should not find in their souls the simple, primitive feeling of human sympathy? Has such a feeling entirely disappeared, and has its place been taken by vainglory, ambition, and cupidity, governing these men in their palaces, meetings, and societies? Has the spreading of that reasonable, egotistical association of people, which we call civilization, destroyed and rendered nugatory the desire for instinctive and loving association? And is this that boasted equality for which so much innocent blood has been shed, and so many crimes have been perpetrated? Is it possible that nations, like children, can be made happy by the mere sound of the word 'equality'?

"Equality before the law? Does the whole life of a people revolve within the sphere of law? Only the thousandth part of it is subject to the law: the rest lies outside of it, in the sphere of the customs and intuitions of society.

"But in society the lackey is better dressed than the minstrel, and insults him with impunity. I am better dressed than the lackey, and insult him with impunity. The porter considers me higher, but the minstrel lower, than himself; when I made the minstrel my companion, he felt that he was on an equality with us both, and behaved rudely. I was impudent to the porter, and the porter acknowledged that he was inferior to me. The waiter was impudent to the minstrel, and the minstrel accepted the fact that he was inferior to the waiter.

100

"And is that government free, even though men seriously call it free, where a single citizen can be thrown into prison because, without harming any one, without interfering with any one, he does the only thing that he can to prevent himself from dying of starvation?

"A wretched, pitiable creature is man with his craving for positive solutions, thrown into this everlastingly tossing, limitless ocean of good and evil, of combinations and contradictions. For centuries men have been struggling and laboring to put the good on one side, the evil on the other. Centuries will pass, and no matter how much the unprejudiced mind may strive to decide where the balance lies between the good and the evil, the scales will refuse to tip the beam, and there will always be equal quantities of the good and the evil on each scale.

"If only man would learn to form judgments, and not to indulge in rash and arbitrary thoughts, and not to make reply to questions that are propounded merely to remain forever unanswered! If only he would learn that every thought is both a lie and a truth!—a lie from the one-sidedness and inability of man to recognize all truth; and true because it expresses one side of mortal endeavor. There are divisions in this everlastingly tumultuous, endless, endlessly confused chaos of the good and the evil. They have drawn imaginary lines over this ocean, and they contend that the ocean is really thus divided.

"But are there not millions of other possible subdivisions from absolutely different standpoints, in other planes? Certainly these novel subdivisions will be made in centuries to come, just as millions of different ones have been made in centuries past.

"Civilization is good, barbarism is evil; freedom, good; slavery, evil. Now, this imaginary knowledge annihilates the instinctive, beatific, primitive craving for the good that is in human nature. And who will explain to me what is freedom, what is despotism, what is civilization, what is barbarism?

"Where are the boundaries that separate them? And whose soul possesses so absolute a standard of good and evil as to measure these fleeting, complicated facts? Whose wit is so great as to comprehend and weigh all the

101

facts in the irretrievable past? And who can find any circumstance in which there is no union of good and evil? And because I know that I see more of one than of the other, is it not because my standpoint is wrong? And who has the ability to separate himself so absolutely from life, even for a moment, as to look upon it from above?

"One, only one infallible Guide we have,—the universal Spirit which penetrates all collectively and as units, which has endowed each of us with the craving for the right; the Spirit which impels the tree to grow toward the sun, which stimulates the flower in autumn-tide to scatter its seed, and which obliges each one of us unconsciously to draw closer together. And this one unerring, inspiring voice rings out louder than the noisy, hasty development of culture.

"Who is the greater man, and who the greater barbarian,—that lord, who, seeing the minstrel's well-worn clothes, angrily left the table, who gave him not the millionth part of his possessions in payment of his labor, and now lazily sitting in his brilliant, comfortable room, calmly opines about the events that are happening in China, and justifies the massacres that have been done there; or the little minstrel, who, risking imprisonment, with a franc in his pocket, and doing no harm to any one, has been going about for a score of years, up hill and down dale, rejoicing men's hearts with his songs, though they have jeered at him, and almost cast him out of the pale of humanity; and who, in weariness and cold and shame, has gone off to sleep, no one knows where, on his filthy straw?"

At this moment, from the city, through the dead silence of the night, far, far away, I caught the sound of the little man's guitar and his voice.

"No," something involuntarily said to me, "you have no right to commiserate the little man, or to blame the lord for his well-being. Who can weigh the inner happiness which is found in the soul of each of these men? There he stands somewhere in the muddy road, and gazes at the brilliant moonlit sky, and gayly sings amid the smiling, fragrant night; in his soul there is no reproach, no anger, no regret. And who knows what is transpiring now in the hearts of all these men within those opulent, brilliant rooms? Who

102

knows if they all have as much unencumbered, sweet delight in life, and as much satisfaction with the world, as dwells in the soul of that little man?

"Endless are the mercy and wisdom of Him who has permitted and formed all these contradictions. Only to thee, miserable little worm of the dust, audaciously, lawlessly attempting to fathom His laws, His designs,— only to thee do they seem like contradictions.

"Full of love He looks down from His bright, immeasurable height, and rejoices in the endless harmony in which you all move in endless contradictions. In thy pride thou hast thought thyself able to separate thyself from the laws of the universe. No, thou also, with thy petty, ridiculous anger against the waiters,—thou also hast disturbed the harmonious craving for the eternal and the infinite." ...

FOOTNOTES:

[49] Hofbrücke, torn down in 1852.

RECOLLECTIONS OF A SCORER.

A STORY.

Well, it happened about three o'clock. The gentlemen were playing. There was the big stranger, as our men called him. The prince was there,—the two are always together. The whiskered bárin was there; also the little hussar, Oliver, who was an actor, and there was the pan.[50] It was a pretty good crowd.

The big stranger and the prince were playing together. Now, here I was walking up and down around the billiard-table with my stick, keeping tally,—ten and forty-seven, twelve and forty-seven.

Everybody knows it's our business to score. You don't get a chance to get a bite of any thing, and you don't get to bed till two o'clock o' nights, but you're always being screamed at to bring the balls.

I was keeping tally; and I look, and see a new bárin comes in at the door. He gazed and gazed, and then sat down on the sofa. Very well!

"Now, who can that be?" thinks I to myself. "He must be somebody."

His dress was neat,—neat as a pin,—checkered tricot pants, stylish little short coat, plush vest, and gold chain and all sorts of trinkets dangling from it.

He was dressed neat; but there was something about the man neater still; slim, tall, his hair brushed forward in style, and his face fair and ruddy,— well, in a word, a fine young fellow.

You must know our business brings us into contact with all sorts of people. And there's many that ain't of much consequence, and there's a good deal of poor trash. So, though you're only a scorer, you get used to telling folks; that is, in a certain way you learn a thing or two.

I looked at the bárin. I see him sit down, modest and quiet, not knowing anybody; and the clothes on him are so bran-new, that thinks I, "Either he's a foreigner,—an Englishman maybe,—or some count just come. And though he's so young, he has an air of some distinction." Oliver sat down next him, so he moved along a little.

They began a game. The big man lost. He shouts to me. Says he, "You're always cheating. You don't count straight. Why don't you pay attention?"

He scolded away, then threw down his cue, and went out. Now, just look here! Evenings, he and the prince plays for fifty silver rubles a game; and here he only lost a bottle of Makon wine, and got mad. That's the kind of a character he is.

Another time he and the prince plays till two o'clock. They don't bank down any cash; and so I know neither of them's got any cash, but they are simply playing a bluff game.

"I'll go you twenty-five rubles," says he.

"All right."

Just yawning, and not even stopping to place the ball,—you see, he was not made of stone,—now just notice what he said. "We are playing for money," says he, "and not for chips."

But this man puzzled me worse than all the rest. Well, then, when the big man left, the prince says to the new bárin, "Wouldn't you like," says he, "to play a game with me?"

"With pleasure," says he.

He sat there, and looked rather foolish, indeed he did. He may have been courageous in reality; but, at all events, he got up, went over to the billiard-table, and did not seem flustered as yet. He was not exactly flustered, but you couldn't help seeing that he was not quite at his ease.

Either his clothes were a little too new, or he was embarrassed because everybody was looking at him; at any rate, he seemed to have no energy. He sort of sidled up to the table, caught his pocket on the edge, began to chalk his cue, dropped his chalk.

Whenever he hit the ball, he always glanced around, and reddened. Not so the prince. He was used to it; he chalked and chalked his hand, tucked up his sleeve; he goes and sits down when he pockets the ball, even though he is such a little man.

They played two or three games; then I notice the prince puts up the cue, and says, "Would you mind telling me your name?"

"Nekhliudof," says he.

Says the prince, "Was your father commander in the corps of cadets?"

"Yes," says the other.

Then they began to talk in French, and I could not understand them. I suppose they were talking about family affairs.

"Au revoir," says the prince. "I am very glad to have made your acquaintance." He washed his hands, and went to get a lunch; but the other stood by the billiard-table with his cue, and was knocking the balls about.

It's our business, you know, when a new man comes along, to be rather sharp: it's the best way. I took the balls, and go to put them up. He reddened, and says, "Can't I play any longer?"

"Certainly you can," says I. "That's what billiards is for." But I don't pay any attention to him. I straighten the cues.

"Will you play with me?"

"Certainly, sir," says I.

I place the balls.

"Shall we play for odds?"

"What do you mean,—'play for odds'?"

"Well," says I, "you give me a half-ruble, and I crawl under the table."

Of course, as he had never seen that sort of thing, it seemed strange to

107

him: he laughs.

"Go ahead," says he.

"Very well," says I, "only you must give me odds."

"What!" says he, "are you a worse player than I am?"

"Most likely," says I. "We have few players who can be compared with you."

We began to play. He certainly had the idea that he was a crack shot. It was a caution to see him shoot; but the Pole sat there, and kept shouting out every time,—

"Ah, what a chance! ah, what a shot!"

But what a man he was! His ideas were good enough, but he didn't know how to carry them out. Well, as usual I lost the first game, crawled under the table, and grunted.

Thereupon Oliver and the Pole jumped down from their seats, and applauded, thumping with their cues.

"Splendid! Do it again," they cried, "once more."

Well enough to cry "once more," especially for the Pole. That fellow would have been glad enough to crawl under the billiard-table, or even under the Blue bridge, for a half-ruble! Yet he was the first to cry, "Splendid! but you haven't wiped off all the dust yet."

I, Petrushka the marker, was pretty well known to everybody.

Only, of course, I did not care to show my hand yet. I lost my second game.

"It does not become me at all to play with you, sir," says I.

He laughs. Then, as I was playing the third game, he stood forty-nine and I nothing. I laid the cue on the billiard-table, and said, "Bárin, shall we play off?"

"What do you mean by playing off?" says he. "How would you have it?"

"You make it three rubles or nothing," says I.

"Why," says he, "have I been playing with you for money?" The fool!

He turned rather red.

Very good. He lost the game. He took out his pocket-book,—quite a new one, evidently just from the English shop,—opened it: I see he wanted to make a little splurge. It is stuffed full of bills,—nothing but hundred-ruble notes.

"No," says he, "there's no small stuff here."

He took three rubles from his purse. "There," says he, "there's your two rubles; the other pays for the games, and you keep the rest for vodka."

"Thank you, sir, most kindly." I see that he is a splendid fellow. For such a one I would crawl under any thing. For one thing, it's a pity that he won't play for money. For then, thinks I, I should know how to work him for twenty rubles, and maybe I could stretch it out to forty.

As soon as the Pole saw the young man's money, he says, "Wouldn't you like to try a little game with me? You play so admirably." Such sharpers prowl around.

"No," says the young man, "excuse me: I have not the time." And he went out.

I don't know who that man was, that Pole. Some one called him Pan or the Pole, and so it stuck to him. Every day he used to sit in the billiard-room, and always look on. He was no longer allowed to take a hand in any game whatever; but he always sat by himself, and got out his pipe, and smoked. But then he could play well.

Very good. Nekhliudof came a second time, a third time; he began to come frequently. He would come morning and evening. He learned to play French carom and pyramid pool,—every thing in fact. He became less bashful, got acquainted with everybody, and played tolerably well. Of course, being a young man of a good family, with money, everybody liked him. The only exception was the "big guest:" he quarrelled with him.

And the whole thing grew out of a trifle.

They were playing pool,—the prince, the big guest, Nekhliudof, Oliver, and some one else. Nekhliudof was standing near the stove talking with some one. When it came the big man's turn to play, it happened that his ball was just opposite the stove. There was very little space there, and he liked to have elbow-room.

Now, either he didn't see Nekhliudof, or he did it on purpose; but, as he was flourishing his cue, he hit Nekhliudof in the chest, a tremendous rap. It actually made him groan. What then? He did not think of apologizing, he was so boorish. He even went further: he didn't look at him; he walks off grumbling,—

"Who's jostling me there? It made me miss my shot. Why can't we have some room?"

Then the other went up to him, pale as a sheet, but quite self-possessed, and says so politely,—

"You ought first, sir, to apologize: you struck me," says he.

"Catch me apologizing now! I should have won the game," says he, "but now you have spoiled it for me."

Then the other one says, "You ought to apologize."

"Get out of my way! I insist upon it, I won't."

And he turned away to look after his ball.

Nekhliudof went up to him, and took him by the arm.

"You're a boor," says he, "my dear sir."

Though he was a slender young fellow, almost like a girl, still he was all ready for a quarrel. His eyes flash fire; he looks as if he could eat him alive. The big guest was a strong, tremendous fellow, no match for Nekhliudof.

110

"Wha-at!" says he, "you call me a boor?" Yelling out these words, he raises his hand to strike him.

Then everybody there rushed up, and seized them both by the arms, and separated them.

After much talk, Nekhliudof says, "Let him give me satisfaction: he has insulted me."

"Not at all," said the other. "I don't care a whit about any satisfaction. He's nothing but a boy, a mere nothing. I'll pull his ears for him."

"If you aren't willing to give me satisfaction, then you are no gentleman."

And, saying this, he almost cried.

"Well, and you, you are a little boy: nothing you say or do can offend me."

Well, we separated them,—led them off, as the custom is, to different rooms. Nekhliudof and the prince were friends.

"Go," says the former; "for God's sake make him listen to reason."

The prince went. The big man says, "I ain't afraid of any one," says he. "I am not going to have any explanation with such a baby. I won't do it, and that's the end of it."

Well, they talked and talked, and then the matter died out, only the big guest ceased to come to us any more.

As a result of this,—this row, I might call it,—he was regarded as quite the cock of the walk. He was quick to take offence,—I mean Nekhliudof,—as to so many other things, however, he was as unsophisticated as a new-born babe.

I remember once, the prince says to Nekhliudof, "Whom do you keep here?"

"No one," says he.

"What do you mean,—'no one'!"

"Why should I?" says Nekhliudof.

"How so,—why should you?"

"I have always lived thus. Why shouldn't I continue to live the same way?"

"You don't say so? Did you ever!"

And saying this, the prince burst into a peal of laughter, and the whiskered bárin also roared. They couldn't get over it.

"What, never?" they asked.

"Never!"

They were dying with laughter. Of course I understood well enough what they were laughing at him for. I keep my eyes open. "What," thinks I, "will come of it?"

"Come," says the prince, "come right off."

"No; not for any thing," was his answer.

"Now, that is absurd," says the prince. "Come along!"

They went out.

They came back at one o'clock. They sat down to supper; quite a crowd of them were assembled. Some of our very best customers,—Atánof, Prince Razin, Count Shustakh, Mirtsof. And all congratulate Nekhliudof, laughing as they do so. They call me in: I see that they are pretty jolly.

"Congratulate the bárin," they shout.

"What on?" I ask.

How did he call it? His initiation or his enlightenment; I can't remember exactly.

"I have the honor," says I, "to congratulate you."

And he sits there very red in the face, yet he smiles. Didn't they have fun with him though!

Well and good. They went afterwards to the billiard-room, all very gay; and Nekhliudof went up to the billiard-table, leaned on his elbow, and said,—

"It's amusing to you, gentlemen," says he, "but it's sad for me. Why," says he, "did I do it? Prince," says he, "I shall never forgive you or myself as long as I live."

And he actually burst into tears. Evidently he did not know himself what he was saying. The prince went up to him with a smile.

"Don't talk nonsense," says he. "Let's go home, Anatoli."

"I won't go anywhere," says the other. "Why did I do that?"

And the tears poured down his cheeks. He would not leave the billiard-table, and that was the end of it. That's what it means for a young and inexperienced man to....

In this way he used often to come to us. Once he came with the prince, and the whiskered man who was the prince's crony; the gentlemen always called him "Fedotka." He had prominent cheek-bones, and was homely enough, to be sure; but he used to dress neatly and ride in a carriage. What was the reason that the gentlemen were so fond of him? I really could not tell.

"Fedotka! Fedotka!" they'd call, and ask him to eat and to drink, and they'd spend their money paying up for him; but he was a thorough-going beat. If ever he lost, he would be sure not to pay; but if he won, you bet he wouldn't fail to collect his money. Often too he came to grief: yet there he was, walking arm in arm with the prince.

"You are lost without me," he would say to the prince. "I am, Fedot,"[51] says he; "but not a Fedot of that sort."

And what jokes he used to crack, to be sure! Well, as I said, they had already arrived that time, and one of them says, "Let's have the balls for three-handed pool."

"All right," says the other.

They began to play at three rubles a stake. Nekhliudof and the prince play, and chat about all sorts of things meantime.

"Ah!" says one of them, "you mind only what a neat little foot she has."

"Oh," says the other, "her foot is nothing; her beauty is her wealth of hair."

Of course they paid no attention to the game, only kept on talking to one another.

As to Fedotka, that fellow was alive to his work; he played his very best, but they didn't do themselves justice at all.

And so he won six rubles from each of them. God knows how many games he had won from the prince, yet I never knew them to pay each other any money; but Nekhliudof took out two greenbacks, and handed them over to him.

"No," says he, "I don't want to take your money. Let's square it: play 'quits or double,'[52]—either double or nothing."

I set the balls. Fedotka began to play the first hand. Nekhliudof seemed to play only for fun: sometimes he would come very near winning a game, yet just fail of it. Says he, "It would be too easy a move, I won't have it so." But Fedotka did not forget what he was up to. Carelessly he proceeded with the game, and thus, as if it were unexpectedly, won.

"Let us play double stakes once more," says he.

"All right," says Nekhliudof.

Once more Fedotka won the game.

"Well," says he, "it began with a mere trifle. I don't wish to win much from you. Shall we make it once more or nothing?"

"Yes."

Say what you may, but fifty rubles is a pretty sum, and Nekhliudof himself began to propose, "Let us make it double or quit." So they played and played.

It kept going worse and worse for Nekhliudof. Two hundred and eighty rubles were written up against him. As to Fedotka, he had his own method: he would lose a simple game, but when the stake was doubled, he would win sure.

As for the prince, he sits by and looks on. He sees that the matter is growing serious.

"Enough!"[53] says he, "hold on."

My! they keep increasing the stake.

At last it went so far that Nekhliudof was in for more than five hundred rubles. Fedotka laid down his cue, and said,—

"Aren't you satisfied for to-day? I'm tired," says he.

Yet I knew he was ready to play till dawn of day, provided there was money to be won. Stratagem, of course. And the other was all the more anxious to go on. "Come on! Come on!"

"No,—'pon my honor, I'm tired. Come," says Fedot; "let's go up-stairs; there you shall have your revanche."

Up-stairs with us meant the place where the gentlemen used to play cards. From that very day, Fedotka wound his net round him so that he began to come every day. He would play one or two games of billiards, and then proceed up-stairs,—every day up-stairs.

What they used to do there, God only knows; but it is a fact that from that time he began to be an entirely different kind of man, and seemed hand in glove with Fedotka. Formerly he used to be stylish, neat in his dress, with his hair slightly curled even; but now it would be only in the morning that he would be any thing like himself; but as soon as he had paid his visit up-stairs, he would not be at all like himself.

Once he came down from up-stairs with the prince, pale, his lips trembling, and talking excitedly.

115

"I cannot permit such a one as he is," says he, "to say that I am not"— How did he express himself? I cannot recollect, something like "not refined enough," or what,—"and that he won't play with me any more. I tell you I have paid him ten thousand, and I should think that he might be a little more considerate, before others, at least."

"Oh, bother!" says the prince, "is it worth while to lose one's temper with Fedotka?"

"No," says the other, "I will not let it go so."

"Why, old fellow, how can you think of such a thing as lowering yourself to have a row with Fedotka?"

"That is all very well; but there were strangers there, mind you."

"Well, what of that?" says the prince; "strangers? Well, if you wish, I will go and make him ask your pardon."

"No," says the other.

And then they began to chatter in French, and I could not understand what it was they were talking about.

And what would you think of it? That very evening he and Fedotka ate supper together, and they became friends again.

Well and good. At other times again he would come alone.

"Well," he would say, "do I play well?"

It's our business, you know, to try to make everybody contented, and so I would say, "Yes, indeed;" and yet how could it be called good play, when he would poke about with his cue without any sense whatever?

And from that very evening when he took in with Fedotka, he began to play for money all the time. Formerly he didn't care to play for stakes, either for a dinner or for champagne. Sometimes the prince would say,—

"Let's play for a bottle of champagne."

"No," he would say. "Let us rather have the wine by itself. Hollo there!

bring a bottle!"

And now he began to play for money all the time; he used to spend his entire days in our establishment. He would either play with some one in the billiard-room, or he would go "up-stairs."

Well, thinks I to myself, every one else gets something from him, why don't I get some advantage out of it?

"Well, sir," says I one day, "it's a long time since you have had a game with me."

And so we began to play. Well, when I won ten half-rubles of him, I says,—

"Don't you want to make it double or quit, sir?"

He said nothing. Formerly, if you remember, he would call me a fool for such a boldness. And we went to playing "quit or double."

I won eighty rubles of him.

Well, what would you think? Since that first time he used to play with me every day. He would wait till there was no one about, for of course he would have been ashamed to play with a mere marker in presence of others. Once he had got rather warmed up by the play (he already owed me sixty rubles), and so he says,—

"Do you want to stake all you have won?"

"All right," says I.

I won. "One hundred and twenty to one hundred and twenty?"

"All right," says I.

Again I won. "Two hundred and forty against two hundred and forty?"

"Isn't that too much?" I ask.

He made no reply. We played the game. Once more it was mine. "Four hundred and eighty against four hundred and eighty?"

I says, "Well, sir, I don't want to wrong you. Let us make it a hundred rubles that you owe me, and call it square."

You ought to have heard how he yelled at this, and yet he was not a proud man at all. "Either play, or don't play!" says he.

Well, I see there's nothing to be done. "Three hundred and eighty, then, if you please," says I.

I really wanted to lose. I allowed him forty points in advance. He stood fifty-two to my thirty-six. He began to cut the yellow one, and missed eighteen points; and I was standing just at the turning-point. I made a stroke so as to knock the ball off of the billiard-table. No—so luck would have it. Do what I might, he even missed the doublet. I had won again.

"Listen," says he. "Peter,"—he did not call me Petrushka then,—"I can't pay you the whole right away. In a couple of months I could pay three thousand even, if it were necessary."

And there he stood just as red, and his voice kind of trembled.

"Very good, sir," says I.

With this he laid down the cue. Then he began to walk up and down, up and down, the perspiration running down his face.

"Peter," says he, "let's try it again, double or quit."

And he almost burst into tears.

"What, sir, what! would you play against such luck?"

"Oh, let us play, I beg of you." And he brings the cue, and puts it in my hand.

I took the cue, and I threw the balls on the table so that they bounced over on to the floor; I could not help showing off a little, naturally. I say, "All right, sir."

But he was in such a hurry that he went and picked up the balls himself, and I thinks to myself, "Anyway, I'll never be able to get the seven hundred

118

rubles from him, so I can lose them to him all the same." I began to play carelessly on purpose. But no—he won't have it so. "Why," says he, "you are playing badly on purpose."

But his hands trembled, and when the ball went towards a pocket, his fingers would spread out and his mouth would screw up to one side, as if he could by any means force the ball into the pocket. Even I couldn't stand it, and I say, "That won't do any good, sir."

Very well. As he won this game I says, "This will make it one hundred and eighty rubles you owe me, and fifty games; and now I must go and get my supper." So I laid down my cue, and went off.

I went and sat down all by myself, at a small table opposite the door; and I look in and see, and wonder what he will do. Well, what would you think? He began to walk up and down, up and down, probably thinking that no one's looking at him; and then he would give a pull at his hair, and then walk up and down again, and keep muttering to himself; and then he would pull his hair again.

After that he wasn't seen for a week. Once he came into the dining-room as gloomy as could be, but he didn't enter the billiard-room. The prince caught sight of him.

"Come," says he, "let's have a game."

"No," says the other, "I am not going to play any more."

"Nonsense! come along."

"No," says he, "I won't come, I tell you. For you it's all one whether I go or not, yet for me it's no good to come here."

And so he did not come for ten days more. And then, it being the holidays, he came dressed up in a dress suit: he'd evidently been into company. And he was here all day long; he kept playing, and he came the next day, and the third....

And it began to go in the old style, and I thought it would be fine to have another trial with him.

"No," says he, "I'm not going to play with you; and as to the one hundred and eighty rubles that I owe you, if you'll come at the end of a month, you shall have it."

Very good. So I went to him at the end of a month.

"By God," says he, "I can't give it to you; but come back on Thursday."

Well, I went on Thursday. I found that he had a splendid suite of apartments.

"Well," says I, "is he at home?"

"He hasn't got up yet," I was told.

"Very good, I will wait."

For a body-servant he had one of his own serfs, such a gray-haired old man! That servant was perfectly single-minded, he didn't know any thing about beating about the bush. So we got into conversation.

"Well," says he, "what is the use of our living here, master and I? He's squandered all his property, and it's mighty little honor or good that we get out of this Petersburg of yours. As we started from the country, I thought it would be as it was with the last bárin (may his soul rest in peace!), we would go about with princes and counts and generals; he thought to himself, 'I'll find a countess for a sweetheart, and she'll have a big dowry, and we'll live on a big scale.' But it's quite a different thing from what he expected; here we are, running about from one tavern to another as bad off as we could be! The Princess Rtishcheva, you know, is his own aunt, and Prince Borotintsef is his godfather. What do you think? He went to see them only once, that was at Christmas-time; he never shows his nose there. Yes, and even their people laugh about it to me. 'Why,' says they, 'your bárin is not a bit like his father!' And once I take it upon myself to say to him,—

"'Why wouldn't you go, sir, and visit your aunt? They are feeling bad because you haven't been for so long.'

120

"'It's stupid there, Demyánitch,' says he. Just to think, he found his only amusement here in the saloon! If he only would enter the service! yet, no: he has got entangled with cards and all the rest of it. When men get going that way, there's no good in any thing; nothing comes to any good.... E-ekh! we are going to the dogs, and no mistake.... The late mistress (may her soul rest in peace!) left us a rich inheritance: no less than a thousand souls, and about three hundred thousand rubles worth of timber-lands. He has mortgaged it all, sold the timber, let the estate go to rack and ruin, and still no money on hand. When the master is away, of course, the overseer is more than the master. What does he care? He only cares to stuff his own pockets.

"A few days ago, a couple of peasants brought complaints from the whole estate. 'He has wasted the last of the property,' they say. What do you think? he pondered over the complaints, and gave the peasants ten rubles apiece. Says he, 'I'll be there very soon. I shall have some money, and I will settle all accounts when I come,' says he.

"But how can he settle accounts when we are getting into debt all the time? Money or no money, yet the winter here has cost eighty thousand rubles, and now there isn't a silver ruble in the house. And all owing to his kind-heartedness. You see, he's such a simple bárin that it would be hard to find his equal: that's the very reason that he's going to ruin,—going to ruin, all for nothing." And the old man almost wept.

Nekhliudof woke up about eleven, and called me in.

"They haven't sent me any money yet," says he. "But it isn't my fault. Shut the door," says he.

I shut the door.

"Here," says he, "take my watch or this diamond pin, and pawn it. They will give you more than one hundred and eighty rubles for it, and when I get my money I will redeem it," says he.

"No matter, sir," says I. "If you don't happen to have any money, it's no consequence; let me have the watch if you don't mind. I can wait for your convenience."

121

I can see that the watch is worth more than three hundred.

Very good. I pawned the watch for a hundred rubles, and carried him the ticket. "You will owe me eighty rubles," says I, "and you had better redeem the watch."

And so it happened that he still owed me eighty rubles.

After that he began to come to us again every day. I don't know how matters stood between him and the prince, but at all events he kept coming with him all the time, or else they would go and play cards up-stairs with Fedotka. And what queer accounts those three men kept between them! this one would lend money to the other, the other to the third, yet who it was that owed the money you never could find out.

And in this way he kept on coming our way for well-nigh two years; only it was to be plainly seen that he was a changed man, such a devil-may-care manner he assumed at times. He even went so far at times as to borrow a ruble of me to pay a hack-driver; and yet he would still play with the prince for a hundred rubles stake.

He grew gloomy, thin, sallow. As soon as he came he used to order a little glass of absinthe, take a bite of something, and drink some port wine, and then he would grow more lively.

He came one time before dinner; it happened to be carnival time, and he began to play with a hussar.

Says he, "Do you want to play for a stake?"

"Very well," says he. "What shall it be?"

"A bottle of Claude Vougeaux? What do you say?"

"All right."

Very good. The hussar won, and they went off for their dinner. They sat down at table, and then Nekhliudof says, "Simon, a bottle of Claude Vougeaux, and see that you warm it to the proper point."

Simon went out, brought in the dinner, but no wine.

"Well," says he, "where's the wine?"

Simon hurried out, brought in the roast.

"Let us have the wine," says he.

Simon makes no reply.

"What's got into you? Here we've almost finished dinner, and no wine. Who wants to drink with dessert?"

Simon hurried out. "The landlord," says he, "wants to speak to you."

Nekhliudof turned scarlet. He sprang up from the table.

"What's the need of calling me?"

The landlord is standing at the door.

Says he, "I can't trust you any more, unless you settle my little bill."

"Well, didn't I tell you that I would pay the first of the month?"

"That will be all very well," says the landlord, "but I can't be all the time giving credit, and having no settlement. There are more than ten thousand rubles of debts outstanding now," says he.

"Well, that'll do, monshoor, you know that you can trust me! Send the bottle, and I assure you that I will pay you very soon."

And he hurried back.

"What was it? Why did they call you out?" asked the hussar.

"Oh, some one wanted to ask me a question."

"Now it would be a good time," says the hussar, "to have a little warm wine to drink."

"Simon, hurry up!"

Simon came back, but still no wine, nothing. Too bad! He left the table, and came to me.

"For God's sake," says he, "Petrushka, let me have six rubles!"

He was pale as a sheet. "No, sir," says I: "by God, you owe me quite too much now."

"I will give forty rubles for six, in a week's time."

"If only I had it," says I, "I should not think of refusing you, but I haven't."

What do you think! He rushed away, his teeth set, his fist doubled up, and ran down the corridor like one mad, and all at once he gave himself a knock on the forehead.

"O my God!" says he, "what has it come to?"

But he did not return to the dining-room; he jumped into a carriage, and drove away. Didn't we have our laugh over it! The hussar asks,—

"Where is the gentleman who was dining with me?"

"He has gone," said some one.

"Where has he gone? What message did he leave?"

"He didn't leave any; he just took to his carriage, and went off."

"That's a fine way of entertaining a man!" says he.

Now, thinks I to myself, it'll be a long time before he comes again after this; that is, on account of this scandal. But no. On the next day he came about evening. He came into the billiard-room. He had a sort of a box in his hand. Took off his overcoat.

"Now let us have a game," says he.

He looked out from under his eyebrows, rather fierce like.

We played a game. "That's enough now," says he: "go and bring me a pen and paper; I must write a letter."

Not thinking any thing, not suspecting any thing, I bring some paper, and put it on the table in the little room.

"It's all ready, sir," says I.

"Very good." He sat down at the table. He kept on writing and writing, and muttering to himself all the time: then he jumps up, and, frowning, says, "Look and see if my carriage has come yet."

It was on a Friday, during carnival time, and so there weren't any of the customers on hand; they were all at some ball. I went to see about the carriage, and just as I was going out of the door, "Petrushka! Petrushka!" he shouted, as if something suddenly frightened him.

I turn round. I see he's pale as a sheet, standing here and looking at me.

"Did you call me, sir?" says I.

He makes no reply.

"What do you want?" says I.

He says nothing. "Oh, yes!" says he. "Let's have another game."

Then says he, "Haven't I learned to play pretty well?"

He had just won the game. "Yes," says I.

"All right," says he; "go now, and see about my carriage." He himself walked up and down the room.

Without thinking any thing, I went down to the door. I didn't see any carriage at all. I started to go up again.

Just as I am going up, I hear what sounds like the thud of a billiard-cue. I go into the billiard-room. I notice a peculiar smell.

I look around; and there he is lying on the floor in a pool of blood, with a pistol beside him. I was so scared that I could not speak a word.

He keeps twitching, twitching his leg; and stretched himself a little. Then he sort of snored, and stretched out his full length in such a strange way. And God knows why such a sin came about,—how it was that it occurred to him to ruin his own soul,—but as to what he left written on this paper, I don't understand it at all. Truly, you can never account for what is going on in the world.

"God gave me all that a man can desire,—wealth, name, intellect, noble aspirations. I wanted to enjoy myself, and I trod in the mire all that was best in me. I have done nothing dishonorable, I am not unfortunate, I have not committed any crime; but I have done worse: I have destroyed my feelings, my intellect, my youth. I became entangled in a filthy net, from which I could not escape, and to which I could not accustom myself. I feel that I am falling lower and lower every moment, and I cannot stop my fall.

"And what ruined me? Was there in me some strange passion which I might plead as an excuse? No!

"My recollections are pleasant. One fearful moment of forgetfulness, which can never be erased from my mind, led me to come to my senses. I shuddered when I saw what a measureless abyss separated me from what I desired to be, and might have been. In my imagination arose the hopes, the dreams, and the thoughts of my youth.

"Where are those lofty thoughts of life, of eternity, of God, which at times filled my soul with light and strength? Where that aimless power of love which kindled my heart with its comforting warmth?...

"But how good and happy I might have been, had I trodden that path which, at the very entrance of life, was pointed out to me by my fresh mind and true feelings! More than once did I try to go from the ruts in which my life ran, into that sacred path.

"I said to myself, Now I will use my whole strength of will; and yet I could not do it. When I happened to be alone, I felt awkward and timid. When I was with others, I no longer heard the inward voice; and I fell all the time lower and lower.

"At last I came to a terrible conviction that it was impossible for me to lift myself from this low plane. I ceased to think about it, and I wished to forget all; but hopeless repentance worried me still more and more. Then, for

126

the first time, the thought of suicide occurred to me....

"I once thought that the nearness of death would rouse my soul. I was mistaken. In a quarter of an hour I shall be no more, yet my view has not in the least changed. I see with the same eyes, I hear with the same ears, I think the same thoughts; there is the same strange incoherence, unsteadiness, and lightness in my thoughts." ...

FOOTNOTES:

[50] Polish name for lord or gentleman.

[51] Fedot, da nyé tot, an untranslatable play on the word.

[52] Kitudubl = Fr. quitte ou double.

[53] asé = assez.

ALBERT.

A STORY.

1857.

I.

Five rich young men went at three o'clock in the morning to a ball in Petersburg to have a good time.

Much champagne was drunk; a majority of the gentlemen were very young; the girls were pretty; a pianist and a fiddler played indefatigably one polka after another; there was no cease to the noise of conversation and dancing. But there was a sense of awkwardness and constraint; every one felt somehow or other—and this is not unusual—that all was not as it should be.

There were several attempts made to make things more lively, but simulated liveliness is much worse than melancholy.

One of the five young men, who was more discontented than any one else, both with himself and with the others, and who had been feeling all the evening a sense of disgust, took his hat, and went out noiselessly on purpose, intending to go home.

There was no one in the ante-room, but in the next room at the door he heard two voices disputing. The young man paused, and listened.

"It is impossible, there are guests in there," said a woman's voice.

"Come, let me in, please. I will not do any harm," urged a man in a gentle voice.

"Indeed I will not without madame's permission," said the woman. "Where are you going? Oh, what a man you are!"

The door was flung open, and on the threshold appeared the figure of a stranger. Seeing a guest, the maid ceased to detain the man; and the stranger, timidly bowing, came into the room with a somewhat unsteady gait.

He was a man of medium stature, with a lank, crooked back, and long dishevelled hair. He wore a short paletot, and tight ragged pantaloons over coarse dirty boots. His necktie, twisted into a string, exposed his long white neck. His shirt was filthy, and the sleeves came down over his lean hands.

But, notwithstanding his thoroughly emaciated body, his face was attractive and fair; and a fresh color even mantled his cheeks under his thin dark beard and side-whiskers. His dishevelled locks, thrown back, exposed a low and remarkably pure forehead. His dark, languid eyes looked unswervingly forward with an expression of serenity, submission, and sweetness, which made a fascinating combination with the expression of his fresh, curved lips, visible under his thin moustache.

Advancing a few steps, he paused, turned to the young man, and smiled. He found it apparently rather hard to smile. But his face was so lighted up by it, that the young man, without knowing why, smiled in return.

"Who is that man?" he asked of the maid in a whisper, as the stranger walked toward the room where the dancing was going on.

"A crazy musician from the theatre," replied the maid. "He sometimes comes to call upon madame."

"Where are you going, Delesof?" some one at this moment called from the drawing-room.

The young man who was called Delesof returned to the drawing-room. The musician was now standing at the door; and, as his eyes fell on the dancers, he showed by his smile and by the beating of his foot how much pleasure this spectacle afforded him.

"Won't you come, and have a dance too?" said one of the guests to him. The musician bowed, and looked at the hostess inquiringly.

"Come, come. Why not, since the gentlemen have invited you?" said the hostess. The musician's thin, weak face suddenly assumed an expression of decision; and smiling and winking, and shuffling his feet, he awkwardly,

130

clumsily went to join the dancers in the drawing-room.

In the midst of a quadrille a jolly officer, who was dancing very beautifully and with great liveliness, accidentally hit the musician in the back. His weak, weary legs lost their equilibrium; and the musician, making ineffectual struggles to keep his balance, measured his length on the floor.

Notwithstanding the sharp, hard sound made by his fall, almost everybody at the first moment laughed.

But the musician did not rise. The guests grew silent, even the piano ceased to sound. Delesof and the hostess were the first to reach the prostrate musician. He was lying on his elbow, and gloomily looking at the ground. When he had been lifted to his feet, and set in a chair, he threw back his hair from his forehead with a quick motion of his bony hand, and began to smile without replying to the questions that were put.

"Mr. Albert! Mr. Albert!" exclaimed the hostess. "Were you hurt? Where? Now, I told you that you had better not try to dance.... He is so weak," she added, addressing her guests. "It takes all his strength."

"Who is he?" some one asked the hostess.

"A poor man, an artist. A very nice young fellow; but he's a sad case, as you can see."

She said this without paying the least heed to the musician's presence. He suddenly opened his eyes as though frightened at something, collected himself, and remarked to those who were standing about him, "It's nothing at all," said he suddenly, arising from the chair with evident effort.

And in order to show that he had suffered no injury, he went into the middle of the room, and was going to dance; but he tottered, and would have fallen again, had he not been supported.

Everybody felt constrained. All looked at him, and no one spoke. The musician's glance again lost its vivacity; and, apparently forgetting that any one was looking, he put his hand to his knee. Suddenly he raised his head, advanced one faltering foot, and, with the same awkward gesture as before, tossed back his hair, and went to a violin-case, and took out the instrument.

"It was nothing at all," said he again, waving the violin. "Gentlemen, we will have a little music."

"What a strange face!" said the guests among themselves.

"Maybe there is great talent lurking in that unhappy creature," said one of them.

"Yes: it's a sad case,—a sad case," said another.

"What a lovely face!... There is something extraordinary about it," said Delesof. "Let us have a look at him."...

II.

Albert by this time, not paying attention to any one, had raised his violin to his shoulder, and was slowly crossing over to the piano, and tuning his instrument. His lips were drawn into an expression of indifference, his eyes were almost shut; but his lank, bony back, his long white neck, his crooked legs, and disorderly black hair presented a strange but somehow not entirely ridiculous appearance. After he had tuned his violin, he struck a quick chord, and, throwing back his head, turned to the pianist who was waiting to accompany him. "Melancholie, G sharp," he said, turning to the pianist with a peremptory gesture. And immediately after, as though in apology for his peremptory gesture, he smiled sweetly, and with the same smile turned to his audience again.

Tossing back his hair with the hand that held the bow, Albert stood at one side of the piano, and, with a flowing motion of the bow, touched the strings. Through the room there swept a pure, harmonious sound, which instantly brought absolute silence.

At first, it was as though a ray of unexpectedly brilliant light had flashed across the inner world of each hearer's consciousness; and the notes of the theme immediately followed, pouring forth abundant and beautiful.

Not one discordant or imperfect note distracted the attention of the listeners. All the tones were clear, beautiful, and full of meaning. All silently, with trembling expectation, followed the development of the theme. From a state of tedium, of noisy gayety, or of deep drowsiness, into which these people had fallen, they were suddenly transported to a world whose existence they had forgotten.

In one instant there arose in their souls, now a sentiment as though they were contemplating the past, now of passionate remembrance of some happiness, now the boundless longing for power and glory, now the feelings of humility, of unsatisfied love, and of melancholy.

Now bitter-sweet, now vehemently despairing, the notes, freely intermingling, poured forth and poured forth, so sweetly, so powerfully, and so spontaneously, that it was not so much that sounds were heard, as that some sort of beautiful stream of poetry, long known, but now for the first time expressed, gushed through the soul.

At each note that he played, Albert grew taller and taller. At a little distance, he had no appearance of being either crippled or peculiar. Pressing the violin to his chin, and with an expression of listening with passionate attention to the tones that he produced, he convulsively moved his feet. Now he straightened himself up to his full height, now thoughtfully leaned forward.

His left hand, curving over spasmodically on the strings, seemed as though it had swooned in its position, while it was only the bony fingers that changed about spasmodically; the right hand moved smoothly, gracefully, without effort.

His face shone with complete, enthusiastic delight; his eyes gleamed with a radiant, steely light; his nostrils quivered, his red lips were parted in rapture.

Sometimes his head bent down closer to his violin, his eyes almost closed, and his face, half shaded by his long locks, lighted up with a smile of genuine blissfulness. Sometimes he quickly straightened himself up, changed from one leg to the other, and his pure forehead, and the radiant look which he threw around the room, were alive with pride, greatness, and the consciousness of power. Once the pianist made a mistake, and struck a false chord. Physical pain was apparent in the whole form and face of the musician. He paused for a second, and with an expression of childish anger stamped his foot, and cried, "Moll, ce moll!" The pianist corrected his mistake; Albert closed his eyes, smiled, and, again forgetting himself and everybody else, gave himself up with beatitude to his work. Everybody who was in the room while Albert was playing preserved an attentive silence, and seemed to live and breathe only in the music.

The gay officer sat motionless in a chair by the window, with his eyes fixed upon the floor, and drawing long heavy sighs. The girls, awed by the universal silence, sat along by the walls, only occasionally exchanging glances expressive of satisfaction or perplexity.

The fat smiling face of the hostess was radiant with happiness. The pianist kept his eyes fixed on Albert's face, and while his whole figure from head to foot showed his solicitude lest he should make some mistake, he did his best to follow him. One of the guests, who had been drinking more heavily than the rest, lay at full length on the sofa, and tried not to move lest he should betray his emotion. Delesof experienced an unusual sensation. It seemed as though an icy band, now contracting, now expanding, were pressed upon his head. The roots of his hair seemed endued with consciousness; the cold shivers ran down his back, something rose higher and higher in his throat, his nose and palate were full of little needles, and the tears stole down his cheeks.

He shook himself, tried to swallow them back and wipe them away without attracting attention, but fresh tears followed and streamed down his face. By some sort of strange association of impressions, the first tones of Albert's violin carried Delesof back to his early youth.

Old before his time, weary of life, a broken man, he suddenly felt as though he were a boy of seventeen again, self-satisfied and handsome, blissfully dull, unconsciously happy. He remembered his first love for his cousin who wore a pink dress, he remembered his first confession of it in the linden alley; he remembered the warmth and the inexpressible charm of the fortuitous kiss; he remembered the immensity and enigmatical mystery of

Nature as it surrounded them then.

In his imagination as it went back in its flight, she gleamed in a mist of indefinite hopes, of incomprehensible desires, and the indubitable faith in the possibility of impossible happiness. All the priceless moments of that time, one after the other, arose before him, not like unmeaning instants of the fleeting present, but like the immutable, full-formed, reproachful images of the past.

He contemplated them with rapture, and wept,—wept not because the time had passed and he might have spent it more profitably (if that time had been given to him again he would not have spent it any more profitably), but he wept because it had passed and would never return. His recollections evolved themselves without effort, and Albert's violin was their mouthpiece. It said, "They have passed, forever passed, the days of thy strength, of love, and of happiness; passed forever, and never will return. Weep for them, shed all thy tears, let thy life pass in tears for these days; this is the only and best happiness that remains to thee."

At the end of the next variation, Albert's face grew serene, his eyes flushed, great clear drops of sweat poured down his cheeks. The veins swelled on his forehead; his whole body swayed more and more; his pale lips were parted, and his whole figure expressed an enthusiastic craving for enjoyment. Despairingly swaying with his whole body, and throwing back his hair, he laid down his violin, and with a smile of proud satisfaction and happiness gazed at the bystanders. Then his back assumed its ordinary curve, his head sank, his lips grew set, his eyes lost their fire; and as though he were ashamed of himself, timidly glancing round, and stumbling, he went into the next room.

III.

Something strange came over all the audience, and something strange was noticeable in the dead silence that succeeded Albert's playing. It was as though each desired, and yet dared not, to acknowledge the meaning of it all.

What did it mean,—this brightly lighted, warm room, these brilliant women, the dawn just appearing at the windows, these hurrying pulses, and the pure impressions made by the fleeting tones of music? But no one ventured to acknowledge the meaning of it all; on the contrary, almost all, feeling incapable of throwing themselves completely under the influence of what the new impression concealed from them, rebelled against it.

"Well, now, he plays mighty well," said the officer.

"Wonderfully," replied Delesof, stealthily wiping his cheek with his sleeve.

"One thing sure, it's time to be going, gentlemen," said the gentleman who had been lying on the sofa, straightening himself up a little. "We'll have to give him something, gentlemen. Let us make a collection."

At this time, Albert was sitting alone in the next room, on the sofa. As he supported himself with his elbows on his bony knees, he smoothed his face with his dirty, sweaty hand, tossed back his hair, and smiled at his own happy thoughts.

A large collection was taken up, and Delesof was chosen to present it. Aside from this, Delesof, who had been so keenly and unwontedly affected by the music, had conceived the thought of conferring some benefit upon this man.

It came into his head to take him home with him, to feed him, to establish him somewhere,—in other words, to lift him from his vile position.

"Well, are you tired?" asked Delesof, approaching him. Albert replied with a smile. "You have creative talent; you ought seriously to devote yourself to music, to play in public."

"I should like to have something to drink," exclaimed Albert, as though suddenly waking up.

Delesof brought him some wine, and the musician greedily drained two glasses.

"What splendid wine!" he exclaimed.

"What a lovely thing that Melancholie is!" said Delesof.

"Oh, yes, yes," replied Albert with a smile. "But pardon me, I do not know with whom I have the honor to be talking; maybe you are a count or a prince. Couldn't you let me have a little money?" He paused for a moment. "I have nothing—I am a poor man: I couldn't pay it back to you."

Delesof flushed, grew embarrassed, and hastened to hand the musician the money that had been collected for him.

"Very much obliged to you," said Albert, seizing the money. "Now let us have some more music; I will play for you as much as you wish. Only let me have something to drink, something to drink," he repeated, as he started to his feet.

Delesof gave him some more wine, and asked him to sit down by him.

"Pardon me if I am frank with you," said Delesof. "Your talent has interested me so much. It seems to me that you are in a wretched position."

Albert glanced now at Delesof, now at the hostess, who just then came into the room.

"Permit me to help you," continued Delesof. "If you need any thing, then I should be very glad if you would come and stay with me for a while. I live alone, and maybe I could be of some service to you."

Albert smiled, and made no reply.

"Why don't you thank him?" said the hostess. "It seems to me that this would be a capital thing for you.—Only I would not advise you," she continued, turning to Delesof, and shaking her head warningly.

"Very much obliged to you," said Albert, seizing Delesof's hand with both his moist ones. "Only now let us have some music, please."

But the rest of the guests were already making their preparations to depart; and as Albert did not address them, they came out into the anteroom.

Albert bade the hostess farewell; and having taken his worn hat with wide brim, and a last summer's alma viva, which composed his only protection against the winter, he went with Delesof down the steps.

As soon as Delesof took his seat in his carriage with his new friend, and became conscious of that unpleasant odor of intoxication and filthiness exhaled by the musician, he began to repent of the step that he had taken, and to curse himself for his childish softness of heart and lack of reason. Moreover, all that Albert said was so foolish and in such bad taste, and he seemed so near a sudden state of beastly intoxication, that Delesof was disgusted. "What shall I do with him?" he asked himself.

After they had been driving for a quarter of an hour, Albert relapsed into silence, took off his hat, and laid it on his knee, then threw himself into a corner of the carriage, and began to snore.... The wheels crunched monotonously over the frozen snow, the feeble light of dawn scarcely made its way through the frosty windows.

Delesof glanced at his companion. His long body, wrapped in his mantle, lay almost lifeless near him. It seemed to him that a long head with large black nose was swaying on his trunk; but on examining more closely he perceived that what he took to be nose and face was the man's hair, and that his actual face was lower down.

He bent over, and studied the features of Albert's face. Then the beauty of his brow and of his peacefully closed mouth once more charmed him. Under the influence of nervous excitement caused by the sleepless hours of the long night and the music, Delesof, as he looked at that face, was once more carried back to the blessed world of which he had caught a glimpse once before that night; again he remembered the happy and magnanimous time of his youth, and he ceased to repent of his rashness. At that moment he loved Albert truly and warmly, and firmly resolved to be a benefactor to him.

IV.

The next morning when Delesof was awakened to go to his office, he saw, with an unpleasant feeling of surprise, his old screen, his old servant, and his clock on the table.

"What did I expect to see if not the usual objects that surround me?" he asked himself.

Then he recollected the musician's black eyes and happy smile; the motive of the Melancholie and all the strange experiences of the night came back into his consciousness. It was never his way, however, to reconsider whether he had done wisely or foolishly in taking the musician home with him. After he had dressed, he carefully laid out his plans for the day: he took some paper, wrote out some necessary directions for the house, and hastily put on his cloak and galoshes.

As he went by the dining-room he glanced in at the door. Albert, with his face buried in the pillow and lying at full length in his dirty, tattered shirt, was buried in the profoundest slumber on the saffron sofa, where in absolute unconsciousness he had been laid the night before.

Delesof felt that something was not right: it disturbed him. "Please go for me to Boriuzovsky, and borrow his violin for a day or two," said he to his man; "and when he wakes up, bring him some coffee, and get him some clean linen and some old suit or other of mine. Fix him up as well as you can, please."

When he returned home in the afternoon, Delesof, to his surprise, found that Albert was not there.

"Where is he?" he asked of his man.

"He went out immediately after dinner," replied the servant. "He took the violin, and went out, saying that he would be back again in an hour; but since that time we have not seen him."

"Ta, ta! how provoking!" said Delesof. "Why did you let him go, Zakhár?"

Zakhár was a Petersburg lackey, who had been in Delesof's service for eight years. Delesof, as a single young bachelor, could not help intrusting him with his plans; and he liked to get his judgment in regard to each of his undertakings.

"How should I have ventured to detain him?" replied Zakhár, playing with his watch-charms. "If you had intimated, Dmitri Ivánovitch, that you wished me to keep him here, I might have kept him at home. But you only spoke of his wardrobe."

"Ta! how vexatious! Well, what has he been doing while I was out?"

Zakhár smiled.

"Indeed, he's a real artist, as you may say, Dmitri Ivánovitch. As soon as he woke up he asked for some madeira: then he began to keep the cook and me pretty busy. Such an absurd.... However, he's a very interesting character. I brought him some tea, got some dinner ready for him; but he would not eat alone, so he asked me to sit down with him. But when he began to play on the fiddle, then I knew that you would not find many such artists at Izler's. One might well keep such a man. When he played 'Down the Little Mother Volga' for us, why, it was enough to make a man weep. It was too good for any thing! The people from all the floors came down into our entry to listen."

"Well, did you give him some clothes?" asked the bárin.

"Certainly I did: I gave him your dress-shirt, and I put on him an overcoat of mine. You want to help such a man as that, he's a fine fellow." Zakhár smiled. "He asked me what rank you were, and if you had had important acquaintances, and how many souls of peasantry you had."

"Very good: but now we must send and find him; and henceforth don't give him any thing to drink, otherwise you'll do him more harm than good."

"That is true," said Zakhár in assent. "He doesn't seem in very robust health: we used to have an overseer who, like him"....

Delesof, who had already long ago heard the story of the drunken overseer, did not give Zakhár time to finish, but bade him make every thing ready for the night, and then go out and bring the musician back.

He threw himself down on his bed, and put out the candle; but it was long before he fell asleep, for thinking about Albert.

"This may seem strange to some of my friends," said Delesof to himself, "but how seldom it is that I can do any thing for any one beside myself! and I ought to thank God for a chance when one presents itself. I will not send him away. I will do every thing, at least every thing that I can, to help him. Maybe he is not absolutely crazy, but only inclined to get drunk. It certainly will not cost me very much. Where one is, there is always enough to satisfy two. Let him live with me a while, and then we will find him a place, or get him up a concert; we'll help him off the shoals, and then there will be time enough to see what will come of it." An agreeable sense of self-satisfaction came over him after making this resolution.

"Certainly I am not a bad man: I might say I am far from being a bad man," he thought. "I might go so far as to say that I am a good man, when I compare myself with others."

He was just dropping off to sleep when the sound of opening doors, and steps in the ante-room, roused him again. "Well, shall I treat him rather severely?" he asked himself; "I suppose that is best, and I ought to do it."

He rang.

"Well, did you find him?" he asked of Zakhár, who answered his call.

"He's a poor, wretched fellow, Dmitri Ivánovitch," said Zakhár, shaking his head significantly, and closing his eyes.

"What! is he drunk?"

"Very weak."

"Had he the violin with him?"

"I brought it: the lady gave it to me."

"All right. Now please don't bring him to me to-night: let him sleep it off; and to-morrow don't under any circumstances let him out of the house."

But before Zakhár had time to leave the room, Albert came in.

V.

"You don't mean to say that you've gone to bed at this time," said Albert with a smile. "I was there again, at Anna Ivánovna's. I spent a very pleasant evening. We had music, told stories; there was a very pleasant company there.

141

Please let me have a glass of something to drink," he added, seizing a carafe of water that stood on the table, "only not water."

Albert was just as he had been the night before,—the same lovely smiling eyes and lips, the same fresh inspired brow, and weak features. Zakhár's overcoat fitted him as though it had been made for him, and the clean, tall, stiffly-starched collar of the dress-shirt picturesquely fitted around his delicate white neck, giving him a peculiarly childlike and innocent appearance.

He sat down on Delesof's bed, smiling with pleasure and gratitude, and looked at him without speaking. Delesof gazed into Albert's eyes, and suddenly felt himself once under the sway of that smile. All desire for sleep vanished from him, he forgot his resolution to be stern: on the contrary, he felt like having a gay time, to hear some music, and to talk confidentially with Albert till morning. Delesof bade Zakhár bring a bottle of wine, cigarettes, and the violin.

"This is excellent," said Albert. "It's early yet, we'll have a little music. I will play whatever you like."

Zakhár, with evident satisfaction, brought a bottle of Lafitte, two glasses, some mild cigarettes such as Albert smoked, and the violin. But, instead of going off to bed as his bárin bade him, he lighted a cigar, and sat down in the next room.

"Let us talk instead," said Delesof to the musician, who was beginning to tune the violin.

Albert sat down submissively on the bed, and smiled pleasantly.

"Oh, yes!" said he, suddenly striking his forehead with his hand, and putting on an expression of anxious curiosity. The expression of his face always foretold what he was going to say. "I wanted to ask you,"—he hesitated a little,—"that gentleman who was there with you last evening.... You called him N. Was he the son of the celebrated N.?"

"His own son," replied Delesof, not understanding at all what Albert could find of interest in him.

"Indeed!" he exclaimed, smiling with satisfaction. "I instantly noticed that there was something peculiarly aristocratic in his manners. I love aristocrats. There is something splendid and elegant about an aristocrat. And that officer who danced so beautifully," he went on to ask. "He also pleased me very much, he was so gay and noble looking. It seems he is called Adjutant N. N."

"Who?" asked Delesof.

"The one who ran into me when we were dancing. He must be a splendid man."

"No, he is a silly fellow," replied Delesof.

"Oh, no! it can't be," rejoined Albert hotly. "There's something very, very pleasant about him. And he's a fine musician," added Albert. "He played something from an opera. It's a long time since I have seen any one who pleased me so much."

"Yes, he plays very well; but I don't like his playing," said Delesof, anxious to bring his companion to talk about music. "He does not understand classic music, but only Donizetti and Bellini; and that's no music, you know. You agree with me, don't you?"

"Oh, no, no! Pardon me," replied Albert with a gentle expression of vindication. "The old music is music; but modern music is music too. And in the modern music there are extraordinarily beautiful things. Now, 'Somnambula,' and the finale of 'Lucia,' and Chopin, and 'Robert'! I often think,"—he hesitated, apparently collecting his thoughts,—"that if Beethoven were alive, he would weep tears of joy to hear 'Somnambula.' It's so beautiful all through. I heard 'Somnambula' first when Viardot and Rubini were here. That was something worth while," he said, with shining eyes, and making a gesture with both hands, as though he were casting something from his breast. "I'd give a good deal, but it would be impossible, to bring it back."

"Well, but how do you like the opera nowadays?" asked Delesof.

"Bosio is good, very good," was his reply, "exquisite beyond words; but she does not touch me here," he said, pointing to his sunken chest. "A singer must have passion, and she hasn't any. She is enjoyable, but she doesn't torture you."

"Well, how about Lablache?"

"I heard him in Paris, in 'The Barber of Seville.' Then he was the only one, but now he is old. He can't be an artist, he is old."

"Well, supposing he is old, still he is fine in morceaux d'ensemble," said Delesof, still speaking of Lablache.

"Who said that he was old?" said Albert severely. "He can't be old. The artist can never be old. Much is needed in an artist, but fire most of all," he declared with glistening eyes, and raising both hands in the air. And, indeed, a terrible inner fire seemed to glow throughout his whole frame. "Ah, my God!" he exclaimed suddenly. "You don't know Petrof, do you,—Petrof, the artist?"

"No, I don't know him," replied Delesof with a smile.

"How I wish that you and he might become acquainted! You would enjoy talking with him. How he does understand art! He and I often used to meet at Anna Ivánovna's, but now she is vexed with him for some reason or other. But I really wish that you might make his acquaintance. He has great, great talent."

"Oh! Does he paint pictures?" asked Delesof.

"I don't know. No, I think not; but he was an artist of the Academy. What thoughts he had! Whenever he talks, it is wonderful. Oh, Petrof has great talent, only he leads a very gay life!... It's too bad," said Albert with a smile. The next moment he got up from the bed, took the violin, and began to play.

"Have you been at the opera lately?" asked Delesof.

Albert looked round, and sighed.

"Ah, I have not been able to!" he said, clutching his head. Again he sat down by Delesof. "I will tell you," he went on to say, almost in a whisper.

144

"I can't go: I can't play there. I have nothing, nothing at all,—no clothes, no home, no violin. It's a wretched life,—a wretched life!" he repeated the phrase. "Yes, and why have I got into such a state? Why, indeed? It ought not to have been," said he, smiling. "Akh! Don Juan."

And he struck his head.

"Now let us have something to eat," said Delesof.

Albert, without replying, sprang up, seized the violin, and began to play the finale of the first act of "Don Juan," accompanying it with a description of the scene in the opera.

Delesof felt the hair stand up on his head, when he played the voice of the dying commander.

"No, I cannot play to-night," said Albert, laying down the instrument. "I have been drinking too much." But immediately after he went to the table, poured out a brimming glass of wine, drank it at one gulp, and again sat down on the bed near Delesof.

Delesof looked steadily at Albert. The latter occasionally smiled, and Delesof returned his smile. Neither of them spoke, but the glance and smile brought them close together into a reciprocity of affection. Delesof felt that he was growing constantly fonder and fonder of this man, and he experienced an inexpressible pleasure.

"Were you ever in love?" he asked suddenly. Albert remained sunk in thought for a few seconds, then his face lighted up with a melancholy smile. He bent over toward Delesof, and gazed straight into his eyes.

"Why did you ask me that question?" he whispered. "But I will tell you all about it. I like you," he added, after a few moments of thought, and glancing around. "I will not deceive you, I will tell you all, just as it was, from the beginning." He paused, and his eyes took on a strange wild appearance. "You know that I am weak in judgment," he said suddenly. "Yes, yes," he continued. "Anna Ivánovna has told you about it. She tells everybody that I am crazy. It isn't true, she says it for a joke; she is a good woman, but I really have not been quite well for some time." Albert paused again, and stood up, gazing with wide-opened eyes at the dark door. "You asked me if I had ever been in love. Yes, I have been in love," he whispered, raising his brows. "That happened long ago; it was at a time when I still had a place at the theatre. I went to play second violin at the opera, and she came into a parquet box at the left."

Albert stood up, and bent over to Delesof's ear. "But no," said he, "why should I mention her name? You probably know her, everybody knows her. I said nothing, but simply looked at her: I knew that I was a poor artist, and she an aristocratic lady. I knew that very well. I only looked at her, and had no thoughts."

Albert paused for a moment, as though making sure of his recollections.

"How it happened I know not, but I was invited once to accompany her on my violin.... Now I was only a poor artist!" he repeated, shaking his head and smiling. "But no, I cannot tell you, I cannot!" he exclaimed, again clutching his head. "How happy I was!"

"What? did you go to her house often?" asked Delesof.

"Once, only once.... But it was my own fault; I wasn't in my right mind. I was a poor artist, and she an aristocratic lady. I ought not to have spoken to her. But I lost my senses, I committed a folly. Petrof told me the truth: 'It would have been better only to have seen her at the theatre.'"

"What did you do?" asked Delesof.

"Ah! wait, wait, I cannot tell you that."

And, hiding his face in his hands, he said nothing for some time.

"I was late at the orchestra. Petrof and I had been drinking that evening, and I was excited. She was sitting in her box, and talking with some general. I don't know who that general was. She was sitting at the very edge of the box, with her arm resting on the rim. She wore a white dress, with pearls on her neck. She was talking with him, but she looked at me. Twice she looked at me. She had arranged her hair in such a becoming way! I stopped playing,

146

and stood near the bass, and gazed at her. Then, for the first time, something strange took place in me. She smiled on the general, but she looked at me. I felt certain that she was talking about me; and suddenly I seemed to be not in my place in the orchestra, but was standing in her box, and seizing her hand in that place. What was the meaning of that?" asked Albert, after a moment's silence.

"A powerful imagination," said Delesof.

"No, no, ... I cannot tell," said Albert frowning. "Even then I was poor. I hadn't any room; and when I went to the theatre, I sometimes used to sleep there."

"What, in the theatre?" asked Delesof.

"Ah! I am not afraid of these stupid things. Ah! just wait a moment. As soon as everybody was gone, I went to that box where she had been sitting, and slept there. That was my only pleasure. How many nights I spent there! Only once again did I have that experience. At night many things seemed to come to me. But I cannot tell you much about them." Albert contracted his brows, and looked at Delesof. "What did it mean?" he asked.

"It was strange," replied the other.

"No, wait, wait!" he bent over to his ear, and said in a whisper,—

"I kissed her hand, wept there before her, and said many things to her. I heard the fragrance of her sighs, I heard her voice. She said many things to me that one night. Then I took my violin, and began to play softly. And I played beautifully. But it became terrible to me. I am not afraid of such stupid things, and I don't believe in them, but my head felt terribly," he said, smiling sweetly, and moving his hand over his forehead. "It seemed terrible to me on account of my poor mind; something happened in my head. Maybe it was nothing; what do you think?"

Neither spoke for several minutes.

"Und wenn die Wolken sie verhüllen,

Die Sonne bleibt doch ewig klar.[54]"

hummed Albert, smiling gently. "That is true, isn't it?" he asked.

"Ich auch habe gelebt und genossen."[55]

"Ah, old man Petrof! how this would have made things clear to you!"

Delesof, in silence and with dismay, looked at his companion's excited and colorless face.

"Do you know the Juristen waltzes?" suddenly asked Albert in a loud voice, and without waiting for an answer, jumped up, seized the violin, and began to play the waltz. In absolute self-forgetfulness, and evidently imagining that a whole orchestra was playing for him, Albert smiled, began to dance, to shuffle his feet, and to play admirably.

"Hey, we will have a good time!" he exclaimed, as he ended, and waved his violin. "I am going," said he, after sitting down in silence for a little. "Won't you come along too?"

"Where?" asked Delesof in surprise.

"Let us go to Anna Ivánovna's again. It's gay there,—bustle, people, music."

Delesof for a moment was almost persuaded. However, coming to his senses, he promised Albert that he would go with him the next day.

"I should like to go this minute."

"Indeed, I wouldn't go."

Albert sighed, and laid down the violin.

"Shall I stay, then?" He looked over at the table, but the wine was gone; and so, wishing him a good-night, he left the room.

Delesof rang. "Look here," said he to Zakhár, "don't let Mr. Albert go anywhere without asking me about it first."

VI.

The next day was a holiday. Delesof, on waking, sat in his parlor, drinking his coffee and reading a book. Albert, who was in the next room, had not yet moved. Zakhár discreetly opened the door, and looked into the dining-room.

"Would you believe it, Dmitri Ivánovitch, there he lies asleep on the bare sofa. I would not send him away for any thing, God knows. He's like a little child. Indeed, he's an artist!"

At twelve o'clock, there was a sound of yawning and coughing on the other side of the door.

Zakhár again crept into the dining-room; and the bárin heard his wheedling voice, and Albert's gentle, beseeching voice.

"Well, how is he?" asked Delesof, when Zakhár came out.

"He feels blue, Dmitri Ivánovitch. He doesn't want to get dressed. He's so cross. All he asks for is something to drink."

"Now, if we are to get hold of him, we must strengthen his character," said Delesof to himself. And, forbidding Zakhár to give him any wine, he again devoted himself to his book; in spite of himself, however, listening all the time for developments in the dining-room.

But there was no movement there, only occasionally were heard a heavy chest cough and spitting. Two hours passed. Delesof, after dressing to go out, resolved to look in upon his guest. Albert was sitting motionless at the window, leaning his head on his hands.

He looked round. His face was sallow, morose, and not only melancholy but deeply unhappy. He tried to welcome his host with a smile, but his face assumed a still more woe-begone expression. It seemed as though he were on the point of tears.

With effort he stood up and bowed. "If I might have just a little glass of simple vodka," he exclaimed with a supplicating expression. "I am so weak. If you please!"

"Coffee will be more strengthening, I would advise you."

Albert's face lost its childish expression; he gazed coldly, sadly, out of the window, and fell back into the chair.

149

"What am I to do now? Wherein am I to blame?" he asked himself.

"Well, how is the musician?" was his first question when he returned home late that evening.

"Bad," was Zakhár's short and ringing reply. "He sighs all the time, and coughs, and says nothing at all, only he has asked for vodka four or five times, and once I gave him some. How can we avoid killing him this way, Dmitri Ivánovitch? That was the way the overseer"....

"Well, hasn't he played on the fiddle?"

"Didn't even touch it. I took it to him, twice—Well, he took it up slowly, and carried it out," said Zakhár with a smile. "Do you still bid me refuse him something to drink?"

"Don't give him any thing to-day; we'll see what'll come of it. What is he doing now?"

"He has shut himself into the parlor."

Delesof went into his library, took down a few French books, and the Testament in German. "Put these books to-morrow in his room; and look out, don't let him get away," said he to Zakhár.

The next morning Zakhár informed his bárin that the musician had not slept a wink all night. "He kept walking up and down his rooms, and going to the sideboard to try to open the cupboard and door; but every thing, in spite of his efforts, remained locked."

Zakhár told how, while he was going to sleep, he heard Albert muttering to himself in the darkness and gesticulating.

Each day Albert grew more gloomy and taciturn. It seemed as though he were afraid of Delesof, and his face expressed painful terror whenever their eyes met. He did not touch either book or violin, and made no replies to the questions put to him.

On the third day after the musician came to stay with him, Delesof returned home late in the evening, tired and worried. He had been on the in his nightdress was standing against the door; Albert in cap and alma viva was trying to pull him away, and was screaming at him in a pathetic voice.

"You have no right to detain me; I have a passport; I have not stolen any thing from you. You must let me go. I will go to the police."

"I beg of you, Dmitri Ivánovitch," said Zakhár, turning to his bárin, and continuing to stand guard at the door. "He got up in the night, found the key in my overcoat-pocket, and he has drunk up the whole decanter of sweet vodka. Was that good? And now he wants to go. You didn't give me orders, and so I could not let him out."

Albert, seeing Delesof, began to pull still more violently on Zakhár. "No one has the right to detain me! He cannot do it," he screamed, raising his voice more and more.

"Let him go, Zakhár," said Delesof. "I do not wish to detain you, and I have no right to, but I advise you to stay till to-morrow," he added, addressing Albert.

"No one has the right to detain me. I am going to the police," screamed Albert more and more furiously, addressing only Zakhár, and not heeding Delesof. "Guard!" he suddenly shouted at the top of his voice.

"Now, what are you screaming like that for? You see you are free to go," said Zakhár, opening the door.

Albert ceased screaming. "How did they dare? They were going to murder me! No!" he muttered to himself as he put on his galoshes. Not offering to say good-by, and still muttering something unintelligible, he went out of the door. Zakhár accompanied him to the gate, and came back.

"Thank the Lord, Dmitri Ivánovitch! Any longer would have been a sin," said he to his bárin. "And now we must count the silver."

Delesof only shook his head, and made no reply. There came over him a lively recollection of the first two evenings which he and the musician had spent together; he remembered the last wretched days which Albert had spent there; and above all he remembered the sweet but absurd sentiment of wonder, of love, and of sympathy, which had been aroused in him by the very first sight of this strange man; and he began to pity him.

"What will become of him now?" he asked himself. "Without money, without warm clothing, alone at midnight!" He thought of sending Zakhár after him, but now it was too late.

"Is it cold out doors?" he asked.

"A healthy frost, Dmitri Ivánovitch," replied the man. "I forgot to tell you that you will have to buy some more firewood to last till spring."

"But what did you mean by saying that it would last?"

VII.

Out of doors it was really cold; but Albert did not feel it, he was so excited by the wine that he had taken and by the quarrel.

As he entered the street, he looked around him, and rubbed his hands with pleasure. The street was empty, but the long lines of lights were still brilliantly gleaming; the sky was clear and beautiful. "What!" he cried, addressing the lighted window in Delesof's apartments; and then thrusting his hands in his trousers pockets under his coat, and looking straight ahead, he walked with heavy and uncertain steps straight up the street.

He felt an absolute weight in his legs and abdomen, something hummed in his head, some invisible power seemed to hurl him from side to side; but he still plunged ahead in the direction of where Anna Ivánovna lived.

Strange, disconnected thoughts rushed through his head. Now he remembered his quarrel with Zakhár, now something recalled the sea and his first voyage in the steamboat to Russia; now the merry night that he had spent with some friend in the wine-shop by which he was passing; then suddenly there came to him a familiar air singing itself in his recollections, and he seemed to see the object of his passion and the terrible night in the theatre.

But notwithstanding their incoherence, all these recollections presented themselves before his imaginations with such distinctness that when he closed his eyes he could not tell which was nearer to the reality: what he was doing, or what he was thinking. He did not realize and he did not feel how his legs moved, how he staggered and hit against a wall, how he looked around him, and how he made his way from street to street.

As he went along the Little Morskaya, Albert tripped and fell. Collecting himself in a moment, he saw before him some huge and magnificent edifice, and he went toward it.

In the sky not a star was to be seen, nor sign of dawn, nor moon, neither were there any street-lights there; but all objects were perfectly distinguishable. The windows of the edifice, which loomed up at the corner of the street, were brilliantly lighted, but the lights wavered like reflections. The building kept coming nearer and nearer, clearer and clearer, to Albert.

But the lights vanished the moment that Albert entered the wide portals. Inside it was dark. He took a few steps under the vaulted ceiling, and something like shades glided by and fled at his approach.

"Why did I come here?" wondered Albert; but some irresistible power dragged him forward into the depths of the immense hall.

There stood some lofty platform, and around it in silence stood what seemed like little men. "Who is going to speak?" asked Albert. No one answered, but some one pointed to the platform. There stood now on the platform a tall, thin man, with bushy hair and dressed in a variegated gown. Albert immediately recognized his friend Petrof.

"How strange! what is he doing here?" said Albert to himself.

"No, brethren," said Petrof, pointing to something, "you did not appreciate the man while he was living among you; you did not appreciate him! He was not a cheap artist, not a merely mechanical performer, not a crazy, ruined man. He was a genius, a great musical genius, who perished among you unknown and unvalued."

Albert immediately understood of whom his friend was speaking; but not wishing to interrupt him, he hung his head modestly. "He, like a sheaf of straw, was wholly consumed by the sacred fire which we all serve," continued

155

the voice. "But he has completely fulfilled all that God gave him; therefore he ought to be considered a great man. You may despise him, torture him, humiliate him," continued the voice, more and more energetically, "but he has been, is, and will be immeasurably higher than you all. He is happy, he is good. He loved you all alike, or cared for you, it is all the same; but he has served only that with which he was so highly endowed. He loved one thing,—beauty, the only infinite good in the world. Oh, yes, what a man he is! Fall all of you before him. On your knees!" cried Petrof in a thundering voice.

But another voice mildly answered from another corner of the hall. "I do not wish to bow my knee before him," said the voice.

Albert instantly recognized Delesof.

"Why is he great? And why should we bow before him? Has he conducted himself in an honorable and righteous manner? Has he brought society any advantage? Do we not know how he borrowed money, and never returned it; how he carried off a violin that belonged to a brother artist, and pawned it?"

"My God! how did he know all that?" said Albert to himself, drooping his head still lower.

"Do we not know," the voice went on, "how he pandered to the lowest of the low, pandered to them for money? Do we not know how he was driven out of the theatre? How Anna Ivánovna threatened to hand him over to the police?"

"My God! that is all true, but protect me," cried Albert. "You are the only one who knows why I did so."

"Stop, for shame!" cried Petrof's voice again. "What right have you to accuse him? Have you lived his life? Have you experienced his enthusiasms?"

"Right! right!" whispered Albert.

"Art is the highest manifestation of power in man. It is given only to the favored few, and it lifts the chosen to such an eminence that the head swims, and it is hard to preserve its integrity. In art, as in every struggle, there

156

are heroes who bring all under subjection to them, and perish if they do not attain their ends."

Petrof ceased speaking; and Albert lifted his head, and tried to shout in a loud voice, "Right! right!" but his voice died without a sound.

"That is not the case with you. This does not concern you," sternly said the artist Petrof, addressing Delesof. "Yes, humble him, despise him," he continued, "for he is better and happier than all the rest of you."

Albert, with rapture in his heart at hearing these words, could not contain himself, but went up to his friend, and was about to kiss him.

"Get thee gone, I do not know you," replied Petrof. "Go your own way, you cannot come here."

"Here, you drunken fellow, you cannot come here," cried a policeman at the crossing.

Albert hesitated, then collected all his forces, and, endeavoring not to stumble, crossed over to the next street.

It was only a few steps to Anna Ivánovna's. From the hall of her house a stream of light fell on the snowy dvor, and at the gate stood sledges and carriages.

Clinging with both hands to the balustrade, he made his way up the steps, and rang the bell.

The maid's sleepy face appeared at the open door, and looked angrily at Albert.

"It is impossible," she cried; "I have been forbidden to let you in," and she slammed the door. The sounds of music and women's voices floated down to him.

Albert sat down on the ground, and leaned his head against the wall, and shut his eyes. At that very instant a throng of indistinct but correlated visions took possession of him with fresh force, mastered him, and carried him off into the beautiful and free domain of fancy.

"Yes! he is better and happier," involuntarily the voice repeated in his imagination.

From the door were heard the sounds of a polka. These sounds also told him that he was better and happier. In a neighboring church was heard the sound of a prayer-bell; and the prayer-bell also told him that he was better and happier.

"Now I will go back to that hall again," said Albert to himself. "Petrof must have many things still to tell me."

There seemed to be no one now in the hall; and in the place of the artist Petrof, Albert himself stood on the platform, and was playing on his violin all that the voice had said before.

But his violin was of strange make: it was composed of nothing but glass, and he had to hold it with both hands, and slowly rub it on his breast to make it give out sounds. The sounds were so sweet and delicious, that Albert felt he had never before heard any thing like them. The more tightly he pressed the violin to his breast, the more sweet and consoling they became. The louder the sounds, the more swiftly the shadows vanished, and the more brilliantly the walls of the hall were illuminated. But it was necessary to play very cautiously on the violin, lest it should break.

Albert played on the instrument of glass cautiously and well. He played things the like of which he felt no one would ever hear again.

He was growing tired, when a heavy distant sound began to annoy him. It was the sound of a bell, but this sound seemed to have a language.

"Yes," said the bell, with its notes coming from somewhere far off and high up, "yes, he seems to you wretched; you despise him, but he is better and happier than you. No one ever will play more on that instrument!"

These words which he understood seemed suddenly so wise, so novel, and so true, to Albert, that he stopped playing, and, while trying not to move, lifted his eyes and his arms toward heaven. He felt that he was beautiful and happy. Although no one was in the hall, Albert expanded his chest, and proudly lifted his head, and stood on the platform so that all might see him.

Suddenly some one's hand was gently laid on his shoulder; he turned around, and in the half light saw a woman. She looked pityingly at him, and shook her head. He immediately became conscious that what he was doing was wrong, and a sense of shame came over him.

"Where shall I go?" he asked her. Once more she gazed long and fixedly at him, and bent her head pityingly. She was the one, the very one whom he loved, and her dress was the same; on her round white neck was the pearl necklace, and her lovely arms were bare above the elbows.

She took him in her arms, and bore him away through the hall. At the entrance of the hall, Albert saw the moon and water. But the water was not below as is usually the case, and the moon was not above; there was a white circle in one place as sometimes happens. The moon and the water were together,—everywhere, above and below, and on all sides and around them both. Albert and his love darted off toward the moon and the water, and he now realized that she whom he loved more than all in the world was in his arms: he embraced her, and felt inexpressible felicity.

"Is not this a dream?" he asked himself. But no, it was the reality, it was more than reality: it was reality and recollection combined.

Then he felt that the indescribable pleasure which he had felt during the last moment was gone, and would never be renewed.

"Why am I weeping?" he asked of her. She looked at him in silence, with pitying eyes. Albert understood what she desired to say in reply. "Just as when I was alive," he went on to say. She, without replying, looked straight forward.

"This is terrible! How can I explain to her that I am alive?" he asked himself in horror. "My God, I am alive! Do understand me," he whispered.

"He is better and happier," said a voice.

But something kept oppressing Albert ever more powerfully. Whether it was the moon or the water, or her embrace or his tears, he could not tell, but he was conscious that he could not say all that it was his duty to say, and that all would be quickly over.

Two guests coming out from Anna Ivánovna's rooms stumbled against Albert lying on the threshold. One of them went back to Anna Ivánovna, and called her. "That was heartless," he said. "You might let a man freeze to death that way."

"Akh! why, that is my Albert. See where he was lying!" exclaimed the hostess. "Annushka, have him brought into the room; find a place for him somewhere," she added, addressing the maid.

"Oh! I am alive, why do you bury me?" muttered Albert, as they brought him unconscious into the room.

FOOTNOTES:

[54]

E'en though the clouds may veil it,

The sun shines ever clear.

[55]

I also have lived and rejoiced.

TWO HUSSARS.

A TALE.

1856.

Jomini, ay, Jomini,

But not a single word of vodka.[56]

D. Davuidof.

At the very beginning of this century, when there were no railways, no macadamized roads, no gas or stearine candles, no low and springy sofas, no unvarnished furniture, no disillusionized young men with eye-glasses, no women philosophers of liberal tendencies, no dear Camilles, such as our time has produced in abundance; in those naïve days when travellers made the journey from Moscow to Petersburg by stage or carriage, and took with them a whole kitchen of domestic preparations, and travelled for a week, night and day, over soft roads, muddy or dusty as the case might be, pinned their faith to Pozharsky cutlets, Valdaï bluebells, and pretzels; when during the long autumn evenings tallow candles burned till they had to be snuffed, and cast their rays on family circles of twenty or thirty people (at balls, wax or spermaceti candles were set up in candelabra); when furniture was placed with stiff precision; when our fathers were still young, not merely by the absence of wrinkles and gray hair, but fought duels for women, and were fain to rush from one end of a room to the other to pick up a handkerchief dropped accidentally or otherwise, and our mothers wore short waists and huge sleeves, and decided family affairs by the drawing of lots; when charming Camilles avoided the light of day; in the naïve period of Masonic lodges, of Martinists, and of the Tugendbund; at the time of the Miloradovitches, Davuidofs, and Pushkins,—a meeting of landed proprietors took place in the governmental city of K., and the election of the college of nobles was drawing to a close.

I.

"Well, all right, it's all the same, be it in the hall," said a young officer dressed in a shuba, and wearing a hussar's helmet, as he dismounted from a travelling sledge in front of the best hotel of the city of K.

"A great meeting, little father, your excellency,—a tremendous crowd," said the hall-boy, who had already learned from the officer's man that it was Count Turbin, and therefore honored him with the address of "your excellency." "Madame Afrimova and her daughters have expressed the intention of going away this evening; you can be accommodated with their room as soon as it is vacated,—No. 11," the hall-boy went on to say, noiselessly showing the count the way, and constantly turning round to look at him.

In the sitting-room, at a small table under a blackened full-length portrait of the Emperor Alexander, sat a number of men, evidently belonging to the local aristocracy, drinking champagne; and on one side were some travelling merchants in blue shubas.

The count entered the room, and calling Blücher, a huge gray boarhound that accompanied him, he threw off his cloak, the collar of which was covered with frost, and, after ordering vodka, sat down at the table in a short blue-satin jacket, and entered into conversation with the gentlemen sitting there. The latter, attracted toward the new-comer by his handsome and frank exterior, offered him a glass of champagne.

The count had begun to drink his glass of vodka; but now he also ordered a bottle of champagne, in order to return the courtesy of his new companions.

The driver came in to ask for vodka-money.

"Sashka,"[57] cried the count, "give it to him."

The driver went out with Sashka, but quickly returned, holding the money in his hands.

"What! little father, 'slency, is that right? I did my best for you. You promised me a half-ruble, and you have only given me a quarter!"

"Sashka, give him a ruble."

Sashka, hanging down his head, gazed at the driver's feet.

"He will have enough," said he in his deep voice. "Besides, I haven't any more money."

The count drew from his pocket-book the two solitary blue notes[58] which were in it, and gave one to the driver, who kissed his hand, and went off. "I have come to the end," said the count, "my last five rubles."

"True hussar style, count," said one of the nobles, whose mustaches, voice, and a certain energetic freedom in the use of his legs, proclaimed him, beyond a peradventure, to be a retired cavalryman. "Are you going to spend some time here, count?"

"I must have some money if I stay, otherwise I should not be very likely to. Besides, there are no spare rooms, the Devil take it, in this cursed tavern."

"I beg of you, count," pursued the cavalryman, "wouldn't you like to come in with me? My room is No. 7. If you wouldn't object to sleep there for the present. We shall be here three days at least. To-day I was at the marshal's: how glad he would be to see you!"

"That's right, count, stay with us," urged another of the table companions, a handsome young man. "What is your hurry? And besides, this happens only once in three years,—these elections. We might get a glimpse of some of our girls, count!"

"Sashka, get me some clean linen. I am going to have a bath," said the count, rising. "And then we will see; perhaps I may decide to pay my respects to the marshal."

Then he called the waiter, and said something to him in an undertone. The waiter replied, with a laugh, "That is within human possibility," and went out.

"Well, then, little father, I have given orders to have my trunk taken to your room," cried the count, as he went out of the door.

"I shall consider it a favor: it delights me," replied the cavalryman as he hastened to the door, and cried, "No.7; don't forget!"

When the count was out of hearing, the cavalryman returned to his place, and drawing his chair nearer to the chinovnik, and looking him straight in his smiling eyes, said,—

"Well, he's the very one."

"What one?"

"I tell you that he's that very same hussar duellist,—let me see, the famous Turbin. He knew me. I'll wager he knew me. I assure you, at Lebedyan he and I were on a spree for three weeks, and were never sober once. That was when I lost my remount. There was one little affair at that time,—we were engaged in it together. Ah, he is a gay lad! isn't he, though?"

"Indeed he is. What pleasant manners he has! There's no fault to be found with him," replied the handsome young man. "How quickly we became acquainted!... He isn't more than twenty-two, is he?"

"He certainly would not seem so, would he?... But he's really more than that. Well, now you want to know who he is, don't you? Who carried off Megunova? He did. He killed Sablin. He kicked Matnyef out of the window. He 'did' Prince Nesterof out of three hundred thousand rubles. He's a regular madcap. You ought to know him,—a gambler, duellist, seducer, but a whole-souled fellow, a genuine hussar. We got talked about a good deal, but if any one really understood what it meant to be a genuine hussar! Those were great times."

And the cavalryman began to tell his comrade of a drinking-bout with the count, which had never taken place, nor could have taken place. It could not have taken place, first, because he had never seen the count before, and had retired from the service two years before the count had entered it; and secondly, because this cavalryman had never served in the cavalry, but had served four years as a very insignificant yunker in the Bielevsky regiment; and just as soon as he was promoted to be ensign, he retired.

But ten years before he had received an inheritance, and actually went to Lebedyan; and there he spent seven hundred rubles with the cavalry officers, and had had made for him an uhlan's uniform with orange lapels, with the intention of entering the uhlans. His thought of entering the cavalry, and his three weeks spent with the officers at Lebedyan, made the very happiest and most brilliant period of his life; so that he began to transfer his thought into a reality. Then, as he added remembrance to it, he began actually to believe in his military past,—which did not prevent him from being a worthy man through his kindness of heart and uprightness.

"Yes, any one who has never served in the cavalry," he went on to say, "will never understand us fellows."

He sat astride of his chair, and, thrusting out his lower lip, went on in a deep voice, "It happens you are riding along in front of the battalion. A devil is under you, not a horse, prancing along; thus you sit on this perfect devil. The battalion commander comes along. 'Lieutenant,' says he, 'I beg of you—your service is absolutely indispensable. You must lead the battalion for the parade.' Very well, and so it goes. You look around, you give a shout, you lead the brave fellows who are under your command. Ah! the deuce take it! 'twas a glorious time!"

The count came back from the bath, all ruddy, and with his hair wet, and went directly to No. 7, where the cavalryman was already sitting in his dressing-gown, with his pipe, and thinking with delight and some little anxiety of the good fortune that had befallen him in sharing his room with the famous Turbin. "Well, now," the thought came into his head, "suppose he should take me, and strip me naked, and carry me outside the town limits, and set me down in the snow, ... or smear me with tar ... or simply ... But, no: he would not do such a thing to a comrade," he said, trying to comfort himself.

"Sashka, give Blücher something to eat," cried the count.

Sashka made his appearance. He had been drinking glasses of vodka ever since his arrival, and was beginning to be genuinely tipsy.

"You have not been able to control yourself. You have been getting drunk, canaillya!... Feed Blücher."

"It won't kill him to fast.... You see, ... he's so plump," replied Sashka, caressing the dog.

166

"Now, none of your impudence. Go, and feed him."

"All you care for is to have your dog fat; but if a man drinks a little glass, then you pitch into him."

"Hey! I'll strike you," cried the count with a voice that made the window-panes rattle, and even scared the cavalryman somewhat.

"You would better ask if Sashka has had any thing to eat to-day. All right, strike away, if a dog is more to you than a man," continued Sashka.

But at that instant he received such a violent blow of the fist across the face that he staggered, struck his head against the partition, and, clutching his nose, leaped through the door, and threw himself down on a bench in the corridor.

"He has broken my teeth," he growled, wiping his bloody nose with one hand, and with the other scratching Blücher's back, as the dog licked him. "He has broken my teeth, Blüchka; and yet he is my count, and I would jump into the fire for him, that's a fact. Because he's my count, do you understand, Blüchka? And do you want something to eat?"

After lying there a while, he got up, gave the dog his dinner, and, almost sobered, went to serve his master, and get him his tea.

"You would simply offend me," said the cavalryman timidly, standing in front of the count, who was lying on the bed with his feet propped against the partition. "Now, you see, I am an old soldier and comrade, I may say; instead of letting you borrow of any one else, it would give me great pleasure to let you have two hundred rubles. I haven't them with me now,—only a hundred,—but I can get the rest to-day; don't refuse, you would simply offend me, count!"

"Thanks, little father," said Turbin, instantly perceiving what sort of relationship would exist between them, and slapping the cavalryman on the shoulder. "Thanks. Well, then, we'll go to the ball if you say so. But now what shall we do? Tell me whom you have in your city: any pretty girls? anybody ready for a spree? Who plays cards?"

167

The cavalryman explained that there would be a crowd of pretty girls at the ball; that the police commissioner,[59] Kolkof, who had just been re-elected, was the greatest hand for sprees, only he lacked the spirit of a genuine hussar, but still was a first-rate fellow; that Ilyushka's chorus of gypsies had been singing at K. ever since the elections began; that Stioshka[60] was the soloist, and that after the marshal's reception everybody went there nowadays. And the stakes were pretty high. "Lukhnof, a visitor here," he said, "is sweeping in the money; and Ilyin, a cornet of uhlans, who rooms in No. 8, has already lost a pile. The game has already begun there. They play there every evening; and he's a wonderfully fine young fellow, I tell you, count, this Ilyin is. There's nothing mean about him—he'd give you his last shirt."

"Then let us go to his room. We will see what sort of men you have," said the count.

"Come on! come on! they will be mighty glad."

II.

Ilyin, the cornet of uhlans, had not long been awake. The evening before, he had sat down at the gambling-table at eight o'clock, and lost for fifteen consecutive hours, till eleven o'clock that day. He had lost a great amount, but exactly how much he did not know, because he had had three thousand rubles of his money, and fifteen thousand belonging to the treasury, which he had long ago mixed up with his own, and he did not dare to settle his accounts lest his anticipations that he had made too great inroads on the public money should be confirmed.

He went to sleep about noon, and slept that heavy, dreamless sleep, peculiar to very young men who have been losing heavily. Waking at six, about the time that Count Turbin had arrived at the hotel, and seeing cards and chalk and soiled tables scattered around him in confusion in the room, he remembered with horror the evening's games, and the last card, a knave, which had lost him five hundred rubles; but, still scarcely believing in the reality, he drew out from under his pillow his money, and began to count it. He recognized a few notes which, with corners turned down and indorsements, had gone from hand to hand around the table; he remembered all the particulars. He had lost his own three thousand rubles, and twenty-five hundred belonging to the treasury had disappeared.

The uhlan had been playing for four nights in succession.

He had come from Moscow, where the public money had been intrusted to him. At K. the post-superintendent had detained him under the pretext that there were no post-horses, but in reality in accordance with his agreement with the hotel-keeper to detain all visitors for a day.

The uhlan, who was a gay young fellow, and had just received from his parent three thousand rubles for his military equipment, was glad to spend a few days in the city of K. during the elections, and counted on having a good time.

He knew a landed proprietor whose family lived there, and he was preparing to call upon him and pay his addresses to his daughter, when the cavalryman appeared, and made his acquaintance. That very evening, without malice prepense, he took him down into the parlor, and introduced him to his friends, Lukhnof and several other gamblers. From that time, the uhlan had kept steadily at gaming, and not only had not called on the proprietor, but had not thought of inquiring further for horses, and for four days had not left his room.

After he had dressed, and taken his tea, he went to the window. He felt an inclination to go out so as to dispel the importunate recollections of the game. He put on his cloak, and went into the street.

The sun had just sunk behind the white houses with their red roofs. It was already twilight. It was warm. The snow was softly falling in big, damp flakes, in the muddy streets. His mind suddenly became filled with unendurable melancholy at the thought that he had spent all that day in sleep, and now the day was done.

"This day which has gone, will never come back again," he said to himself.

"I have wasted my youth," he suddenly exclaimed, not because he really felt that he had wasted his youth,—he did not think about it at all,—but simply this phrase came into his head.

"What shall I do now?" he reasoned; "borrow of some one, and go away?"

A lady was passing along the sidewalk.

"What a stupid woman!" he said to himself for some reason.

"There's no one I can borrow of. I have wasted my youth."

He came to a block of stores. A merchant in a fox-skin shuba was standing at the door of his shop, and inviting custom.

"If I hadn't taken the eight, I should have won."

A little old beggar-woman followed him, snivelling.

"I have no one to borrow of."

A gentleman in a bear-skin shuba passed him. A policeman was standing on the corner.

"What can I do that will make sensation? Fire a pistol at them? No! That would be stupid. I have wasted my youth. Akh! what a splendid harness that is hanging in that shop! I should like to be riding behind a troïka!... Ekh! you fine fellows![61] I am going back. Lukhnof will be there pretty soon, and we'll have a game."

He returned to the hotel, and once more counted his money. No, he was not mistaken the first time; twenty-five hundred rubles of public money were missing, just as before.

"I will put up twenty-five rubles first; the next time, a quarter stake; then on seven, on fifteen, on thirty, and on sixty ... three thousand. I will buy that harness, and start. He won't give me any odds, the villain! I have wasted my youth!"

This was what was passing through the uhlan's mind just as Lukhnof himself came into the room.

"Well, have you been up long, Mikháïlo Vasílyitch?" inquired Lukhnof, deliberately removing from his thin nose his gold eye-glasses, and carefully wiping them with a red silk handkerchief.

"No, only just this minute. I had a splendid sleep!"

"A new hussar has just come. He is staying with Zavalshevsky. Had you heard about it?"

"No, I hadn't. Well, no one seems to be here yet. I believe they have gone to call on Priakhin. They'll be here very soon."

In fact, in a short time there came into the room an officer of the garrison, who was always hovering round Lukhnof; a Greek merchant with a huge hooked nose, cinnamon complexion, and deep-set black eyes; a stout, puffy proprietor, a brandy-distiller who gambled all night long, and always made his stakes on the basis of half a ruble. All of these wished to begin playing as promptly as possible, but the more daring players said nothing about it; Lukhnof, in particular, with perfect equanimity, told stories of rascality in Moscow.

"Just think of it," said he, "Moscow, the metropolis, the capital; and there they go out at night with crooks, dressed like demons; and they scare the stupid people, and rob pedestrians, and that is the end of it. Do the police notice it? No! It is astonishing!"

The uhlan listened attentively to the tales of these highwaymen, but finally got up and unobtrusively ordered cards to be brought. The stout proprietor was the first to notice it.

"Well, gentlemen, we are wasting golden moments. To work, let us to work!"

"Yes, you won by the half-ruble last evening, and so you like it," exclaimed the Greek.

"It's a good time to begin," said the garrison officer.

Ilyin looked at Lukhnof. Lukhnof, returning his gaze, went on calmly with his story of the robbers who dressed themselves up like devils. "Will you start the bank?" asked the uhlan.

"Isn't it rather early?"

"Byélof!" cried the uhlan, reddening for some reason or other; "bring me something to eat.... I haven't had any dinner to-day, gentlemen. Bring some champagne, and distribute the cards."

A this moment, the count and Zavalshevsky entered. It proved that Turbin and Ilyin were in the same division. They immediately struck up an acquaintance, drank a glass of champagne, clinking their glasses together, and in five minutes were calling each other "thou."

It was evident that Ilyin made a very pleasant impression on the count. The count smiled whenever he looked at him, and was amused at his freshness.

"What a fine young uhlan!" he said, "what a mustache! what a splendid mustache!"

Ilyin's upper lip bore the first down of a mustache, that was as yet almost white.

"You were preparing to play, were you not?" asked the count. "Well, I should like to win from you, Ilyin. I think that you must be a master," he added smiling.

"Yes, we were just starting in," replied Lukhnof, opening a pack of cards.... "Aren't you going to join us, count?"

"No, I won't to-night. If I did there wouldn't be any thing left of any of you! When I take a hand I always break the bank. But I haven't any money just now. I lost at Volotchok, at the station-house. It was by some sort of infantry-man who wore rings; what a cheat he was! and he cleaned me out completely."

"Were you long there at the station?" asked Ilyin.

"I staid there twenty-two hours. I shall not forget that station, curse it! and the superintendent won't forget it either."

"Why?"

"I got there, you see; the superintendent comes out, rascally face, the liar! 'There are no horses,' said he. Well, now I must tell you, I have made a rule in such cases: when there are no horses, I keep on my shuba, and go straight to the superintendent's room,—not the waiting-room, mind you, but the superintendent's own room,—and I have all the windows and doors opened, as though it were stifling. Well, that's what I did here. Cold! you remember how cold it has been this last month; twenty degrees below. The superintendent began to remonstrate. I knock his teeth in for him. There was some old woman there; and some young girls and peasant-women[62] set up a piping, were going to seize their pots and fly to the village.... I go to the door, and say, 'Let me have horses, and I'll go away: if you don't, I won't let you out, I'll freeze you all to death.'"

"What an admirable way!" said the puffy proprietor, bursting out into a laugh. "That's the way one would freeze out cockroaches."

"But I wasn't sufficiently on my guard: the superintendent and all his women managed to get out and run away. Only the old woman remained on the oven as my hostage. She kept sniffing, and offering prayers to God. Then we entered into negotiations. The superintendent came back, and, standing at a distance, tried to persuade me to let the old woman go. But I set Blücher on him: Blücher is a magnificent dog to take care of superintendents. Even then the rascal did not let me have horses till the next morning. And then came along that footpad! I went into the next room, and began to play. Have you seen Blücher?—Blücher! Fiu!" Blücher came running in. The players received him with flattering attention, although it was evident that they were anxious to get to work at entirely different matters.

"By the way, gentlemen, why don't you begin your game? I beg of you, don't let me interfere with you. You see I am a chatterbox," said Turbin. "Whether you love or not, 'tis an excellent thing."

III.

Lukhnof took two candles, brought out a huge dark-colored pocket-book full of money; slowly, as though performing some sacrament, opened it on the table; took out two one-hundred-ruble notes, and laid them on the cards.

"There, just the same as last evening; the bank begins with two hundred," said he, adjusting his glasses, and opening a pack of cards.

"Very well," said Ilyin, not glancing at him, or interrupting his conversation with Turbin.

The game began. Lukhnof kept the bank with mechanical regularity, occasionally pausing, and deliberately making notes, or looking sternly over his glasses, and saying in a weak voice, "Throw."

The stout proprietor talked louder than the rest, making various calculations at the top of his voice, while he wet his clumsy fingers and dog-eared his cards.

The garrison officer silently wrote in a fine hand his account on a card, turned down small corners, pressing them against the table.

The Greek sat next the banker, attentively following the game with his deep black eyes, as though waiting for something.

Zavalshevsky, as he stood by the table, would suddenly become all of a tremble, draw from his trousers-pocket a blue note or a red,[63] lay a card on it, pound on it with his palm, and say, "Bring me luck, little seven!" then he would bite his mustache, change from one leg to the other, and be in a continual state of excitement until the card came out.

Ilyin, who had been eating veal and cucumbers placed near him on the haircloth sofa, briskly wiped his hands on his coat, and began to put down one card after another.

Turbin, who had taken his seat at first on the sofa, immediately noticed that something was wrong. Lukhnof did not look at the uhlan, or say any thing to him; but occasionally his eyes for an instant rested on the uhlan's hands. The most of his cards lost.

"If I could only trump that little card," exclaimed Lukhnof in reference

174

to one of the stout proprietor's cards. He was still making half-ruble wagers.

"Trump Ilyin's instead: what would be the use of trumping mine?" replied the proprietor.

And, in point of fact, Ilyin's cards were trumped oftener than the others'. He nervously tore up his losing card under the table, and with trembling hands chose another.

Turbin arose from the sofa, and asked the Greek to give him his place next the banker. The Greek changed places; and the count, taking his chair, and not moving his eyes, began to watch Lukhnof's hands attentively.

"Ilyin," said he suddenly in his ordinary voice, which, entirely contrary to his desire, drowned out the others, "why do you stick to those routine cards? You don't know how to play!"

"Supposing I don't, it's all the same."

"You'll lose that way surely. Let me play against the bank for you."

"No, excuse me, I beg of you. I'm always this way. Play for yourself if you like."

"I have told you that I am not going to play. But I should like to play for you. I hate to see you losing so."

"Ah, well! you see it's my luck."

The count said nothing more, and leaning on his elbow began once more to watch the banker's hand just as attentively as before.

"Shameful!" he suddenly cried in a loud voice, dwelling on the word.

Lukhnof glared at him.

"Shameful, shameful!" he repeated still louder, staring straight into Lukhnof's eyes.

The game continued.

"That is not right!" said Turbin again, as Lukhnof trumped one of Ilyin's

175

high cards.

"What displeases you, count?" politely asked the banker with an air of indifference.

"Because you give Ilyin a simplum, and turn down your corners. That's what is shameful!"

Lukhnof made a slight motion with his shoulders and brows, signifying that he was resigned to any fate, and then he went on with the game.

"Blücher, fiu!" cried the count, rising; "over with him!" he added quickly. Blücher, bumping against the sofa with his back, and almost knocking the garrison officer from his feet, came leaping toward his master, looking at every one and wagging his tail as though he would ask, "Who is misbehaving here, hey?"

Lukhnof laid down the cards, and moved his chair away. "This is no way to play," said he. "I detest dogs. What kind of a game can you have if a whole pack of hounds is to be brought in?"

"Especially that kind of dog: they are called blood-suckers, if I am not mistaken," suggested the garrison officer.

"Well, are we to play or not, Mikháïlo Vasílyitch?" asked Lukhnof, addressing the uhlan.

"Don't bother us, count, I beg of you," said Ilyin, turning to Turbin.

"Come here for a moment," said Turbin, taking Ilyin's arm, and drawing him into the next room.

There the count's words were perfectly audible, though he spoke in his ordinary tone. But his voice was so powerful that it could always be heard three rooms off.

"Are you beside yourself? Don't you see that that man with the glasses is a cheat of the worst order?"

"Hey? Nonsense! Be careful what you say."

176

"No nonsense! but quit it, I tell you. It makes no difference to me. Another time I myself would have plucked you; but now I am sorry to see you ruining yourself. Have you any public money left?"

"No. What makes you think so about him?"

"Brother, I have been over this same road, and I know the ways of these professional gamblers. I tell you that the man in the glasses is a cheat. Quit, please. I ask you as a comrade."

"All right; I'll have just one more hand, and then have done with it."

"I know what that 'one more' means: very well, we will see."

They returned to the gaming-table. In one deal he laid down so many cards, and they were trumped so badly, that he lost a large amount.

Turbin rested his hand in the middle of the table, and said, "That's enough! now let us be going."

"No, I can't go yet; leave me, please," said Ilyin in vexation, shuffling the bent cards and not looking at Turbin.

"All right! the Devil be with you! Lose all you've got, if that please you; but it's time for me to be going.—Come, Zavalshevsky, let us go to the marshal's."

And they went out. No one spoke, and Lukhnof did not make the bank until the noise of their feet and of Blücher's paws had died away down the corridor.

"That's a madcap," said the proprietor, smiling.

"Well, now he won't bother us any more," said the garrison officer in a hurried whisper.

And the game went on.

IV.

The band, composed of the marshal's domestic serfs, were stationed in the butler's pantry, which had been put in order on account of the ball, and, having turned up the sleeves of their coats, had begun at the signal of their leader to play the ancient polonaise "Aleksandr, Yelisaviéta;" and under the soft, brilliant light of the wax candles, the couples began to move in tripping measure through the great ballroom; a governor-general of Catherine's time, with a star, taking out the gaunt wife of the marshal, the marshal with the governor's wife, and so on through all the hierarchy of the government in various combinations and variations,—when Zavalshevsky in a blue coat with a huge collar, and epaulets on his shoulders, and wearing stockings and pumps, and exhaling about him an odor of jasmine with which he had plentifully drenched his mustaches, the facings of his coat, and his handkerchief, entered with the handsome count, who wore tight-fitting blue trousers and a red pelisse embroidered with gold, and wearing on his breast the cross of Vladímir and a medal of 1812.

The count was of medium height, but had an extremely handsome figure. His clear blue eyes of remarkable brilliancy, and dark hair which was rather long and fell in thick ringlets, gave his beauty a peculiar character.

The count's presence at the ball was not unexpected. The handsome young man who had seen him at the hotel had already spoken of him to the marshal.

The impressions made by this announcement were of various kinds, but on the whole were not altogether pleasant.

"I suppose this young man will turn us into ridicule," was what the old women and the men said to themselves.

"Suppose he should run off with me," was what the wives and young ladies thought, with more or less apprehension.

As soon as the polonaise was finished, and the couples had made each other low bows, once more the women formed little groups by themselves, and the men by themselves. Zavalshevsky, proud and happy, led the count up to the hostess.

The marshal's wife, conscious of a certain inward trepidation lest this hussar should make her the cause of some scandal before everybody, said

178

proudly and scornfully, as she turned away, "Very glad to see you. I hope that you will dance." And then she looked at the count mistrustfully with an expression that seemed to say, "Now, if you insult any woman, then you are a perfect scoundrel after this."

The count, however, quickly overcame this prejudice by his amiability, his politeness, and his handsome jovial appearance; so that in five minutes the expression on the face of the marshal's wife plainly declared to all who stood around her, "I know how to manage all these men. He immediately realized whom he was talking with. And now he will be charming to me all the rest of the evening."

Moreover, just then the governor, who had known his father, came up to the count, and very graciously drew him to one side, and entered into conversation with him, which still more pleased the fashionable society of the town, and raised the count in their estimation.

Then Zavalshevsky presented the count to his sister, a plump young widow, who, ever since the count entered the room, had kept her big black eyes fastened upon him.

The count asked the little widow for the waltz which at that moment the musicians had struck up, and it was his artistic dancing that conquered the last vestiges of the popular prejudice.

"Ah, he's a master at dancing!" said a stout lady, following the legs in blue trousers which were flashing through the ballroom, and mentally counting, "One, two, three; one, two, three,—he's a master."

"How gracefully he moves his feet! how gracefully!" said another guest, who did not stand very high in the governmental society. "How does he manage to not hit any one with his spurs? Wonderful, very skilful!"

The count, by his skill in dancing, eclipsed the three best dancers of the city. These were, a governor's aide, a tall albino, who was famous for his rapid dancing and because he held the lady pressed very close to his breast; secondly, the cavalryman, who was famous for his graceful swaying during the waltz, and for his frequent but light tapping with his heels; and thirdly, a civilian of

179

whom everybody said, that, though he was not very strong-minded, yet he was an admirable dancer and the life of all balls.

In point of fact, this civilian from the beginning to the end of a ball invariably invited all the ladies in the order in which they sat, did not cease for a moment to dance, and only occasionally paused to wipe his weary but still radiant face with his cambric handkerchief, which would become wet through.

The count had surpassed them all, and had danced with the three principal ladies,—with the stout one, who was rich, handsome, and stupid; with the middle-sized one, who was lean, and not particularly good-looking, but handsomely dressed; and with the little one, who was not pretty, but very witty.

He had danced also with others,—with all the pretty women, and there were many pretty women there.

But the little widow, Zavalshevsky's sister, pleased the count more than all the rest; with her he danced a quadrille and a schottische and a mazurka.

At first, when they took their places for the quadrille, he overwhelmed her with compliments, comparing her to Venus and Diana, and to a rosebush, and to some other flower besides.

To all these amenities the little widow only bent her white neck, modestly dropped her eyes, and, looking at her white muslin dress, changed her fan from one hand to the other.

When, at last, she said, "This is too much, count; you are jesting," etc., her voice, which was rather guttural, betrayed such naïve simplicity of heart and amusing naturalness that the count, as he looked at her, actually compared her, not to a flower or to a rosebush, but to some kind of a pinkish-white wild-flower, exuberant and odorless, growing alone on a virgin snow-drift in some far, far-distant land.

Such a strange impression was made upon the count by this union of naïveté and unconventionality together with fresh beauty, that several times, in the pauses of the conversation, when he looked silently into her eyes or contemplated the loveliness of her arms and neck, the desire came over him with such vehemence to take her into his arms and kiss her again and again, that he was really obliged to restrain himself.

The little widow was quite satisfied with the impression which she perceived that she had made; but there was something in the count's behavior that began to disquiet her, and fill her with apprehensions, though the young hussar was not only flatteringly amiable, but even, to an extravagant degree, deferential in his treatment of her.

He ran to get orgeat for her, picked up her handkerchief, snatched a chair from the hands of a scrofulous young proprietor, who was also anxious to pay her attention, and who was not quick enough. But perceiving that these assiduities, which were fashionable at that period, had little effect in making the lady well-disposed, he began to amuse her by telling her ridiculous anecdotes: he assured her that he was ready at a moment's notice to stand on his head, or to crow like a cock, or to jump out of the window, or to fling himself into a hole in the ice.

This procedure was a brilliant success: the little widow became very gay; she rippled with laughter, displaying her marvellous white teeth, and became entirely satisfied with her cavalier. The count each moment grew more and more enchanted with her, so that at the end of the quadrille he was really in love with her.

After the quadrille, when she was approached by her former admirer, a young man of eighteen, the son of a very rich proprietor, the same scrofulous young man from whom Turbin had snatched away the chair, she received him with perfect coolness, and not one-tenth part of the constraint was noticeable in her which she felt when she was with the count.

"You are very kind," she said, all the time gazing at Turbin's back, and unconsciously reckoning how many yards[64] of gold-lace were used for his whole jacket. "You are very kind; you promised to come to take me for a walk, and to bring me some comfits."

"Well, I did come, Anna Fedorovna, but you weren't at home, and I left the very best comfits for you," said the young man, in a voice that was very thin, considering his height.

"You always are provided with excuses; I don't need your comfits. Please do not think"....

"I begin to see, Anna Fedorovna, how you have changed toward me, and I know why. But it is not right," he added, but without finishing his remark, evidently owing to some powerful interior emotion, which caused his lips to tremble strangely.

Anna Fedorovna did not heed him, and continued to follow Turbin with her eyes. The marshal, at whose house the ball was given,—a big, stout old man, who had lost his teeth,—came up to the count, and, taking him by the arm, invited him into his library to smoke and drink if he so desired.

As soon as Turbin disappeared, Anna Fedorovna felt that there was absolutely nothing for her to do in the ballroom, and slipping her hand through the arm of a dried-up old maid, who was a friend of hers, went with her into the dressing-room.

"Well, what do you think of him? Is he nice?" asked the old maid.

"Only it's terrible—the way he follows you up!" said Anna Fedorovna, going to the mirror, and contemplating herself in it.

Her face was aglow, her eyes were full of mischief, her color was heightened; then suddenly imitating one of the ballet-dancers whom she had seen during election time, she pirouetted round on one toe, and, laughing her guttural but sweet laugh, she leaped up in the air, crossing her knees.

"What a man he is! he even asked me for a souvenir," she confided to her friend. "But he will ne-e-ver get one," she said, singing the last words, and lifting one finger in the lilac-colored glove that reached to her elbow.

In the library where Turbin was conducted by the marshal, stood various kinds of vodka, liqueurs, edibles,[65] and champagne. In a cloud of tobacco-smoke the nobility were sitting, or walking up and down, talking about the elections.

"When the whole of the high nobility of our district has honored him with an election," exclaimed the newly elected isprávnik who was already tolerably tipsy, "he certainly ought not to fail in his duties toward society in general."

The conversation was interrupted by the count's coming. All were presented to him, and the isprávnik especially pressed his hand long between both of his, and asked him several times to go with him after the ball to the new tavern, where he would treat the gentlemen of the nobility, and where they would hear the gypsies sing.

The count accepted his invitation, and drank with him several glasses of champagne.

"Why aren't you dancing, gentlemen?" he asked, as he was about to leave the library.

"We aren't dancers," replied the isprávnik, laughing. "We prefer the wine, count; and besides, all these young ladies have grown up under my eyes, count. But still, I do sometimes take part in a schottische, count. I can do it, count."

"Come on then for a while," said Turbin. "Let us have some sport before we go to the gypsies."

"What say you, gentlemen? Let us come! Let us delight our host!"

And the three gentlemen who, since the beginning of the ball, had been drinking in the library and had very red faces, began to draw on their gloves, some of black kid, another of knit silk, and were just going with the count to the ballroom, when they were detained by the scrofulous young man, who, pale as a sheet, and scarcely able to refrain from tears, came straight up to Turbin.

"You have an idea, because you are a count, you can run into people as if you were at a fair," said he, with difficulty drawing his breath; "hence it isn't fitting"—

Once more the stream of his speech was interrupted by the involuntary

183

trembling of his lips.

"What?" cried Turbin, frowning suddenly, "what?... You're a baby," he cried, seizing him by the arm, and squeezing it so that the blood rushed to the young man's head, not so much from vexation as from fright. "What is it? Do you want to fight? If so, I am at your service."

Turbin had scarcely let go of his arm, which he had squeezed so powerfully, when two nobles seized the young man by the sleeve, and carried him off through a back door.

"What! have you lost your wits? You've surely been drinking too much. We shall have to tell your papa. What's the matter with you?" they asked.

"No, I haven't been drinking; but he ran into me, and did not apologize. He's a hog, that's what he is," whined the young man, now actually in tears.

Nevertheless they paid no attention to him, but carried him off home.

"Never mind, count," said the isprávnik and Zavalshevsky assuringly. "He's a mere child. They still whip him: he's only sixteen years old. It's hard to tell what is to be done with him. What fly stung him? And his father is such an honorable man! He's our candidate."

"Well, the Devil take him if he refuses"....

And the count returned to the ballroom, and, as gayly as before, danced the schottische with the pretty little widow, and laughed heartily when he saw the antics of the gentlemen who had come with him out of the library. There was a general burst of merriment all through the ballroom when the isprávnik tripped, and measured his length on the floor in the midst of the dancers.

V.

Anna Fedorovna, while the count was in the library, went to her brother, and, for the very reason of her conviction that she ought to pretend to feel very little interest in the count, she began to question him.

"Who is this hussar that has been dancing with me? Tell me, brother."

The cavalryman explained, to the best of his ability, what a great man

184

this hussar was, and in addition he told his sister that the count had stopped there simply because his money had been stolen on the route: he himself had loaned him a hundred rubles, but that was not enough. Couldn't his sister let him have two hundred more? Zavalshevsky asked her not to say any thing about this to any one, and, above all, not to the count.

Anna Fedorovna promised to send the money the next day, and to keep it a secret; but somehow or other, during the schottische, she had a terrible desire to offer the count as much money as he needed.

She deliberated, blushed, and at last, mastering her confusion, thus addressed herself to the task:—

"My brother told me, count, that you had met with a misfortune on the road, and hadn't any money. Now, if you need some, wouldn't you take some of me? I should be terribly glad."

But after she had thus spoken, Anna Fedorovna suddenly was overcome with fright, and blushed. All the gayety had instantly vanished from the count's face.

"Your brother is a fool!" said he in a cutting tone. "You know, when a man insults a man, then they fight a duel; but when a woman insults a man, then what do they do? Do you know?"

Poor Anna Fedorovna blushed to her ears with confusion. She dropped her eyes, and made no reply.

"They kiss the woman in public," said the count softly, bending over to whisper in her ear. "Permit me, however, to kiss your little hand," he added almost inaudibly, after a long silence, having some pity on his lady's confusion.

"Ah! only not quite yet," urged Anna Fedorovna, with a deep sigh.

"But when, then? To-morrow I am going away early.... But really, you owe it to me."

"Well, then, of course it is impossible," said Anna Fedorovna smiling.

"Only give me a chance to see you before to-morrow, so that I may kiss your hand. I will find one."

"How will you find one?"

"That is my affair. I can do any thing to see you.... Is it agreed?"

"Agreed."

The schottische came to an end; they danced through the mazurka, and in it the count did marvels, purloining handkerchiefs, bending on one knee, and clinking his spurs in an extraordinary manner, after the Warsaw style, so that all the old men came from their boston to look into the ballroom; and the cavalryman who was the best dancer confessed himself outdone. After they had eaten supper, they danced still the gross vater, and began to disperse.

The count all this time did not take his eyes from the little widow. He had not been insincere when he declared his readiness to throw himself into a hole in the ice.

Whether it was caprice or love or stubbornness, but that evening all the strength of his mind had been concentrated into one desire,—to see and to love her.

As soon as he perceived that Anna Fedorovna was taking her farewell of the hostess, he hastened to the servants' quarters, and thence, without his shuba, to the place where the carriages were drawn up.

"Anna Fedorovna Zaïtsova's equipage," he cried.

A high four-seated carriage with lanterns moved out, and started to drive up to the doorstep.

"Stop!" shouted the count to the coachman, rushing up toward the carriage through snow that was knee-deep.

"What is wanted?" called the driver.

"I want to get into the carriage," replied the count, opening the door as the carriage moved, and trying to climb in.

"Stop, you devil! stupid! Vaska![66] stop!" cried the coachman to the

186

postilion, and reining in the horses. "What are you getting into another person's carriage for? This belongs to the Lady Anna Fedorovna, and not to your grace."

"Hush up, blockhead! Na! there's a ruble for you; now come down and shut the door!" said the count.

But as the coachman did not move, he lifted the steps himself, and, shutting the window, managed to pull the door to.

In this, as in all ancient carriages, especially those upholstered in yellow galloon, there was an odor of mustiness and burnt bristles.

The count's legs were wet to the knees from melting snow, and almost freezing in his thin boots and trousers; and his whole body was penetrated by a cold like that of winter.

The coachman was grumbling on his box, and seemed to be getting ready to get down. But the count heard nothing and felt nothing. His face was aglow, his heart was beating violently. He convulsively clutched the yellow strap, thrust his head out of the side-window, and his whole being was concentrated in expectation.

He was not doomed to wait long. At the door-steps, they shouted, "Zaïtsova's carriage!" The coachman shook his reins, the carriage swung on its high springs; the lighted windows of the house passed one after another by the carriage-windows.

"See here, rogue, if you tell the lackey that I am here," said the count, thrusting his head through the front window, and addressing the coachman, "you'll feel my whip; but if you hold your tongue, I will give you ten rubles more."

He had scarcely time to close the window, when the carriage shook again still more violently, and then the wheels came to a stop.

He drew back as far as possible into the corner; he ceased to breathe; he even shut his eyes, so apprehensive was he, lest his passionate expectation should be disappointed.

The door was opened; one after the other, with a creak, the steps were let down; a woman's dress rustled, and the close atmosphere of the carriage was impregnated by the odor of jasmine; a woman's dainty feet hurried up the steps, and Anna Fedorovna, brushing against the count's leg with the skirt of her cloak, which was loosely thrown about her, silently, and with a deep sigh, took her place on the cushioned seat next him.

Whether she saw him or not, no one could decide, not even Anna Fedorovna herself: but when he took her hand, and said, "Now I will kiss your little hand anyway," she evinced very little dismay. She said nothing, but let him take her hand, which he covered with kisses, not stopping at the glove.

The carriage rolled off.

"Tell me something. You are not angry?" said he to her.

She silently sank back into her corner, but suddenly, for some reason or other, burst into tears, and let her head fall on his breast.

VI.

The newly elected ispravnik, with his company, the cavalryman, and other members of the nobility, had already been listening for some time to the gypsies, and drinking at the new tavern, when the count, in a blue-lined bearskin shuba which had belonged to Anna Fedorovna's late husband, joined them.

"Little father, your excellency! we have almost given up expecting you," said a squint-eyed black gypsy with brilliant teeth, who met him in the entry and divested him of his shuba. "We haven't met since we were at Lebedyan.... Stioshka has pined away on account of you."

Stioshka, a slender young gypsy-girl[67] with a cherry red bloom on her cinnamon-colored cheeks, with brilliant deep black eyes, shaded by long eyelashes, also hurried to meet him.

"Ah! dear little count![68] my sweetheart! This is a pleasure," she exclaimed through her teeth, with a joyous smile.

Ilyushka himself came to greet Turbin, pretending that he was very glad to see him. The old women, the wives, the young girls, hastened to the spot and surrounded the guest.

One would have said that he was a relative or a god-brother to them.

Turbin kissed all the young gypsy girls on the lips; the old women and the men kissed him on the shoulder or on the hand.

The gentlemen were also very glad of the count's arrival; the more because the festivity, having passed its apogee, was now becoming tame; every one began to feel a sense of satiety. The wine, having lost its exhilarating effect on the nerves, only served to load the stomach. Everybody had discharged the last cannon of his wildness, and was looking around moodily. All the songs had been sung, and ran in the heads of each, leaving a mere impression of noise and confusion.

Whatever any one did that was strange and wild, the rest began to look upon it as nothing very entertaining or amusing.

The isprávnik stretched out on the floor in shameless fashion at the feet of some old woman, kicked his leg in the air, and began to cry,—

"Champagne!... The count has come!... Champagne!... He has come!... Now give us champagne!... I will make a bath of champagne, and swim in it! Gentlemen of the nobility, I love your admirable society!... Stioshka, sing 'The Narrow Road.'"

The cavalryman was also very gay, but in a different fashion. He was sitting in a corner of a sofa with a tall, handsome gypsy, Liubasha; and with the consciousness that intoxication was beginning to cloud his eyes, he kept blinking them, and swinging his head, and repeating the same words over and over again: he was proposing in a whisper to the gypsy to fly with him somewhere.

Liubasha, smiling, listened to him as though what he said were very amusing to her, and at the same time rather melancholy. Occasionally she cast her glances at her husband, the squint-eyed Sashka, who was standing behind a chair near her. In reply to the cavalryman's declaration of love, she bent over to his ear, and begged him to buy her some perfume and a ribbon without any one knowing it, so that the others should not see it.

"Hurrah!" cried the cavalryman when the count came in.

The handsome young man, with an expression of anxiety, was walking up and down the room with solicitously steady steps, and humming an air from the "Revolt in the Seraglio."

An old paterfamilias, dragged out to see the gypsies through the irresistible entreaties of the gentlemen of the nobility, who had told him that if he staid away every thing would go to pieces, and in that case they had better not go, was lying on a sofa where he had stretched himself out immediately on his arrival; and no one paid any attention to him.

A chinovnik, who had been there before, had taken off his coat, was sitting with his legs on the table, and was rumpling up his hair, and thus proving that he understood how to be dissipated.

As soon as the count came in, the official unbuttoned his shirt-collar, and lifted his legs still higher. The count's arrival generally gave new life to the festivities.

The gypsy girls, who had been scattered about the room, again formed their circle. The count seated Stioshka, the soloist, on his knee, and ordered more champagne to be brought. Ilyushka, with his guitar, stood in front of the soloist, and began the plyaska, that is, the gypsy song and dance, "When I walk upon the Street," "Hey! you Hussars," "Do you hear, do you understand?" and others of the usual order.

Stioshka sang splendidly. Her flexible, sonorous contralto, with its deep chest notes, her smiles while she was singing, her mischievous, passionate eyes, and her little foot which involuntarily kept time to the measure of the song, her despairing wail at the end of each couplet,—this all touched some resonant but tender chord. It was evident that she lived only in the song that she was singing.

Ilyushka, in his smile, his back, his legs, his whole being, carrying out

190

in pantomime the idea expressed in the song, accompanied it on his guitar, and, fixing his eyes upon her as though he were hearing her for the first time, attentively and carefully lifted and drooped his head with the rhythm of the song.

Then he suddenly straightened himself up as the singer sang the last note, and, as though he felt himself superior to every one else in the world, with proud deliberation kicked the guitar, turned it over, stamped his foot, tossed back his locks, and looked at the chorus with a frown.

All his body, from his neck to his toes, began to dance in every sinew.

And twenty powerful, energetic voices, each trying to outdo the other in making strange and extraordinary noises, were lifted in union.

The old women sprang down from their chairs, waving their handkerchiefs, and showing their teeth, and crying in rhythmic measure, each louder than the other. The bassos, leaning their heads on one side, and swelling their necks, bellowed from behind their chairs.

When Stioshka emitted her high notes, Ilyushka brought his guitar nearer to her as though trying to aid her; and the handsome young man, in his enthusiasm, cried out that now they struck B-flat.

When they came to the national dance, the Plyasovaya, and Duniasha, with shoulders and bosom shaking, stepped in front of the count, and was passing on, Turbin leaped from his place, took off his uniform, and, remaining only in his red shirt, boldly joined her, keeping up the same measure, and cutting with his feet such antics, that the gypsies laughed and exchanged glances of approval.

The isprávnik, who was sitting Turkish fashion, pounded his chest with his fist, and cried "Vivat!" and then, seizing the count by the leg, began to tell him that out of two thousand rubles, he had only five hundred left and that he might do whatever he pleased, if only the count would permit him.

The old paterfamilias woke up, and wanted to go home, but they would not let him. The handsome young man asked a gypsy girl to waltz with him.

The cavalryman, anxious to exalt himself by his friendship with the count, got up from his corner, and embraced Turbin. "Ah, my turtle-dove!" he cried. "Why must you leave us so soon? ha?" The count said nothing, being evidently absorbed in thought. "Where did you go? Ah, you rascal, I know where you went!"

This familiarity somehow displeased the Count Turbin. Without smiling, he looked in silence into the cavalryman's face, and suddenly gave him such a terrible and grievous affront that the cavalryman was mortified, and for some time did not know what to make of such an insult, whether it were a joke or not a joke. At last he made up his mind that it was a joke; he smiled, and returned to his gypsy, assuring her that he would really marry her after Easter.

Another song was sung, a third, they danced again; the round of gayety was kept up, and every one continued to feel gay. There was no end to the champagne.

The count drank a great deal. His eyes seemed to grow rather moist, but he did not grow dizzy; he danced still better than the rest, spoke without any thickness, and even joined in a chorus, and supported Stioshka when she sang "The sweet emotion of friendship."

In the midst of the dance and song the merchant, who kept the hotel, came to beg the guests to go home, as it was three o'clock in the morning.

The count took the landlord by the throat, and ordered him to dance the prisiadka. The merchant refused. The count snatched a bottle of champagne, and standing the merchant on his head ordered him to stay so, and then amid general hilarity poured the whole bottle over him.

The dawn was already breaking. All were pale and weary except the count.

"At all events, I must go to Moscow," said he, suddenly rising. "Come with me, all of you, to my room, children.... See me off, and let us have some tea."

192

All accompanied him with the exception of the sleeping proprietor, who still remained there; they piled into three sledges that were waiting at the door, and drove off to the hotel.

VII.

"Have the horses put in!" cried the count, as he entered the sitting-room of the hotel with all his friends including the gypsies.

"Sashka,—not the gypsy Sashka, but mine,—tell the superintendent that if the horses are poor I will flog him. Now give us some tea. Zavalshevsky, make some tea; I am going to Ilyin's; I want to find how things have gone with him," added Turbin; and he went out into the corridor, and directed his steps to the uhlan's room.

Ilyin was just through playing, and, having lost all his money down to his last kopek, had thrown himself face down on the worn-out haircloth sofa, and was picking the hairs out one by one, sticking them in his mouth, biting them into two, and spitting them out again.

Two tallow candles, one of which was already burnt down to the paper, stood on the card-cluttered ombre-table, and mingled their feeble rays with the morning light which was beginning to shine through the window.

The uhlan's mind was vacant of all thought: that strange thick fog of the gambling-passion muffled all the capabilities of his mind so that there was not even room for regret.

Once he endeavored to think what was left for him to do, how he should get away without a kopek, how he should pay back the fifteen thousand rubles of public money that he had lost in gambling, what his colonel would say, what his mother would say, what his comrades would say; and such fear came over him, and such disgust at himself, that, in his anxiety to rid himself of the thought of it, he arose and began to walk up and down through the room, trying only to walk on the cracks of the floor; and then once more he began to recall all the least details of the evening.

He vividly imagined that he was winning the whole back again: he takes a nine, and lays down a king of spades on two thousand rubles; a queen lies at the right, at the left an ace, at the right a king of diamonds—and all was lost! but if he had had a six at the right and a king of diamonds at the left, then he would have won it all back, he would have staked all again on P, and would have won back his fifteen thousand rubles, then he would have bought a good pacer of the colonel, an extra pair of horses, and a phaëton. And what else besides? Ah! indeed it would have been a splendid, splendid thing!

Again he threw himself down on the sofa, and began to bite the hairs once more.

"Why are they singing songs in No. 7?" he wondered. "It must be, they are having a jollification in Turbin's room. I'm of a good mind to go there, and have a little drink."

Just at this moment the count came in.

"Well, have you been losing, brother, hey?" he cried.

"I will pretend to be asleep, otherwise I shall have to talk with him, and I really want to sleep now."

Nevertheless Turbin went up to him, and laid his hand caressingly on his head.... "Well, my dear little friend, have you been losing? have you had bad luck? Tell me."

Ilyin made no reply.

The count took him by the arm.

"I have been losing. What is it to you?" muttered Ilyin, in a sleepy voice expressing indifference and vexation; he did not change his position.

"Every thing?"

"Well, yes. What harm is there in it? All! What is it to you?"

"Listen: tell me the truth, as to a comrade," said the count, who, under the influence of the wine that he had been drinking, was disposed to be tender, and continued to smooth the other's hair. "You know I have taken a fancy to you. Tell me the truth. If you have lost the public money, I will help

194

you; if you don't, it will be too late.... Was it public money?"

Ilyin leaped up from the sofa.

"If you wish me to tell you, don't speak to me so, because ... and I beg of you don't speak to me.... I will blow my brains out—that's the only thing that's left for me now!" he exclaimed with genuine despair, letting his head sink into his hands, and bursting into tears, although but the moment before he had been calmly thinking about his horses.

"Ekh! you're a pretty young girl! Well, who might not have the same thing happen to him? It isn't as bad as it might be; perhaps we can straighten things out: wait for me here."

The count hastened from the room.

"Where is the pomyeshchik[69] Lukhnof's room?" he demanded of the hall-boy.

The hall-boy offered to show the count the way. The count in spite of the objections of the lackey, who said that his master had only just come in and was preparing to retire, entered the room.

Lukhnof in his dressing-gown was sitting in front of a table, counting over a number of packages of bank-notes piled up before him. On the table was a bottle of Rheinwein, of which he was very fond. He had procured himself this pleasure from his winnings.

Coldly, sternly, Lukhnof looked at the count over his glasses, affecting not to recognize him.

"It seems that you do not know me," said the count, proceeding toward the table with resolute steps.

Lukhnof recognized the count, and asked,—

"What is your pleasure?"

"I wish to play with you," said Turbin, sitting down on the sofa.

"Now?"

"Yes."

"Another time I should be most happy, count; but now I am tired, and am getting ready to go to bed. Won't you have some wine? It is excellent wine."

"But I wish to play with you for a little while now."

"I am not prepared to play any more. Maybe some of the other guests will. I will not, count! I beg of you to excuse me."

"Then you will not?"

Lukhnof shrugged his shoulders as though to express his regret at not being able to fulfil the count's desires.

"Will you not play under any consideration?"

The same gesture.

"I am very desirous of playing with you.... Say, will you play, or not?"

Silence.

"Will you play?" asked the count a second time.

The same silence, and a quick glance over his glasses at the count's face, which was beginning to grow sinister.

"Will you play?" cried the count in a loud voice, striking his hand on the table so violently that the bottle of Rheinwein toppled over and the wine ran out. "You have been cheating, have you not? Will you play? I ask you the third time."

"I have told you, no! This is truly strange, count, ... perfectly unjustifiable, to come this way, and put your knife at a man's throat," remarked Lukhnof, not lifting his eyes.

A brief silence followed, during which the count's face grew paler and paler. Suddenly Lukhnof received a terrible blow on the head, which stunned him. He fell back on the divan, trying to grasp the money, and screamed in a penetratingly despairing tone, such as was scarcely to be expected from him, he was always so calm and imposing in his deportment.

Turbin gathered up the remaining bank-notes that were lying on the table, pushed away the servant who had come to his master's assistance, and with quick steps left the room.

"If you wish satisfaction, I am at your service; I shall be in my room for half an hour yet,—No. 7," added the count, turning back as he reached the door.

"Villain! thief!" cried a voice from within the room.... "I will have satisfaction at law!"

Ilyin, who had not paid any heed to the count's promise to help him, was still lying on the sofa in his room, drowned in tears of despair.

The count's caresses and sympathy had awakened him to a consciousness of the reality, and now, amidst the fog of strange thoughts and recollections which filled his mind, it made itself more and more felt.

His youth, rich in hopes, honor, his social position, the dreams of love and friendship, were all destroyed forever. The fountain of his tears began to run dry, a too calm feeling of hopelessness took possession of him; and the thought of suicide, now bringing no sense of repulsion or terror, more and more frequently recurred to him.

At this moment the count's firm steps were heard.

On Turbin's face were still visible the last traces of his recent wrath, his hands trembled slightly; but in his eyes shone a kindly gayety and self-satisfaction.

"There! It has been won back for you!" he cried, tossing upon the table several packages of bank-notes. "Count them; are they all there? Then come as soon as possible to the sitting-room; I am going off right away," he added, as though he did not perceive the tremendous revulsion of joy and gratefulness which rushed over the uhlan's face. Then, humming a gypsy song, he left the room.

VIII.

Sashka, tightening his girdle, was waiting for the horses to be harnessed, but was anxious to go first and get the count's cloak, which, with the collar, must have been worth three hundred rubles, and return that miserable blue-lined shuba to that rascally man who had exchanged with the count at the marshal's. But Turbin said that it was not necessary, and went to his room to change his clothes.

The cavalryman kept hiccoughing as he sat silently by his gypsy maiden. The isprávnik called for vodka, and invited all the gentlemen to come and breakfast with him, promising them that his wife would, without fail, dance the national dance with the gypsies.

The handsome young man was earnestly arguing with Ilyushka that there was more soul in the piano-forte, and that it was impossible to take B-flat on the guitar. The chinovnik was gloomily drinking tea in one corner, and apparently the daylight made him feel ashamed of his dissipation.

The gypsies were conversing together in Romany, and urging that they should once more enliven the gentlemen; to which Stioshka objected, declaring that it would only vex the barorai,—that is, in Romany, count or prince, or rather great bárin.

For the most part, the last spark of the orgy was dying out.

"Well, then, one more song for a farewell, and then home with you," exclaimed the count, fresh, gay, and radiant above all the others, as he came into the room ready dressed in his travelling suit.

The gypsies had again formed their circle, and were just getting ready to sing, when Ilyin came in with a package of bank-notes in his hand, and drew the count to one side.

"I had only fifteen thousand rubles of public money, but you gave me sixteen thousand three hundred," said the uhlan; "this is yours, of course."

"That's a fine arrangement. Let me have it."

Ilyin handed him the money, looking timidly at the count, and opened his mouth to say something; but then he reddened so painfully that the tears came into his eyes, and he seized the count's hand, and began to squeeze it.

"Away with you, Ilyushka ... listen to me! Now, here's your money, but you must accompany me with your songs to the city limits!" And he threw on his guitar the thirteen hundred rubles which Ilyin had brought him. But the count had forgotten to repay the cavalryman the one hundred rubles which he had borrowed of him the evening before.

It was now ten o'clock in the morning. The little sun was rising above the housetops, the streets were beginning to fill with people, the merchants had long ago opened their shops, nobles and chinovniks were riding up and down through the streets, and ladies were out shopping, when the band of gypsies, the isprávnik, the cavalryman, the handsome young fellow, Ilyin, and the count who was wrapped up in his blue-lined bear-skin shuba, came out on the door-steps of the hotel.

It was a sunny day, and it thawed. Three hired tróïkas, with their tails knotted, and splashing through the liquid mud, pranced up to the steps; and the whole jolly company prepared to take their places. The count, Ilyin, Stioshka, Ilyushka, and Sashka the count's man,[70] mounted the first sledge.

Blücher was beside himself with delight, and, wagging his tail, barked at the shaft-horse.

The other gentlemen, together with the gypsies, men and women, climbed into the other sledges. From the very hotel the sledges flew off side by side, and the gypsies set up a merry chorus and song.

The tróïkas, with the songs and jingling bells, dashed through the whole length of the city to the gates, compelling all the equipages which they met to rein up on the very sidewalks.

Merchants and passers-by who did not know them, and especially those who did, were filled with astonishment to see nobles of high rank, in the midst of "the white day," dashing through the streets with intoxicated gypsies, singing at the tops of their voices.

When they reached the city limits, the tróïkas stopped, and all the party

199

took farewell of the count.

Ilyin, who had drunk considerable at the leave-taking, and had all the time been driving the horses, suddenly became melancholy, and began to urge the count to stay just one day more; but when he was assured that this was impossible, quite unexpectedly threw himself into his arms, and began to kiss his new friend, and promised him that as soon as he got to camp, he would petition to be transferred into the regiment of hussars in which Count Turbin served.

The count was extraordinarily hilarious; he tipped into a snow-drift the cavalryman, who, since morning, had definitely taken to saying thou to him; he set Blücher on the isprávnik; he took Stioshka into his arms, and threatened to carry her off with him to Moscow; but at last he tucked himself into the sledge, and stationed Blücher by his side, who was always ready to ride. Sashka took his place on the box, after once more asking the cavalryman to secure the count's cloak from them, and to send it to him. The count cried "Go on,"[71] took off his cap, waved it over his head, and whistled in post-boy fashion to the horses. The tróïkas parted company.

As far as the eye could see, stretched a monotonous snow-covered plain, over which wound the yellowish muddy ribbon of the road.

The bright sunlight, dancing, glistened on the melting snow, which was covered with a thin crust of transparent ice, and pleasantly warmed the face and back.

The steam arose from the sweaty horses. The bells jingled.

A peasant[72] with a creaking sledge, heavily loaded, slowly turned out into the slushy snow, twitching his hempen reins, and tramping with his well-soaked sabots.[73]

A stout, handsome peasant woman, with a child wrapped in a sheep-skin on her lap, who was seated on another load, used the end of her reins to whip up a white mangy-tailed old nag.

Suddenly the count remembered Anna Fedorovna.

"Turn round!" he cried.

The driver did not understand.

"Turn round and drive back; back to the city! Be quick about it." The tróïka again passed the city gate, and quickly drew up in front of the boarded steps of the Zaïtsova dwelling.

The count briskly mounted the steps, passed through the vestibule and the parlor, and finding the widow still asleep he took her in his arms, lifting her from her bed, and kissed her sleeping eyes again and again, and then darted back to the sledge.

Anna Fedorovna awoke from her slumber, and demanded, "What has happened?"

The count took his seat in his sledge, shouted to the driver, and now no longer delaying, and thinking not of Lukhnof nor of the little widow, nor of Stioshka, but only of what was awaiting him in Moscow, rapidly left the city of K. behind him.

IX.

A score of years have passed. Much water has run since then, many men have died, many children have been born, many have grown up and become old; still more thoughts have been born and perished. Much that was beautiful and much that was ugly in the past have disappeared; much that is beautiful in the new has been brought forth, and still more that is incomplete and abortive of the new has appeared in God's world.

Count Feódor Turbin was long ago killed in a duel with some foreigner whom he struck on the street with his long whip. His son, who was as like him as two drops of water, had already reached the age of two or three and twenty, and was a lovely fellow, already serving in the cavalry.

Morally the young Count Turbin was entirely different from his father. There was not a shadow of those fiery, passionate, and in truth be it said, corrupt inclinations, peculiar to the last century.

Together with intelligence, cultivation, and inherited natural gifts, a love for the proprieties and amenities of life, a practical view of men and circumstances, wisdom and forethought, were his chief characteristics.

The young count made admirable progress in his profession; at twenty-three he was already lieutenant.... When war broke out, he came to the conclusion that it would be more for his interests to enter the regular army; and he joined a regiment of hussars as captain of cavalry, where he soon was given command of a battalion.

In the month of May, 1848, the S. regiment of hussars was on its way through the government of K., and the very battalion which the young Count Turbin commanded was obliged to be quartered for one night at Morozovka, Anna Fedorovna's village. Anna Fedorovna was still alive, but was now so far from being young that she no longer called herself young, which, for a woman, means much.

She had grown very stout, and this, it is said, restores youth in a woman. But that was not the worst of it: over her pale, stout flesh was a net-work of coarse, flabby wrinkles. She no longer went to the city, she even found it hard to mount into her carriage; but still she was just as good-natured and as completely vacant-minded as ever,—the truth might safely be told, now that it was no longer palliated by her beauty.

Under her roof lived her daughter Liza, a rustic Russian belle of twenty-three summers, and her brother, our acquaintance the cavalryman, who had spent all his patrimony in behalf of others, and now, in his old age, had taken refuge with Anna Fedorovna.

The hair on his head had become perfectly gray; his upper lip was sunken, but the mustache that it wore was carefully dyed. Wrinkles covered not only his brow and cheeks, but also his nose and neck; and yet his weak bow-legs gave evidence of the old cavalryman.

Anna Fedorovna's whole family and household were gathered in the small parlor of the ancient house. The balcony door and windows, looking out into a star-shaped garden shaded by lindens, were open. Anna Fedorovna, in her gray hair and a lilac-colored gown,[74] was sitting on the sofa, before

202

a small round mahogany table, shuffling cards. The old brother, dressed in spruce white pantaloons and a blue coat, had taken up his position near the window, knitting strips of white cotton on a fork, an occupation which his niece had taught him, and which gave him great enjoyment, as he had nothing else to do, his eyes not being strong enough to enable him to read newspapers, which was his favorite occupation. Near him Pímotchka, a protégée of Anna Fedorovna, was studying her lessons under the guidance of Liza, who with wooden knitting-needles was knitting stockings of goat-wool for her uncle.

The last rays of the setting sun, as always at this time, threw under the linden alley their soft reflections on the last window-panes and the little étagère which stood near it.

In the garden it was so still that one could hear the swift rush of a swallow's wings, and so quiet in the room that Anna Fedorovna's gentle sigh, or the old man's cough as he kept changing the position of his legs, was the only sound.

"How does this go, Lízanka? show me, please. I keep forgetting," said Anna Fedorovna, pausing in the midst of her game of patience. Liza, without stopping her work, went over to her mother, and, glancing at the cards, "Ah!" says she. "You have mixed them all up, dear mamasha," said she, arranging the cards. "That is the way they should be placed. Now they come as you desired," she added, secretly withdrawing one card.

"Now you are always managing to deceive me! You said that it would go."

"No, truly; it goes, I assure you. It has come out right."

"Very well, then; very well, you rogue! But isn't it time for tea?"

"I have just ordered the samovár heated. I will go and see about it immediately. Shall we have it brought here?... Now, Pímotchka, hasten and finish your lessons, and we will go and take a run."

And Liza started for the door.

"Lízotchka! Lízanka!" cried her uncle, steadfastly regarding his fork, "again it seems to me I have dropped a stitch. Arrange it for me, my darling."[75]

"In a moment, in a moment. First I must have the sugar broken up."

And in point of fact, within three minutes, she came running into the room, went up to her uncle, and took him by the ear.

"That's to pay you for dropping stitches," said she laughing. "You have not been knitting as I taught you."

"Now, that'll do, that'll do, adjust it for me; there seems to be some sort of a knot."

Liza took the fork, pulled out a pin from her kerchief, which was blown back a little by the breeze coming through the window, picked it out a couple of times, and handed it back to her uncle.

"Now you must kiss me for that," said she, putting up her rosy cheek toward him, and re-adjusting her kerchief. "You shall have rum in your tea to-day. To-day is Friday, you see."

And again she went to the tea-room.

"Uncle dear, come and look! some hussars are riding up toward the house!" her ringing voice was heard to say. Anna Fedorovna and her brother hastened into the tea-room, the windows of which faced the village, and looked at the hussars. Very little was to be seen; through the cloud of dust it could be judged only that a body of men was advancing.

"What a pity, sister," remarked the uncle to Anna Fedorovna, "what a pity that we are so cramped, and the wing is not built yet, so that we might invite the officers here. Officers of the hussars! they are such glorious, gay young fellows! I should like to have a glimpse at them."

"Well, I should be heartily glad, but you know yourself that there is nowhere to put them: my sleeping-room, Liza's room, the parlor, and then your room,—judge for yourself. Mikháïlo Matveef has put the stárosta's[76] house in order for them; he says it will be nice there."

"But we must find you a husband, Lízotchka, among them,—a glorious hussar!" said the uncle.

"No, I do not want a hussar: I want an uhlan. Let me see, you served among the uhlans, didn't you, uncle?... I don't care to know these hussars. They say they are desperate fellows."

And Liza blushed a little, and then once more her ringing laugh was heard. "There's Ustiushka running: we must ask her what she saw," said she. Anna Fedorovna sent to have Ustiushka brought in.

"She has no idea of sticking to her work, she must always be running off to look at the soldiers," said Anna Fedorovna.... "Now, where have they lodged the officers?"

"With the Yeremkins, your ladyship. There are two of them, such lovely men! One of them is a count, they tell me."

"What's his name?"

"Kazárof or Turbínof. I don't remember, excuse me."

"There now, you're a goose, you don't know how to tell any thing at all. You might have remembered his name!"

"Well, I'll run and find out."

"I know that you are quite able to do that. But no, let Danílo go.— Brother, go and tell him to go; have him ask if there is not something which the officers may need; every thing must be done in good form; have them understand that it is the lady of the house who has sent to find out."

The old people sat down again in the tea-room, and Liza went to the servants' room to put the lumps of sugar in the sugar-bowl. Ustiushka was telling them there about the hussars.

"O my dear young lady, what a handsome man he is! that count!" she said, "absolutely a little cherubim,[77] with black eyebrows. You ought to have such a husband as that; what a lovely little couple you would make!" The other maids smiled approvingly; the old nurse, sitting by the window with her stocking, sighed, and, drawing a long breath, murmured a prayer.

"It seems to me that the hussars have given you a great deal of pleasure," said Liza. "You are a master hand at description. Bring me the mors,[78] Ustiushka, please; we must give the officers something sour to drink." And Liza, laughing, went out with the sugar-bowl.

"But I should like to see what sort of a man this hussar is,—whether he is brunet or blondin. And I imagine he would not object to making our acquaintance. But he will go away, and never know that I was here and was thinking about him. And how many have passed by me in this way! No one ever sees me except uncle and Ustiushka! How many times I have arranged my hair, how many pairs of cuffs I have put on, and yet no one ever sees me or falls in love with me," she thought with a sigh, contemplating her white, plump hand.

"He must be tall, and have big eyes, and a nice little black mustache.... No! I am already over twenty-two, and no one has ever fallen in love with me except the pock-marked Iván Ipátuitch. And four years ago I was still better-looking; and so my girlhood has gone, and no one is the better for it. Ah! I am an unhappy country maiden!"

Her mother's voice, calling her to bring the tea, aroused the country maiden from this momentary revery.

She shook her little head, and went into the tea-room.

The best things always happen unexpectedly; and the more you try to force them, the worse they come out. In the country it is rare that any attempt is made to impart education, and therefore when a good one is found it is generally a surprise. And thus it happened, in a notable degree, in the case of Liza. Anna Fedorovna, through her own lack of intelligence and natural laziness, had not given Liza any education at all; had not taught her music, nor the French language which is so indispensable. But the girl had fortunately been a healthy, bright little child: she had intrusted her to a wet-nurse and a day-nurse; she had fed her, and dressed her in print dresses and goat-skin shoes, and let her run wild and gather mushrooms and berries; had her taught reading and arithmetic by a resident seminarist. And thus, as fate would have it, at the age of sixteen, she found in her daughter a companion, a soul who was always cheerful and good-natured, and the actual mistress of the house.

Through her goodness of heart, Anna Fedorovna always had in her house some protégée, either a serf or some foundling. Liza, from the time she was ten years old, had begun to take care of them; to teach them, clothe them, take them to church, and keep them still when they were inclined to be mischievous.

Then her old broken-down but good-natured uncle made his appearance, and he had to be taken care of like a child. Then the domestic servants and the peasants began to come to the young mistress with their desires and their ailments; and she treated them with elderberry, mint, and spirits of camphor. Then the domestic management of the house fell into her hands entirely. Then came the unsatisfied craving for love, which found expression only in nature and religion.

Thus Liza, by chance, grew into an active, good-naturedly cheerful, self-poised, pure, and deeply religious young woman.

To be sure, she had her little fits of jealousy and envy when she saw, all around her in church, her neighbors dressed in new, fashionable hats that came from K.; she was sometimes vexed to tears by her old, irritable mother, and her caprices; she had her dreams of love in the most absurd and even the crudest forms, but her healthy activity, which she could not shirk, drove them away; and now, at twenty-two, not a single spot, not a single compunction, had touched the fresh, calm soul of this maiden, now developed into the fulness of perfect physical and moral beauty.

Liza was of medium height, rather plump than lean; her eyes were brown, small, with a soft dark shade on the lower lid; she wore her flaxen hair in a long braid.

In walking she took long steps, and swayed like a duck, as the saying is.

The expression of her face, when she was occupied with her duties, and nothing especially disturbed her, seemed to say to all who looked into it, "Life in this world is good and pleasant to one who has a heart full of love, and a pure conscience."

Even in moments of vexation, of trouble, of unrest, or of melancholy, in spite of her tears, of the drawing-down of the left brow, of the compressed lips, of the petulance of her desires, even then in the dimples of her cheeks, in the corners of her mouth, and in her brilliant eyes, so used to smile and rejoice in life,—even then there shone a heart good and upright, and unspoiled by knowledge.

X.

It was still rather warm, though the sun was already set, when the battalion arrived at Morozovka. In front of them, along the dusty village street, trotted a brindled cow, separated from the herd, bellowing, and occasionally stopping to look round, and never once perceiving that all she had to do was to turn out and let the battalion pass.

Peasants, old men, women, children, and domestic serfs, crowding both sides of the road, gazed curiously at the hussars.

Through a thick cloud of dust the hussars rode along on raven-black horses, curvetting and occasionally snorting.

At the right of the battalion, gracefully mounted on beautiful black steeds, rode two officers. One was the commander, Count Turbin; the other a very young man, who had recently been promoted from the yunkers; his name was Polózof.

A hussar, in a white kittel, came from the best of the cottages, and, taking off his cap, approached the officers.

"What quarters have been assigned to us?" asked the count.

"For your excellency?" replied the quartermaster, his whole body shuddering. "Here at the stárosta's; he has put his cottage in order. I tried to get a room at the mansion,[79] but they said no; the proprietress is so ill-tempered."

"Well, all right," said the count, dismounting and stretching his legs as he reached the stárosta's cottage. "Tell me, has my carriage come?"

"It has deigned to arrive, your excellency," replied the quartermaster, indicating with his cap the leathern carriage-top which was to be seen inside the gate, and then hastening ahead into the entry of the cottage, which was crowded with the family of serfs, gathered to have a look at the officer.

He even tripped over an old woman, as he hastily opened the door of the neatly cleaned cottage, and stood aside to let the count pass.

The cottage was large and commodious, but not perfectly clean. The German body-servant,[80] dressed like a bárin, was standing in the cottage, and, having just finished setting up the iron bed, was taking out clean linen from a trunk.

"Phu! what a nasty lodging!" exclaimed the count in vexation. "Diádenko! Is it impossible to find me better quarters at the proprietor's or somewhere?"

"If your excellency command, I will go up to the mansion," replied Diádenko; "but the house is small and wretched, and seems not much better than the cottage."

"Well, that's all now. You can go."

And the count threw himself down on the bed, supporting his head with his hands.

"Johann!" he cried to his body-servant; "again you have made a hump in the middle. Why can't you learn to make a bed decently?"

Johann was anxious to make it over again.

"No, you need not trouble about it now!... Where's my dressing-gown?" he proceeded to ask in a petulant voice. The servant gave him the dressing-gown.

The count, before he put it on, examined the skirt. "There it is! You have not taken that spot out! Could it be possible for any one to be a worse servant than you are?" he added, snatching the garment from the servant's hands, and putting it on. "Now tell me, do you do this way on purpose? Is tea ready?"

"I haven't had time to make it," replied Johann.

"Fool!"

After this, the count took a French novel which was at hand, and read for some time without speaking; but Johann went out into the entry to blow up the coals in the samovár.

It was plain to see that the count was in a bad humor; it must have been owing to weariness, to the dust on his face, to his tightly-fitting clothes, and to his empty stomach. "Johann!" he cried again, "give me an account of those ten rubles. What did you get in town?"

The count looked over the account which the servant handed him, and made some dissatisfied remarks about the high prices paid.

"Give me the rum for the tea."

"I did not get any rum," said Johann.

"Delightful! How many times have I told you always to have rum?"

"I didn't have money enough."

"Why didn't Polózof buy it? You might have got some from his man."

"The cornet Polózof? I do not know. He bought tea and sugar."

"Beast! Get you gone. You are the only man who has the power to exhaust my patience! You know that I always take rum in my tea when I am on the march."

"Here are two letters one of the staff brought for you," said the body-servant.

The count, as he lay on the bed, tore open the letters, and began to read them. At this moment the cornet came in with gay countenance, having quartered the battalion.

"Well, how is it, Turbin? It's first-rate here, seems to me. I am tired out, I confess it. It has been a warm day."

"First-rate! I should think so! A dirty, stinking hut! and no rum, thanks to you. Your stupid did not buy any, nor this one either. You might have said something anyway!"

And he went on with his reading. After he had read the letter through, he crumpled it up, and threw it on the floor.

"Why didn't you buy some rum?" the cornet in a whisper demanded of his servant in the entry. "Didn't you have any money?"

"Well, why should we be always the ones to spend the money? I have enough to spend for without that, and his German does nothing but smoke his pipe,—that's all."

The second letter was evidently not disagreeable, because the count smiled as he read it.

"Who's that from?" asked Polózof, returning to the room, and trying to arrange for himself a couch on the floor, near the oven.

"From Mina," replied the count gayly, handing him the letter. "Would you like to read it? What a lovely woman she is! Now, she's better than our young ladies, that's a fact. Just see what feeling and what wit in that letter! There's only one thing that I don't like,—she asks me for money!"

"No, that's not pleasant," replied the cornet.

"Well it's true I promised to give her some; but this expedition—And besides, if I am commander of the battalion, at the end of three months I will send some to her. I should not regret it; she's really a lovely woman. Isn't she?" he asked with a smile, following with his eyes Polózof's expression as he read the letter.

"Horribly misspelled, but sweet; it seems to me she really loves you," replied the cornet.

"Hm! I should think so! Only these women truly love when they do love."

"But who was that other letter from?" asked the cornet, pointing to the one which he had read.

"That? Oh, that's from a certain man, very ugly, to whom I owe a gambling debt, and this is the third time that he has reminded me of it. I can't pay it to him now. It's a stupid letter," replied the count, evidently nettled by the recollection of it.

The two officers remained silent for some little time. The cornet, who, it seemed, had come under Turbin's influence, drank his tea without speaking, though he occasionally cast a glance at the clouded face of the handsome count, who gazed steadily out of the window. He did not venture to renew the conversation.

"Well, then, I think it can be accomplished without difficulty," suddenly exclaimed the count, turning to Polózof, and gayly nodding his head. "If we who are in the line get promoted this year, yes, and if we take part in some engagement, then I can overtake my former captains of the guard."

They were drinking their second cup of tea, and the conversation was still dwelling on this theme, when the old Danílo came with the message from Anna Fedorovna.

"And she would also like to know whether you are not pleased to be the son of Feódor Ivánovitch Turbin," he added, on his own responsibility, as he had found out the officer's name, and still remembered the late count's visit to the city of K. "Our mistress,[81] Anna Fedorovna, used to be very well acquainted with him."

"He was my father. Now tell the lady that I am very much obliged, but that I need nothing; only, if it would not be possible to give me a cleaner room in the mansion, say, or somewhere."

"Now, why did you do that?" asked Polózof after Danílo had gone. "Isn't it just the same thing? For one night isn't it just as well here? And it will put them to inconvenience."

"There it is again! It seems to me we have had enough of being sent round among these smoky hovels.[82] It's easy enough to see that you are not a practical man. Why shouldn't we seize the opportunity, when we can, of sleeping, even if it's for only one night, like decent men? And they, contrary to what you think, will be mighty glad. There's only one thing objectionable. If this lady used to know my father," continued the count, with a smile that discovered his white gleaming teeth,—"somehow I always feel a little ashamed of my late papasha; there's always some scandalous story, or some debt or other. And so I can't endure to meet any of my father's acquaintances. However, that was an entirely different age," he added seriously.

"Oh! I did not tell you," rejoined Polózof. "I recently met Ilyin, the brigade commander of uhlans. He is very anxious to see you; he is passionately fond of your father."

"I think that he is terrible trash, that Ilyin. But the worst is that all these gentlemen who imagine that they knew my father in order to make friends with me, insist upon telling me, as though it were very pleasant for me to hear, about escapades of his that make me blush. It is true I am not impulsive, and I look upon things dispassionately; while he was too hot-spirited a man, and sometimes he played exceedingly reprehensible tricks. However, that was all due to his time. In our day and generation, maybe, he would have been a very sensible man, for he had tremendous abilities; one must give him credit for that."

In a quarter of an hour the servant returned, and brought an invitation for them to come and spend the night at the mansion.

XI.

As soon as Anna Fedorovna learned that the officer of hussars was the son of Count Feódor Turbin, she was thrown into a great state of excitement.

"Oh! great heavens![83] he is my darling! Danílo! run, hurry, tell them the lady invites them to stay at her house," she cried, in great agitation, and hastening to the servants' room. "Lízanka! Ustiushka! You must have your room put in order, Liza. You can go into your uncle's room; and you, brother,—brother, you can sleep to-night in the parlor. It's for only one night."

"That's nothing, sister! I would sleep on the floor."

213

"He must be a handsome fellow, I think, if he's like his father. Only let me see him, the turtle-dove! You shall see for yourself, Liza. Ah! his father was handsome! Where shall we put the table? Let it go there," said Anna Fedorovna, running about here and there. "There now, bring in two beds; get one from the overseer, and get from the étagère the glass candlestick which my brother gave me for my birthday, and put in a wax candle."

At last all was ready. Liza, in spite of her mother's interference, arranged her room in her own way for the two officers.

She brought out clean linen sheets, fragrant of mignonnette, and had the beds made; she ordered a carafe of water and candles near it on the little table. She burned scented paper in the girls' room, and moved her own little bed into her uncle's chamber.

Anna Fedorovna gradually became calm, and sat down again in her usual place; she even took out her cards; but instead of shuffling them, she leaned on her fat elbow, and gave herself up to her thoughts.

"How time has gone! how time has gone!" she exclaimed in a whisper. "It is long! long! isn't it? I seem to see him now! Akh! he was a scamp!"

And the tears came into her eyes. "Now here is Lízanka, but she isn't at all what I was at her age. She is a nice girl; but no, not quite...."

"Lízanka, you had better wear your mousselin-de-laine dress this evening."

"But are you going to invite them down-stairs, mamasha? You had better not do it," rejoined Liza, with a feeling of invincible agitation at the thought of seeing the officers. "You had better not, mamasha!"

In point of fact, she did not so much desire to see them, as she felt apprehensive of some painful pleasure awaiting her, as it seemed to her.

"Perhaps they themselves would like to make our acquaintance, Lízotchka," said Anna Fedorovna, glancing at her daughter's hair, and at the same time thinking, "No, not such hair as I had at her age. No, Lízotchka, how much I could wish for you!" And she really wished something very excellent

214

for her daughter, but she could scarcely look forward to a match with the count; she could not desire such a relationship as she herself had formed with his father; but that something good would come of it, she wished very, very much for her daughter. She possibly had the desire to live over again in her daughter's happiness all the life which she lived with the late count.

The old cavalryman was also somewhat excited by the count's coming. He went to his room, and shut himself up in it. At the end of a quarter of an hour, he re-appeared dressed in a Hungarian coat and blue pantaloons; and with a troubled-happy expression of countenance, such as a girl wears when she puts on her first ball-dress, he started for the room assigned to the guests.

"We shall have a glimpse of some of the hussars of to-day, sister. The late count was indeed a genuine hussar. We shall see! we shall see!"

The officers had by this time come in by the back entrance, and were in the room that had been put at their service.

"There now," said the count, stretching himself out in his dusty boots on the bed which had just been made for him, "if we aren't better off here than we were there in that hovel with the cockroaches!"

"Better? of course; but think what obligations we are putting ourselves under to the people here."

"What rubbish! You must always be a practical man. They are mighty glad to have us, of course. Fellow!" cried the count, "ask some one to put a curtain up at this window, else there'll be a draught in the night."

At this moment the old man came in to make the acquaintance of the officers. Though he was somewhat confused, he did not fail to tell how he had been a comrade of the late count's, who had been very congenial to him, and he even went so far as to say that more than once he had been under obligations to the late count. Whether he meant, in speaking of the obligations to the late count, a reference to the hundred rubles which the count had borrowed and never returned, or to his throwing him into the snow-drift, or to the slap in the face, the old man failed to explain.

However, the count was very urbane with the old cavalryman, and thanked him for his hospitality.

"You must excuse us if it is not very luxurious, count,"—he almost said "your excellency," as he had got out of the habit of meeting with men of rank. "My sister's house is rather small. As for the window here, we will find something to serve as a curtain right away, and it will be first-rate," added the little old man; and under the pretext of going for a curtain, but really because he wanted to give his report about the officers as quickly as possible, he left the room. The pretty little Ustiushka came, bringing her mistress's shawl to serve as a curtain. She was also commissioned to ask if the gentlemen would not like some tea.

The cheerful hospitality had had a manifestly beneficent influence upon the count's spirits. He laughed and jested with Ustiushka gayly, and went to such lengths that she even called him a bad man; he asked her if her mistress was pretty, and in reply to her question whether he would like some tea, replied that she might please bring him some, but above all, as his supper was not ready, he would like some vodka now, and a little lunch, and some sherry if there was any.

The old uncle was in raptures over the young count's politeness, and praised to the skies the young generation of officers, saying that the men of the present day were far preferable to those of the past.

Anna Fedorovna could not agree to that,—no one could be any better than Count Feódor Ivánovitch,—and she was beginning to grow seriously angry, and remarked dryly, "For you, brother, the one who flatters you last is the best! Without any question, the men of our time are better educated, but still Feódor Ivánovitch could dance the schottische, and was so amiable that everybody in his day, you might say, was stupid compared to him! only he did not care for any one else beside me. Oh, certainly there were fine men in the old time!"

At this moment came the message requesting the vodka, the lunch, and the sherry.

"There now, just like you, brother! You never do things right. We ought to have had supper prepared.... Liza, attend to it, that's my darling."

Liza hastened to the storeroom for mushrooms and fresh cream butter, and told the cook to prepare beef cutlets.

"How much sherry is there? Haven't you any left, brother?"

"No, sister; I never have had any."

"What! no sherry? but what is it you drink in your tea?"

"That is rum, Anna Fedorovna."

"Isn't that the same thing? Give them some of that. It is all the same, it'll make no difference. Or would it not be better to invite them down here, brother? You know all about it. They would not be offended, I imagine, would they?"

The cavalryman assured her that he would answer for it that the count, in his goodness of heart, would not decline, and that he would certainly bring them.

Anna Fedorovna went off to put on, for some reason or other, her gros-grain dress and a new cap; but Liza was so busy that she had no time to take off her pink gingham dress with wide sleeves. Moreover, she was terribly wrought up; it seemed to her that something astonishing, like a very low black cloud, was sweeping down upon her soul.

This count-hussar, this handsome fellow, seemed to her an absolutely novel and unexpected but beautiful creature. His character, his habits, his words, it seemed to her, must be something extraordinary, such as had never come into the range of her experience. All that he thought and said must be bright and true; all that he did must be honorable; his whole appearance must be beautiful. She could have no doubt of that. If he had demanded not merely a lunch and sherry, but even a bath in spirits of salvia, she would not have been surprised, she would not have blamed him, and she would have been convinced that this was just and reasonable.

The count immediately accepted when the cavalryman brought him his sister's invitation; he combed his hair, put on his coat, and took his cigar-case.

"Will you come?" he asked of Polózof.

"Indeed we had better not go," replied the cornet; "ils feront des frais pour nous recevoir."

"Rubbish! it will make them happy. Besides, I have been making inquiries ... there's a pretty daughter here.... Come along," said the count in French.

"Je vous en prie, messieurs," said the cavalryman, merely for the sake of giving them to understand that he also could speak French, and understood what the officers were saying.

XII.

Liza, red in the face and with downcast eyes, was ostensibly occupied with filling up the teapot, and did not dare to look at the officers as they entered the room.

Anna Fedorovna, on the contrary, briskly jumped up and bowed, and without taking her eyes from the count's face began to talk to him, now finding an extraordinary resemblance to his father, now presenting her daughter, now offering him tea, meats, or jelly-cakes.

No one paid any attention to the cornet, thanks to his modest behavior; and he was very glad of it, because it gave him a chance, within the limits of propriety, to observe and study the details of Liza's beauty, which had evidently come over him with the force of a surprise.

The uncle listening to his sister's conversation had a speech ready on his lips, and was waiting for a chance to relate his cavalry experiences.

The count smoked his cigar over his tea, so that Liza had great difficulty in refraining from coughing, but he was very talkative and amiable; at first, in the infrequent pauses of Anna Fedorovna's conversation, he introduced his own stories, and finally he took the conversation into his own hands.

One thing struck his listeners as rather strange: in his talk he often used words, which, though not considered reprehensible in his own set, were here rather audacious, so that Anna Fedorovna was a little abashed, and Liza blushed to the roots of her hair. But this the count did not notice, and continued to be just as natural and amiable as ever.

Liza filled the glasses in silence, not putting them into the hands of the guests, but pushing them toward them; she had not entirely recovered from her agitation, but listened eagerly to the count's anecdotes.

The count's pointless tales, and the pauses in the conversation, gradually re-assured her. The bright things that she had expected from him were not forthcoming, nor did she find in him that surpassing elegance for which she had confusedly hoped. Even as soon as the third glass of tea, when her timid eyes once encountered his, and he did not avoid them, but continued almost too boldly to stare at her, with a lurking smile, she became conscious of a certain feeling of hostility against him; and she soon discovered that there was not only nothing out of the ordinary in him, but that he was very little different from those whom she had already seen; in fact, that there was no reason to be afraid of him. She noticed that he had long and neat finger-nails, but otherwise there was no mark of special beauty about him.

Liza suddenly, not without some inward sorrow, renouncing her dream, regained her self-possession; and only the undemonstrative cornet's glance, which she felt fixed upon her, disquieted her.

"Perhaps it is not the count, but the other," she said to herself.

XIII.

After tea, the old lady invited her guests into the other room, and again sat down in her usual place. "But perhaps you would like to rest, count?" she asked. "Well, then, what would you like to amuse yourselves with, my dear guests?" she proceeded to ask after she had been assured to the contrary. "You play cards, do you not, count?—Here, brother, you might take a hand in some game or other."...

"Why, you yourself can play préférence," replied the cavalryman. "You had better take a hand, then. The count will play, will he not? And you?"

The officers were agreeable to every thing that might satisfy their amiable hosts.

Liza brought from her room her old cards which she used for divining whether her mother would speedily recover of a cold, or whether her uncle would return on such and such a day from the city if he chanced to have gone there, or whether her neighbor would be in during the day, and other like things. These cards, though they had been in use for two months, were less soiled than those which Anna Fedorovna used for the same purpose.

"Perhaps you are not accustomed to playing for small stakes," suggested the uncle. "Anna Fedorovna and I play for half-kopeks, and then she always gets the better of all of us."

"Ah! make your own arrangements. I shall be perfectly satisfied," said the count.

"Well, then, be it in paper kopeks for the sake of our dear guests; only let me gain, as I am old," said Anna Fedorovna, settling herself in her chair, and adjusting her mantilla. "Maybe I shall win a ruble of them," thought Anna Fedorovna, who in her old age felt a little passion for cards.

"If you would like, I will teach you to play with tablets," said the count, "and with the miséries. It is very jolly."

Everybody was delighted with this new Petersburg fashion. The uncle went so far as to assert that he knew it, and that it was just the same thing as boston, but that he had forgotten somewhat about it.

Anna Fedorovna did not comprehend it at all; and it took her so long to get into it, that she felt under the necessity of smiling and nodding her head assuringly, to give the impression that she now understood, and that now it was all perfectly clear to her. But there was no little amusement created when in the midst of the game Anna Fedorovna, with ace and king blank, called "misérie," and remained with the six. She even began to grow confused, smiled timidly, and hastened to assure them that she had not as yet become accustomed to the new way.

Nevertheless they put down the points against her, and many of them too; the more because the count, through his practice of playing on large stakes, played carefully, led very prudently, and never at all understood what the cornet meant by sundry raps with his foot under the table, or why he made such stupid blunders in playing.

Liza brought in more jelly-cakes, three kinds of preserves, and apples cooked in some manner with port-wine; and then, standing behind her mother's chair, she looked on at the game, and occasionally watched the officers, and especially the count's white hands with their delicate long finger-nails, as he with such skill, assurance, and grace, threw the cards, and took the tricks.

Once more Anna Fedorovna, with some show of temper going beyond the others, bid as high as seven, and lost three points; and when, at her brother's instigation, she tried to make some calculation, she found herself utterly confused and off the track.

"It's nothing, mamasha; you'll win it back again," said Liza, with a smile, anxious to rescue her mother from her ridiculous position. "Some time you'll put a fine on uncle: then he will be caught."

"But you might help me, Lízotchka," cried Anna Fedorovna, looking with an expression of dismay at her daughter; "I don't know how this"....

"But I don't know how to play this either," rejoined Liza, carefully calculating her mother's losses. "But if you go on at this rate, mamasha, you will lose a good deal, and Pímotchka will not have her new dress," she added in jest.

"Yes, in this way it is quite possible to lose ten silver rubles," said the cornet, looking at Liza, and anxious to draw her into conversation.

"Aren't we playing for paper money?" asked Anna Fedorovna, gazing round at the rest.

"I don't know, I am sure," replied the count. "But I don't know how to reckon in bank-notes. What are they? what do you mean by bank-notes?"[84]

"Why, no one nowadays reckons in bank-notes," explained the

cavalryman, who was playing like a hero and was on the winning side.

The old lady ordered some sparkling wine, drank two glasses herself, grew quite flushed, and seemed to abandon all hope. One braid of her gray hair escaped from under her cap, and she did not even put it up. It was evident that she thought herself losing millions, and that she was entirely ruined. The cornet kept nudging the count's leg more and more emphatically. The count was noting down the old lady's losses.

At last the game came to an end. In spite of Anna Fedorovna's efforts to bring her reckoning higher than it should be, and to pretend that she had been cheated in her account, and that it could not be correct, in spite of her dismay at the magnitude of her losses, at last the account was made out, and she was found to have lost nine hundred and twenty points.

"Isn't that equal to nine paper rubles?" she asked again and again; and she did not begin to realize how great her forfeit was, until her brother, to her horror, explained that she was "out" thirty-two and a half paper rubles, and that it was absolutely necessary for her to pay it.

The count did not even sum up his gains, but, as soon as the game was over, arose and went over to the window where Liza was arranging the lunch, and putting potted mushrooms on a plate. There he did with perfect calmness and naturalness what the cornet had been anxious and yet unable to effect all the evening,—he engaged her in conversation about the weather.

The cornet at this time was brought into a thoroughly unpleasant predicament. Anna Fedorovna, in the absence of the count and Liza, who had managed to keep her in a jovial frame of mind, became really angry.

"Indeed, it is too bad that we have caused you to lose so heavily," said Polózof, in order to say something. "It is simply shameful."

"I should think these tablets and miséries were something of your own invention. I don't know any thing about them. How many paper rubles does the whole amount to?" she demanded.

"Thirty-two rubles, thirty-two and a half," insisted the cavalryman, who, from the effect of having been on the winning side, was in a very waggish frame of mind. "Give him the money, sister.... Give it to him."

"I will give all I owe, only you must not ask for any more. No, I shall never win it back in my life."

And Anna Fedorovna went to her room, all in excitement, hurried back, and brought nine paper rubles. Only on the old man's strenuous insistence she was induced to pay the whole sum. Polózof had some fear that the old lady would pour out on him the vials of her wrath if he entered into conversation with her. He silently, without attracting attention, turned away, and rejoined the count and Liza, who were talking at the open window.

On the table, which was now spread for the supper, stood two tallow candles, whose flame occasionally flickered in the gentle breeze of the mild May night. Through the window opening into the garden came a very different light from that which filled the room. The moon, almost at its full, already beginning to lose its golden radiance, was pouring over the tops of the lofty lindens, and making brighter and brighter the delicate fleecy clouds that occasionally overcast it.

From the pond, the surface of which, silvered in one place by the moon, could be seen through the trees, came the voices of the frogs. In the sweet-scented lilac-bush under the very window, which from time to time slowly shook its heavy-laden blossoms, birds were darting and fluttering.

"What marvellous weather!" said the count, as he joined Liza, and sat down in the low window-seat. "I suppose you go to walk a good deal, don't you?"

"Yes," rejoined Liza, not experiencing the slightest embarrassment in the count's company. "Every morning, at seven o'clock, I make the tour of the estate, and sometimes I take a walk with Pímotchka,—mamma's protégée."

"It's pleasant living in the country," cried the count, putting his monocle to his eye, and gazing first at the garden, and then at Liza. "But don't you like to take a walk on moonlight nights?"

"No. Three years ago my uncle and I used to go out walking every

223

moonlight night. He had some sort of strange illness,—insomnia. Whenever there was a full moon, he could not sleep. His room like this opens into the garden, and the window is low. The moon shines right into it."

"Strange," remarked the count. "Then this is your room."

"No, I only sleep there for this one night. You occupy my room."

"Is it possible? ... oh, good heavens![85] I shall never in the world forgive myself for the trouble that I have caused," said the count, casting the monocle from his eye as a sign of sincerity.... "If I had only known that I was going to"....

"How much trouble was it? On the contrary, I am very glad. My uncle's room is so nice and jolly: there's a low window there. I shall sit down in it before I go to bed, or perhaps I shall go down, out into the garden, and take a little walk."

"What a glorious girl!" said the count to himself, replacing the monocle, and staring at her, and while pretending to change his seat in the window, trying to touch her foot with his. "And how shrewdly she gave me to understand that I might meet her in the garden at the window, if I would come down!"

Liza even lost in the count's eyes a large share of her charm, so easy did the conquest of her seem to him.

"And how blissful it must be," said the count dreamily, gazing into the shadow-haunted alley, "to spend such a night in the garden with the object of one's love!"

Liza was somewhat abashed by these words, and by a second evidently deliberate pressure upon her foot. Before she thought, she made some reply for the sake of dissimulating her embarrassment.

She said, "Yes, it is splendid to walk in the moonlight."

There was something disagreeable about the whole conversation. She put the cover on the jar from which she had been taking the mushrooms, and was just turning from the window, when the cornet came toward her, and she felt a curiosity to know what kind of a man he was.

"What a lovely night!" said he.

"They can only talk about the weather," thought Liza.

"What a wonderful view!" continued the cornet, "only I should think it would be tiresome," he added through a strange propensity, peculiar to him, of saying things sure to offend the people who pleased him very much.

"Why should you think so? Always the same cooking and always the same dress might become tiresome; but a lovely garden can never be tiresome when you enjoy walking, and especially when there's a moon rising higher and higher. From my uncle's room you can see the whole pond. I shall see it from there to-night."

"And you haven't any nightingales at all, have you?" asked the count, greatly put out, because Polózof had come and prevented him from learning the exact conditions of the rendezvous.

"Oh, yes, we always have them; last year the hunters caught one; and last week there was one that sang beautifully, but the district inspector[86] came along with his bells, and scared him away.... Three years ago my uncle and I used to sit out in the covered alley, and listen to one for two hours at a time."

"What is this chatterbox telling you about?" inquired the old uncle, joining the trio. "Aren't you ready for something to eat?"

At supper, the count by his reiterated praise of the viands, and his appetite, succeeded somewhat in pacifying Anna Fedorovna's unhappy state of mind. Afterwards the officers made their adieux, and went to their room. The count shook hands with the old cavalier, and, to Anna Fedorovna's surprise, with her, without offering to kiss her hand; and he also squeezed Liza's hand, at the same time looking straight into her eyes, and craftily smiling his pleasing smile. This glance again somewhat disconcerted the maiden. "He is very handsome," she said to herself, "only he is quite too conceited."

225

XIV.

"Well, now, aren't you ashamed?" exclaimed Polózof, when the two officers had reached the privacy of their chamber. "I tried to lose, and I kept nudging you under the table. Now aren't you really ashamed? The poor old lady was quite beside herself."

The count burst into a terrible fit of laughter.

"A most amusing dame! How abused she felt!"

And again he began to laugh so heartily that even Johann, who was standing in front of him, cast down his eyes to conceal a smile. "And here is the son of an old family friend! Ha, ha, ha!" continued the count in a gale of laughter.

"No, indeed, it is not right. I felt really sorry for her," said the cornet.

"What rubbish! How young you are! What! did you think that I was going to lose? Why should I lose? I only lose when I don't know any better. Ten rubles, brother, will come in handy. You must look on life in a practical way, or else you will always be a fool."

Polózof made no answer: in the first place, he wanted to think by himself about Liza, who seemed to him to be an extraordinarily pure and beautiful creature.

He undressed, and lay down on the clean soft bed which had been made ready for him.

"How absurd all these honors and the glory of war!" he thought to himself, gazing at the window shaded by the shawl, through the interstices of which crept the pale rays of the moon. "Here is happiness—to live in a quiet nook, with a gentle, bright, simple-hearted wife; that is enduring, true happiness."

But somehow he did not communicate these imaginations to his friend; and he did not even speak of the rustic maiden, though he felt sure that the count was also thinking about her.

"Why don't you undress?" he demanded of the count, who was walking up and down the room.

"Oh, I don't feel like sleeping! Put out the candle if you like," said he. "I can undress in the dark."

And he continued to walk up and down.

"He does not feel sleepy," repeated Polózof, who after the evening's experiences felt more than ever dissatisfied with the count's influence upon him, and disposed to revolt against it. "I imagine," he reasoned, mentally addressing Turbin, "what thoughts are now trooping through that well-combed head of yours. And I saw how she pleased you. But you are not the kind to appreciate that simple-hearted, pure-minded creature. Mina is the one for you, you want the epaulets of a colonel.—Indeed, I have a mind to ask him how he liked her."

And Polózof was about to address him, but he deliberated: he felt that not only he was not in the right frame of mind to discuss with him if the count's glance at Liza was what he interpreted it to be, but that he should not have the force of mind necessary for him to disagree with him, so accustomed was he to submit to an influence which for him grew each day more burdensome and unrighteous.

"Where are you going?" he asked, as the count took his cap and went to the door.

"I am going to the stable; I wish to see if every thing is all right."

"Strange!" thought the cornet; but he blew out the candle, and, trying to dispel the absurdly jealous and hostile thoughts that arose against his former friend, he turned over on the other side.

Anna Fedorovna meantime, having crossed herself, and kissed her brother, her daughter, and her protégée, as affectionately as usual, also retired to her room.

Long had it been since the old lady had experienced in a single day so many powerful sensations. She could not even say her prayers in tranquillity;

all the melancholy but vivid remembrances of the late count, and of this young dandy who had so ruthlessly taken advantage of her, kept coming up in her mind.

Nevertheless she undressed as usual, and drank a half glass of kvas which stood ready on the little table near the bed, and lay down. Her beloved cat came softly into the room. Anna Fedorovna called her, and began to stroke her fur, and listen to her purring; but still she could not go to sleep.

"It is the cat that disturbs me," she said to herself, and pushed her away. The cat fell to the floor softly, and, slowly waving her bushy tail, got upon the oven;[87] and then the maid, who slept in the room on the floor, brought her felt, and put out the candle, after lighting the night-lamp.

At last the maid began to snore; but sleep still refused to come to Anna Fedorovna, and calm her excited imagination. The face of the hussar constantly arose before her mental vision, when she shut her eyes; and it seemed to her that it appeared in various strange guises in her room, when she opened her eyes and looked at the commode, at the table, and her white raiment hanging up in the feeble light of the night-lamp. Then it seemed hot to her in the feather-bed, and the ticking of the watch on the table seemed unendurable; exasperating to the last degree, the snoring of the maid. She wakened her, and bade her cease snoring.

Again the thoughts of the old count and of the young count, and of the game of préférence, became strangely mixed in her mind. Now she seemed to see herself waltzing with the former count; she saw her own round white shoulders, she felt on them some one's kisses, and then she saw her daughter in the young count's embrace.

Once more Ustiushka began to snore....

"No, it's somehow different now, the men aren't the same. He was ready to fling himself into the fire for my sake. Yes, I was worth doing it for! But this one, have no fear, is sound asleep like a goose, instead of wooing. How his father fell on his knees, and said, 'Whatever you desire I will do, I could kill myself in a moment; what do you desire?' And he would have killed himself, if I had bade him!"...

Suddenly the sound of bare feet was heard in the corridor; and Liza with a shawl thrown over her came in pale and trembling, and almost fell on her mother's bed....

After saying good-night to her mother, Liza had gone alone to the room that had been her uncle's. Putting on a white jacket, throwing a handkerchief round her thick long braids, she put out the light, opened the window, and curled up in a chair, turning her dreamy eyes to the pond which was now all shining with silver brilliancy.

All her ordinary occupations and interests came up before her now in an entirely different light. Her capricious old mother, unreasoning love for whom had become a part of her very soul, her feeble but amiable old uncle, the domestics, the peasants who worshipped their young mistress, the milch cows and the calves; all this nature which was forever the same in its continual death and resurrection, amid which she had grown up, with love for others, and with the love of others for her,—all this that gave her that gentle, agreeable peace of mind,—suddenly seemed to her something different; it all seemed to her dismal, superfluous.

It was as though some one said to her, "Fool, fool! For twenty years you have been occupied in trivialities, you have been serving others without reason, and you have not known what life, what happiness, were!"

This was what she thought now as she gazed down into the depths of the motionless moonlit garden, and the thought came over her with vastly more force than ever before. And what was it that induced this train of thought? It was not in the least a sudden love for the count, as might easily be supposed. On the contrary, he did not please her. It might rather have been the cornet of whom she was thinking; but he was homely, poor, and taciturn.

"No, it isn't that," she said to herself.

Her ideal was so charming! It was an ideal which might have been loved in the midst of this night, in the midst of this nature, without infringing its supernal beauty; an ideal not in the least circumscribed by the necessity of reducing it to coarse reality.

In days gone by, her lonely situation, and the absence of people who might have attracted her, caused that all the strength of the love which Providence has implanted impartially in the hearts of each one of us, was still intact and potential in her soul. But now she had been living too long with the pathetic happiness of feeling that she possessed in her heart this something, and occasionally opening the mysterious chalice of her heart, of rejoicing in the contemplation of its riches, ready to pour out without stint on some one all that it contained.

God grant that she may not have to take this melancholy delight with her to the tomb! But who knows if there be any better and more powerful delight, or if it is not the only true and possible one?

"O Father in heaven," she thought, "is it possible that I have lost my youth and my happiness, and that they will never return?... Will they never return again? is it really true?"

She gazed in the direction of the moon at the bright far-off sky, studded with white wavy clouds, which, as they swept on toward the moon, blotted out the little stars.

"If the moon should seize that little cloud above it, then it means that it is true," she thought. A thin smoke-like strip of cloud passed over the lower half of the brilliant orb, and gradually the light grew fainter on the turf, on the linden tops, on the pond: the black shadows of the trees grew less distinct. And as though to harmonize with the gloomy shade which was enveloping nature, a gentle breeze stirred through the leaves, and brought to the window the dewy fragrance of the leaves, the moist earth, and the blooming lilacs.

"No, it is not true!" she said, trying to console herself; "but if the nightingale should sing this night, then I should take it to mean that all my forebodings are nonsense, and that there is no need of losing hope."

And long she sat in silence, as though expecting some one, while once more all grew bright and full of life; and then again and again the clouds passed over the moon, and all became sombre.

230

She was even beginning to grow drowsy, as she sat there by the window, when she was aroused by the nightingale's melodious trills clearly echoing across the pond. The rustic maiden opened her eyes. Once more, with a new enjoyment, her whole soul was dedicated to that mysterious union with the nature which so calmly and serenely spread out before her.

She leaned on both elbows. A certain haunting sensation of gentle melancholy oppressed her heart; and tears of pure, deep love, burning for satisfaction, good consoling tears, sprang to her eyes.

She leaned her arms on the window-sill, and rested her head upon them. Her favorite prayer seemed of its own accord to arise in her soul, and thus she fell asleep with moist eyes.

The pressure of some one's hand awakened her. She started up. But the touch was gentle and pleasant. The hand squeezed hers with a stronger pressure.

Suddenly she realized the true state of things, screamed, tore herself away; and trying to make herself believe that it was not the count who, bathed in the brilliant moonlight, was standing in front of her window, she hastened from the room.

<u>XV.</u>

It was indeed the count. When he heard the maiden's cry, and the cough of the watchman who was coming from the other side of the fence in reply to the shriek, he had the sensation of being a thief caught in the act, and started to run across the dew-drenched grass, so as to hide in the depths of the garden.

"Oh, what a fool I was!" he said instinctively. "I frightened her. I ought to have been more gentle, to have wakened her by gentle words. Oh! I am a beast, a blundering beast."

He paused and listened. The watchman had come through the wicket-gate into the garden, dragging his cane along the sanded walk.

He must hide. He went toward the pond. The frogs made him tremble

231

as they hastily sprang from under his very feet into the water. There, notwithstanding his wet feet, he crouched down on his heels, and, began to recall all he had done,—how he had crept through the hedge, found her window, and at last caught a glimpse of a white shadow; how several times, while on the watch for the least noise, he had hastened away from the window; how at one moment it seemed to him that doubtless she was waiting for him with vexation in her heart that he was so dilatory, and the next how impossible it seemed that she would make an appointment with him so easily; and how, finally coming to the conclusion, that, through the embarrassment naturally felt by a country maiden, she was only pretending to be asleep, he had resolutely gone up to the window, and seen clearly her position, and then suddenly, for some occult reason, had run away again; and only after a powerful effort of self-control, being ashamed of his cowardice, he had gone boldly up to her and touched her on the hand.

The watchman again coughed, and, shutting the squeaky gate, went out of the garden. The window in the young girl's room was shut, and the wooden shutters inside were drawn.

The count was terribly disappointed to see this. He would have given a good deal to have a chance to begin it all over again; he would not have acted so stupidly.

"A marvellous girl! what freshness! simply charming! And so I lost her. Stupid beast that I was."

However, as he was not in the mood to go to sleep yet, he walked, as chance should lead, along the path, through the linden alley, with the resolute steps of a man who has been angry. And now for him also this night brought, as its gifts of reconciliation, a strange, calming melancholy, and a craving for love.

The clay path, here and there dotted with sprouting grass or dry twigs, was lighted by patches of pale light where the moon sent its rays straight through the thick foliage of the lindens. Here and there a bending bough, apparently overgrown with gray moss, gleamed on one side. The silvered foliage occasionally rustled.

At the house there was no light in the windows; all sounds were hushed, only the nightingale filled with his song all the immensity of silent and glorious space.

"My God! what a night! what a marvellous night!" thought the count, breathing in the fresh fragrance of the garden. "Something makes me feel blue, as though I were dissatisfied with myself and with others, and dissatisfied with my whole life. But what a splendid, dear girl! Perhaps she was really offended." Here his fancies changed. He imagined himself there in the garden with this district maiden in various and most remarkable situations; then his mistress Mina supplanted the maiden's place.

"What a fool I am! I ought simply to have put my arm around her waist, and kissed her."

And with this regret the count returned to his room. The cornet was not yet asleep. He immediately turned over in bed, and looked at the count.

"Aren't you asleep?" asked the count.

"No."

"Shall I tell you what happened?"

"Well."

"No, I'd better not tell you.... Yes, I will too. Move your legs over a little."

And the count, who had already given up vain regret for his unsuccessful intrigue, sat down with a gay smile on his comrade's bed. "Could you imagine that the young lady of the house gave me a rendezvous?"

"What is that you say?" screamed Polózof, leaping up in bed.

"Well, now listen."

"But how? When? It can't be!"

"See here: while you were making out your accounts in préférence, she told me that she would this night be sitting at the window, and that it was

233

possible to get in at that window. Now, this is what it means to be a practical man: while you were there reckoning up with the old woman, I was arranging this little affair. You yourself heard her say right out in your presence, that she was going to sit at the window to-night, and look at the pond."

"Yes, but she said that without any meaning in it."

"I am not so sure whether she said it purposely or otherwise. Maybe she did not wish to come at it all at once, only it looked like that. But a wretched piece of work came out of it. Like a perfect fool I spoilt the whole thing," he added, scornfully smiling at himself.

"Well, what is it? Where have you been?"

The count told him the whole story, with the exception of his irresolute and repeated advances. "I spoilt it myself; I ought to have been bolder. She screamed, and ran away from the window."

"Then she screamed and ran away?" repeated the cornet, replying with a constrained smile to the count's smile, which had such a long and powerful influence upon him.

"Yes, but now it's time to go to sleep."

Polózof again turned his back to the door, and lay in silence for ten minutes. God knows what was going on in his soul; but when he turned over again, his face was full of passion and resolution.

"Count Turbin," said he in a broken voice.

"Are you dreaming, or not?" replied the count calmly. "What is it, cornet Polózof?"

"Count Turbin, you are a scoundrel," cried Polózof, and he sprang from the bed.

XVI.

The next day the battalion departed. The officers did not see any of the household, or bid them farewell. Neither did they speak together.

It was understood that they were to fight their duel when they came to the next halting-place. But Captain Schultz, a good comrade, an admirable horseman, who was loved by everybody in the regiment, and had been chosen by the count for his second, succeeded in arranging the affair in such a manner that not only they did not fight, but that no one in the regiment knew about the matter; and Turbin and Polózof, though their old relations of friendship were never restored, still said "thou," and met at meals and at the gaming-table.

FOOTNOTES:

[56] From the poem entitled, "The Song of an Old Hussar," in which a veteran contrasts the mighty days of the past with the dilettanti present. Denis Vasilyevitch Davuidof, who was an officer of hussars, died in 1839.—Tr.

[57] Diminished diminutive of Aleksandr.

[58] Blue notes were five rubles.

[59] isprávnik.

[60] Diminutive of Stepanida, Stephanie.

[61] golúbchiki, little pigeons.

[62] babas.

[63] Five or ten rubles.

[64] arshins.

[65] zakuski.

[66] Diminutive of Vasili.

[67] tsiganotchka.

[68] grafchik! golubchik!

[69] Landed proprietor.

[70] denshchik.

[71] próshol.

[72] muzhík.

[73] lapti.

[74] katsavéïka.

[75] golúbchik.

[76] Village elder.

[77] kherubimchik.

[78] A sour beverage made of cranberries.

[79] barsky dvor.

[80] kammerdiener.

[81] báruinya.

[82] kúrnaya izbá, a peasant's hut without chimney.

[83] bátiuzhki moï!

[84] Assignatsii.

[85] Akh! Bozhe moï!

[86] stanovói.

[87] The lezhanka, a part of the oven built out as a sort of couch.

THREE DEATHS

A TALE.

1859.

I.

It was autumn.

Along the highway came two equipages at a brisk pace. In the first carriage sat two women. One was a lady, thin and pale. The other, her maid, with a brilliant red complexion, and plump. Her short, dry locks escaped from under a faded cap; her red hand, in a torn glove, put them back with a jerk. Her full bosom, incased in a tapestry shawl, breathed of health; her restless black eyes now gazed through the window at the fields hurrying by them, now rested on her mistress, now peered solicitously into the corners of the coach.

Before the maid's face swung the lady's bonnet on the rack; on her knees lay a puppy; her feet were raised by packages lying on the floor, and could almost be heard drumming upon them above the noise of the creaking of the springs, and the rattling of the windows.

The lady, with her hands resting in her lap and her eyes shut, feebly swayed on the cushions which supported her back, and, slightly frowning, struggled with a cough.

She wore a white nightcap, and a blue neckerchief twisted around her delicate pale neck. A straight line, disappearing under the cap, parted her blonde hair, which was smoothly pomaded; and there was a dry, deathly appearance about the whiteness of the skin in this simple parting. The withered and rather sallow skin was loosely drawn over her delicate and pretty features, and there was a hectic flush on the cheeks and cheek-bones. Her lips were dry and restless, her thin eyelashes had lost their curve, and a cloth travelling capote made straight folds over her sunken chest. Although her eyes were closed, her face gave the impression of weariness, irascibility, and habitual suffering.

The lackey, leaning back, was napping on the coach-box. The hired driver,[88] shouting in a clear voice, urged on his four powerful and sweaty horses, occasionally looking back at the other driver, who was shouting just behind them in an open barouche. The tires of the wheels, in their even and rapid course, left wide parallel tracks on the limy mud of the highway.

The sky was gray and cold, a moist mist was falling over the fields and the road. It was suffocating in the carriage, and smelt of eau-de-cologne and dust. The invalid leaned back her head, and slowly opened her eyes. Her great eyes were brilliant, and of a beautiful dark color. "Again!" said she, nervously pushing away with her beautiful attenuated hand the end of her maid's cloak, which occasionally hit against her knee. Her mouth contracted painfully.

Matriósha raised her cloak in both hands, lifting herself up on her strong legs, and then sat down again, farther away. Her fresh face was suffused with a brilliant scarlet.

The invalid's handsome dark eyes eagerly followed the maid's motions; and then with both hands she took hold of the seat, and did her best to raise herself a little higher, but her strength was not sufficient.

Again her mouth became contracted, and her whole face took on an expression of unavailing, angry irony.

"If you would only help me.... Ah! It's not necessary. I can do it myself. Only have the goodness not to put those pillows behind me.... On the whole, you had better not touch them, if you don't understand!"

The lady closed her eyes, and then again, quickly raising the lids, gazed at her maid.

Matriósha looked at her, and gnawed her red lower lip. A heavy sigh escaped from the sick woman's breast; but the sigh was not ended, but was merged in a fit of coughing. She scowled, and turned her face away, clutching her chest with both hands. When the coughing fit was over, she once more

239

shut her eyes, and continued to sit motionless. The coach and the barouche rolled into the village. Matriósha drew her fat hand from under her shawl, and made the sign of the cross.

"What is this?" demanded the lady.

"A post-station, madame."

"Why did you cross yourself, I should like to know?"

"The church, madame."

The lady looked out of the window, and began slowly to cross herself, gazing with all her eyes at the great village church, in front of which the invalid's carriage was now passing.

The two vehicles came to a stop together at the post-house. The sick woman's husband and the doctor dismounted from the barouche, and came to the coach.

"How are you feeling?" asked the doctor, taking her pulse.

"Well, my dear, aren't you fatigued?" asked the husband, in French. "Wouldn't you like to go out?"

Matriósha, gathering up the bundles, squeezed herself into the corner, so as not to interfere with the conversation.

"No matter, it's all the same thing," replied the invalid. "I will not get out."

The husband, after standing there a little while, went into the post-house. Matriósha, jumping from the carriage, tiptoed across the muddy road, into the enclosure.

"If I am miserable, there is no reason why the rest of you should not have breakfast," said the sick woman, smiling faintly to the doctor, who was standing by her window.

"It makes no difference to them how I am," she remarked to herself as the doctor, turning from her with slow step, started to run up the steps of

240

the station-house. "They are well, and it's all the same to them. O my God!"

"How now, Eduard Ivánovitch," said the husband, as he met the doctor, and rubbing his hands with a gay smile. "I have ordered my travelling-case brought; what do you say to that?"

"That's worth while," replied the doctor.

"Well now, how about her?" asked the husband with a sigh, lowering his voice and raising his brows.

"I have told you that she cannot reach Moscow, much less Italy, especially in such weather."

"What is to be done, then? Oh! my God! my God!"

The husband covered his eyes with his hand.... "Give it here," he added, addressing his man, who came bringing the travelling-case.

"You'll have to stop somewhere on the route," replied the doctor, shrugging his shoulders.

"But tell me, how can that be done?" rejoined the husband. "I have done every thing to keep her from going: I have spoken to her of our means, and of our children whom we should have to leave behind, and of my business. She would not hear a word. She has made her plans for living abroad, as though she were well. But if I should tell her what her real condition is, it would kill her."

"Well, she is a dead woman now: you may as well know it, Vasíli Dmítritch. A person cannot live without lungs, and there is no way of making lungs grow again. It is melancholy, it is hard, but what is to be done about it? It is my business and yours to make her last days as easy as possible. It is the confessor that is needed here."

"Oh, my God! Now just perceive how I am situated, in speaking to her of her last will. Let come whatever may, yet I cannot speak of that. And yet you know how good she is."

"Try at least to persuade her to wait until the roads are frozen," said the

241

doctor, shaking his head significantly: "something might happen during the journey."

"Aksiúsha, oh, Aksiúsha!" cried the superintendent's daughter, throwing a cloak over her head and tiptoeing down the muddy back steps. "Come along. Let us have a look at the Shirkínskaya lady: they say she's got lung-trouble, and they're taking her abroad. I never saw how any one looked in consumption."

Aksiúsha jumped down from the door-sill; and the two girls, hand in hand, hurried out of the gates. Shortening their steps, they walked by the coach, and stared in at the lowered window. The invalid bent her head toward them; but when she saw their inquisitiveness, she frowned and turned away.

"Oh, de-e-ar!" said the superintendent's daughter, vigorously shaking her head.... "How wonderfully pretty she used to be, and how she has changed! It is terrible! Did you see? Did you see, Aksiúsha?"

"Yes, but how thin she is!" assented Aksiúsha. "Let us go by and look again; we'll make believe go to the well. Did you see, she turned away from us; still I got a good view of her. Isn't it too bad, Masha?"

"Yes, but what terrible mud!" replied Masha, and both of them started to run back within the gates.

"It's evident that I have become a fright," thought the sick woman.... "But we must hurry, hurry, and get abroad, and there I shall soon get well."

"Well, and how are you, my dear?" inquired the husband, coming to the carriage with still a morsel of something in his mouth.

"Always one and the same question," thought the sick woman, "and he's even eating!"

"It's no consequence," she murmured between her teeth.

"Do you know, my dear, I am afraid that this journey in such weather will only make you worse. Eduard Ivánovitch says the same thing. Hadn't we better turn back?"

She maintained an angry silence.

"The weather will improve maybe, the roads will become good, and that would be better for you; then at least we could start all together."

"Pardon me. If I had not listened to you so long, I should at this moment be at Berlin and have entirely recovered."

"What's to be done, my angel? it was impossible, as you know. But now if you would wait a month, you would be ever so much better; I could finish up my business, and we could take the children with us."

"The children are well, and I am ill."

"But just see here, my love, if in this weather you should grow worse on the road.... At least we should be at home."

"What is the use of being at home?... Die at home?" replied the invalid peevishly.

But the word die evidently startled her, and she turned upon her husband a supplicating and inquiring look. He dropped his eyes, and said nothing.

The sick woman's mouth suddenly contracted in a childish fashion, and the tears sprang to her eyes. Her husband covered his face with his handkerchief, and silently turned from the carriage.

"No, I will go," cried the invalid; and lifting her eyes to the sky, she clasped her hands, and began to whisper incoherent words. "My God! why must it be?" she said, and the tears flowed more violently. She prayed long and fervently, but still there was just the same sense of constriction and pain in her chest, just the same gray melancholy in the sky and the fields and the road; just the same autumnal mist, neither thicker nor more tenuous, but ever the same in its monotony, falling on the muddy highway, on the roofs, on the carriage, and on the sheep-skin coats of the drivers, who were talking in strong, gay voices, as they were oiling and adjusting the carriage.

II.

The coach was ready, but the driver loitered. He had gone into the driver's cottage,[89] where it was warm, close, dark, and suffocating; smelling of human occupation, of cooking bread, of cabbage, and of sheep-skin garments.

Several drivers were in the room; the cook was engaged near the oven, on top of which lay a sick man wrapped up in pelts.

"Uncle Khveódor! hey! Uncle Khveódor," called a young man, the driver, in a tulup, and with his knout in his belt, coming into the room, and addressing the sick man.

"What do you want, rattlepate? What are you calling to Fyédka[90] for?" demanded one of the drivers. "There's your carriage waiting for you."

"I want to borrow his boots. Mine are worn out," replied the young fellow, tossing back his curls and straightening his mittens in his belt. "Why? is he asleep? Say, Uncle Khveódor!" he insisted, going to the oven.

"What is it?" a weak voice was heard saying, and a blowsy, emaciated face was lifted up from the oven.

A broad, gaunt hand, bloodless and covered with hairs, pulled up his overcoat over the dirty shirt that covered his bony shoulder. "Give me something to drink, brother; what is it you want?"

The young fellow handed him a small dish of water.

"I say, Fyédya," said he, hesitating, "I reckon you won't want your new boots now; let me have them? Probably you won't need them any more."

The sick man dropping his weary head down to the lacquered bowl, and dipping his thin, hanging mustache in the brown water, drank feebly and eagerly.

His tangled beard was unclean; his sunken, clouded eyes were with difficulty raised to the young man's face. When he had finished drinking, he tried to raise his hand to wipe his wet lips, but his strength failed him, and he wiped them on the sleeve of his overcoat. Silently, and breathing with difficulty through his nose, he looked straight into the young man's eyes, and tried to collect his strength.

"Maybe you have promised them to some one else?" said the young

244

driver. "If that's so, all right. The worst of it is, it is wet outside, and I have to go out to my work, and so I said to myself, 'I reckon I'll ask Fyédka for his boots; I reckon he won't be needing them.' But maybe you will need them,—just say"....

Something began to bubble up and rumble in the sick man's chest; he bent over, and began to strangle, with a cough that rattled in his throat.

"Now I should like to know where he would need them?" unexpectedly snapped out the cook, angrily addressing the whole hovel. "This is the second month that he has not crept down from the oven. Just see how he is all broken up! and you can hear how it must hurt him inside. Where would he need boots? They would not think of burying him in new ones! And it was time long ago, God pardon me the sin of saying so. Just see how he chokes! He ought to be taken from this hovel to another, or somewhere. They say there's hospitals in the city; but what's you going to do? he takes up the whole room, and that's too much. There isn't any room at all. And yet you are expected to keep neat."

"Hey! Seryóha, come along, take your place, the people are waiting," cried the head man of the station, coming to the door.

Seryóha started to go without waiting for his reply, but the sick man during his cough intimated by his eyes that he was going to speak.

"You can take the boots, Seryóha," said he, conquering the cough and getting his breath a little. "Only, do you hear, buy me a stone when I am dead," he added hoarsely.

"Thank you, uncle; then I will take them, and as for the stone,—éï-éï!—I will buy you one."

"There, children, you are witnesses," the sick man was able to articulate, and then once more he bent over and began to choke.

"All right, we have heard," said one of the drivers. "But run, Seryóha, or else the stárosta will be after you again. You know Lady Shirkínskaya is sick."

Seryóha quickly pulled off his ragged, unwieldy boots, and flung them under the bench. Uncle Feódor's fitted his feet exactly, and the young driver could not keep his eyes off them as he went to the carriage.

"Ek! what splendid boots! Here's some grease," called another driver with the grease-pot in his hand, as Seryóha mounted to his box and gathered up the reins. "Get them for nothing?"

"So you're jealous, are you?" cried Seryóha, lifting up and tucking around his legs the tails of his overcoat. "Off with you, my darlings," he cried to the horses, cracking his knout; and the coach and barouche with their occupants, trunks, and other belongings, were hidden in the thick autumnal mist, and rapidly whirled away over the wet road.

The sick driver remained on the oven in the stifling hovel, and, not being able to throw off the phlegm, by a supreme effort turned over on the other-side, and stopped coughing.

Till evening there was a continual coming and going, and eating of meals in the hovel, and the sick man was not noticed. Before night came on, the cook climbed upon the oven, and pulled off the sheep-skin from his legs.

"Don't be angry with me, Nastásya," murmured the sick man. "I shall soon leave you your room."

"All right, all right, it's of no consequence. But what is the matter with you, uncle? Tell me."

"All my innards are gnawed out, God knows what it is!"

"And I don't doubt your gullet hurts you when you cough so?"

"It hurts me all over. My death is at hand, that's what it is. Okh! Okh! Okh!" groaned the sick man.

"Now cover up your legs this way," said Nastásya, comfortably arranging the overcoat so that it would cover him, and then getting down from the oven.

During the night the hovel was faintly lighted by a single taper. Nastásya and a dozen drivers were sleeping, snoring loudly, on the floor and the benches.

Only the sick man feebly choked and coughed, and tossed on the oven.

In the morning no sound was heard from him.

"I saw something wonderful in my sleep," said the cook, as she stretched herself in the early twilight the next morning. "I seemed to see Uncle Khveódor get down from the oven, and go out to cut wood. 'Look here,' says he, 'I'm going to help you, Násya;' and I says to him, 'How can you split wood?' but he seizes the hatchet, and begins to cut so fast, so fast that nothing but chips fly. 'Why,' says I, 'ain't you been sick?'—'No,' says he, 'I am well,' and he kind of lifted up the axe, and I was scared; and I screamed and woke up. He can't be dead, can he?—Uncle Khveódor! hey, uncle!"

Feódor did not move.

"Now he can't be dead, can he? Go and see," said one of the drivers who had just waked up. The emaciated hand, covered with reddish hair, that hung down from the oven, was cold and pale.

"Go tell the superintendent; it seems he is dead," said the driver.

Feódor had no relatives. He was a stranger. On the next day they buried him in the new burying-ground behind the grove; and Nastásya for many days had to tell everybody of the dream which she had seen, and how she had been the first to discover that Uncle Feódor was dead.

III.

Spring had come.

Along the wet streets of the city swift streamlets ran purling between bits of ice; bright were the colors of people's dresses and the tones of their voices, as they hurried along. In the walled gardens, the buds on the trees were bourgeoning, and the fresh breeze swayed their branches with a soft gentle murmur. Everywhere transparent drops were forming and falling....

The sparrows chattered incoherently, and fluttered about on their little wings. On the sunny side, on the walls, houses, and trees, all was full of life and brilliancy. The sky, and the earth, and the heart of man overflowed with youth and joy.

247

In front of a great seignorial mansion, in one of the principal streets, fresh straw was laid; in the house lay that same invalid whom we saw hastening abroad.

Near the closed doors of the house stood the sick lady's husband, and a lady well along in years. On a sofa sat the confessor, with cast-down eyes, holding something wrapped up under his stole.[91] In one corner, in a Voltaire easy-chair, reclined an old lady, the sick woman's mother, weeping violently.

Near her the maid stood holding a clean handkerchief, ready for the old lady's use when she should ask for it. Another maid was rubbing the old lady's temples, and blowing on her gray head underneath her cap.

"Well, Christ be with you, my dear," said the husband to the elderly lady who was standing with him near the door: "she has such confidence in you; you know how to talk with her; go and speak with her a little while, my darling, please go!"

He was about to open the door for her; but his cousin held him back, putting her handkerchief several times to her eyes, and shaking her head.

"There, now she will not see that I have been weeping," said she, and, opening the door herself, went to the invalid.

The husband was in the greatest excitement, and seemed quite beside himself. He started to go over to the old mother, but after taking a few steps he turned around, walked the length of the room, and approached the priest.

The priest looked at him, raised his brows toward heaven, and sighed. The thick gray beard also was lifted and fell again.

"My God! my God!" said the husband.

"What can you do?" exclaimed the confessor, sighing and again lifting up his brows and beard, and letting them drop.

"And the old mother there!" exclaimed the husband, almost in despair. "She will not be able to endure it. You see, she loved her so, she loved her so,

248

that she.... I don't know. You might try, holy father,[92] to calm her a little, and persuade her to go away."

The confessor arose and went over to the old lady.

"It is true, no one can appreciate a mother's heart," said he, "but God is compassionate."

The old lady's face was suddenly convulsed, and a hysterical sob shook her frame.

"God is compassionate," repeated the priest, when she had grown a little calmer. "I will tell you, in my parish there was a sick man, and much worse than Márya Dmítrievna, and he, though he was only a shopkeeper,[93] was cured in a very short time, by means of herbs. And this very same shopkeeper is now in Moscow. I have told Vasíli Dmítrievitch about him; it might be tried, you know. At all events, it would satisfy the invalid. With God, all things are possible."

"No, she won't get well," persisted the old lady. "Why should God have taken her, and not me?"

And again the hysterical sobbing overcame her so violently that she fainted away.

The invalid's husband hid his face in his hands, and rushed from the room.

In the corridor the first person whom he met was a six-year-old boy, who was chasing his little sister with all his might and main.

"Do you bid me take the children to their mamma?" inquired the nurse.

"No, she is not able to see them. They distract her."

The lad stopped for a moment, and after looking eagerly into his father's face, he cut a dido with his leg, and with merry shouts ran on. "I'm playing she's a horse, papásha," cried the little fellow, pointing to his sister.

Meantime, in the next room, the cousin had taken her seat near the sick woman, and was skilfully bringing the conversation by degrees round so as to prepare her for the thought of death. The doctor stood by the window, mixing some draught.

The invalid in a white dressing-gown, all surrounded by cushions, was sitting up in bed, and gazed silently at her cousin.

"Ah, my dear!" she exclaimed, unexpectedly interrupting her, "don't try to prepare me; don't treat me like a little child! I am a Christian woman. I know all about it. I know that I have not long to live; I know that if my husband had heeded me sooner, I should have been in Italy, and possibly, yes probably, should have been well by this time. They all told him so. But what is to be done? it's as God saw fit. We all of us have sinned, I know that; but I hope in the mercy of God, that all will be pardoned, ought to be pardoned. I am trying to sound my own heart. I also have committed many sins, my love. But how much I have suffered in atonement! I have tried to bear my sufferings patiently"....

"Then shall I have the confessor come in, my love? It will be all the easier for you, after you have been absolved," said the cousin.

The sick woman dropped her head in token of assent. "O God! pardon me a sinner," she whispered.

The cousin went out, and beckoned to the confessor. "She is an angel," she said to the husband, with tears in her eyes. The husband wept. The priest went into the sick-room; the old lady still remained unconscious, and in the room beyond all was perfectly quiet. At the end of five minutes the confessor came out, and, taking off his stole, arranged his hair.

"Thanks be to the Lord, she is calmer now," said he. "She wishes to see you."

The cousin and the husband went to the sick-room. The invalid, gently weeping, was gazing at the images.

"I congratulate you, my love," said the husband.

"Thank you. How well I feel now! what ineffable joy I experience!" said the sick woman, and a faint smile played over her thin lips. "How merciful God is! Is it not so? He is merciful and omnipotent!" And again with an eager prayer she turned her tearful eyes towards the holy images.

Then suddenly something seemed to occur to her mind. She beckoned to her husband.

"You are never willing to do what I desire," said she in a weak and querulous voice.

The husband, stretching his neck, listened to her submissively.

"What is it, my love?"

"How many times I have told you that these doctors don't know any thing! There are uneducated women doctors: they make cures. That's what the good father said.... A shopkeeper.... send for him"....

"For whom, my love?"

"Good heavens! you can never understand me." And the dying woman frowned, and closed her eyes.

The doctor came to her, and took her hand. Her pulse was evidently growing feebler and feebler. He made a sign to the husband. The sick woman remarked this gesture, and looked around in fright. The cousin turned away to hide her tears.

"Don't weep, don't torment yourselves on my account," said the invalid. "That takes away from me my last comfort."

"You are an angel!" exclaimed the cousin, kissing her hand.

"No, kiss me here. They only kiss the hands of those who are dead. My God! my God!"

That same evening the sick woman was a corpse, and the corpse in the coffin lay in the parlor of the great mansion. In the immense room, the doors of which were closed, sat the clerk,[94] and with a monotonous voice read the Psalms of David through his nose.

251

The bright glare from the wax candles in the lofty silver candelabra fell on the white brow of the dead, on the heavy waxen hands, on the stiff folds of the cerement which brought out into awful relief the knees and the feet.

The clerk, not varying his tones, continued to read on steadily, and in the silence of the chamber of death his words rang out and died away. Occasionally from distant rooms came the voice of children and their romping.

"*Thou hidest thy face, they are troubled; thou takest away their breath, they die and return to their dust.*

"*Thou sendest forth thy Spirit, they are created; and thou renewest the face of the earth.*

"*The glory of the Lord shall endure forever: the Lord shall rejoice in his works.*"

The face of the dead was stern and majestic. But there was no motion either on the pure cold brow, or the firmly closed lips. She was all attention. But did she perhaps now understand these grand words?

IV.

At the end of a month, over the grave of the dead a stone chapel was erected. Over the driver's there was as yet no stone, and only the fresh green grass sprouted over the mound that served as the sole record of the past existence of a man.

"It will be a sin and a shame, Seryóha," said the cook at the station-house one day, "if you don't buy a gravestone for Khveódor. You kept saying, 'It's winter, winter,' but now why don't you keep your word? I heard it all. He has already come back once to ask why you don't do it; if you don't buy him one, he will come again, he will choke you."

"Well, now, have I denied it?" urged Seryóha. "I am going to buy him a stone, as I said I would. I can get one for a ruble and a half. I have not forgotten about it; I'll have to get it. As soon as I happen to be in town, then I'll buy him one."

"You ought at least to put up a cross, that's what you ought to do," said an old driver. "It isn't right at all. You're wearing those boots now."

"Yes. But where could I get him a cross? You wouldn't want to make one out of an old piece of stick, would you?"

"What is that you say? Make one out of an old piece of stick? No; take your axe, go out to the wood a little earlier than usual, and you can hew him out one. Take a little ash-tree, and you can make one. You can have a covered cross. If you go then, you won't have to give the watchman a little drink of vodka. One doesn't want to give vodka for every trifle. Now, yesterday I broke my axletree, and I go and hew out a new one of green wood. No one said a word."

Early the next morning, almost before dawn, Seryóha took his axe, and went to the wood.

Over all things hung a cold, dead veil of falling mist, as yet untouched by the rays of the sun.

The cast gradually grew brighter, reflecting its pale light over the vault of heaven still covered by light clouds. Not a single grass-blade below, not a single leaf on the topmost branches of the tree-top, waved. Only from time to time could be heard the sounds of fluttering wings in the thicket, or a rustling on the ground broke in upon the silence of the forest.

Suddenly a strange sound, foreign to this nature, resounded and died away at the edge of the forest. Again the noise sounded, and was monotonously repeated again and again, at the foot of one of the ancient, immovable trees. A tree-top began to shake in an extraordinary manner; the juicy leaves whispered something; and the warbler, sitting on one of the branches, flew off a couple of times with a shrill cry, and, wagging its tail, finally perched on another tree.

The axe rang more and more frequently; the white chips, full of sap, were scattered upon the dewy grass, and a slight cracking was heard beneath the blows.

The tree trembled with all its body, leaned over, and quickly straightened itself with a fearful shudder on its base.

For an instant all was still, then once more the tree bent over; a crash was heard in its trunk; and tearing the thicket, and dragging down the branches, it plunged toward the damp earth.

The noise of the axe and of footsteps ceased.

The warbler uttered a cry, and flew higher. The branch which she grazed with her wings shook for an instant, and then came to rest like all the others with their foliage.

The trees, more joyously than ever, extended their branches over the new space that had been made in their midst.

The first sunbeams, breaking through the cloud, gleamed in the sky, and shone along the earth and heavens.

The mist, in billows, began to float along the hollows; the dew, gleaming, played on the green foliage; translucent white clouds hurried along their azure path.

The birds hopped about in the thicket, and, as though beside themselves, voiced their happiness; the juicy leaves joyfully and contentedly whispered on the tree-tops; and the branches of the living trees slowly and majestically waved over the dead and fallen tree.

FOOTNOTES:

[88] yamshchik.

[89] izbá.

[90] Fyédka and Fyédya are diminutives of Feódor, Theodore.

[91] Called epitrachilion in the Greek Church.

[92] bátiushka.

[93] meshchánin.

[94] diachók.

A PRISONER IN THE CAUCASUS.

I.

A Russian of rank was serving as an officer in the army of the Caucasus. His name was Zhilin.

There came to him one day a letter from his home. His aged mother wrote him: "I am now getting along in years, and before I die I should like to see my beloved son. Come and bid me farewell, lay me in the ground, and then with my blessing return again to your service. And I have been finding a bride for you, and she is intelligent and handsome and has property. If you like, you can marry and settle down together."

Zhilin cogitated, "It is very true: the old lady has been growing feeble; maybe I shall not have a chance to see her again. Let us go, and if the bride is pretty—then I might marry."

He went to his colonel, got his leave of absence, took his farewell of his comrades, gave the soldiers of his command nine gallons[95] of vodka as a farewell treat, and made his arrangements to depart.

There was war at that time in the Caucasus. The roads were not open for travel either by day or night. If any of the Russians rode or walked outside of the fortress, the Tatars were likely either to kill him or carry him off to the mountains. And it was arranged that twice a week an escort of soldiers should go from fortress to fortress. In front and behind marched the soldiers, and the travellers rode in the middle.

It was now summer-time. At sunrise the baggage-train was made up behind the fortification; the guard of soldiery marched ahead, and the procession moved along the road.

Zhilin was on horseback, and his effects were on a cart that formed part of the train.

They had twenty-five versts[96] to travel. The train marched slowly;

sometimes the soldiers halted; sometimes a wagon-wheel came off, or a horse balked, and all had to stop and wait.

The sun was already past the zenith, but the train had only gone half way, so great were the dust and heat. The sun was baking hot, and nowhere was there shelter. A bald steppe; not a tree or a shrub on the road.

Zhilin rode on ahead, occasionally stopping and waiting till the train caught up with him. He would listen, and hear the signal on the horn to halt again. And Zhilin thought, "Would I better go on alone without the soldiers? I have a good horse under me; if I fall in with the Tatars, I can escape. Or shall I wait?"

He kept stopping and pondering. And just then another officer, also on horseback, rode up to him; his name was Kostuilin, and he had a musket.

He said, "Zhilin, let us ride on ahead together. I am so hungry that I cannot stand it any longer, and the heat too,—you could wring my shirt out!" Kostuilin was a heavy, stout, ruddy man, and the sweat was dripping from him.

Zhilin reflected, and said, "And your musket is loaded?"

"It is."

"All right, let us go. Only one condition: not to separate."

And they started on up the road. They rode along the steppe, talking and looking on each side. There was a wide sweep of view. As soon as the steppe came to an end, the road went into a pass between two mountains.

And Zhilin said, "I must ride up on that mountain, and reconnoitre, otherwise you see they might come down from the mountain and surprise us."

But Kostuilin said, "What is there to reconnoitre? Let us go ahead."

Zhilin did not heed him.

"No," says he, "you wait for me here below. I'll just glance around."

And he spurred his horse up the mountain to the left.

The horse that Zhilin rode was a hunter; he had bought him out of a drove of colts, paying a hundred rubles for him, and he had himself trained him. He bore him up the steep slope as on wings. He had hardly reached the summit when before him less than seven hundred feet distant mounted Tatars were standing,—thirty men.

He saw them, and started to turn back, but the Tatars had caught sight of him; they set out in pursuit of him, unstrapping their weapons as they gallop. Zhilin dashes down the precipice with all the speed of his horse, and cries to Kostuilin, "Fire your gun!" and to his horse he says, though not aloud, "Little mother, carry me safely, don't stumble; if you trip, I am lost. If we get back to the gun, we won't fall into their hands."

But Kostuilin, instead of waiting for him, as soon as he saw the Tatars, galloped on with all his might toward the fortress. With his whip he belabored his horse, first on one side, then on the other; all that could be seen through the dust, was the horse switching her tail.

Zhilin saw that his case was desperate. The gun was gone; nothing was to be done with a sabre alone. He turned his horse back toward the train; he thought he might escape that way.

But in front of him, he sees that six are galloping down the steep. His horse is good, but theirs are better; and besides, they have got the start of him. He started to wheel about, and was going to dash ahead again, but his horse had got momentum, and could not be held back; he flew straight down toward them.

He sees a red-bearded Tatar approaching him on a gray mare. He is gaining on him; he gnashes his teeth; he is getting his gun ready.

"Well," thinks Zhilin, "I know you devils; if you should take me prisoner, you would put me in a hole, and flog me with a whip. I won't give myself up alive."

Now, Zhilin was not of great size, but he was an uhlan. He drew his sabre, spurred his horse straight at the red-bearded Tatar. He says to himself, "Either I will crush him with my horse, or I will hack him down with my sabre."

Zhilin, however, did not reach the place on horseback; suddenly behind him, gun-shots were fired at the horse. The horse fell headlong, and pinned Zhilin's leg to the ground.

He tried to arise; but already ill-smelling Tatars were sitting on him, and pinioning his hands behind his back.

He burst from them, knocking the Tatars over; but three others had dismounted from their horses, and began to beat him on the head with their gun-stocks.

His sight failed him, and he staggered.

The Tatars seized him, took from their saddles extra saddle-girths, bent his arms behind his back, fastened them with a Tatar knot, and lifted him up.

They took his sabre from him, pulled off his boots, made a thorough search of him, pulled out his money and his watch, tore his clothes all to pieces.

Zhilin glanced at his horse. The poor beast lay as he had fallen, on his side, and was kicking, vainly trying to rise. In his head was a hole, and from the hole the black blood was pouring; the dust for an arshin around was wet with it.

A Tatar went to the horse to remove the saddle. He was still kicking, so the man took out his dagger, and cut his throat. The throat gave a whistling sound, a trembling ran over the body, and all was over.

The Tatars took off the saddle and the other trappings. The one with the red beard mounted his horse, and the others lifted Zhilin behind him to keep him from falling; they fastened him with the reins to the Tatar's belt, and thus they carried him off to the mountains.

Zhilin sat behind, swaying and bumping his face against the stinking

Tatar's back.

All that he could see before him was the healthy Tatar back, and the sinewy neck, and a smooth-shaven nape, showing blue beneath the cap.

Zhilin's head ached; the blood trickled into his eyes. And it was impossible for him to get a more comfortable position on the horse, or wipe away the blood. His arms were so tightly bound that his collar-bones ached. They rode long from mountain to mountain; they forded a river; then they entered a highway, and rode along a valley. Zhilin tried to follow the route that they took him; but his eyes were glued together with blood, and it was impossible for him to turn round.

It began to grow dark; they crossed still another river, and began to climb a rocky mountain. There was an odor of smoke. The barking of dogs was heard.

They had reached an aul.[97]

The Tatars dismounted. The Tatar children came running up, and surrounded Zhilin, whistling and exulting. Finally they began to fling stones at him.

The Tatar drove away the children, lifted Zhilin from the horse, and called a servant.

A Nogáï, with prominent cheek-bones, came at the call. He wore only a shirt. The shirt was torn; his whole breast was bare. The Tatar said something to him. The servant brought a foot-stock. It consisted of two oaken blocks provided with iron rings, and in one of the rings was a clamp with a lock. They unfastened Zhilin's arms, put on the stock, and took him to a barn, pushed him in, and shut the door.

Zhilin fell on the manure. As he lay there, he felt round in the darkness, and when he had found a place that was less foul, he stretched himself out.

II.

Zhilin scarcely slept that night. The nights were short. He saw through a crack that it was growing light. Zhilin got up, widened the crack, and managed to look out.

Through the crack he could see a road leading down from the mountain; at the right, a Tatar saklia[98] with two trees near it. A black dog was lying on the road; a she-goat with her kids was walking by, all of them shaking their tails.

He saw coming down the mountain a young Tatar girl in a variegated shirt, ungirdled, in pantalettes and boots; her head was covered with a kaftan, and on it she bore a great tin water-jug.

She walked along, swaying and bending her back, and holding by the hand a little Tatar urchin, with shaven head, who wore a single shirt.

After the Tatar maiden had passed with her water-jug, the red-bearded Tatar of the evening before came out, wearing a silk beshmet, a silver dagger in his belt, and sandals on his bare feet. On his head was a high cap of sheep-skin, dyed black, and with the point hanging down. He came out, stretched himself, stroked his red beard. He paused, gave some order to the servant, and went off somewhere.

Then two children on horseback came along on their way to the watering-trough. The hind-quarters of the horses were wet.

Other shaven-headed youngsters, with nothing but shirts on, and nothing on their legs, formed a little band, and came to the barn; they got a dry stick, and stuck it through the crack.

Zhilin growled "ukh" at them. The children began to cry, and scatter in every direction as fast as their legs would carry them; only their bare knees glistened. But Zhilin began to be thirsty; his throat was parched. He said to himself, "I wonder if they won't come to look after me?"

Suddenly the barn-doors are thrown open.

The red Tatar came in, and with him another, of slighter stature and of dark complexion. His eyes were bright and black, his cheeks ruddy, his little beard well trimmed, his face jolly and always enlivened with a grin.

The dark man's clothing was still richer: a silk beshmet of blue silk, embroidered with gold lace. In his belt, a great silver dagger; handsome morocco slippers embroidered with silver, and over the fine slippers he wore a larger pair of stout ones. His cap was tall, of white lamb's wool.

The red Tatar came in, muttered something, gave vent to some abusive language, and then stood leaning against the wall, fingering his dagger, and scowling under his brows at Zhilin, like a wolf.

But the dark Tatar, nervous and active, and always on the go, as though he were made of springs, came straight up to Zhilin, squatted down on his heels, showed his teeth, tapped him on the shoulder, began to gabble something in his own language, winked his eyes, and, clucking his tongue, kept saying, "A fine Russ, a fine Russ!"[99]

Zhilin did not understand him, and said, "Drink; give me some water."

The dark one grinned.

"A fine Russ!" and all the time he kept babbling.

Zhilin signified by his hands and lips that they should give him water.

The dark one understood, grinned, put his head out of the door, and cried, "Dina!"

A young girl came running in,—a slender, lean creature of thirteen, with a face like the dark man's. Evidently she was his daughter.

She was dressed in a long blue shirt with wide sleeves and without a belt. On the bottom, on the breast, and on the cuffs it was relieved with red trimmings. She wore on her legs pantalettes and slippers, and over the slippers another pair with high heels. On her neck was a necklace wholly composed of half-ruble pieces. Her head was uncovered; she had her hair in a black braid, and on the braid was a ribbon, and to the ribbon were attached various ornaments and a silver ruble.

Her father gave her some command. She ran out, and quickly returned, bringing a little tin pitcher. After she had handed him the water, she also squatted on her heels in such a way that her knees were higher than her shoulders.

She sits that way, and opens her eyes, and stares at Zhilin while he drinks, as though he were some wild beast.

Zhilin offered to return the pitcher to her. She darted away like a wild goat. Even her father laughed.

He sent her after something else. She took the pitcher, ran out, and brought back some unleavened bread on a small round board, and again squatted down, and stared without taking her eyes from him.

The Tatars went out, and again bolted the door.

After a while the Nogáï also comes to Zhilin, and says, "Aï-da, khozyáïn, aï-da!"

But he does not know Russian either. Zhilin, however, perceived that he wished him to go somewhere.

Zhilin hobbled out with his clog; it was impossible to walk, so he had to drag one leg. The Nogáï led the way for him.

He sees before him a Tatar village, of half a score of houses, and the native mosque with its minaret.

In front of one house stood three horses saddled. Lads held them by the bridle. From this house came the dark Tatar, and waved his hand, signifying that Zhilin was to come to him. He grinned, and kept saying something in his own tongue, and went into the house.

Zhilin followed him.

The room was decent; the walls were smoothly plastered with clay. Against the front wall were placed feather-beds; on the sides hung costly rugs; on the rugs were guns, pistols, and sabres, all silver-mounted.

On one side a little oven was set in, on a level with the floor.

The floor was of earth, clean as a threshing-floor, and the whole of the front portion was covered with felt; rugs were distributed over the felt, and on the rugs were down pillows.

On the rugs were sitting some Tatars in slippers only,—the dark Tatar, the red-bearded one, and three guests. Behind their backs, down cushions were placed; and before them on wooden plates were pancakes of millet-flour, and melted butter in a cup, and the Tatar beer, called buza, in a pitcher. They ate with their fingers, and all dipped into the butter.

The dark man leaped up, bade Zhilin sit on one side, not on a rug but on the bare floor; going back again to his rug, he handed his guests cakes and buza.

The servant showed Zhilin his place; he himself took off his shoes, placed them by the door in a row with the slippers of the other guests, and took his seat on the felt as near as possible to his masters; and while they eat he looks at them, and his mouth waters.

After the Tatars had finished eating, a Tatar woman entered, dressed in the same sort of shirt as the girl wore, and in pantalettes; her head was covered with a handkerchief. She carried out the butter and the cakes, and brought a handsome finger-bowl, and a pitcher with a narrow nose.

The Tatars finished washing their hands, then they folded their arms, knelt down, and puffed on all sides, and said their prayers. They talked in their own tongue.

Then one of the guests, a Tatar, approached Zhilin, and began to speak to him in Russian. "Kazi Muhamet made you prisoner," said he, pointing to the red-bearded Tatar; "and he has given you to Abdul Murat," indicating the dark one. "Abdul Murat is now your master."[100]

Zhilin said nothing.

Abdul Murat began to talk, all the time pointing toward Zhilin, and grinned as he talked-: "soldat Urus, korosho Urus."

The interpreter went on to say, "He commands you to write a letter home, and have them send money to ransom you. As soon as money is sent, he will set you free."

264

Zhilin pondered a little, and then said, "Does he wish a large ransom?"

The Tatars took counsel together, and then the interpreter said,—

"Three thousand silver rubles."

"No," replied Zhilin, "I can't pay that."

Abdul leaped up, began to gesticulate and talk to Zhilin; he seemed all the time to think that Zhilin understood him.

The interpreter translated his words. "He means," says he, "how much will you give?"

Zhilin after pondering a little said, "Five hundred rubles."

Then the Tatars all began to talk at once. Abdul began to scream at the red-bearded Tatar. He grew so excited as he talked, that the spittle flew from his mouth.

But the red-bearded Tatar only frowned, and clucked with his tongue.

When all became silent again, the interpreter said, "Five hundred rubles is not enough to buy you of your master. He himself has paid two hundred for you. Kazi Muhamet was in debt to him. He took you for the debt. Three thousand rubles; it is no use to send less. But if you don't write, they will put you in a hole, and flog you with a whip."

"Ekh!" thinks Zhilin, "the more cowardly one is, the worse it is for him." He leaped to his feet, and said,—

"Now you tell him, dog that he is, that if he thinks he is going to frighten me, then I will not give him a single kopek nor will I write. I am not afraid of you, and you will never make me afraid of you, you dog!" The interpreter translated this, and again they all began to talk at once.

They gabbled a long time, then the dark one got up and came to Zhilin.

"Urus," says he, "jigit, jigit Urus!"

The word jigit among them signifies a brave young man. And he grinned, said something to the interpreter, and the interpreter said, "Give a thousand rubles." Zhilin would not give in. "I will not pay more than five hundred. But if you kill me, you will get nothing at all."

The Tatars consulted together, sent out the servant, and they themselves looked first at the door, then at Zhilin.

The servant returned, followed by a rather stout man in bare feet and almost stripped. His feet also were in stocks.

Zhilin made an exclamation: he recognized Kostuilin.

And they brought him in, and placed him next his comrade; the two began to talk together, and the Tatars looked on and listened in silence.

Zhilin told how it had gone with him; Kostuilin told how his horse had stood stock still, and his gun had missed fire, and that this same Abdul had overtaken him and captured him.

Abdul listened, pointed to Kostuilin, and muttered something. The interpreter translated his words to mean that they now both belonged to the same master, and that the one who paid the ransom first would be freed first. "Now," says he to Zhilin, "you lose your temper so easily, but your comrade is calm; he has written a letter home; they will send five thousand silver rubles. And so he will be well fed, and he won't be hurt."

And Zhilin said, "Let my comrade do as he pleases. Maybe he is rich. But I am not rich; I will do as I have already told you. Kill me if you wish, but it would not do you any good, and I will not pay you more than five hundred rubles."

They were silent.

Suddenly Abdul leaped up, brought a little chest, took out a pen, a sheet of paper, and ink, and pushed them into Zhilin's hands, then tapped him on the shoulder, and said by signs, "Write." He had agreed to take the five hundred rubles.

"Wait a moment," said Zhilin to the interpreter. "Tell him that he must feed us well, clothe us, and give us good decent foot-wear, and let us stay together. We want to have a good time. And lastly, that he take off these clogs."

He looked at his Tatar master, and smiled. The master also smiled, and when he learned what was wanted, said,—

"I will give you the very best clothes: a cherkeska[101] and boots, fit for a wedding. And I will feed you like princes. And if you want to live together, why, you can live in the barn. But it won't do to take away the clogs: you would run away. Only at night will I have them taken off." Then he jumped up, tapped him on the shoulder: "You good, me good."

Zhilin wrote his letter, but he put on it the wrong address so that it might never reach its destination. He said to himself, "I shall run away."

They took Zhilin and Kostuilin to the barn, strewed corn-stalks, gave them water in a pitcher, and bread, two old cherkeski, and some worn-out military boots. It was evident that they had been stolen from some dead soldier. When night came they took off their clogs, and locked them up in the barn.

III.

Thus Zhilin and his comrade lived a whole month. Their master was always on the grin.

"You, Iván, good—me, Abdul, good."

But he gave them wretched food; unleavened bread made of millet-flour, cooked in the form of cakes, but often not heated through.

Kostuilin wrote home again, and was anxiously awaiting the arrival of the money, and lost his spirits. Whole days at a time, he sat in the barn, and counted the days till his money should arrive, or else he slept.

But Zhilin had no expectation that his letter would reach its destination, and he did not write another.

"Where," he asked himself,—"where would my mother get the money for my ransom? And besides, she lived for the most part on what I used to send her. If she made out to raise five hundred rubles, she would be in want till the end of her days. If God wills it, I may escape."

And all the time he kept his eyes open, and made plans to elude his captors.

He walked about the aul; he amused himself by whistling; or else he sat down and fashioned things, either modelling dolls out of clay or plaiting baskets of osiers, for Zhilin was a master at all sorts of handiwork.

One time he had made a doll with nose, and hands and feet, and dressed in a Tatar shirt, and he set the doll on the roof. The Tatar women were going for water. Dina, the master's daughter, caught sight of the doll. She called the Tatar girls. They set down their jugs, and looked and laughed.

Zhilin took the doll, and offered it to them. They keep laughing, but don't dare to take it.

He left the doll, went to the barn, and watched what would take place.

Dina ran up to the doll, looked around, seized the doll, and fled.

The next morning at dawn he sees Dina come out on the doorstep with the doll. And she has already dressed it up in red rags, and was rocking it like a little child, and singing a lullaby in her own language.

An old woman came out, gave her a scolding, snatched the doll away, broke it in pieces, and sent Dina to her work.

Zhilin made another doll, a still better one, and gave it to Dina.

One time Dina brought a little jug, put it down, took a seat, and looked at him. Then she laughed, and pointed to the jug.

"What is she so gay about?" thinks Zhilin.

He took the jug, and began to drink. He supposed that it was water, but it was milk.

He drank up the milk.

"Good," says he. How delighted Dina was! "Good, Iván, good!"

And she jumped up, clapped her hands, snatched the jug, and ran away. And from that time she began to bring him secretly fresh milk every day.

Now, sometimes the Tatars would make cheesecakes out of goat's milk, and dry them on their roofs. Then she used to carry some of these cakes secretly to him. And another time, when her father had killed a sheep, she brought him a piece of mutton in her sleeve. She threw it down, and ran away.

One time there was a tremendous shower, and for a whole hour the rain poured as from buckets; and all the brooks grew roily. Wherever there had been a ford, the depth of the water increased to seven feet, and bowlders were rolled along by it. Everywhere torrents were rushing, the mountains were full of the roaring.

Now, when the shower was over, streams were pouring all through the village. Zhilin asked his master for a knife, whittled out a cylinder and some paddles, and made a water-wheel, and fastened manikins at the two ends.

The little girls brought him some rags, and he dressed up the manikins, one like a man, the other like a woman. He fastened them on, and put the wheel in a brook. The wheel revolved, and the dolls danced.

The whole village collected: the little boys and the little girls, the women, and even the Tatars, came and clucked with their tongues. "Aï, Urus! aï, Iván!"

Abdul had a Russian watch, which had been broken. He took it, and showed it to Zhilin, and clucked with his tongue. Zhilin said,—

"Let me have it, I will fix it."

He took it, opened the penknife, took it apart. Then he put it together again, and gave it back. The watch ran.

The Tatar was delighted, brought him his old beshmet which was all in rags, and gave it to him. Nothing else to be done,—he took it, and used it as a covering at night.

From that time, Zhilin's fame went abroad, that he was a "master." Even from distant villages, they came to him. One brought him a gun-lock or a pistol to repair, another a watch.

His master furnished him with tools,—a pair of pincers and gimlets and a little file.

One time a Tatar fell ill; they came to Zhilin: "Come cure him!"

Zhilin knew nothing of medicine. He went, looked at the sick man, said to himself, "Perhaps he will get well, anyway." He went into the barn, took water and sand, and shook them up together. He whispered a few words to the water in presence of the Tatars, and gave it to the sick man to drink.

Fortunately for him, the Tatar got well.

Zhilin had by this time learned something of their language. And some of the Tatars became accustomed to him; when they wanted him, they called him by name, "Iván, Iván;" but others always looked at him as though he was a wild beast.

The red-bearded Tatar did not like Zhilin; when he saw him, he scowled and turned away, or else insulted him.

There was another old man among them; he did not live in the aul, but came down from the mountain. Zhilin never saw him except when he came to the mosque to prayer. He was of small stature; on his cap, he wore a white handkerchief as an ornament. His beard and mustaches were trimmed; they were white as wool, and his face was wrinkled and brick-red. His nose was hooked like a hawk's, and his eyes were gray and cruel, and he had no teeth except two tusks.

He used to come in his turban, leaning on his staff, and glare like a wolf; whenever he saw Zhilin, he would snort, and turn his back.

One time Zhilin went to the mountain to see where the old man lived. He descended a narrow path, and sees a little stone-walled garden. On the other side of the wall are cherry-trees, peach-trees, and a little hut with a flat roof.

270

He went nearer; he sees bee-hives made of straw, and bees flying and humming around them. And the old man is on his knees before the hives, hammering something.

Zhilin raised himself up, so as to get a better view, and his clog made a noise.

The old man looked up,—squealed; he pulled his pistol from his belt, and fired at Zhilin, who had barely time to hide behind the wall.

The old man came to make his complaint to Zhilin's master. Abdul called him in, grinned, and asked him:

"Why did you go to the old man's?"

"I didn't do him any harm. I wanted to see how he lived."

Abdul explained it to the old man; but he was angry, hissed, mumbled something, showed his tusks, and threatened Zhilin with his hands.

Zhilin did not understand it all; but he made out that the old man wished Abdul to kill the two Russians, and not have them in the aul.

The old man went off.

Zhilin began to ask his master, "Who is that old man?" And the master replied,—

"He is a great man. He used to be our first jigit; he has killed many Russians. He used to be rich. He had three wives and eight sons. All lived in one village. The Russians came, destroyed his village, and killed seven of his sons. One son was left, and surrendered to the Russians. The old man went and gave himself up to the Russians also. He lived among them three months, found his son, killed him with his own hand, and escaped. Since that time he has stopped fighting. He went to Mecca to pray to God, and that's why he wears a turban. Whoever has been to Mecca is called a hadji, and wears a chalma. But he does not love you Russians. He has bade me kill you, but I don't intend to kill you. I have paid out money for you, and besides, Iván, I have come to like you. And so far from wishing to kill you, I would rather not let you go from me at all, if I had not given my word."

He laughed, and began to repeat in Russian, "Tvoyá Iván, khorósh, moyá, Abdul, khorósh."

IV.

Thus Zhilin lived a month. In the daytime he walked about the aul or did some handiwork, but when night came, and it grew quiet in the aul, he burrowed in his barn. It was hard work digging because of the stones, and he sometimes had to use his file on them; and thus he dug a hole under the wall big enough to crawl through.

"Only," he thought, "I must know the region a little first, so as to escape in the right direction. And the Tatars wouldn't tell me any thing."

He waited till one time when his master was absent, then he went after dinner behind the aul to a mountain. His idea was to reconnoitre the country.

But when Abdul returned he commanded a small boy to follow Zhilin, and not take his eyes from him. The little fellow tagged after Zhilin, and kept crying,—

"Don't go there. Father won't allow it. I will call the men if you go!"

Zhilin began to reason with him. "I am not going far," says he,—"only to that hill: I must get some herbs. Come with me; I can't run away with this clog. To-morrow I will make you a bow and arrows."

He persuaded the lad, they went together. To look at, the mountain is not far, but it was hard work with the clog; he went a little distance at a time, pulling himself up by main strength.

Zhilin sat down on the summit, and began to survey the ground.

To the south behind the barn lay a valley through which a herd was grazing, and another aul was in sight at the foot of it. Back of the village was another hill still steeper, and back of that still another. Between the mountains lay a further stretch of forest, and then still other mountains constantly rising higher and higher. And higher than all, stood snow-capped peaks white as sugar, and one snowy peak rose like a dome above them all.

To the east and west also were mountains. In every direction the smoke of auls was to be seen in the ravines.

"Well," he said to himself, "this is all their country."

He began to look in the direction of the Russian possessions. At his very feet was a little river, his village surrounded by gardens. By the river some women, no larger in appearance than little dolls, were standing and washing. Behind the aul was a lower mountain, and beyond it two other mountains covered with forests. And between the two mountains a plain stretched far, far away in the blue distance; and on the plain lay what seemed like smoke.

Zhilin tried to remember in what direction, when he lived at home in the fortress, the sun used to rise, and where it set. He looked. "Just about there," says he, "in that valley, our fortress ought to be. There, between those two mountains, I must make my escape."

The little sun began to slope toward the west. The snowy mountains changed from white to purple; the wooded mountains grew dark; a mist arose from the valley; and the valley itself, where the Russian fortress must be, glowed in the sunset as though it were on fire. Zhilin strained his gaze. Something seemed to hang waving in the air, like smoke arising from chimneys.

And so it seemed to him that it must be from the fortress itself,—the Russian fortress.

It was already growing late. The voice of the mulla calling to prayer was heard. The herds began to return; the kine were lowing. The little lad kept repeating, "Let us go!" but Zhilin could not tear himself away.

They returned home.

"Well," thinks Zhilin, "now I know the place; I must make my escape."

He proposed to make his escape that very night. The nights were dark; it was the wane of the moon.

Unfortunately the Tatars returned in the evening. Usually they came in driving the cattle with them, and came in hilarious. But this time they had no cattle; but they brought a Tatar, dead on his saddle. It was Kazi Muhamet's brother. They rode in solemnly, and collected for the burial.

Zhilin also went out to look.

They did not put the dead body in a coffin, but wrapped it in linen, and placed it under a plane-tree in the village, where it lay on the sward.

The mulla came; the old men gathered together, their caps bound around with handkerchiefs. They took off their shoes, and sat in rows on their heels before the dead.

In front was the mulla, behind him three old men in turbans, and behind them the rest of the Tatars. The mulla lifted the dead man's head, and said, "Allah!" (That means God.) He said this one word, and let the head fall back. All were silent; they sat motionless.

Again the mulla lifted the head, saying, "Allah!" and all repeated it after him,—

"Allah!"

Then silence again.

The dead man lay on the sward; he was motionless, and they sat as though they were dead. Not one made a motion. The only sound was the rustling of the foliage of the plane-tree, stirred by the breeze.

Then the mulla offered a prayer. All got to their feet; they took the dead body in their arms, and carried it away.

They brought it to a pit. The pit was not a mere hole, but was hollowed out under the earth like a cellar.

They took the body under the armpits and by the legs, doubled it up, and let it down gently, shoved it forcibly under the ground, and laid the arms along the belly. The Nogáï brought a green osier. They laid it in the pit; then they quickly filled it up with earth, and over the dead man's head they placed a gravestone. They smoothed the earth over, and again sat around the grave in

274

rows. There was a long silence.

"Allah! Allah! Allah!"

They sighed and got up. The red-bearded Tatar gave money to the old men, then he got up, struck his forehead three times with a whip, and went home.

The next morning Zhilin sees the red-haired Tatar leading a mare through the village, and three Tatars following him. They went behind the village. Kazi Muhamet took off his beshmet, rolled up his sleeves,—his hands were powerful,—took out his dagger, and sharpened it on a whetstone. The Tatars held back the mare's head. Kazi Muhamet approached, and cut the throat; then he turned the animal over, and began to flay it, pulling away the hide with his mighty fists.

The women and maidens came, and began to wash the intestines and the lights. Then they cut up the mare, and carried the meat to the hut. And the whole village collected at the Kazi Muhamet's to celebrate the dead.

For three days they feasted on the mare and drank buza. Thus they celebrated the dead. All the Tatars were at home.

On the fourth day about noon, Zhilin sees that they are collecting for some expedition. Their horses are brought out. They put on their gear, and started off, ten men of them, under the command of the Kazi Muhamet; only Abdul staid at home. There was a new moon, but the nights were still dark.

"Now," thinks Zhilin, "to-day we must escape." And he tells Kostuilin.

But Kostuilin was afraid. "How can we escape? We don't know the way."

"I know the way."

"But we should not get there during the night."

"Well, if we don't get there we will spend the night in the woods. I have some cakes. What are you going to do? It will be all right if they send you the money, but you see, your friends may not collect so much. And the Tatars are now angry because the Russians have killed one of their men. They say they are thinking of killing us."

Kostuilin thought and thought. "All right, let us go!"

V.

Zhilin crept down into his hole, and widened it so that Kostuilin also could get through, and then they sat and waited till all should be quiet in the aul.

As soon as the people were quiet in the aul, Zhilin crept under the wall, and came out on the other side. He whispers to Kostuilin, "Crawl under."

Kostuilin also crept under, but in doing so he hit a stone with his leg, and it made a noise.

Now, the master had a brindled dog as a watch,—a most ferocious animal; they called him Ulyashin.

Zhilin had been in the habit of feeding him. Ulyashin heard the noise, and began to bark and jump about, and the other dogs joined in.

Zhilin gave a little whistle, threw him a piece of cake. Ulyashin recognized him, began to wag his tail, and ceased barking.

Abdul had heard the disturbance, and cried from within the hut:—

"Háït! háït! Ulyashin."

But Zhilin scratched the dog behind the ears. The dog makes no more sound, rubs against his legs, and wags his tail.

They wait behind the corner.

All became silent again; the only sound was the bleating of a sheep in the fold, and far below them the water roaring over the pebbles.

It is dark, but the sky is studded with stars. Over the mountain the young moon hung red, with its horns turned upward.

In the valleys a mist was rising, white as milk. Zhilin started up, and said to his comrade in Tatar, "Well, brother, aï-da!"

They set out again.

But as they get under way, they hear the call of the mulla on the minaret:—

"Allah! Bis'm Allah! el Rakhman!"

"That means, the people will be going to the mosque."

Again they sat down and hid under the wall.

They sat there long, waiting until the people should pass. Again it grew still.

"Now for our fate!"

They crossed themselves, and started.

They went across the dvor, and down the steep bank to the stream, crossed the stream, proceeded along the valley. The mist was thick, and closed in all around them, but above their heads the stars could still be seen.

Zhilin used the stars to guide him which way to go. It was cool in the mist, it was easy walking, only their boots were troublesome,—they were worn at the heels. Zhilin took his off, threw them away, and walked barefoot. He sprang from stone to stone, and kept glancing at the stars.

Kostuilin began to grow weary. "Go slower," says he; "my boots chafe me, my whole foot is raw."

"Then take them off, it will be easier."

Kostuilin began to go barefoot, but that was still worse; he kept scraping his feet on the stones and having to stop.

Zhilin said to him, "You may cut your feet, but you will save your life; but if you are caught they will kill you, which would be worse."

Kostuilin said nothing, but crept along, groaning. For a long time they went down the valley. Suddenly they hear dogs barking at the right. Zhilin halted, looked around, climbed up the bank, and felt about with his hands.

"Ekh!" says he, "we have made a mistake; we have gone too far to the right. Here is one of the enemy's villages. I could see it from the hill. We must go back to the left, up the mountain. There must be a forest there."

But Kostuilin objected. "Just wait a little while, let us get breath. My feet are all blood."

"Eh, brother! they will get well. You should walk more lightly. This way."

And Zhilin turned back toward the left, and up hill toward the forest.

Kostuilin kept halting and groaning. Zhilin tried to hush him up, and still hastened on.

They climbed the mountain. And there they found the forest. They entered it; their clothes were all torn to pieces on the thorns. They found a little path through the woods. They walked along it.

"Halt!"

There was the sound of hoofs on the path. They stopped to listen. It sounded like the tramping of a horse: then it also stopped. They set out once more; again the tramping hoofs. When they stopped, it stopped.

Zhilin crept ahead, and investigated a light spot on the path.

Something is standing there. It may be a horse, or it may not, but on it there is something strange, not at all like a man.

It snorted—plainly! "What a strange thing!"

Zhilin gave a slight whistle. There was a dash of feet from the path into the forest, a crackling in the underbrush, and something rushed along like a hurricane, with a crashing of dry boughs.

Kostuilin almost fell to the ground in fright. But Zhilin laughed, and said,—

"That was a stag. Do you hear how it crashes through the woods with its horns? We frightened him, and he frightened us."

They went on their way. Already the Great Bear was beginning to set;

the dawn was not distant. And they were in doubt whether they should come out right or not. Zhilin was inclined to think that they were on the right track, and that it would be about ten versts farther before they reached the Russian fortress, but there is no certain guide; you could not tell in the night.

They came to a little clearing. Kostuilin sat down and said,—

"Do as you please, but I will not go any farther; my legs won't carry me."

Zhilin tried to persuade him.

"No," says he, "I won't go, I can't go."

Zhilin grew angry; he threatens him, he scolds him.

"Then I will go on without you. Good-by!"

Kostuilin jumped up and followed. They went four versts farther. The fog began to grow thicker in the forest. Nothing could be seen before them; the stars were barely visible.

Suddenly they hear the tramping of a horse just in front of them; they can hear his shoes striking on the stones.

Zhilin threw himself down on his belly, and tried to listen by laying his ear to the ground.

"Yes, it is,—it is some one on horseback coming in our direction."

They slipped off to one side of the road, crouched down in the bushes, and waited. Zhilin crept close to the path, and looked.

He sees a mounted Tatar riding along, driving a cow. The man is muttering to himself. When the Tatar had ridden by, Zhilin returned to Kostuilin.

"Well, God has saved us. Up with you! Come along!"

Kostuilin tried to rise, and fell back.

"I can't; by God, I can't. My strength is all gone."

The man was as though he were drunk. He was all of a sweat; and as they

279

were surrounded by the cold fog, and his feet were torn, he was quite used up. Zhilin tried to lift him by main force. Then Kostuilin cried, "Aï! it hurt."

Zhilin was frightened to death.

"What are you screaming for? Don't you know that Tatar is near? He will hear you." But he said to himself, "Now he is really played out, what can I do with him? I can't abandon a comrade. Now," says he, "get up; climb on my back. I will carry you if you can't walk any longer." He took Kostuilin on his shoulders, holding him by the thighs, and went along the path with his burden. "Only," says he, "don't put your hands on my throat, for Christ's sake! Lean on my shoulders."

It was hard for Zhilin. His feet were also bloody, and he was weary. He stopped, and made it a little easier for himself by setting Kostuilin down, and getting him better mounted. Then he went on again.

Evidently the Tatar had heard them when Kostuilin screamed. Zhilin caught the sound of some one following them and shouting in his language. Zhilin put into the bushes. The Tatar aimed his gun; he fired it off, but missed; began to whine in his native tongue, and galloped up the path.

"Well," says Zhilin, "we are lost, brother. The dog,—he will be right back with a band of Tatars on our track.... If we don't succeed in putting three versts between us, we are lost." And he thinks to himself, "The devil take it, that I had to bring this clod along with me! Alone, I should have got there long ago."

Kostuilin said, "Go alone. Why should you be lost on my account?"

"No, I will not go; it would not do to abandon a comrade." He lifted him again on his shoulder, and started on. Thus he made a verst. It was forest all the way, and no sign of outlet. But the fog was now beginning to lift, and seemed to be floating away in little clouds: not a star could be seen. Zhilin was tired out.

A little spring gushed out by the road: it was walled in with stones. There he stopped, and dropped Kostuilin.

"Let me rest a little," says he, "and get a drink. We will eat our cakes. It can't be very far now."

He had just stretched himself out to drink, when the sound of hoofs was heard behind them. Again they hid in the bushes at the right under the crest, and crouched down.

They heard Tatar voices. The Tatars stopped at the very spot where they had turned in from the road. After discussing a while, they seemed to be setting dogs on the scent.

The refugees hear the sound of a crashing through the bushes: a strange dog comes directly to them. He stops and barks.

The Tatars followed on their track. They are also strangers.

They seized them, bound them, lifted them on horses, and carried them off.

After they had ridden three versts, Abdul, with two Tatars, met them. He said something to their new captors. They were transferred to Abdul's horses, and were brought back to the aul.

Abdul was no longer grinning, and he said not a word to them.

They reached the village at daybreak; the prisoners were left in the street. The children gathered around them, tormenting them with stones and whips, and howling.

The Tatars gathered around them in a circle, and the old man from the mountain was among them. They began to discuss. Zhilin made out that they were deciding on what should be done with them. Some said that they ought to be sent farther into the mountains, but the old man declared that they must be killed. Abdul argued against it. Says he, "I have paid out money for them, I shall get a ransom for them."

But the old man said, "They won't pay any thing; it will only be an injury to us. And it is a sin to keep Russians alive. Kill them, and that is the end of it."

They separated. Abdul came to Zhilin, and reported the decision.

"If," says he, "the ransom is not sent in two weeks, you will be flogged. And if you try to run away again, I will kill you like a dog. Write your letter, and write it good!"

Paper was brought them; they wrote their letters. Clogs were put on their feet again; they were taken behind the mosque.... There was a pit twelve feet[102] deep, and they were thrust down into this pit.

VI.

Life was made utterly wretched for them. Their clogs were not taken off even at night, and they were not let out at all.

Unbaked dough was thrown down to them as though they were dogs, and water was let down in a jug. In the pit it was damp and suffocating.

Kostuilin became ill, and swelled up, and had rheumatism all over his body, and he groaned or slept all the time.

Even Zhilin lost his spirits; he sees that they are in desperate straits. And he does not know how to get out.

He had begun to make an excavation, but there was nowhere to hide the earth; Abdul discovered it, and threatened to kill him.

He was squatting down one time in the pit, and thinking about life and liberty, and he grew sad.

Suddenly a cake[103] fell directly into his lap, then another, and some cherries followed. He looked up, and there was Dina. She peered down at him, laughed, and then ran away. And Zhilin began to conjecture, "Couldn't Dina help me?"

He cleared out a little place in the pit, picked up some clay, and made some dolls. He made men and women, horses and dogs; he said to himself, "When Dina comes, I will give them to her."

But Dina did not make her appearance on the next day. And Zhilin hears the trampling of horses' hoofs: men came riding up: the Tatars collected

282

at the mosque, arguing, shouting, and talking about the Russians.

The voice of the old man was heard. Zhilin could not understand very well, but he made out that the Russians were somewhere near, and the Tatars were afraid that they would attack the aul, and they did not know what to do with the prisoners.

They talked a while, and went away. Suddenly Zhilin heard a rustling at the edge of the pit.

He sees Dina squatting on her heels, with her knees higher than her head; she leaned over, her necklace hung down and swung over the pit. And her little eyes twinkled like stars. She took from her sleeve two cheesecakes, and threw them down to him. Zhilin accepted them, and said, "Why did you stay away so long? I have been making you some dolls. Here they are." He began to toss them up to her one at a time.

But she shook her head, and would not look at them. "I can't take them," said she. She said nothing more for a time, but sat there: then she said, "Iván, they want to kill you."

She made a significant motion across her throat.

"Who wants to kill me?"

"Father. The old man has ordered him to. But I am sorry for you."

And Zhilin said, "Well, then, if you are sorry for me, bring me a long stick." She shook her head, meaning that it was impossible.

He clasped his hands in supplication to her. "Dina, please! Bring one to me, Dínushka!"

"I can't," said she. "They would see me; they are all at home." And she ran away.

Afterwards, Zhilin was sitting there in the evening, and wondering what he should do. He kept raising his eyes. He could see the stars, but the moon was not yet up. The mulla uttered his call, then all became silent.

Zhilin began already to doze, thinking to himself, "The little maid is afraid."

Suddenly a piece of clay fell on his head; he glanced up; a long pole was sliding over the edge of the pit, it slid out, began to descend toward him, it reached the bottom of the pit. Zhilin was delighted. He seized it, pulled it along,—it was a strong pole. He had noticed it before on Abdul's roof.

He gazed up; the stars were shining high in the heavens, and Dina's eyes, at the edge of the pit, gleamed in the darkness like a cat's.

She craned her head over, and whispered, "Iván, Iván." And she waved her hands before her face, meaning, "Softly, please."

"What is it?" said Zhilin.

"All have gone, there are only two at home."

And Zhilin said, "Well, Kostuilin, let us go, let us make our last attempt. I will help you."

Kostuilin, however, would not hear to it.

"No," says he, "it is not meant for me to get away from here. How could I go when I haven't even strength to turn over?"

"All right, then. Good-by.[104] Don't think me unkind."

He kissed Kostuilin.

He clasped the pole, told Dina to hold it firmly, and tried to climb up. Twice he fell back,—his clog so impeded him. Kostuilin boosted him; he managed to get to the top: Dina pulled on the sleeves of his shirt with all her might, laughing heartily.

Zhilin pulled up the pole, and said, "Carry it back to its place, Dina, for if they found it they would flog you."

She dragged off the pole, and Zhilin began to go down the mountain. When he had reached the bottom of the cliff, he took a sharp stone, and tried to break the padlock of his clog. But the lock was strong; he could not strike it fairly.

He hears some one hurrying down the hill, with light, skipping steps. He thinks, "That is probably Dina again."

Dina ran to him, took a stone, and says, "Let me try it."

She knelt down, and began to work with all her might. But her hands were as delicate as osiers. She had no strength. She threw down the stone, and burst into tears.

Zhilin again tried to break the lock, and Dina squatted by his side, and leaned against his shoulder. Zhilin glanced up, and saw at the left behind the mountain a red glow like a fire; it was the moon just rising.

"Well," he says to himself, "I must cross the valley and get into the woods before the moon rises." He stood up, and threw away the stone. No matter for the clog—he must take it with him.

"Good-by," says he. "Dínushka, I shall always remember you."

Dina clung to him, reached with her hands for a place to stow away some cakes. He took the cakes.

"Thank you," said he: "you are a thoughtful darling. Who will make you dolls after I am gone?" and he stroked her hair.

Dina burst into tears, hid her face in her hands, and scrambled up the hillside like a kid. He could hear, in the darkness, the jingling of the coins on her braids.

Zhilin crossed himself, picked up the lock of his clog so that it might not make a noise, and started on his way, dragging his leg all the time, and keeping his eyes constantly on the glow where the moon was rising.

He knew the way. He had eight versts to go in a direct course, but he would have to strike into the forest before the moon came entirely up. He crossed the stream, and now the light was increasing behind the mountain.

He proceeded along the valley: it was growing light. He walks along, constantly glancing around; but still the moon was not visible. The glow was now changing to white light, and one side of the valley grew brighter and brighter. The shadow crept away from the mountain till it reached its very foot.

Zhilin still hurried along, all the time keeping to the shadow.

He hurries as fast as he can, but the moon rises still faster; and now, at the right, the mountain-tops are illuminated.

He struck into the forest just as the moon rose above the mountains. It became as light and white as day. On the trees all the leaves were visible. It was warm and bright on the mountain-side; every thing seemed as though it were dead. The only sound was the roaring of a torrent far below. He walked along in the forest; he had met no one. Zhilin found a little spot in the forest where it was still darker, and began to rest.

While he rested he ate one of his cakes. He procured a stone and once more tried to break the padlock, but he only bruised his hands, and failed to break the lock.

He arose and went on his way. When he had gone a verst his strength gave out, his feet were sore. He had to walk ten steps at a time, and then rest.

"There's nothing to be done for it," says he to himself. "I will push on as long as my strength holds out; for if I sit down, then I shall not get up again. If I do not reach the fortress before it is daylight, then I will lie down in the woods and spend the day, and start on to-morrow night again."

He walked all night. Once he passed two Tatars on horseback, but he heard them at some distance, and hid behind a tree.

Already the moon was beginning to pale, the dew had fallen, it was near dawn, and Zhilin had not reached the end of the forest.

"Well," says he to himself, "I will go thirty steps farther, strike into the forest, and sit down."

He went thirty steps, and sees the end of the forest. He went to the edge; it was broad daylight. Before him, as on the palm of his hand, were the steppe and the fortress; and on the left, not far away on the mountain-side, fires were burning, or dying out; the smoke rose, and men were moving around the watch-fires.

He looks, and sees the gleaming of fire-arms: Cossacks, soldiers!

Zhilin was overjoyed.

He gathered his remaining strength, and walked down the mountain. And he says to himself, "God help me, if a mounted Tatar should get sight of me on this bare field! I should not escape him, even though I am so near." Even while these thoughts are passing through his mind, he sees at the left, on a hillock not fourteen hundred feet away, three Tatars on the watch. They caught sight of him,—bore down upon him. Then his heart failed within him. Waving his arms, he shouted at the top of his voice, "Brothers! help, brothers!"

Our men heard him,—mounted Cossacks dashed out toward him. The Cossacks were far off, the Tatars near. And now Zhilin collected his last remaining energies, seized his clog with his hand, ran toward the Cossacks, and, without any consciousness of feeling, crossed himself and cried, "Brothers, brothers, brothers!"

The Cossacks were fifteen in number.

The Tatars were dismayed. Before they reached him, they stopped short. And Zhilin reached the Cossacks.

The Cossacks surrounded him, and questioned him: "Who are you?" "What is your name?" "Where did you come from?"

But Zhilin was almost beside himself; he wept, and kept on shouting, "Brothers, brothers!"

The soldiers hastened up, and gathered around him; one brought him bread, another kasha-gruel, another vodka, another threw a cloak around him, still another broke his chains.

The officers recognized him, they brought him into the fortress. The soldiers were delighted, his comrades pressed into Zhilin's room.

Zhilin told them what had happened to him, and he ended his tale with the words,—

"That's the way I went home and got married! No, I see that such is not to be my fate."

And he remained in the service in the Caucasus.

At the end of a month Kostuilin was ransomed for five thousand rubles.

He was brought home scarcely alive.

FOOTNOTES:

[95] Four vedros, equivalent exactly to 8.80 gallons.

[96] Sixteen and a half miles.

[97] Aul = Tatar's village.—Author's note.

[98] A mountain-hut in the Caucasus.

[99] Urus in Tatar.

[100] khozyáïn.

[101] A sort of long Circassian cloak.

[102] Five arshins, 11.65 feet.

[103] lepyóshka.

[104] proshchaï.

About Author

In the 1870s Tolstoy experienced a profound moral crisis, followed by what he regarded as an equally profound spiritual awakening, as outlined in his non-fiction work A Confession (1882). His literal interpretation of the ethical teachings of Jesus, centering on the Sermon on the Mount, caused him to become a fervent Christian anarchist and pacifist. Tolstoy's ideas on nonviolent resistance, expressed in such works as The Kingdom of God Is Within You (1894), were to have a profound impact on such pivotal 20th-century figures as Mahatma Gandhi and Martin Luther King Jr. Tolstoy also became a dedicated advocate of Georgism, the economic philosophy of Henry George, which he incorporated into his writing, particularly Resurrection (1899).

Origins

The Tolstoys were a well-known family of old Russian nobility who traced their ancestry to a mythical nobleman named Indris described by Pyotr Tolstoy as arriving "from Nemec, from the lands of Caesar" to Chernigov in 1353 along with his two sons Litvinos (or Litvonis) and Zimonten (or Zigmont) and a druzhina of 3000 people. While the word "Nemec" has been long used to describe Germans only, at that time it was applied to any foreigner who didn't speak Russian (from the word nemoy meaning mute). Indris was then converted to Eastern Orthodoxy under the name of Leonty and his sons – as Konstantin and Feodor, respectively. Konstantin's grandson Andrei Kharitonovich was nicknamed Tolstiy (translated as fat) by Vasily II of Moscow after he moved from Chernigov to Moscow.

Because of the pagan names and the fact that Chernigov at the time was ruled by Demetrius I Starshy some researches concluded that they were Lithuanians who arrived from the Grand Duchy of Lithuania, then part of the State of the Teutonic Order. At the same time, no mention of Indris was ever found in the 14th – 16th-century documents, while the Chernigov Chronicles used by Pyotr Tolstoy as a reference were lost. The first documented members of the Tolstoy family also lived during the 17th century, thus Pyotr

Tolstoy himself is generally considered the founder of the noble house, being granted the title of count by Peter the Great.

Life and career

Tolstoy was born at Yasnaya Polyana, a family estate 12 kilometres (7.5 mi) southwest of Tula, Russia, and 200 kilometers (120 mi) south of Moscow. He was the fourth of five children of Count Nikolai Ilyich Tolstoy (1794–1837), a veteran of the Patriotic War of 1812, and Countess Mariya Tolstaya (née Volkonskaya; 1790–1830). After his mother died when he was two and his father when he was nine, Tolstoy and his siblings were brought up by relatives. In 1844, he began studying law and oriental languages at Kazan University, where teachers described him as "both unable and unwilling to learn." Tolstoy left the university in the middle of his studies, returned to Yasnaya Polyana and then spent much of his time in Moscow, Tula and Saint Petersburg, leading a lax and leisurely lifestyle. He began writing during this period, including his first novel Childhood, a fictitious account of his own youth, which was published in 1852. In 1851, after running up heavy gambling debts, he went with his older brother to the Caucasus and joined the army. Tolstoy served as a young artillery officer during the Crimean War and was in Sevastopol during the 11-month-long siege of Sevastopol in 1854–55, including the Battle of the Chernaya. During the war he was recognised for his bravery and courage and promoted to lieutenant. He was appalled by the number of deaths involved in warfare, and left the army after the end of the Crimean War.

His conversion from a dissolute and privileged society author to the non-violent and spiritual anarchist of his latter days was brought about by his experience in the army as well as two trips around Europe in 1857 and 1860–61. Others who followed the same path were Alexander Herzen, Mikhail Bakunin and Peter Kropotkin. During his 1857 visit, Tolstoy witnessed a public execution in Paris, a traumatic experience that would mark the rest of his life. Writing in a letter to his friend Vasily Botkin: "The truth is that the State is a conspiracy designed not only to exploit, but above all to corrupt its citizens ... Henceforth, I shall never serve any government anywhere." Tolstoy's concept of non-violence or Ahimsa was bolstered when he read a

German version of the Tirukkural. He later instilled the concept in Mahatma Gandhi through his A Letter to a Hindu when young Gandhi corresponded with him seeking his advice.

His European trip in 1860–61 shaped both his political and literary development when he met Victor Hugo, whose literary talents Tolstoy praised after reading Hugo's newly finished Les Misérables. The similar evocation of battle scenes in Hugo's novel and Tolstoy's War and Peace indicates this influence. Tolstoy's political philosophy was also influenced by a March 1861 visit to French anarchist Pierre-Joseph Proudhon, then living in exile under an assumed name in Brussels. Apart from reviewing Proudhon's forthcoming publication, La Guerre et la Paix (War and Peace in French), whose title Tolstoy would borrow for his masterpiece, the two men discussed education, as Tolstoy wrote in his educational notebooks: "If I recount this conversation with Proudhon, it is to show that, in my personal experience, he was the only man who understood the significance of education and of the printing press in our time."

Fired by enthusiasm, Tolstoy returned to Yasnaya Polyana and founded 13 schools for the children of Russia's peasants, who had just been emancipated from serfdom in 1861. Tolstoy described the school's principles in his 1862 essay "The School at Yasnaya Polyana". Tolstoy's educational experiments were short-lived, partly due to harassment by the Tsarist secret police. However, as a direct forerunner to A.S. Neill's Summerhill School, the school at Yasnaya Polyana can justifiably be claimed the first example of a coherent theory of democratic education.

Towards the end of his career, Tolstoy was selected to receive the first Nobel Prize in Literature in 1901, but turned down the honor in October of the same year, worrying that the prize money would bring unwanted complications to his life.

Personal life

The death of his brother Nikolay in 1860 had an impact on Tolstoy, and led him to a desire to marry. On 23 September 1862, Tolstoy married Sophia Andreevna Behrs, who was 16 years his junior and the daughter of a court physician. She was called Sonya, the Russian diminutive of Sofia, by her family and friends. They had 13 children, eight of whom survived childhood:

Count Sergei Lvovich Tolstoy (1863–1947), composer and ethnomusicologist

Countess Tatyana Lvovna Tolstaya (1864–1950), wife of Mikhail Sergeevich Sukhotin

Count Ilya Lvovich Tolstoy (1866–1933), writer

Count Lev Lvovich Tolstoy (1869–1945), writer and sculptor

Countess Maria Lvovna Tolstaya (1871–1906), wife of Nikolai Leonidovich Obolensky

Count Peter Lvovich Tolstoy (1872–1873), died in infancy

Count Nikolai Lvovich Tolstoy (1874–1875), died in infancy

Countess Varvara Lvovna Tolstaya (1875–1875), died in infancy

Count Andrei Lvovich Tolstoy (1877–1916), served in the Russo-Japanese War

Count Michael Lvovich Tolstoy (1879–1944)

Count Alexei Lvovich Tolstoy (1881–1886)

Countess Alexandra Lvovna Tolstaya (1884–1979)

Count Ivan Lvovich Tolstoy (1888–1895)

The marriage was marked from the outset by sexual passion and emotional insensitivity when Tolstoy, on the eve of their marriage, gave her his diaries detailing his extensive sexual past and the fact that one of the serfs on his estate had borne him a son. Even so, their early married life was happy and allowed Tolstoy much freedom and the support system to compose War and Peace and Anna Karenina with Sonya acting as his secretary, editor, and financial manager. Sonya was copying and handwriting his epic works time after time. Tolstoy would continue editing War and Peace and had to have clean final drafts to be delivered to the publisher.

However, their later life together has been described by A.N. Wilson as one of the unhappiest in literary history. Tolstoy's relationship with his wife deteriorated as his beliefs became increasingly radical. This saw him seeking to reject his inherited and earned wealth, including the renunciation of the copyrights on his earlier works.

Some of the members of the Tolstoy family left Russia in the aftermath of the 1905 Russian Revolution and the subsequent establishment of the Soviet Union, and many of Leo Tolstoy's relatives and descendants today live in Sweden, Germany, the United Kingdom, France and the United States. Among them are Swedish jazz singer Viktoria Tolstoy and the Swedish landowner Christopher Paus, whose family owns the major estate Herresta outside Stockholm.

One of his great-great-grandsons, Vladimir Tolstoy (born 1962), is a director of the Yasnaya Polyana museum since 1994 and an adviser to the President of Russia on cultural affairs since 2012. Ilya Tolstoy's great-grandson, Pyotr Tolstoy, is a well-known Russian journalist and TV presenter as well as a State Duma deputy since 2016. His cousin Fyokla Tolstaya (born Anna Tolstaya in 1971), daughter of the acclaimed Soviet Slavist Nikita Tolstoy (ru) (1923–1996), is also a Russian journalist, TV and radio host.

Novels and fictional works

Tolstoy is considered one of the giants of Russian literature; his works include the novels War and Peace and Anna Karenina and novellas such as Hadji Murad and The Death of Ivan Ilyich.

Tolstoy's earliest works, the autobiographical novels Childhood, Boyhood, and Youth (1852–1856), tell of a rich landowner's son and his slow realization of the chasm between himself and his peasants. Though he later rejected them as sentimental, a great deal of Tolstoy's own life is revealed. They retain their relevance as accounts of the universal story of growing up.

Tolstoy served as a second lieutenant in an artillery regiment during the Crimean War, recounted in his Sevastopol Sketches. His experiences in battle helped stir his subsequent pacifism and gave him material for realistic depiction of the horrors of war in his later work.

His fiction consistently attempts to convey realistically the Russian society in which he lived. The Cossacks (1863) describes the Cossack life and people through a story of a Russian aristocrat in love with a Cossack girl. Anna Karenina (1877) tells parallel stories of an adulterous woman trapped by the conventions and falsities of society and of a philosophical landowner (much like Tolstoy), who works alongside the peasants in the fields and seeks to reform their lives. Tolstoy not only drew from his own life experiences but also created characters in his own image, such as Pierre Bezukhov and Prince Andrei in War and Peace, Levin in Anna Karenina and to some extent, Prince Nekhlyudov in Resurrection.

War and Peace is generally thought to be one of the greatest novels ever written, remarkable for its dramatic breadth and unity. Its vast canvas includes 580 characters, many historical with others fictional. The story moves from family life to the headquarters of Napoleon, from the court of Alexander I of Russia to the battlefields of Austerlitz and Borodino. Tolstoy's original idea for the novel was to investigate the causes of the Decembrist revolt, to which it refers only in the last chapters, from which can be deduced that Andrei Bolkonsky's son will become one of the Decembrists. The novel explores Tolstoy's theory of history, and in particular the insignificance of individuals such as Napoleon and Alexander. Somewhat surprisingly, Tolstoy did not consider War and Peace to be a novel (nor did he consider many of the great Russian fictions written at that time to be novels). This view becomes less surprising if one considers that Tolstoy was a novelist of the realist school who considered the novel to be a framework for the examination of social and political issues in nineteenth-century life. War and Peace (which is to Tolstoy really an epic in prose) therefore did not qualify. Tolstoy thought that Anna Karenina was his first true novel.

After Anna Karenina, Tolstoy concentrated on Christian themes, and his later novels such as The Death of Ivan Ilyich (1886) and What Is to Be Done? develop a radical anarcho-pacifist Christian philosophy which led to his excommunication from the Russian Orthodox Church in 1901. For all the praise showered on Anna Karenina and War and Peace, Tolstoy rejected the two works later in his life as something not as true of reality.

In his novel Resurrection, Tolstoy attempts to expose the injustice of man-made laws and the hypocrisy of institutionalized church. Tolstoy also explores and explains the economic philosophy of Georgism, of which he had become a very strong advocate towards the end of his life.

Tolstoy also tried himself in poetry with several soldier songs written during his military service and fairy tales in verse such as Volga-bogatyr and Oaf stylized as national folk songs. They were written between 1871 and 1874 for his Russian Book for Reading, a collection of short stories in four volumes (total of 629 stories in various genres) published along with the New Azbuka textbook and addressed to schoolchildren. Nevertheless, he was skeptical about poetry as a genre. As he famously said, "Writing poetry is like ploughing and dancing at the same time". According to Valentin Bulgakov, he criticised poets, including Alexander Pushkin, for their "false" epithets used "simply to make it rhyme".

Critical appraisal by other authors

Tolstoy's contemporaries paid him lofty tributes. Fyodor Dostoyevsky, who died thirty years before Tolstoy's death, thought him the greatest of all living novelists. Gustave Flaubert, on reading a translation of War and Peace, exclaimed, "What an artist and what a psychologist!" Anton Chekhov, who often visited Tolstoy at his country estate, wrote, "When literature possesses a Tolstoy, it is easy and pleasant to be a writer; even when you know you have achieved nothing yourself and are still achieving nothing, this is not as terrible as it might otherwise be, because Tolstoy achieves for everyone. What he does serves to justify all the hopes and aspirations invested in literature." The 19th-century British poet and critic Matthew Arnold opined that "A novel by Tolstoy is not a work of art but a piece of life."

Later novelists continued to appreciate Tolstoy's art, but sometimes also expressed criticism. Arthur Conan Doyle wrote "I am attracted by his earnestness and by his power of detail, but I am repelled by his looseness of construction and by his unreasonable and impracticable mysticism." Virginia

Woolf declared him "the greatest of all novelists." James Joyce noted that "He is never dull, never stupid, never tired, never pedantic, never theatrical!" Thomas Mann wrote of Tolstoy's seemingly guileless artistry: "Seldom did art work so much like nature." Vladimir Nabokov heaped superlatives upon The Death of Ivan Ilyich and Anna Karenina; he questioned, however, the reputation of War and Peace, and sharply criticized Resurrection and The Kreutzer Sonata.

Religious and political beliefs

After reading Schopenhauer's The World as Will and Representation, Tolstoy gradually became converted to the ascetic morality upheld in that work as the proper spiritual path for the upper classes: "Do you know what this summer has meant for me? Constant raptures over Schopenhauer and a whole series of spiritual delights which I've never experienced before. ... no student has ever studied so much on his course, and learned so much, as I have this summer"

In Chapter VI of A Confession, Tolstoy quoted the final paragraph of Schopenhauer's work. It explained how the nothingness that results from complete denial of self is only a relative nothingness, and is not to be feared. The novelist was struck by the description of Christian, Buddhist, and Hindu ascetic renunciation as being the path to holiness. After reading passages such as the following, which abound in Schopenhauer's ethical chapters, the Russian nobleman chose poverty and formal denial of the will:

But this very necessity of involuntary suffering (by poor people) for eternal salvation is also expressed by that utterance of the Savior (Matthew 19:24): "It is easier for a camel to go through the eye of a needle, than for a rich man to enter into the kingdom of God." Therefore, those who were greatly in earnest about their eternal salvation, chose voluntary poverty when fate had denied this to them and they had been born in wealth. Thus Buddha Sakyamuni was born a prince, but voluntarily took to the mendicant's staff; and Francis of Assisi, the founder of the mendicant orders who, as a youngster at a ball, where the daughters of all the notabilities were sitting together, was asked: "Now Francis, will you not soon make your choice from these beauties?"

and who replied: "I have made a far more beautiful choice!" "Whom?" "La povertà (poverty)": whereupon he abandoned every thing shortly afterwards and wandered through the land as a mendicant.

In 1884, Tolstoy wrote a book called What I Believe, in which he openly confessed his Christian beliefs. He affirmed his belief in Jesus Christ's teachings and was particularly influenced by the Sermon on the Mount, and the injunction to turn the other cheek, which he understood as a "commandment of non-resistance to evil by force" and a doctrine of pacifism and nonviolence. In his work The Kingdom of God Is Within You, he explains that he considered mistaken the Church's doctrine because they had made a "perversion" of Christ's teachings. Tolstoy also received letters from American Quakers who introduced him to the non-violence writings of Quaker Christians such as George Fox, William Penn and Jonathan Dymond. Tolstoy believed being a Christian required him to be a pacifist; the consequences of being a pacifist, and the apparently inevitable waging of war by government, are the reason why he is considered a philosophical anarchist.

Later, various versions of "Tolstoy's Bible" would be published, indicating the passages Tolstoy most relied on, specifically, the reported words of Jesus himself.

Tolstoy believed that a true Christian could find lasting happiness by striving for inner self-perfection through following the Great Commandment of loving one's neighbor and God rather than looking outward to the Church or state for guidance. His belief in nonresistance when faced by conflict is another distinct attribute of his philosophy based on Christ's teachings. By directly influencing Mahatma Gandhi with this idea through his work The Kingdom of God Is Within You (full text of English translation available on Wikisource), Tolstoy's profound influence on the nonviolent resistance movement reverberates to this day. He believed that the aristocracy were a burden on the poor, and that the only solution to how we live together is through anarchism.

He also opposed private property in land ownership and the institution of marriage and valued the ideals of chastity and sexual abstinence (discussed in Father Sergius and his preface to The Kreutzer Sonata), ideals also held by the young Gandhi. Tolstoy's later work derives a passion and verve from the depth of his austere moral views. The sequence of the temptation of Sergius in Father Sergius, for example, is among his later triumphs. Gorky relates how Tolstoy once read this passage before himself and Chekhov and that Tolstoy was moved to tears by the end of the reading. Other later passages of rare power include the personal crises that were faced by the protagonists of The Death of Ivan Ilyich, and of Master and Man, where the main character in the former or the reader in the latter are made aware of the foolishness of the protagonists' lives.

Tolstoy had a profound influence on the development of Christian anarchist thought. The Tolstoyans were a small Christian anarchist group formed by Tolstoy's companion, Vladimir Chertkov (1854–1936), to spread Tolstoy's religious teachings. Philosopher Peter Kropotkin wrote of Tolstoy in the article on anarchism in the 1911 Encyclopædia Britannica:

Without naming himself an anarchist, Leo Tolstoy, like his predecessors in the popular religious movements of the 15th and 16th centuries, Chojecki, Denk and many others, took the anarchist position as regards the state and property rights, deducing his conclusions from the general spirit of the teachings of Jesus and from the necessary dictates of reason. With all the might of his talent, Tolstoy made (especially in The Kingdom of God Is Within You) a powerful criticism of the church, the state and law altogether, and especially of the present property laws. He describes the state as the domination of the wicked ones, supported by brutal force. Robbers, he says, are far less dangerous than a well-organized government. He makes a searching criticism of the prejudices which are current now concerning the benefits conferred upon men by the church, the state, and the existing distribution of property, and from the teachings of Jesus he deduces the rule of non-resistance and the absolute condemnation of all wars. His religious arguments are, however, so well combined with arguments borrowed from a dispassionate observation of the present evils, that the anarchist portions of his works appeal to the religious and the non-religious reader alike.

During the Boxer Rebellion in China, Tolstoy praised the Boxers. He was harshly critical of the atrocities committed by the Russians, Germans, Americans, Japanese, and other western troops. He accused them of engaging in slaughter when he heard about the lootings, rapes, and murders, in what he saw as Christian brutality. Tolstoy also named the two monarchs most responsible for the atrocities; Nicholas II of Russia and Wilhelm II of Germany. Tolstoy, a famous sinophile, also read the works of Chinese thinker and philosopher, Confucius. Tolstoy corresponded with the Chinese intellectual Gu Hongming and recommended that China remain an agrarian nation and warned against reform like what Japan implemented.

The Eight-Nation Alliance intervention in the Boxer Rebellion was denounced by Tolstoy as were the Philippine–American War and the Second Boer War between the British Empire and the two independent Boer republics. The words "terrible for its injustice and cruelty" were used to describe the Czarist intervention in China by Tolstoy. Confucius's works were studied by Tolstoy. The attack on China in the Boxer Rebellion was railed against by Tolstoy. The war against China was criticized by Leonid Andreev and Gorkey. To the Chinese people, an epistle, was written by Tolstoy as part of the criticism of the war by intellectuals in Russia. The activities of Russia in China by Nicholas II were described in an open letter where they were slammed and denounced by Leo Tolstoy in 1902. Tolstoy corresponded with Gu Hongming and they both opposed the Hundred Day's Reform by Kang Youwei and agreed that the reform movement was perilous. Tolstoys' ideology on non violence shaped the anarchist thought of the Society for the Study of Socialism in China. Lao Zi and Confucius's teachings were studied by Tolstoy. Chinese Wisdom was a text written by Tolstoy. The Boxer Rebellion stirred Tolstoy's interest in Chinese philosophy. The Boxer and Boxer wars were denounced by Tolstoy.

In hundreds of essays over the last 20 years of his life, Tolstoy reiterated the anarchist critique of the state and recommended books by Kropotkin and Proudhon to his readers, whilst rejecting anarchism's espousal of violent revolutionary means. In the 1900 essay, "On Anarchy", he wrote; "The Anarchists are right in everything; in the negation of the existing order, and in the assertion that, without Authority, there could not be worse violence than that of Authority under existing conditions. They are mistaken only in thinking that Anarchy can be instituted by a revolution. But it will be instituted only by there being more and more people who do not require the protection of governmental power ... There can be only one permanent revolution—a moral one: the regeneration of the inner man." Despite his misgivings about anarchist violence, Tolstoy took risks to circulate the prohibited publications of anarchist thinkers in Russia, and corrected the proofs of Kropotkin's "Words of a Rebel", illegally published in St Petersburg in 1906.

Tolstoy was enthused by the economic thinking of Henry George, incorporating it approvingly into later works such as Resurrection (1899), the book that played a major factor in his excommunication.

In 1908, Tolstoy wrote A Letter to a Hindu outlining his belief in non-violence as a means for India to gain independence from British colonial rule. In 1909, a copy of the letter was read by Gandhi, who was working as a lawyer in South Africa at the time and just becoming an activist. Tolstoy's letter was significant for Gandhi, who wrote Tolstoy seeking proof that he was the real author, leading to further correspondence between them.

Reading Tolstoy's The Kingdom of God Is Within You also convinced Gandhi to avoid violence and espouse nonviolent resistance, a debt Gandhi acknowledged in his autobiography, calling Tolstoy "the greatest apostle of non-violence that the present age has produced". The correspondence between Tolstoy and Gandhi would only last a year, from October 1909 until Tolstoy's death in November 1910, but led Gandhi to give the name Tolstoy Colony to his second ashram in South Africa. Besides nonviolent resistance, the two men shared a common belief in the merits of vegetarianism, the subject of several of Tolstoy's essays.

Tolstoy also became a major supporter of the Esperanto movement. Tolstoy was impressed by the pacifist beliefs of the Doukhobors and brought their persecution to the attention of the international community, after they burned their weapons in peaceful protest in 1895. He aided the Doukhobors in migrating to Canada. In 1904, during the Russo-Japanese War, Tolstoy condemned the war and wrote to the Japanese Buddhist priest Soyen Shaku in a failed attempt to make a joint pacifist statement.

Towards the end of his life, Tolstoy become more and more occupied with the economic theory and social philosophy of Georgism. He spoke of great admiration of Henry George, stating once that "People do not argue with the teaching of George; they simply do not know it. And it is impossible to do otherwise with his teaching, for he who becomes acquainted with it cannot but agree." He also wrote a preface to George's Social Problems. Tolstoy and George both rejected private property in land (the most important source of income of the passive Russian aristocracy that Tolstoy so heavily criticized) whilst simultaneously both rejecting a centrally planned socialist economy. Some assume that this development in Tolstoy's thinking was a move away from his anarchist views, since Georgism requires a central administration to collect land rent and spend it on infrastructure. However, anarchist versions of Georgism have also been proposed since. Tolstoy's 1899 novel Resurrection explores his thoughts on Georgism in more detail and hints that Tolstoy indeed had such a view. It suggests the possibility of small communities with some form of local governance to manage the collective land rents for common goods; whilst still heavily criticising institutions of the state such as the justice system.

Death

Tolstoy died in 1910, at the age of 82. Just prior to his death, his health had been a concern of his family, who were actively engaged in his care on a daily basis. During his last few days, he had spoken and written about dying. Renouncing his aristocratic lifestyle, he had finally gathered the nerve to separate from his wife, and left home in the middle of winter, in the dead of night. His secretive departure was an apparent attempt to escape unannounced from Sophia's jealous tirades. She was outspokenly opposed to many of his teachings, and in recent years had grown envious of the attention which it seemed to her Tolstoy lavished upon his Tolstoyan "disciples".

Tolstoy died of pneumonia at Astapovo train station, after a day's rail journey south. The station master took Tolstoy to his apartment, and his personal doctors were called to the scene. He was given injections of morphine and camphor.

The police tried to limit access to his funeral procession, but thousands of peasants lined the streets. Still, some were heard to say that, other than knowing that "some nobleman had died", they knew little else about Tolstoy.

According to some sources, Tolstoy spent the last hours of his life preaching love, nonviolence, and Georgism to his fellow passengers on the train. (Source: Wikipedia)

CPSIA information can be obtained
at www.ICGtesting.com
Printed in the USA
BVHW031158180719
553829BV00005B/232/P